What people are saying about

The Intrigues of Jennie Lee

The Intrigues of Jennie Lee is marvelous in so many ways.. excellent take on the twisted, dangerous politics of 1930s Britain and a rattling good read.
C.J. Sansom, author of *Dominion* and the Shardlake mysteries.

The Intrigues of Jennie Lee

A Novel

The Intrigues of Jennie Lee

A Novel

Alex Rosenberg

TOP HAT
BOOKS

Winchester, UK
Washington, USA

JOHN HUNT PUBLISHING

First published by Top Hat Books, 2020
Top Hat Books is an imprint of John Hunt Publishing Ltd., No. 3 East St., Alresford,
Hampshire SO24 9EE, UK
office@jhpbooks.com
www.johnhuntpublishing.com
www.tophat-books.com

For distributor details and how to order please visit the 'Ordering' section on our website.

Text copyright: Alex Rosenberg 2019

ISBN: 978 1 78904 458 4
978 1 78904 459 1 (ebook)
Library of Congress Control Number: 2019948220

A CIP catalogue record for this book is available from the British Library.

Design: Stuart Davies

UK: Printed and bound by CPI Group (UK) Ltd, Croydon, CR0 4YY
US: Printed and bound by Thomson-Shore, 7300 West Joy Road, Dexter, MI 48130

We operate a distinctive and ethical publishing philosophy in
all areas of our business, from our global network of authors to
production and worldwide distribution.

Also by Alex Rosenberg

The Girl from Krakow
ISBN-10: 1477830812, ISBN-13: 978-1477830819

Autumn in Oxford.
ISBN-10: 9781503939073, ISBN-13: 978-1503939073

The Atheist's Guide to Reality
ISBN-10: 9780393344110, ISBN-13: 978-0393344110

*How History Gets Things Wrong: The Neuroscience of our Addiction
to Story Telling*
ISBN-10: 0262537990, ISBN-13: 978-0262537995

Preface

Almost all persons mentioned in this work really lived. They actually committed most of political acts and led *almost all* of the private lives credited to them here, at least before the British political upheaval of August 1931. A ***Dramatis Personae*** follows the narrative.

Chapter One

Ramsay MacDonald knew he was a handsome, even charismatically attractive man. That January of 1904, he was thirty-seven, manly, tall, with piercing eyes, a mop of curly dark hair, dramatically streaked white and grey, and a fashionably wide, dark moustache that extended half an inch beyond either side of his mouth.

MacDonald was the leader of the Labour Party. He'd been its parliamentary candidate for Leicester, three hundred miles south, in England, repeatedly unsuccessful but unbowed. Now, he was traveling across the politically more fertile ground of the Scottish coal country, speaking at meetings, making friends among union men still suspicious of socialism, convincing people his party stood a chance. MacDonald had been doing this for more than a decade. It wouldn't be long now, he felt, before he'd find his way into parliament.

Between the steel trusses of the great railway bridge over the Firth of Forth, the North Sea looked forbidding from his unheated second-class railway carriage. An hour later, at 4:30, the winter gloom had already been enveloped by night when MacDonald alighted on the Cowdenbeath platform; just beyond the railway bridge twenty feet above the High Street, slicing the town in half. Set on a plane between rolling hills, Cowdenbeath was surrounded by coal pits so extensive that after only fifty years or so they were beginning to produce a noticeable subsidence at one end of the High Street. Nowhere in the Scottish coalfields was more fertile ground for Ramsay MacDonald's evangelical socialism.

The miner's union had booked him into a convenient local hotel, a temperance hotel. That was no objection so far as MacDonald was concerned. Like the other buildings on the street, the Arcade Hotel was an unimpressive two-storey stone building. He noticed the small attached Arcade Theatre next to the hotel and chuckled. He heard his Scottish forbears whisper: *A hotel, even a temperance hotel, hard by a theatre? It had to be a brothel.*

The gas-lit glow from the two windows to the left of the entry door was inviting in the early darkness of that late mid-winter afternoon. MacDonald entered and smiled at the man standing behind a small raised counter that didn't look much like a registration desk. The man looked up and smiled expectantly.

"Good evening."

"I'm Ramsay MacDonald. I believe I've been booked in by—"

"It's Mr MacDonald of the Labour Party, James."

It was a young woman's voice from the vicinity of the fireplace, a half dozen feet away in what passed for the hotel's lounge.

The woman came to the desk, wiping her hands on an apron and extending both to their guest. It was a warmer greeting than a Scotsman expected or proffered. She looked MacDonald over, seeming to nod to herself as though she liked what she saw.

"I'm Euphemia Lee. This is my husband, James Lee."

The pair looked more like Edinburgh intelligentsia than coalfield hoteliers. He was thin, slight, studious in his spectacles, with thick dark hair in need of cutting, combed down to the right. James Lee wore a tie, albeit askew from his detachable collar, above a tweed waistcoat, buttoned against the cold. His wife was almost as tall as her husband, decidedly pretty with chestnut hair cut short above the shoulders, quite out of fashion. James Lee had also extended his hand.

"So pleased to meet you."

MacDonald had to decide whose hand to grasp.

He took the man's and said, "Pleased to meet you too, sir."

As MacDonald signed the woman came forward and grasped the Gladstone bag at his foot.

"I'll show you to your room, Mr MacDonald."

2

She was mounting the stair before he could protest. *Well, too small a hotel for a porter, I warrant, but it's no woman's place to carry a guest's bag.* Stranger still, Euphemia Lee didn't just unlock the door to his room, she entered, placed the bag on a bureau and opened it. Then she turned to MacDonald, stood and stared hard at him. There was no mistaking the look. MacDonald flushed, went to the door to usher her out. She left with a smile too wide merely to signal hospitality.

Have I indeed come to a brothel? The thought made him smile only briefly. It was followed by a rush of images, emotions, flashes of warmth coursing through his body, and finally by thoughts he'd been raised to call "unworthy." This had happened before, often enough for MacDonald to think he understood it.

Successful political men exuded a personal magnetism that harnessed people, women especially, to their causes. The temptations had ruined more than one promising career: Charles Parnell's, Randolph Churchill's.

He tried to visualise the frankness he'd seen in Euphemia Lee's look. But he couldn't. *You're probably imagining it anyway. Still, she's a breagh lass.* The Gaelic came back to him. Then he opened his bag and took out the speech he'd prepared for the meeting of the local branch of the Labour Party and the Fife and Kinross Miners Association.

* * *

The three were returning from the evening meeting at which MacDonald had spoken, warmly and powerfully, of the need for unity, solidarity, the role of the unions, but also of the Christian roots of socialism as against the secular champions of the cause. James Lee was feeling more optimistic than he had for a long time.

"So, the Prime Minister has really promised you unopposed seats at the next elections? How many?"

"Well, as many as he thinks he'll lose to the Conservatives if we split the Liberal vote. I think we can hope for upwards of twenty-five seats."

"A real political party then."

MacDonald didn't reply. He was tired, but pleased with the evening. Euphemia Lee was walking between them and now he found himself wondering if the way she brushed against him was accidental, and whether her hand had really grazed his. He wasn't hoping, just wondering. Surely he'd just mistaken that first glance in his room, fantasised her interest.

James Lee spoke again,

"You'll be staying tomorrow night, Mr MacDonald?"

The other man nodded.

"There's a Gilbert and Sullivan company at the theatre tomorrow evening. *Mikado* I think."

"I regret, music is not one of my passions, Mr Lee. And I've an early train to Glasgow the next morning."

"Sorry to hear it, sir. I never miss a concert myself."

They reached the hotel and stepped into the lobby.

"I'll bid you good evening." Ramsay MacDonald nodded to them both.

* * *

It was near nine the next evening as MacDonald prepared to retire. It had been a good day; a visit to Fife and Kinross Miner's Union hall, the mining school, then supper with the priest at the Catholic Parish hall. Labour couldn't neglect the devout who'd come across the Irish Sea for the work.

He'd already dimmed the only lamp in the room, but MacDonald could still hear laugher and even snatches of song from the theatre next door. As he brought his nightshirt over his head, there was a knock at the door. His first thought was that he had no dressing gown to put on.

"Who is it?"

The voice was Euphemia Lee's.

"Please open. It's cold out here."

He turned the key and before he could open the door, she darted in.

Ramsay MacDonald had never seen a woman completely naked before, not even his wife. Yet there one was, reflecting the light of the gas lamp like a figure in a painting by Alma Tadema. Before he could say a word the woman had embraced him and then began pulling him towards the bed. The single word, "But..." was stifled by the kiss while the rest of his body responded with a swiftness he had never experienced.

Several things happened to Ramsay MacDonald's body in the next hour he could never have imagined. Things were done to it, things that were beyond his ken. What's more he found himself responding to her in ways he might have previously described as unspeakable but the woman treated as delightful. And all accompanied by Arthur Sullivan's catchy tunes wafting in from the theatre next door.

When at last they could hear the curtain-call ovations through the thin walls separating the hotel from the theatre next door, Euphemia Lee stole from the bed and slipped out of the room.

* * *

"Well, James, our little experiment in eugenics seems to have worked."

Euphemia tried to make the observation sound light, quelling the tremulousness from her voice. The Lees were readying for bed, some six weeks after Mr MacDonald's visit. Euphemia was giving her hair the obligatory 100 strokes; James was folding his trousers over a chair.

Once she had stopped trying to ignore the meaning of the morning sickness, she began to struggle with how to break this news to her husband. This seemed the best way, a dispassionate reminder of their compact, their conspiracy. Her back to him, James could not see the dread in her eyes.

James Lee turned to her as she continued to brush. He had not absorbed his wife's drift. He'd not heard the words 'experiment' and 'eugenics'. Or he'd misheard.

"Sorry, dear, come again?"

She faced him. She would have to repeat herself, this time more plainly.

"James, I'm pregnant. Our scheme has played out as we'd hoped."

Her husband heard the words, and then he absorbed them. She'd said it clearly enough. He hadn't misheard. There was no point saying "What?" But it was all he could say. Reaching out to a bureau with both hands, he steadied himself. Then the heat began to rise from his body. Suddenly he was perspiring freely in the unheated bedroom. He lurched over to the bed, sat heavily and brought his hands to his temples.

Then, the word she'd spoke came back to him, that bloodless term 'eugenics,' one they'd heard first spoken at a Fabian lecture in Edinburgh a few years before. Yes, he and Euphemia had approved. It was scientific, rational, in accord with the foundations of their socialism. There had been his 'difficulty' impotence, from the first night of their marriage. She had been more than understanding, wonderful in her acceptance, support and patience. Over and over, she had told him she'd wait, she loved him regardless. It mattered, of course, but mainly because they wanted children, not because they needed the carnal bond. Eugenics had suggested a solution. Now, in his mortification, he could not pretend they hadn't had the conversation, months ago, hadn't made the decision, the agreement, so abstract, so bloodless, at the time, about events so hypothetical, so distant in the future they made no difference. They had agreed that they could wait, wait a lifetime if they had to, to consummate their happy marriage. But meanwhile, Euphemia's childbearing years were passing. Like many a Scottish couple they'd married late. She was already in her early thirties. The intelligence of eugenics had helped them decide. Euphemia was to be given license to solve their problem provided she could do so discreetly and with someone of the right stock. Resolved, they had been glad to put the matter aside. It was not spoken of again.

Now, the recollection of his acquiesce drained all his anger into a silent dishonour. He slumped down from the edge of their bed to the floor, dropping his head to his knees. Euphemia approached, bewildered by the combination of her gladness and her husband's deep chagrin. He felt her hand on his shoulder and decided that sobbing would not do. He'd face matters as they were and make the best of things, take pleasure in the boy, raise him to be his own son. The child would certainly be a boy.

Jennie Lee was born seven months later.

Chapter Two

The train ride south to London from Glasgow was providing no distraction. Anticipation had given way to monotony, and monotony to doubt. *Is this what you really wanted, Jennie? Do you even have much of an idea of what you're in for, member of parliament for North Lanark?*

Shining on a platform, campaigning at doorsteps, outwitting hecklers—Tories or Communists—at meetings, it had been great fun. She'd been doing that sort of thing since the age of fifteen. From the beginning, Jennie knew the crowds came for the novelty of it, a wee slip of a girl on the platform with all those wizened and burly figures. But they stayed to listen. And she held them in a thrall. Standing for parliament was all of a piece with what she'd been doing for almost ten years.

But now it'll have consequences.

Jennie was hurtling towards a future for which she was quite unprepared. *How should I act, what should I say?* To be constantly scrutinised by everyone around her, older, powerful, male, all of them laughing at her, patronising her or worse, gulling her like a child? The answer came unbidden: *Isn't that what you are, a child? Not twenty-five and elected to parliament?* Would anyone take her seriously, let alone take her for an MP? Overwhelmed by fear she resolved to get out at the next stop, Leeds, to turn round and go home.

It wasn't just fear, there was the debate she'd had with herself from the moment she'd been proposed as a parliamentary candidate. The anarchist in her had silently assailed the hypocrisy of standing, or worse, winning a seat. There was all that arcana of legislative detail she didn't even really believe in: pettifogging legalism, haggling over minutia, solicitors arguing with barristers over the place of a comma and the meaning of a word, when all the real power was wielded in the capitalists' clubs and boardrooms.

She decided definitively. She'd get off at Leeds. She had to. It was the only way to escape.

Through the compartment window, her gloom was matched by the sodden midlands landscape sweeping past the train, a monochrome of grey and dull brown, spindly frozen trees at narrow grade crossings bereft of traffic in the cratered lanes. Beyond them, the endless undulations of open fields, vacant but for an occasional sheep seemingly frozen to the ground where it stood.

A sudden splash of rainwater against the window made her turn away instinctively to protect her herself. Then she was back in the warm, dry second-class compartment. *You're going to blub, right there. Get a grip!* Jennie squared herself in the seat.

The middle-aged man sitting across took out a packet of cigarettes and offered one. She accepted. But her curt response to pleasantries encouraged no more of them. She knew that riding alone, as she had so often in the last years traveling the Labour Party speaking circuit in Scotland and beyond, she was a magnet for attention, and even presumption. Young, pretty, but with no evident interests in primly feminine style, her manner did not signal clearly to men how she wanted to be treated. And once the Scottish lass with the tastes of a cosmopolitan bohemian began to speak, people were even more perplexed. Jennie hadn't allowed bourgeois expectations to constrain her. Smoking in public, accepting a cigarette from a stranger wasn't done, she knew. But she'd never cared before. Would she have to start caring?

You've never given in to fear before! Don't start now. It wasn't to be the first time Jennie had broken into a man's world. She was not twelve when she'd interrupted a man for the first time. There were half a dozen seated round the hearth arguing socialism on a Sunday afternoon in the winter of 1916 in her parents' home along the miners' terraces. Jennie's parents had given up hotel work and her dad had returned to the pits. He'd become a miners' union leader.

One among the men had praised the disgraced cabinet minister, Winston Churchill for going into the trenches with the Royal Scots Fusiliers. Sitting behind them and listening, Jennie had recognised the name. She came forward and interrupted,

"Isn't he the bastard who sent troops to shoot the Welsh miners at Tondypandy?"

Shocked as much by the interruption as by the oath in the mouth of a girl, the men had glared in her direction as the speaker spoke harshly,

"It's not your place to contradict your elders, lassie."

The man looked to James Lee to reprove his daughter with slap across the face. Instead he'd smiled and brought his arm round his daughter.

"Quite right, my girl."

Thereafter James Lee had treated his daughter as an equal in political discussion at his table and round his hearth and made his weekly guests do so as well.

Suddenly the train was in a tunnel, turning the gloom to blackness that made the window into a mirror. She looked at her reflection in the carriage window. *Steady on, Jennie, you're not getting out at Leeds. You'll just have to start all over again at Westminster.*

* * *

There was a more immediate problem though, one waiting for her train at Euston. Would it be just Charlie Trevelyan alone, or would he come with his wife, Lady Mary? His invitation to stay till she found digs in London was natural enough. But in what capacity would she be a guest, protégé, friend of the family, political ally, discreet and occasional liaison? Or member of parliament for North Lanark? She'd have to begin as she meant to go on.

She'd met Charlie two years before, on a channel ferry, bound for a socialist conference they were both to attend in Brussels. He was old enough to be Jennie's father, but at fifty-eight still almost dashingly handsome. Only once they were off the ferry at Ostend did she learn, and not from him, that Charlie was the honourable Charles Trevelyan, heir to the 2d baronetcy of Wallington, whatever that was. Despite his wealth and social status, Trevelyan had been a cabinet minister in the first, short-lived Labour government back in 1924. He was a rare figure, a wealthy landowner on the left of the Labour Party. More than once in the succeeding two years, they had found themselves together under the same dingy hotel roof, at party conferences and before Labour bi-election rallies. Twice he had gallantly given her diner, and afterwards she had discreetly rewarded his gallantry.

It hadn't been her first time by any means. In university she'd been no less free than the men in her year. She was discreet but willing to take a boy home (if she could sneak him past her landlady), or to sneak into his digs. Armed with a letter from her mother to Marie Stopes' Edinburgh address, Jennie had secured a diaphragm. It had put her on a level playing field.

Taking Charlie Trevelyan to her bed was how Jennie described it to herself, though the bed was usually in his grander suite in the party meeting hotel. Doing so was her introduction to the uncomplicated attitude towards casual sexual recreation adopted by the British upper class across much of the political spectrum. And when at last she'd met Charlie's wife, Lady Mary Katherine Trevelyan, her friendly but knowing smile told Jennie she was perfectly at ease with her husband's dalliances.

* * *

The train glided into Euston Station, hissing steam from its brakes up toward the compartment windows. Almost before it had come to a complete stop, passengers were alighting, striding purposefully down the platform. This was London.

There he was, just beyond the barrier, unruly grey hair over a high forehead, chiselled features, a strong straight nose, a natural smile every politician envied, and dressed, she noticed, to receive a parliamentary delegation. Beside Charlie stood the formidable wife, ten years younger, nearly as tall as her husband, chestnut hair piled and twisted beneath a wide-brimmed hat. Lady Mary was carrying flowers. Jennie was relieved. She would be glad to be their guest, not just his.

The Trevelyans' London home was a large, un-detached, red-brick, three-storey house on Great College Street, literally in the clock-tower shadow of the Palace of Westminster. As the butler took on the burden of one winter coat after another, Lady Mary began scanning the post lying on a buffet at the entry.

"A couple for you, Jennie, delivered from the House..." She paused and her eyebrows rose. "And one from the palace?" Catching her breath, Lady Mary looked inquiringly towards Jennie. "My, but you travel in rich company for a stalwart of the Labour Party!"

She handed Jennie the creamy envelope and a letter opener, inviting her to open the message before them.

Jennie decided she had to do as Lady Mary's gesture bid her. She opened the envelope and scanned the note. Then she read it aloud.

"Dearest Jennie, how wonderful that my childhood playmate should rise to the station of a Member of Parliament. Do warn me of your maiden speech and I shall certainly find my way to the Ladies' gallery. Best wishes, Elizabeth, Duchess of York."

"Childhood playmate? Whatever is she talking about?"

Charles Trevelyan's look combined quizzicality with a tinge of envy unbecoming to a left-wing politician, an incipient republican for that matter.

Jennie's train of thought had gone back almost fifteen years till it was snapped back by the question.

"Oh, we've known each other since the war, when she was just Bowes-Lyons."

"Lady Elizabeth Bowes-Lyons, daughter of the earl of Strathmore and Kinghorne," they were both reminded by Lady Mary, who evidently knew her Debrett's *Peerage*. She softened but couldn't keep the incredulousness out of her voice.

"How did you meet?" She had to gulp away the 'how*ever*' in her question.

"When I was a girl I went to visit a wounded cousin who was convalescing at Glamis Castle. They had a fire and flood. I helped her save a lot of furnishings and we became friends."

Lady Mary was doing her sums.

"A girl? A wee child!" She feigned a Scots accent. "You were ten in the war."

"Twelve, actually, when we met. She was only fifteen. We haven't met more than a half dozen times since the war. Once or twice in Edinburgh when I was at the 'varsity, and not since she married the Duke. But we've stayed in touch, rather."

"You know she almost snared the Prince of Wales himself before settling on the younger brother," Lady Mary observed to no one in particular. Then she turned to Jennie. "In any case, you're to take the oath at tonight's sitting. You'd better know the form." Lady Mary rose. "It's a bit of bowing...and swearing loyalty to your royal friend's father-in-law. Are you up for that, Jennie?" The younger woman smiled and nodded. "Now, let's imagine the Speaker's chair is there." She gestured to the far end of the long sitting room. "You'll enter from the lobby...with your two sponsors." Lady Mary gestured Jennie to the sliding doors on the opposite end of the room, where her host and hostess came to either side and they walked together across the room to an imaginary dispatch box. Lady Mary put a hand to Jennie's back. "This is where you bow to the Speaker...three times."

* * *

Was it urgent business or curiosity about a young woman firebrand that filled the House of Commons that late afternoon? Conservatives affected to take no notice, but Labour members waved order papers as she came to the bar of the house. On one side Robert Smillie, her father's oldest political friend, looked like a rumpled don. On the other, James Maxton, perhaps the most radical MP in the country—wraith-thin, his long hair running down to his shoulders—was dressed even less formally than her other sponsor. *I might as well be waiving the Red Flag. Or singing it*, she thought.

There, before the great mace, she bowed thrice, but did not take up the bible, nor would she invoke the almighty, except as the law required. She raised her right hand. "I, Jennie Lee, do swear that I will be faithful and bear true allegiance to His Majesty King George, his heirs and successors, according to law. So help me God." And then under her breath, Jennie, as if to counteract the spell, sang the words of *The Red Flag*, words she'd learned as a small girl:

> *Then raise the scarlet standard high.*
> *Beneath its shade we'll live and die,*
> *Though cowards flinch and traitors sneer,*
> *We'll keep the red flag flying here.*

She could not yet know all the famous political figures—Labour, Conservative, Liberal—that now crowded round her with their congratulations. But she recognised Ramsay MacDonald, as the elderly man strode the few steps from the opposition front bench and extended a hand that was cold to the touch. There was an unwonted smile on his face.

"Ah, Miss Lee. You're very welcome to the house. We're so glad to have your voice on our benches."

Jennie didn't notice, nor would she have been able to place the woman standing on the other side, behind the government front bench, who now drew a sharp breath, and muttered, to no one in particular, "So, Oedipus meets Laius, King of Thebes."

"What's that you say, Lady Astor?" said the member next to her.

"Nothing dear, nothing at all." She stepped to the aisle and went up to make the acquaintance of the new member for North Lanark.

Chapter Three

It wasn't until she made her maiden speech a few weeks later, that Sir Oswald Mosley—Tom, to his friends—noticed Jennie Lee. He listened to her speech with interest, amusement and agreement, of course. Politically, they were on the same side, the very left of the Labour Party. But that wasn't what drew him so strongly to her. It wasn't her looks, either, though she was more than pretty, alluring in a way that showed no effort. It was the complete difference between Jennie Lee and all the women he'd bedded that made her so damned attractive.

Sitting on the Labour front benches, he had to twist his body to look at her standing behind and above him in the backbenches. At first, she had looked at her notes, then, warming to her subject, she let the pages fall. *Was this for effect?* he wondered. She made no effort to disguise a lowland Scot's accent, nor to look anything like the other half dozen, matronly women MPs. Dark brown hair naturally curled but not bobbed to her shoulders, deep-set eyes, wearing a belted dress that did not hide her figure, she seemed very tall, looming over the back benches. Turning from left to right as she began to speak, sometimes arms akimbo, sometimes hammering the right hand down on the left, Jennie Lee was a splendid sight to Mosley. Her face, alternately bitter with sarcasm, wreathed in anger, was steadily beautiful in a way he found irresistible.

He might have seen her before, Mosley realised, once or twice at Labour Party meetings in the last few years. But he'd never taken any notice. Now, quavering slightly, she unleashed bolts of invective against the Chancellor of the Exchequer, Winston Churchill. This Miss Lee was impossible to ignore—by turns formidable, impudent, brave, reckless, smart, impetuous. A woman after his own heart, and also his head. He knew he'd have to add Jennie Lee to his—what was the right word for these

16

women Tom drew to himself—his seraglio? He wanted to think of them as friends, but he knew that most others wouldn't think of his lovers that way.

* * *

The Chancellor's budget speech was always the highlight of the Parliamentary year. The 600 or so MPs would have to crowd into the four wainscoted banks of benches. Winston Churchill's had been designed as a bribe to the voters, in the election everyone knew was coming in the fall of 1929.

Now, after several days debate, Churchill relaxed. No one had managed to land a blow on his policies. The Chancellor hadn't reckoned with Jennie Lee's maiden speech.

She'd been listening to the debate with increasing anger. Three days in, she rose, caught the Speaker's eye, and in a maiden speech made Churchill's complacent reassurances sound foolish. On the Labour frontbench, Tom Mosley looked like he enjoyed every minute of it.

It was an evening sitting late in April. The house was filling as the professional men came into the chamber after a day in the courts, offices and boardrooms. Those with no need to work and no theatre tickets for the evening were sauntering in from supper parties, several still in dinner jackets. Lady Astor was already in her accustomed seat two rows up from the government bench, in a black sack suit and tricorn hat calculated to convey her high-minded distain for the politicians surrounding her. Surveying the scene, Lady Nancy caught sight of something unusual. There, above the floor of the House, in the Ladies' gallery, sat Elizabeth, the Duchess of York. *Whatever is she doing here?* King George V's daughter-in-law had never before shown any interest in politics. Jennie too had noticed her friend. No one detected the smiles they exchanged.

Jennie had been trying to catch the Speaker's eye for a quarter of an hour, rising repeatedly from her seat along the bench at the back of the chamber. She had already learned that to hold the House she had to entertain. To win it over she had to make members laugh at Churchill. She wanted to scold, to shout, to hector. But she knew she had to mock.

When at last her turn came, members on both benches noticed. The word filtered to the smoking rooms, "Jennie Lee is up," and the House began to fill.

"Mister Speaker." Shouting out the words overmastered a moment's fright.

Having secured a drop in the hum of conversation, she looked down briefly at a sheaf of papers in her hand. She began coolly.

"In his entertaining speech the Chancellor spoke in the warmest terms about the working class and congratulated himself on its increased living standards. He particularly noted the increased consumption of motorcycles and silk garments."

She lingered over the words 'silk garments,' forcing everyone's memory back to Churchill's words.

"I have yet to see such finery in my constituency, still less to be run over by a miner in silk pyjamas astride his Norton motorcycle."

Now she would puncture the laughter.

"What I have seen are children who go to bed wearing every stitch of clothing they own just to survive a freezing night with no coal in the grate at all. What I have seen, with my own eyes, are underfed, underpaid miners, heaving a cart filled with tons of coal up a grade because the mine owner, who drives something rather grander than a motorcycle, won't harness the cart to a pit pony or even the meanest little engine."

A rather large Tory backbencher shouted out, "And put a brace of miners out of work?"

Jennie looked across and behind Churchill lounging on the government front bench.

"Perhaps the honourable member could employ them to help him on with his silken garments, or dress the Chancellor of the Exchequer when it comes to that."

The House began to roar at this riposte and even Churchill smiled. Most MPs knew of Churchill's boast that his skin was too sensitive for anything save silk underclothes

She turned back to look at Churchill, sprawled across the front benches, folding and refolding his order paper, whispering with Stanley Baldwin, the Prime Minister, now back to making a show of indifference at her remarks. Jennie came to the end of her speech: a peroration she'd memorised, one as unparliamentarily in its tone as she could contrive without incurring the Speaker's banishment.

Jennie addressed Churchill directly, "You stand before us and, with a straight face, insist that a shilling more in the old age pension will destroy our financial position, undermine our trade, overburden industry, make it impossible for the working classes to purchase more tea, more sugar, more silk garments! You say to us the government is doing everything that economic circumstances allow! No. That is cant, corruption and incompetence!"

She sat down, trembling with anger, but feeling the whole House's intake of breath, the hiss of exchanged whispers.

Then shouts of "Unparliamentary language!" "Shame!" "Withdraw!" spread across the Tory benches on the other side of the chamber.

The Labour benches were subdued. Had they been listening? *Why are they silent? Surely I've only said what they've been thinking right along. All that noise on the Tory side, just mock indignation, Jennie. Pay no heed. But why are my lot silent?* Was it just because they'd never heard a woman, a young woman, a girl, give as good as she got? Suddenly it came to her that there'd never been a moment's stage fright after the first moment she had risen to speak.

* * *

Jennie did not wait to hear the next speaker. Nor did she feel the tug of the others on the bench, warm in their encouragement, as she rose to leave the chamber. She simply felt relief, the sort of satisfaction that comes after an examination one had well and thoroughly prepared for. She descended to the floor of the house, bowed to the Speaker and walked out.

She didn't notice Tom Mosley's eye following her down each tread of the stair, over to the mace, where she bowed, and out into the lobby of the palace of Westminster. He had savoured every moment of her triumph. In fact, he'd fallen completely in love with her, or rather with the idea of having her. But it was not, Tom Mosley recognised, the moment to approach her. His instincts about women were unerring.

As she descended the stairs to the Lady Members' Room, Jennie heard a heavy tread of steps behind her. She turned to see Winston Churchill's somewhat breathless but beaming face. He reached her and before she could say a word, put his hand on her arm.

"I say, what a debut! Marvellous the way you took the wind out of my sail." Jennie was about to thank him and move off. But keeping his hand on her arm, Churchill continued. "You must continue to speak like that in the house. There are too few voices like yours."

His look of pleasure was evidently sincere. Still, Jennie felt the need to be unhanded. Without a word she lifted his fingers off her arm. Churchill immediately saw that he had been carried away by his warmth. He drew back slightly and looked down at her arm.

"I do beg your pardon."

"It's quite alright, Mr Churchill."

"Pray, call me Winston. We're all members of the same club here."

"I doubt it," she paused to try on his Christian name, "Winston." It sounded like false bonhomie. Together they mounted the stairs to a broad landing.

"You were supposed to be offended by my remarks. Weren't you?"

"Oh, I disagreed with them, heartily. But offended? No. It's politics, my dear. That was what you were meant to do." He paused, gauging whether she'd understood. When Jennie nodded, he went on. "Not enough of that sort of thing from your side."

They both turned to see Lady Nancy Astor descending the stair behind them. She reached them and grasped Jennie by the arm Churchill had grasped, but much more firmly.

"Come away, Miss Lee. You can't afford to be seen with this... this...four flusher."

Jennie was no happier to be manhandled by Lady Astor. She jerked the arm away again.

"Why not? Winston's being perfectly charming." Jennie's tone was ever so slightly supercilious.

Lady Astor failed to notice.

"Winston, is it?" She literally tisked. "Well, I suppose you're safe from being mauled by the sexless blowhard, drunk or sober."

By now, Churchill had moved back up the stair. Whether through distain or embarrassment he had not replied to Nancy Astor's implicit accusations.

The two women continued down the stair in silence.

Then Jennie spoke. "I'm sorry, Lady Astor, but I fear I need to be the judge of whom I'm seen with." They were walking side by side along the wide corridor.

"Yes, of course, Miss Lee." The older woman nodded her head. "It was sheer bloody-minded of me He's quite harmless, actually, unlike most of the men in this place."

Jennie stopped. "What do you mean, Lady Astor?

"Only that almost all of them will want to take advantage. Even those who don't try will still want to. And the more important they are, the more they're given to womanising."

"Except for Churchill?"

"Horrible man. But he's kept his marriage vows."

Jennie laughed. "Is that why you called him undersexed?"

"Actually, I said 'sexless,' Miss Lee." She paused. "But I suppose it comes to the same thing. Still, I don't think he's an… invert, so it's the only explanation."

Invert had for 30 years been the polite term for men like Oscar Wilde.

By now they had reached the Lady Members' Room. It was the only space accorded the half dozen or so women among the 615 MPs at Westminster, and nowhere near the only ladies' room in the entire palace. As they entered, Nancy Astor's maid approached with a salver and a note upon it. Lady Astor reached for the envelope, her eyes widening as she scanned the return address.

"Simkins, this letter is for Miss Lee, not for me." She passed the salver to Jennie.

"So sorry, milady." Her servant blushed.

"Natural mistake, Simkins. It's from Buckingham Palace." She turned to Jennie. "Who do you know at the palace, Miss Lee?" One didn't ask a direct question like that, Nancy Astor knew well enough. But she was quite unable to supress the curiosity.

"Only a servant," Jennie lied, putting the envelope in the battered leather case she'd left on her desk.

Lady Astor gave the girl a sharp look. "One who steals Buckingham Palace notepaper?" She was not fooled. There had to be a connection between the note Miss Lee had received and the singular presence of the Duchess of York in the Strangers' Gallery. But what did this have to do with the intelligence about Jennie Lee's parentage that Nancy Astor was already in possession of?

She turned to her lady's maid. "Time to dress for the Connaught party, Simkins." The two went off to a corner of the room where a screen and a clothes tree stood. Moments later she came out in a shimmering Balenciaga gown and choker, pulled a fox stole over her shoulders and strode from the room.

Chapter Four

The next afternoon Jennie ventured into the Smoking Room, just to see whether anyone had remembered her speech of the night before. The Smoking Room, the terrace overlooking the Thames, the member's restaurant—these were all places Lady Astor had sternly warned Jennie away from.

* * *

The noble lady had taken Jennie firmly by the hand, that first day she'd been sworn in, too firmly, Jennie thought, though she decided not to ask to be unhanded.

"Come with me, young lady." It was the tone of a head teacher with a stroppy pupil.

Nancy Astor led her away from the House of Commons chamber through the palace and down a broad flight of marble stairs. At the bottom they turned underneath the stair into a windowless corridor. They arrived at an unlabelled door that Lady Astor threw open.

"The Lady Members' Room," she spoke with finality and stepped aside for Jennie to enter.

There were six women in the room to whom Jennie was now formally presented. The four Tory ladies were older, moneyed, married. A couple sat for constituencies their late husbands had filled. Another was, like Lady Astor, the titled wife of a wealthy husband, ennobled and now sitting in the House of Lords. Three of the women in the room were Labour MPs, who gathered round Jennie to welcome her.

Jennie peered round the dark, close room, poorly lit, with rather shabby furniture: a few small desks, one chesterfield, a coat tree and a screen. The wainscoting darkened the space into a gloom. The only natural light in the room fell from a clerestory window that opened on an interior courtyard of the palace.

"Why are we cooped up in here?" Jennie asked to no one in particular.

"What do you mean cooped up?" It was one of the Labour members, the woman closest in age to Jennie, but still ten years older. Jennie knew the name, Ellen Wilkinson, *Red Ellen* she was called, owing to the colour of her hair and her politics.

Jennie turned to face her. "Lady Nancy and I passed some very nice public rooms on the way here."

Before she could answer Lady Astor declaimed, "No woman of virtue would be seen in the Smoking Room of the House." None of the other women spoke up to disagree with her. The silence was Nancy Astor's signal to offer a diatribe. "What members get up to in those places, drinking, swearing, bawdy stories, and swarming over any female foolish enough to allow herself to be lured into the place...Stay away, Miss Lee!"

Jennie had let the matter drop, but she knew Lady Astor's injunction would not deter her.

* * *

Sauntering alone into the member's Smoking Room, Jennie was soon standing at the bar, the focus of an orbit of a half dozen members, the youngest perhaps twenty years her senior, all of them safely Labour men, all of them fawning in their compliments.

The room was large, unashamedly masculine in its heavy leather furniture. There were long tables at which members sat playing backgammon and chess, and smaller ones for those sharing tea or a pint, or something stronger. Every one seemed to have a cigar, pipe or cigarette in his hand. *Well, it is the smoking room*, Jennie thought. The rather ugly applique on every wall, under pictures of parliamentary worthies, made the room look decidedly Victorian, aggressively so. There were large windows that overlooked the terrace and the invisible Thames below, racks of newspapers, a billiards table and a bar behind which stewards stood in white jackets.

Lady Astor had been right. Standards in the smoking room seemed rather louche. Jennie couldn't help thinking, *Must all your compliments have to be laced with innuendo?* But she smiled agreeably. Thankfully, no one in the claque surrounding her was smoking a cigar. She found she was enjoying herself. *This is what a gentlemen's club must be like...and what do you know, I'm a member.*

Through the tobacco smoke, she noticed someone staring at her. He was magnetically handsome. Standing very erect, he was well built, with dark hair over a broad forehead, heavy brows, penetrating eyes, a moustache between chiselled cheekbones. Yes, this was the same man who had been sitting on the Labour front bench, twisting to watch her speak the night before. He evidently knew that he was striking to look at. Even standing with his hands in his suit coat pockets, he had the bearing of a guardsman, beautifully dressed in a Saville Row double-breasted. *Could he really be a Labour member?* She tried to place him. *Looks more like a Tory toff.* And he was staring at her with a smile that made his carnal interest frank. *Who are you?* She looked about her. *Can't ask this lot who he is!* She didn't want to meet him surrounded by these men anyway. Evidently he didn't wish to meet her then and there either. When he was sure she had noticed him, he nodded and walked out of the room.

Of course! Suddenly, Jennie knew who this was, though no newspaper photograph did him justice. But the descriptions, the word portraits she'd read in the papers, should have been enough. It was Mosley, Sir Oswald Mosley, 6th Baronet Mosley of someplace or other, Jennie couldn't remember. Like Jennie now, he'd once been the youngest member of the House of Commons, elected at nineteen just after the Great War. Over a period of three or four years beginning in 1924, he'd moved from the

Conservative Party all the way across the spectrum to Jennie's left-wing of Labour. Their paths had never crossed. She thought she might just change that. The chance came much sooner than she expected.

* * *

Less than a week later, Jennie found herself at Charlie Trevelyan's home, invited for dinner. She'd managed to find something to wear at a shop just below her dingy little flat in Soho. It specialised in the sort of evening dress a deb would cast off after a single wearing that made it no longer fashionable. The long gown, in dark violet, backless and with a cowl front, was close enough fitting to show what there was of a boyish figure, but long enough to cover rather shabby pumps. It made her look taller than her five feet seven inches, but alas, no older.

There were to be eight for dinner: Sir Charles and Lady Mary Trevelyan; a Cambridge economist named Keynes and his ballerina wife, Lydia; a conservative MP, introduced as Captain Harold Macmillan, and his wife Lady Dorothy Cavendish—odd, she'd introduced herself that way, not as Mrs Macmillan. Jennie was the seventh. The eighth was apparently late.

The name Keynes meant something to Jennie. He'd made a mark writing a book about the Treaty of Versailles, and then another one, a slashing attack on Churchill for returning Britain to the gold standard. Keynes was in his late 40s, thin enough to bend in a stiff breeze, his tone something between avuncular and condescending. His wife looked every inch the dancer, but initially said almost nothing. The other couple, closer to Jennie's age, seemed ill matched. He was tall and reticent, stooped, with a slight limp. *He's Captain Macmillan, so a war injury?* Jennie wondered. The wife was fashionable and effusive.

The guests, host and hostess were all in the drawing room, indulging in the new craze for American cocktails, when the butler announced the last member of the dinner party:

"Sir Oswald Mosley."

Charlie Trevelyan stepped forward, extending his hand. "So glad you were able to come Mosley. I think you know every one, except perhaps Miss Lee, the—"

"The new member for North Lanark," Mosley finished the sentence with a smile. Apparently he even knew her precise constituency. *However did he learn I'd be here tonight?* Jennie wondered.

"How nice to meet you, Miss Lee. Splendid maiden speech!" He smiled warmly, indeed magnetically, and took her hand.

Lady Trevelyan was watching Mosley as one might observe a predatory falcon.

"You don't know each other already?" They both shook their heads. Lady Mary observed, "I'd have thought your politics would have thrown you together before now."

"How so?" Jennie invited her to explain.

"You're both Independent Labour Party, aren't you?"

"Is that right?" Jeannie looked towards Mosley with surprise and pleasure.

"Well, there's no other way I could get into the Labour Party." Unlike the Conservatives and Liberals, Labour was a confederation of disparate groups. "I don't qualify for union membership. I'm certainly no Fabian and I won't join a co-op. So the Independent Labour Party was my only way in."

Charlie Trevelyan now sought to bring the tall captain, Macmillan, into the conversation. "How about you, Macmillan? You don't seem any more attached to the Tory party than Mosley was before he quit."

Macmillan was about to reply when he was interrupted by his wife.

"Politics. What a bore." She downed her second martini and lurched slightly to the drinks tray.

To break the embarrassed silence, she turned to the others

and asked, "Have you seen the new Arnold Bennett play, at the Theatre Royale? That Charles Laughton is a scream."

Jennie smiled. "Charles Laughton? He's got a flat in the place where I live."

"I say, Miss Lee, make a play for him, do! You've the looks for it." Lady Dorothy's directness didn't seem to shock anyone. But Jennie felt the need to change the subject.

"Actually, the building's had a more distinguished occupant than the Laughton's. Karl Marx lived there when he first came to Britain."

"Is that why you lodge there, politics?" Annoyance tinged Lady Dorothy's voice.

The butler announced dinner and the company put down their drinks. In pairs they moved out of the brightly lit salon to a darkened room, in the middle of which a table had been laid. Over a brilliant white tablecloth, cluttered with beautifully polished silver, each of the eight places glittered. Going in, Jennie found herself briefly on the arm of Tom Mosley. They looked at the place cards and took their seats.

The party made a start at the dining table etiquette of alternating small talk to one's right and left as the courses succeeded one another. Months later, Jennie would reflect on how beautifully each of them managed to tip toe through the mine fields of what they must have known about each other. The dinner was her introduction to the complexities of cosmopolitan life in the capital. Each party round the table bore an almost open secret, one Jennie knew or would soon learn without asking. Lady Dorothy Cavendish had been carrying on an affair with another MP. Her lover was her husband's best friend, and Captain Macmillan, who looked ashen that night, would contemplate suicide within months. Keynes was a homosexual married *en blanc* to the beautiful ballerina sitting across from him, with her own chequered taste for men. At one end of the table, Charlie Trevelyan was Jennie's sometime lover. At the other end was his complaisant wife. As for Mosley, Jennie was about to become one of his almost open secrets.

By the savoury course, Mosley decided that Lady Dorothy's injunction against politics had lasted long enough.

Looking across to Keynes, Mosley observed, "Look here, you're the only man at the table not an MP." Keynes looked up, daubing his mouth. Mosley continued. "Ever think of standing? You've certainly got strong opinions."

Keynes thought for a moment. The others fell silent, really interested in his answer. How much of the truth could he tell? That he'd be laughed out of his circle, the Bloomsbury group, if he stood?

He replied coolly, "No discipline, Mosley. Won't take the whips."

"Sorry, Keynes, not good enough. Party discipline's never stopped me. "

"Stopped you? It provokes you, Tom!" Lady Trevelyan laughed. "You're as bad as Churchill. Crossing the floor to Labour after you were elected as a Conservative!"

"I'll have to cross back again to equal Winston's record for ratting and re-ratting." He used the word Churchill had employed to describe his two escapes from sinking political ships, in 1904 and 1924.

Lady Mary teased. "Would you do it, Tom?"

Mosley put down his napkin and thought for a moment. "If I had to, to get anything done. There are a million unemployed men in this country and no one's interested in finding them work." Mosley glanced towards Jennie, gauging the effect of his words. She smiled, nodding her concurrence. She was about to speak when Mosley went on. "Winston understands there's no point being in politics without at least a chance at power. In fact, power is the only thing that makes the whole filthy business interesting."

"Filthy?" Macmillan asked.

"Squalid!" There was disdain in Mosley's tone. "I've met too many men at Westminster who are there just for what they can get out of it. And the jobbers you've to deal with...Belisha, Mond, Shinwell..." He fell silent for a moment while the others contemplated his list. There was one from each party on it— Liberal, Conservative, Labour, but all Jews. No one round the table took exception. Was this acquiescence, embarrassment or cowardice Jennie wondered? Casual anti-Semitism was fashionable. Probably it meant nothing. Meanwhile Macmillan and Keynes frowned at each other, but good manners kept them from remonstrance.

At this point, Dorothy Cavendish lost patience. "I suppose one just can't escape politics at this table. Do you think the ladies can retire now, Lady Mary?" She looked towards Lady Trevelyan and rose to pre-empt a demur.

"Quite right," Lady Mary concurred. "Let's leave the gentlemen to their port and politics."

Jennie remained seated. "I'll stay on if I may."

She addressed herself to Lady Mary. It was something she'd done before at the few formal dinner parties.

Lady Mary nodded. "Suit yourself." Then she led the two other women from the dining room.

* * *

There was a complicated little dance as the men moved to vacated seats on either side of their host. Macmillan, who'd been seated in the middle of the table, took a seat at Charlie Trevelyan's immediate left. Before Keynes could take one of the empty places closer to the others Mosley rose, offered his to Keynes and came round the table to sit next to Jennie. She noticed. When they had settled, the butler brought a tray of drinks, a box of cigars and a silver cigarette case to the table. Trevelyan and Keynes both reached into the box and a cigar nipper was handed round.

Mosley took up the cigarette box and offered one to Jennie, who took it.

Freed from any further conversational constraint, Trevelyan turned to party politics. "Well, comes the flapper election." It was to be the first election with full woman's suffrage. "Will the ladies change things, Jennie?"

She laughed at the fact obvious to all. "I shall at least be allowed to vote for myself." Then she thought for a minute. "I don't think it will change things much. For 40 years Tories wouldn't grant woman the vote because the suffragettes were all real socialists. ILP, my lot. But most women are conservative."

"There's a pity." It was Macmillan, the only member of the Conservative party in the room.

"You're right, Miss Lee." Keynes spoke through a funnel of blue grey smoke as he tried to get his cigar started. "If they vote Labour, it'll be because they reckon old Ramsay MacDonald'll be as niggardly with their money as the proprietor of a coal mine."

Everyone laughed at the image, but each for a different reason. Jennie remembered that the Labour leader had helped break the general strike in '26 and destroyed the coal miners union.

The table fell to discussing the details of industrial policy — Keynes giving a little lecture on economics, Macmillan suddenly enthusiastic in agreement, Charlie Trevelyan shaking his head at Keynes' political naiveté.

But Jennie was no longer listening closely. She was instead preoccupied by the feeling of Mosley's hand on her thigh, warming it through the thin gown. She should have removed it instantly. *Why are you letting him do this?* The reply came back in her thoughts. *It's only a bit of fun.* How far up her leg would she allow it to go? The feelings were becoming increasingly pleasurable as the hand moved slowly up her thigh. Jennie had to decide where to draw the line. *Not here. Not yet.*

Suddenly the conversation shifted. Trevelyan was asking Mosley a question. "Mosley, I hear your good Lady Cynthia has been adopted as the Labour candidate for Stoke-on-Trent. Is that right?"

"Yes, Cimmie is standing."

"Is that quite fair? Husband and wife both on the Labour benches."

"Front benches too, if I can contrive it," Mosley replied in a smug tone.

Jennie decided it was time to end the little under-the-table game. It wasn't the casual mention of an absent wife. She already knew enough about political marriages not to be terribly surprised. But she'd be embarrassed if Keynes or Charlie noticed. They'd be too discreet to let on in any way if they were to. Perhaps they'd already noticed.

It was certainly too late to remonstrate with Mosley, even by a glance of anger. His hand had been caressing the flesh beneath her gown for too long now. She should have removed his hand immediately if his advance had really been unwelcome.

You're playing with fire, and not yet burned, girl. Stop now! The thought made her stand up quickly, so quickly if the other men had been looking, they would have seen Mosley's hand drop from her lap. She stubbed out her cigarette.

"Thank you, Sir Charles. I'll join the ladies after all."

* * *

Jennie decided to walk home along the Embankment, to lean against the wind coming up the Thames, to think her way back to Soho. She knew well enough she'd have to decide how she felt about this man she'd allowed to grope her.

There were knots of homeless men camped beneath the stone barrier that broke the weather coming off the river. These wretched souls wouldn't trouble Jennie, she knew. They might as well have been her North Lanark constituents—hungry, wet, cold, all their anger stewed down into hopeless resignation: no threat to the lone young woman passing along their cardboard shelters. Often before she would stop, talk a while, leave a half crown. For once Jennie hardly noticed them. It was Tom Mosley on her mind.

She had been steadily antagonised by his talk: the naked attraction to power, the casual anti-Semitism, the evident political opportunism. And yet he was handsome, very handsome, more striking, more attractive up close, in evening clothes, exuding a faint musk, than he'd been twenty feet away from her in the Smoking Room of the House. She'd enjoyed her effect on him as much as she'd savoured the titillation of his fingers. It had been heightened by the brazen risk they both ran, sitting there in that formal dining room, men in dinner jackets on each side of them, leaning back, puffing at cheroots and Havanas. Once or twice Keynes had looked downwards, beneath the table-top. Had he actually noticed?

Even in the chill coming off the Thames she was able to relive the sheer pleasure of the touch upon her thigh.

It wouldn't have been the first time she'd used someone and allowed herself to be used. She'd slept with Charlie Trevelyan, there across the table, more than once. It had been almost companionable however, warmth in chill hotel rooms on wintry nights in gloomy midland mill towns. She had no use for double standards. Jennie was prepared to treat men on a level, but she had to get as good as she gave—boys at the 'varsity, comrades from the picket line. But she had liked them. This would be different. Mosley struck her as brazen. And she'd never taken a lover she wasn't quite certain she could cope with.

Jennie literally shuddered and wrapped the coat tighter against a fresh gust. Lost in her thoughts, she'd gone too far along the Embankment. Jennie turned back to Northumberland Avenue, up through Trafalgar Square on her way to Soho.

Chapter Five

The next day, writs were issued for a general election to be held six weeks hence, at the end of May. With a safe seat in North Lanark, Jennie was drafted into speaking across Scotland and Northern England for every Labour Party candidate who had a chance and needed the young people's votes.

Wherever she went, doorstep to doorstep with a local candidate, the scene repeated itself: The withered, threadbare woman at her doorstep, pushing hungry children back from the door—dirty, shoeless, unclothed children she would not let Jennie meet. Behind her an older child dressed in faded calico hopsacking carried her youngest, older and younger both sucking hard on thumbs. Once Jennie had asked for the man of the house and was told he'd been out of work so long he was ashamed to come to the door. She didn't make the same request again.

Speaking a half dozen times a day, to groups that ranged from doorsteps and street corners to halls packed with hundreds, Jennie made the same speech over and over. It was full of radical promises that three months in Westminster had convinced her the old men of the Labour Party's leadership didn't really want to keep, even if they did win.

But they did win.

Jennie woke up in Glasgow on the morning of the 31st of May, 1929 to discover that her party had beaten the Tories: 287 Labour members of parliament against 260 Conservatives, with the balance of power—fifty-nine seats—held by Lloyd George's Liberal party.

Her party's victory wouldn't mean much to her, Jennie thought. She'd just be another backbench MP, occasionally indulging her outrage braying into a political vacuum, with no influence whatever over events. But that was not how things turned out.

* * *

Almost immediately, parliament was recalled. Back at her London flat for the first time in six weeks, Jennie found a third buff envelope, heavy with gold embossing. It carried a very kind, but now rather firm invitation from the Duchess of York. Evidently, her previous notes had not been merely polite correspondence with an old chum. Elizabeth Bowes-Lyons really wanted to see Jennie.

* * *

They'd never have met but for the Great War, then in its second full summer. And of course there was the fire that broke out, one late summer day in 1916. Someone, almost certainly a servant, had been careless, smoking under the sombre hennin towers circling the timbered roof of the massive central keep of the forbidding Glamis Castle north of Dundee.

The Earl of Strathmore had offered to take in wounded men at the castle, almost immediately after they had begun streaming back from the Black Watch; his son Fergus' regiment in 1914. Fergus was to die in the trenches the next year. Of course, the Earl's hospitality was only extended to "other ranks" — private soldiers and non-commissioned officers — on the understanding these men would not be so disfigured by their injuries to cause disquiet to the Earl's youngest daughter, Elizabeth Bowes-Lyons.

The fire broke out under the roof of Glamis castle sometime in the afternoon of the 16th of September 1916. Her mother, the countess, gone for the day, Elizabeth was playing chatelaine. There were about a dozen soldiers in the house. A few had visitors. One of these was a twelve-year-old girl, Jennie Lee, up from Cowdenbeath fifty miles to the south.

It was only the powerful pump of the Dundee brigade's machine that saved the castle, spreading a wet coat across the entire roof, while its men fought the fire's source in the servants' quarters beneath it.

Just when everyone was breathing a sigh of relief that the castle had been saved, the real catastrophe began. With a loud report, water began spilling in cascades out between the roof and the exterior walls. The water tank under the roof had burst and was now adding to what the fire truck had pumped out and was still sluicing down from the roof.

Standing in the park surveying the damage high above, the fifteen-year-old Elizabeth immediately understood what had happened.

"It's the water tank. It's flooding the castle!"

She rushed back into the house followed by a dozen of those nearest her. The tank's contents were spilling down the stairs from storey to storey, with the strength of a salmon run in flood. Above the stair the broad ceilings were straining with the weight, and walls were beginning to stain as the water seeped everywhere. Standing at the landing between the ground and first floors, Elizabeth took command.

"Brooms, mops, hurry! Anything that will move the water off the floors."

Among the staff and the soldiers frantically channelling the flow with whatever came to hand, Elizabeth noticed a young girl. As she worked, her head was turning from side to side surveying the paintings on the wall. Then she addressed Elizabeth.

"Should na' something be done to save 'em — the pictures and rugs, the furniture we can move? What if the ceilings collapse from the water?"

She was right. Elizabeth called the footmen and some of the soldiers together. The young girl joined in as they began rescuing furniture, pictures, rugs, anything that was threatened by the flood of cold water and could be moved. For the next three hours, a dozen maids, soldiers, guests swept, sloshed, brushed water down the stairs, until someone managed to turn off the source of the water that filled the roof tank.

By ten that night, they'd done what they could. Wet, exhausted, but slightly exhilarated by the madcap adventure she'd been through, Elizabeth found herself sitting on steps outside the carriage entrance of the vast brownstone of Glamis Castle. Next to her was the young girl who'd been through the entire afternoon and evening, never flagging, always there in the thick of things, smart, effective, not just doing things, but thinking what needed doing, and how things could be done better. Elizabeth looked at her and the girl looked back, smiling.

"How old are you?"

The girl answered, "I'll be twelve in a month or so."

"No." Elizabeth spoke in disbelief. She put out her hand. "I'm Elizabeth Bowes-Lyons. What's your name?"

The girl smiled and reached for the hand, shaking it firmly, as between victorious teammates. "Jennie Lee. I'm visiting my cousin, Corporal Pollock. He's one of the wounded." The name Bowes-Lyons evidently meant nothing to the girl.

"Did you come alone?"

"Yes, I did." She paused to explain. "I was here with my mum last month. She couldn't come today, but I wanted to."

"She let you travel all this way alone?"

"I guess she couldn't really stop me. I had the fare."

"But you'll never get home tonight. Last train to Edinburgh was at four. Your parents will worry themselves sick. Do they have a telephone?"

"No, they don't."

"Can you send a telegram?"

"I suppose, but the station in town must be closed, and besides, I can't afford it."

"We'll see to it in the morning. Meanwhile, you'll stay as my guest."

"Your guest?" Jennie looked at the older girl, as wet and bedraggled as herself. "Who are you?"

* * *

So began an unlikely friendship: the earl's ninth child and the miner's daughter. Jennie came back to Glamis several more times that autumn. Once her cousin was sent back to his regiment in October of 1916, she assumed her welcome to Glamis had expired. But early the next summer came the summons:

> *Dear Jennie,*
> *Come, do your patriotic duty! Help me deal with the hoards of*
> *wounded at the castle.*
> *Elizabeth*

She'd enclosed return railway tickets, first class.

And Jennie went, spending weeks at Glamis each of the next two years. Often out of doors in the rainy, windswept Scottish summers, the two girls, Jennie and Elizabeth, keeping soldiers walking the grounds, talking, about their wars, their lives, their futures.

By the summer of 1918, they both felt as if the Great War had been going on all their lives. Jennie was now fourteen and Elizabeth seventeen, a gulf that should have been much larger than the gap that had been between them at twelve and fifteen, but wasn't.

Right from the start, the friends had argued about things—to begin with the war, then politics, and finally, when they were older, men. Jennie was eager to convince, and Elizabeth glad to find someone prepared to disagree. From the first, Elizabeth was struck at how much more she envied her friend's life than Jennie coveted hers. She couldn't even bring herself to believe Jennie's indifference to the castle's comforts. When, at eighteen, Jennie left home for university in Edinburgh, Elizabeth tried briefly to live the younger girl's life vicariously. But within a year she was betrothed to a Royal and sustained contact with Jennie was no longer feasible. In 1923 Elizabeth Bowes-Lyons had married the King's younger son, Albert, and became the Duchess of York. Meetings would now be noticed by equerries and ladies in waiting. Both understood. Even their correspondence, once steady, had dwindled to Christmas greetings. Now Elizabeth — no, not Elizabeth, but the Duchess of York, had begun writing again.

* * *

It was a surprisingly modest teashop up Kensington Church Street Elizabeth had suggested. As Jennie walked up from the Notting Hill tube stop, she was on the lookout for the Duchess's Daimler. It had to be a Daimler, she told herself. *She's the King's daughter-in-law. She'll be expecting a curtsy, won't she? Surely not in a teashop!* The large car was impossible to miss. Someone had tried to park it discreetly round the corner on Bedford Gardens. The chauffer was standing beside the black behemoth at the kerb, smoking, not a dozen yards down the side street from the teashop's entry. He smiled and touched his cap as she passed. Somehow, he knew Jennie was the person the Duchess was waiting for.

The bell on the door made a noise loud enough for the half dozen ladies taking tea to look up at Jennie. The lace curtains of the shop window prevented the daylight from illuminating the room, except where direct sun lit up the drab green walls. Tall, thin, unsmiling women in grey smocks and white servant's caps were gliding silently between the tables, at which sat ladies distinctly older than Jennie. Watching them, Jennie couldn't help wondering how many unemployed men each was supporting.

Her friend rose from a small table in a half-hidden alcove as

Jennie entered the shop, signalling to her. Elizabeth reached out to hold her by both arms, preventing any incipient curtsy. "At last!" she sighed.

Jennie looked her up and down. She was glad to see her friend not yet looking matronly. At 30, perhaps her face was a little rounder, but the slight cleft in the chin was still just visible. Her small eyes remained mischievous and there was no visible tracery of small veins across Elizabeth's still fine complexion.

Jennie was about to reply, almost despite herself, "Your grace," but the Duchess was shaking her head.

"Elizabeth." She whispered the command.

Was it informality she craved, or did she not wish to be recognised? The Duchess of York was trying hard to look like Mrs Elizabeth Windsor, just an affluent Scottish lady, cloche hat, shingled hairstyle, and the still fashionable woman's version of the Great War trench coat. Was she too cold, even in the shop, to take it off, Jennie wondered, or was she dressed underneath for another occasion? Never mind. Jennie would keep her coat on too.

Elizabeth looked towards the table. "I've ordered a cream tea, if that's alright."

Next to the table stood a three-foot-high serving stand, holding two plates of small sandwiches and pastries at each of its levels. Glancing at them, Jennie realised she was hungry. The teapot on the table was covered with a cosy. Plainly, Elizabeth had been waiting for Jennie. The women sat and Elizabeth took off the cosy.

"I'll be mum." Jennie nodded a smile and reached for one of the crustless sandwiches on the stand.

Elizabeth began. "Will you speak again soon...in the House?"

"Not likely. The whole new intake will have to give their maiden speeches. I'm already an old member, since I was seated in last parliament."

"Now your side is the government, I expect you'll get a chance to speak more."

"Less, I fear. My leader certainly doesn't want to hear what I have to say."

"Why ever not, Jennie?"

"Because I believe in socialism and he doesn't."

"That's not the King's opinion." She looked round subversively. "Hates MacDonald. Thinks he's a raving Bolshie." They both smiled at the idea. "I expect it's the war."

MacDonald had given up the Labour leadership in 1914 because he'd opposed the Great War from the outset—his finest hour, Jennie's family had agreed.

Jennie enjoyed the thought of the King's discomfiture.

"Well, he's stuck with old Ramshackle Mac now." It was the left's disobliging nickname for their party's leader.

Elizabeth looked round before continuing. She was evidently anxious not to be overheard.

"He didn't want MacDonald as PM in the worst way. Tried to get the Tories to do a deal with the Liberals to keep your lot out."

"But that's outrageous. Labour won the most seats."

"Well, he thought that since between them Conservatives and Liberals had a majority, they could keep MacDonald from becoming PM again."

Jennie's eyes widened. "It's quite unconstitutional, Elizabeth."

"Just what Mr Baldwin said." Elizabeth continued in a whisper. "Told the King shutting Labour out wasn't 'fair play.'"

Stanley Baldwin, the outgoing Conservative, had done this once before, in 1924, letting Labour govern with only a plurality in the House of Commons.

"It was good politics the last time he did it," Jennie observed. "MacDonald didn't last six months. Tories brought down his government and won the next election on a monstrous fraud."

Elizabeth nodded. "Yes, I do remember. That Zinoviev letter forgery."

Days before that election, a Tory newspaper had published

a forged letter from Russia to British communists, supporting Labour policies.

Speaking quietly, Jennie wondered aloud, "How did you hear any of this? It would have been between the King and Stanley Baldwin."

"The King was so upset after his audience with Baldwin he couldn't help talking about it with David and Albert."

These were the King's sons, the Prince of Wales and the Duke of York, Elizabeth's husband. "And then at dinner that evening the King was still livid." Jennie said nothing, not wanting to staunch her flow of court gossip. "The Prince said giving Labour another chance was fair-play. The King interrupted him and said 'To devil with fair-play. That was Baldwin's argument when he insisted I send for MacDonald and his lot.'"

"Baldwin would have had to do a deal with Lloyd George, if he was to keep out Labour." Lloyd George, the wartime prime minister, had been forced from office after selling knighthoods to finance his party. It had been the great scandal of the early '20s.

"Well, I'm only glad they kept out that randy old goat..." Both women knew about the wartime prime minister's reputation as a womaniser.

Jennie nodded her head. "They're all like that. I was seated next one at a dinner in May, mauled me under the table, he did."

Elizabeth nodded. "I've a cousin who's like that. MP, married, got two kids. Keeps a flat in Ebury Street just for his...trysts. Terrifically good-looking. I can see how he manages it."

Jennie replied knowingly, "All those political wives in London hanging about with nothing to do."

Elizabeth's voice rose, her eyebrow lifted. She knew she was going to shock.

"But this one also sleeps with his sister-in-law and his mother-in-law!"

"How the blazes do you know this, Elizabeth?"

"No one in that family seems to make much of a secret of it. It's that randy Oswald Mosley: married to Lord Curzon's daughter, sleeps with the rest of the family."

"But that's the very man who tried to seduce me at that dinner party last spring!" Jennie's tone was a combination of amusement and anger. "Trouble is, now MacDonald has put him in the cabinet. He's the only one in government with any idea what to do about unemployment. If it came out about the wife and her mother, he'd be ruined in the party...and his policies too."

"Somehow I doubt it ever will come out."

"Why not?" Jennie wondered. "Double standard?"

"No, no, wrong end of the stick. Wives do it too. Won't ever come out. Conspiracy of silence among the press lords. Private lives off limits. They won't publish a word. Besides, they carry on the same way, many of them."

Both women fell silent. *Well, one less thing for a politician to worry about,* Jennie found herself thinking.

Elizabeth was introspective. After a moment, she spoke, almost wistfully. "Nothing like that at the palace anymore, not since naughty old Edward VII." Then she turned back to Jennie. "What I wouldn't give for a little bad behaviour. Jennie, court life's so boring. It's killing me."

"Looks pretty glamorous in the papers." Jennie wanted to comfort her friend.

"Endlessly standing round at wreath-layings? Unveiling cornerstones? Try holding yourself motionless in a receiving line with a smile painted on your face while a thousand people pump your wrist." She stopped, her frown turned to a brief sob. "I'm going to be doing this for the next thirty years. I don't think I can face it!"

She pulled a hankie from her sleeve and wiped at the two tears that had run down each cheek.

Jennie knew what she wanted to say. They'd covered this

ground in their last meetings five years before, when Elizabeth's engagement was announced. She hadn't needed to warn her friend what she was giving up, marrying the King's second son. Elizabeth knew perfectly well. She'd already declined the Duke's proposals a half dozen times when she finally gave way. The words she wouldn't say formed themselves, *Going to give up being Duchess of York, going to run away, ducky?* Her friend deserved the sarcastic, admonitory, recriminating, belligerent question. She should never have sold herself into Royal bondage. But Jennie couldn't, wouldn't make her feel worse. Instead she reached out her hand to her friend in an unvoiced apology for the unkind thought.

"What about your baby?" The Duchess' daughter was three years old. "She gives pleasure, no?"

"Yes, yes. I love Lilibet." It was her pet name for her daughter. "And Albert too." Was that addition something she had to say, Jennie wondered?

"What can I do to help—" Jennie had again almost said, "Your grace" before stopping herself. Her hand had remained covering her friend's.

"Well, you could start by meeting me a little more often." Regaining her composure, Elizabeth smiled. "I just need someone to talk to, confide in, share the way I feel about things."

Surely there's someone in your circle? Why me? Jennie thought. Elizabeth seemed to read her mind as she went on.

"All those years I listened to you prattle on against the war, when we were kids, later when you were in university arguing for socialism, I couldn't quite take it seriously. I don't know what I thought...it was just you being contrary to everything everyone else was saying. But now I don't wonder you were right all a long, or at least mostly...well, partly right."

"I'll be happy to fill your head with contrary thoughts."

"In return I may be able to offer the odd titbit or two, a scrap of intelligence here and there."

Nothing that might interest me, surely, Jennie couldn't help thinking. The British Royal family hadn't wielded real political power for a century or so.

"What do you mean, Elizabeth?"

"There's a good deal of loose talk at the palace. Lots of angry voices at table, usually about matters of state. Besides, the King is ill, and when he dies," she gulped at the *lèse-majesté*, "David's to become King, and he's terrifically indiscreet."

David was Albert's older brother, the Prince of Wales.

"King tried to teach the Prince his job, giving him the boxes." The locked red boxes with royal crests came to the palace daily from Downing Street, filled with dispatches, state papers, communications to and from the Prime Minister. But David just leaves them open with the secret papers spread about. Can't be bothered."

Now, this is interesting. Jennie drew her breath. "Well, Elizabeth, palace life doesn't sound quite so dull after all."

"So the King's stopped doing it. Doesn't think David is," she paused, looking for the right word, "sound." Jennie was silent. This was intoxicating.

"Steady on, Elizabeth. I'm thrilled to be in on your little... secrets. But I'm not going to ask you to spy on anyone for me."

"Humour me, ducky!" The words were spoken in mock cockney.

* * *

Afterwards Jennie didn't know quite what to think. She felt slightly sorry for her friend, for the choices she'd been fated, by birth, class, formation, to make, saddened about the life she now led in consequence. *Funny that, your feeling sorry for a duchess.* Poor Elizabeth Bowes-Lyons had never really been allowed to be anything but frivolous. Jennie had a hard time blaming her. But the girl wasn't foolish or feckless. *She has a mind of her own. Must have! She's still seeing you, Jennie.*

Walking away down the narrow street, back to the Notting Hill Gate tube station, Jennie asked herself why she was still keeping up with Elizabeth. *What is she to you, girl? Why haven't you dropped her in all these years?* It was rather simple, Jennie realised. Despite her own reverse snobbery, she rather liked Elizabeth. They shared enough of a past to remain friends.

Chapter Six

Tom Mosley hadn't expected to be dropped from Nancy Astor's circle just because he'd joined the Labour Party, or even when he joined the Labour cabinet. Still, he wouldn't have minded much if he had been excluded. This latest invitation for a weekend at Cliveden, her vast estate twenty-five miles west of London, wasn't really welcome at all. It would be hard to find a drink. Lady Astor was teetotal. And she'd invited Tom's wife, Lady Cynthia—Cimmie. That's what everyone called Lady Mosley.

He'd tried to discourage her from going, but Cimmie wouldn't hear of it. She'd been in the Astor circle since before the war, when her father, Lord Curzon, was Viceroy of India, and her late mother, an American heiress like Lady Nancy, had been Vicereine. Besides, now that Cimmie too was an MP—yet another woman in parliament, albeit a Labour member—she had even more in common with Lady Astor: politics.

Still, it was damned inconvenient Cimmie coming along, Tom couldn't help thinking. There'd be no bed-hopping for him, not even with a willing chambermaid.

* * *

Early Saturday morning Mosley rose and dressed to ride. Cimmie would sleep in and take a tray in her bedroom.

Striding out beyond the deep shadows of the building, the silence of the world was broken only by the crunch of the fine white gravel beneath his riding boots.

Who should be saddling up when he got to the stables but Nancy Astor? In unvoiced agreement, they rode into the lush park of the estate and down the slope to the Thames. There they stopped, held by the sparkle of the water reflecting a low morning sun as it moved slowly under trees still in leaf. Turning, their eyes traced the track back up beyond the copse to the vast palace at the brow of the hill. It stood there, the façade still in a purple shade, on its pedestal throne, overawing the woods that surrounded it.

Lady Astor broke the silence. "So, now you're in that damned socialist government."

Tom Mosley nodded, satisfaction on his smile.

Gazing round, surveying her domain, she continued, "Will your lot try to take all this away from me?"

Mosley laughed. "Not bloody likely. Too frightened to do much of anything, MacDonald is." She nodded in agreement. "Doesn't have the votes to begin with. Doesn't have the taste for it either."

"He's no revolutionary, that's for certain. Can't say the same for his spawn."

"His spawn? I suppose there are lots of serious socialists in the Labour Party. Lots of them in the ILP. Me, for one." He grinned mischievously. The ILP—Independent Labour Party was one of the constituents of the British Labour Party, the most left wing of its component groups.

"You're no socialist, Tom." Her laugh mocked him. She'd made Mosley angry for a moment. Now she needed to share something with him, something that would get him back on side again. "When I said spawn, I was speaking literally, not figuratively."

"I'd hardly describe Malcolm MacDonald as Bolshie." This was Ramsay MacDonald's son, who had won a seat in the '29 election.

"No, I meant his other child in the Commons, the love child…" She let the words hang in a silence, broken only by the sound of leather saddles shifting under their rider's weight.

"What rot are you talking, Nancy?"

"Just some wild story I heard from Chips Channon."

"What's that, then? Out with it!"

"It's that Bolshie girl MP from Scotland, Jennie Lee. Channon says MacDonald's her father."

"Astonishing!"

"What's more, she doesn't know!"

"How the blazes did he find out?"

"Channon is a snob, a cad, a nosey parker...and very amusing." She chortled. "It was right here at Cliveden last winter, just after she won her bi-election, before she made that appalling maiden speech."

Mosley recalled it. "Rather witty, I thought. So, who told Channon?"

"Well, MacDonald was here for the weekend. In the library one afternoon writing letters, when Channon walked in. Ramsay finished and left his letters on a salver for the footman. Brazen Chips couldn't resist looking through them. Wasn't interested in the official ones. But he noticed one to a woman in Scotland. So he took it off the tray, went up to his room and steamed it open, the scoundrel! There it was in black and white...MacDonald telling the mother about Miss Lee's speech."

They began riding slowly down the towpath at the Thames' edge, ducking every so often under the willows.

"Doesn't make him her father." Mosley observed.

"He quoted Shakespeare—'How sharper than a serpent's tooth to have a thankless child.' Enough for you?"

"Not at all. She was attacking Winston Churchill in that speech, not the leader of her own party! Perhaps Winston is her father and MacDonald knows the secret."

"Don't be silly. Winston is the only one of you who's never strayed."

Spot on, Mosley thought. "Right. That's why he'll never be PM. Not enough sex-drive."

Lady Astor resisted the temptation to blackguard Churchill further. It would be more fun to tell Mosley everything she knew or surmised. Then she could watch the ambitious Mosley intrigued against his prime minister.

"Actually, what MacDonald said in the letter, after quoting Shakespeare, was how glad he was she wasn't attacking her father for once, but giving the Conservatives a hard time. Then he ended the letter with 'burn after reading.' Enough for you?"

"But Nancy. You said the Lee girl doesn't know the PM is her father? How did you learn that?"

"Woman's intuition, dear. I watched them that day in the House when she took the oath. She frowned when he offered his hand. She's abusive about him in the Lady Members' Room."

"Nancy, why are you telling me this? Sowing seeds of distrust in my party?

"Your party?" She scoffed. "Your party is the party of oversexed politicians who just can't resist the women that can't resist them." She rode away at a canter.

A few moments later she slowed down, allowing Mosley to catch up. He spoke. "Whatever became of MacDonald's letter, Nancy. Did Channon ever put it into the post?"

"No. He was too proud of his naughtiness. Gave it to me." Lady Astor rode forward, afraid of showing the pleasure on her face.

Mosley rode after her as she pulled the reins on her horse into a walk. "Nancy, will you give me that letter?"

"Why, Tom?"

"Keep my leader safe from blackmail?" There was enough of the interrogative in his voice to make Lady Astor suppress a laugh. Suddenly, she saw, there was more mischief to be made giving MacDonald's letter to an overly ambitious member of his cabinet than keeping it herself.

* * *

None among the guests at Cliveden that weekend seemed to notice the Wall Street sell-off the previous Thursday and Friday.

At any rate, no one mentioned it. But after Black Tuesday of the following week, the financial panic in New York was on most people's minds.

October 30th, the day after the Wall Street crash, Jennie was sitting in a corner of one of the Westminster smoking rooms with the only other woman MP she'd yet warmed to. Ellen Wilkinson was a dozen years older than Jennie, a veteran militant who'd helped found the British Communist party in 1920. Disgusted by its slavishness to Moscow, she'd moved to Labour, been elected for the first time in 1924 and was now a minor member of MacDonald's government. A head shorter than Jennie, "Red Ellen" she was called, for her politics and her hair, which fell from her brow in almost crimson ringlets.

The two women had *The Financial Times* spread out on the coffee table in front of them. It was a far cry from the Labour Party paper, *The Daily Herald*, but they needed to understand the crash and were vainly seeking the explanation in the FT's salmon-coloured pages.

Suddenly, there were two men standing over them, casting shadows on the small print of the flimsy newsprint. Both women looked up and Ellen smiled.

"Wise, Bevan...come and sit." She patted the places next to them.

The men smiled and chose facing chairs instead.

"Jennie, let me introduce two of the new intake. Frank Wise, MP for Leicester East, and Aneurin Bevan, who sits for Ebbw Vale in Wales."

The first was in his early 40s, thin, with a long face that started at a balding dome and ended in a cleft chin. His smile was bright and his eyes kind. Wise was dressed rather formally for a Labour politician, Jennie thought, right down to the fob and chain that ran across his waistcoat. In fact he looked to Jennie like someone who would take *The Financial Times*.

The other, Bevan, was younger, late 20s or early 30s, a bear of a man, a thick mop of hair parted to the right, oval face with wide-set eyes and strong brows, thoroughly Welsh from the moment he spoke. Grasping her hand just short of too firmly, he pumped vigorously. When this man smiled his whole face seemed to move. Bevan was wearing a rather loud tie and a pin stripe double-breasted, chosen to be noticed, Jennie thought, but obviously bought off the peg.

"Help us, Wise." Wilkinson indicated the newspaper spread out before them. "We're trying to figure out the Wall Street crash."

The older man moved his hand dismissively over the pages.

"Easy to explain...after it's happened." The others waited, inviting him to continue. "No one wanted to be the last fool."

Bevan looked at him. "Last fool?"

Before Wise could say anything, Jennie interjected. "Left holding the bag."

She looked to the other man, who smiled and nodded her to go on. She liked that.

"So, Frank," she tried out the Christian name, "you think it was just a bubble, popped when the stock market ran out of fools to buy the stuff?"

"Short run, yes...Jennie." He returned the complement of using her first name. "But I think it's a symptom of something serious."

Ellen Wilkinson nodded to the newsprint on the table. "Not what your favourite economist thinks, Frank." Wise raised his eyebrows. "There's a quote by Keynes somewhere in the *FT* from him. Says the crash won't have any real effects. You don't agree, Wise?"

"I don't, actually. Been watching wheat prices."

"Wise knows about wheat prices," Ellen said to Jennie. "He advises the Soviet trade delegation here." She looked back at him. "Go on."

"Too many bumper crops all over the world—America,

Australia, Argentina, even Russia. Wheat prices are starting to collapse."

Bevan didn't mind admitting he was lost. "So?"

Wise replied, "Farming is half the American economy." He waited to hear if Bevan needed more.

Jennie understood immediately. She would finish his explanation, and see whether Wise would approve. She wanted his approval.

"Farm prices go down, everyone poorer. Everyone buys less. Result: a slump."

Frank Wise beamed. "Got it in one, Miss Lee."

Why had he reverted to surnames, she wondered? Was she putting him off with her interruptions?

"Jennie, please."

Ellen shook her head. "Still don't see the connection to the crash."

Better let Wise answer, thought Jennie.

"Someone in America twigged to the wheat price decline, someone with a lot of stock. Decided everyone was going to get poorer, all businesses would suffer. Started unloading stock. Others noticed. Then contagion took over."

"Glad we're not in the wheat business." Ellen brightened. "As for Yanks wealthy enough to dabble in stocks, I'm not going to lose any sleep worrying about them."

Frank shook his head. "Don't you see, Miss Wilkinson, it's the worst news possible for MacDonald. Knocks his policy over completely."

"I don't see it actually." Ellen looked at him frankly. "Just a lot of paper profits going up in smoke. Why should it mean anything to us?"

"Look, for ten years now, since the Great War, 'responsible' politicians," each detected Wise's ironical reference to MacDonald, "have agreed that the only way to get the unemployed back to work is to get our exports—coal, textiles, railway engines, ships—back to pre-Great War levels. That's why the Labour Party leadership helped crush the general strike in '26, to keep wages down so we could sell abroad cheaper." The recollection angered all three of his listeners, but they were silent. "Well, selling the Yanks anything is going to be quite impossible now."

Nye and Ellen spoke one word in unison. "Why?"

But Jennie had twigged, and she couldn't be stopped.

"The Americans have less money now. They are going to stop buying, stop buying from us." She stopped, looked at Wise, who smiled, nodding her on. "Same goes for every other country. They'll have to cut their orders for British goods, till MacDonald or whoever is prime minister realises export can't solve the unemployment problem." There was an ominous silence among them.

Bevan broke it. "You're saying things are going to get worse?"

Frank Wise nodded his head in regret. "Lots worse."

Chapter Seven

Every morning that gloomy winter of 1929-30, Jennie would wake up perplexed about what to do. There was Frank Wise. There was Aneurin Bevan. *As if politics weren't hard enough, even for an ideologue, now there's men to make matters more complicated.*

Almost from the day they met her, both Frank Wise and Nye Bevan had contrived to find themselves sharing the busy-work of Jennie's backbench life—parliamentary committees, sittings of the House, endless splinter group meetings, political journalism. She had detected their interests immediately.

One long weekend she made the slog back to her Scottish constituency. A day or two in North Lanark—amongst the indomitable women standing before cold grey tenements, the haggard men nursing pints to stay warm in dank public houses—had replenished Jennie's store of indignation. She didn't share their cheery confidence about what Labour would do for them now it was in power. But she certainly couldn't say so. All that weekend she'd been able to keep her mind firmly focused on politics. But now, as her train pulled out of Glasgow that Monday morning, something else intruded, persistently. The demand that she decide between the two men—Nye and Frank—became incessant and distracting. Carried along by the motion of the carriage shifting from one side to the other, she found herself longing. It was the longing that solved her problem.

* * *

Jennie had always been a magnet for men, ever since university in Edinburgh. She enjoyed it, the only attractive, unafraid, outspoken woman in a young man's world. It wasn't just the verbal swordplay, the cut and thrust of sectarian student politics. She liked the attention, the flirting. She'd let the chase take its course often enough, if she was attracted to a man. She'd no trouble admitting to herself that availability gave her power over men, and that she wanted it. But it wasn't the only thing she liked about what, with mock censoriousness, her crowd called fornication. She knew she had to take care, not just to minimise the obvious risks, but to keep her emotional freedom too. She'd always been able to keep her feelings under control. *Or perhaps you never really had feelings strong enough to test your control?* Now, Jennie knew, things were different. Her feelings were out of her control, and she didn't mind.

Sitting through the eight hours back to King's Cross, letting herself mull over Frank Wise and Aneurin Bevan, she came to two conclusions: She knew what she wanted. She knew what she wanted to want. And they weren't the same thing at all.

* * *

Nye Bevan was flamboyant, fun, attentive, shared her politics, her upbringing as a miner's child. He was her age, and he loved her, of that Jennie was pretty certain. When he made advances she had no trouble keeping him just this side of out of control. When she gave in, as she did from time to time, she could feel his need for her.

Bevan's style was slightly garish—patterned ties over Tattersall shirts, under pinstripe double-breasted suits. His wide face was handsome in a rugged way and his Welsh accent was poetry to Jennie's ear. Standing next to him, she felt in the presence of a friendly bear, one ready to encircle her, lift her off the ground, crush her in an enthusiastic hug. Bevan's thick brown hair looked like it needed cutting within minutes of leaving a barber's chair. Jennie was forever tempted to trim his bushy eyebrows. His eyes were perpetually mischievous in their glint, and he couldn't resist a smile, even for political opponents on the opposition benches.

Nye Bevan was a stalwart, who would never turn his back on the workers of the Welsh coal valleys, where he had laboured himself from fourteen. But he wouldn't deny himself fun, pleasure, and even notorious company. He had become something of a darling for the erratic reactionary newspaper magnate Lord Beaverbrook, accepting his invitations to dinner, to the theatre, to parties. And whenever he could he tried to take Jennie along.

From the first, Jennie and Nye recognised how similar were their backgrounds in the coal towns of Scotland and Wales. It made them share so much they could reliably predict one another's thoughts. Jennie recalled an evening in the fall of '29 soon after their first meeting. They were nursing drinks on the terrace of the Commons, overlooking the slow waters of the Thames, the lights twinkling in the office buildings across Westminster Bridge. The division bell had just sounded, breaking the spell and calling them back into the chamber for a vote. Jennie put down her drink, looked at Bevan.

"Nye, we could be brother and sister."

Without a pause, but smiling, he had replied, "Mmm, with a tendency to incest."

Jennie Lee and Aneurin Bevan were indeed well matched. She liked him terrifically. She believed in his star. She wanted to want him. But Jennie didn't want him.

She wanted Frank Wise. Frank was twenty years older, lean, balding, dressed like a City banker, with the slight fastidiousness of a senior civil servant. In fact, he had been one in the Great War, and carried a 'bangle' — Companion of the Order of the Bath — for his services to Lloyd George's government. He was erudite, experienced, accomplished, influential, without feeling the need to show it. Frank was quiet where Aneurin was garrulous, deep where Aneurin made waves, thoughtful where Aneurin was impetuous. He listened to Jennie, heard her out, took her more seriously than anyone she'd known before. He was a thoughtful, careful, passionate lover. And he was married. Jennie couldn't have Frank, not the way she could have Aneurin Bevan, as a husband. In truth, she didn't want Frank that way—married to him. She just wanted Frank.

It all could have been very convenient for Jennie. Nye Bevan was there for the taking. It would have been a match made in political heaven. It would have been fun, too, and there'd be no one to hurt or harm. Nothing to hide either. She wouldn't have to give up a thing to marry Nye. But she couldn't.

Soon enough Nye knew that she loved Frank, and he was willing for the moment at least to remain a comrade, a friend, a brother.

* * *

Frank had fallen in love with her. In the worst way, she realised.

The evening they first fell into bed together, after walking through quiet Whitehall streets at the end of a late night sitting of the House, neither had really expected the other to want it. She'd invited him in for a drink, knowing he'd have to refuse, and he'd accepted, knowing he should have refused. After the second small scotch she'd leaned across her chesterfield, pulled him slowly toward her, by his necktie no less, and kissed him.

Frank had responded warmly. But then straightened up. "Jennie. I have to tell you, I'm married."

"Frank, I knew that. Nye Bevan was particularly keen I knew."

"Blighter." Frank couldn't help a sardonic laugh. "What else did he say?"

"Well, he didn't volunteer any more, out of loyalty to you, I suspect." She paused. "But I made him answer some questions."

"Such as?"

"The obvious ones—name, age, what she's like." Jennie stopped again. "Whether he thought you loved her. He didn't know much."

"Well, I'm prepared to satisfy your curiosity." He pulled out a cigarette case, offered Jennie one, and lit them both with a wooden match.

"Tell me what's she's like. Do you love her?"

"Dorothy..." He thought a moment. "Formidable lady. J.P., educated, but no bluestocking. Keeps our place in Bucks beautifully. There's four kids. Three girls and a boy. The oldest two girls are in school now, here in London. They stay in town with me most weekends. Dorothy's a great help with politics. She's been chair of the Mid-Bucks Labour Party. I'm terrifically grateful to her."

"But you don't love her..." Wise was silent, so Jennie answered for him: "Anymore."

"Never sure I did. Admire her awfully. But it's not like this."

"Frank, can this just be a fling...please?"

"I don't know." It was all he could say.

Jennie knew. It couldn't be a fling, not for her. But it had to be clandestine. She didn't mind that, not at all, and not just for his sake. She couldn't have anyone think she was someone else's creature, a dependency, a satellite in some man's orbit. That was the marvellous thing about Frank. He loved her. But from the first he treated her as an equal, never condescending, never humouring, ready to take her arguments seriously, to argue against them when he disagreed, credit her when she changed his mind. All this despite the differences in their ages, experience, education. Somehow, it was important to Frank that his lover have her own, independent standing.

* * *

Frank Wise had been right about effects of the Wall Street crash. Within weeks it had turned the steady overhang of unemployment in heavy industry into a torrent of job losses. Month by month, almost a quarter of the British workforce were driven into a miserable dependence on pay-outs from the dwindling National Insurance Scheme. Every Labour constituency was haemorrhaging work, and then communities began losing their entire local economy. From week to week, more and more shopkeepers and tradesmen found themselves vagrants, sometimes even beggars, cap in hand shuffling from street corners at the command of coppers. Jennie saw it wherever she spoke.

At their wit's end, MPs on the left of the Labour Party increasingly rejected the caution of their own cabinet ministers. Day after day, they'd meet in the same rooms with the same back benchers, all obsessively working over the same terrain, turning over every policy, ploy, plan that might make a difference. All knew equally well that nothing they could do would spur MacDonald's government into real action.

Night after night Jennie would come out of the house with Frank seething, blocked, defeated, powerless before the magnitude of her own government's indifference.

"Frank, is there anything anyone can do?" Her tone was plaintive, as though she were supplicating, beseeching.

Wise had to say something, anything that might lift her gloom even a little.

"Only hope is Mosley." Jennie looked at him, bighting her lip, but he didn't notice. "MacDonald has given him unemployment as his responsibility in cabinet. He's talking to the right people—Keynes for example. He just has to get them to listen."

* * *

By the early winter of 1930 Jennie had moved to Guilford Street, a few steps from the tube at Russell Square and close to Frank Wise's larger flat in Bloomsbury.

Jennie and Frank woke together after one of the first nights they were able to share in her new flat.

She slipped out of the bed, not bothering to cover her body against the draft, dropped a coin in the gas fire and moved into the kitchen to make two cups of tea. Coming back with the cups, she had to circumnavigate the clothes each had shed the night before in their path towards the bed. Frank lifted the covers to her and she slid back under the warn eiderdown, passing him a cup.

"How ever can you prance round in the cold without a stitch, Jennie?" Frank's body was still buried beneath the quilt.

"This wouldn't even be a chill morning in Fife."

His look was serious. "Dorothy suspects about us, I fear."

"However did she…" Jennie didn't finish the sentence. There were a hundred ways a wife might find out about these things, she knew, no matter how discreet one were.

Frank was prepared to answer her question. "Came to the House one day on a shopping trip up to London from Bucks."

The Wise's owned a ramshackle 19th century pile south of Oxford. It required much of Dorothy's attention, as did the two younger children.

"She was in the Ladies' Gallery. Saw us walking out of the Commons together and 'just knew.' That's what she said anyway."

"Surely no one would have given us away." She'd been assured by no less than the Duchess of York that it wasn't done, not even between political enemies in Westminster. Coupling was one's private life and not to be tread upon. Besides, no grouping in the house had a corner on conventional morality. Everyone knew that the outcome of public disclosure was tit-for-tat, and that nothing spread about could stay private for long.

"Don't think anyone told her. That's why I rather credited her intuition."

"You admitted it to her?"

"No. Denied it absolutely!"

She kept her face impassive. She wasn't going to condemn his dissimulation. In fact she was glad of it.

But Frank looked ashamed of himself. She realised she had to reassure him.

"You did the right thing."

Relief spread across Frank's face and he moved towards her in a way she did not misinterpret. Jennie decided to toy with him briefly.

"Frank, tell me why we need to get off the gold standard."

Later, in the languor of a late morning lie-in, Jennie decided that he had very much done the right thing, not admitting the affair to his wife. She knew she loved Frank, needed him in her life in a way she had never needed anyone else. But she knew with equal certainty that she didn't want to marry him. Jennie didn't want to be *his*, or anyone's just yet, wasn't ready to live with anyone as anything like a wife. *You're twenty-five. You need your freedom, don't you, Jennie?* The question answered itself. She felt too young to be settled. She looked over at Frank, facing her but dozing. Not for the first time she thought, *If you were a couple, he'd have to take the lead, even if you still had a political life at all.* But it wasn't merely that, she knew. *You won't make the promise of fidelity, exclusiveness that you're not ready to keep.* She could feel it in her body and now expressed it to herself in unspoken words. *You're too vital an animal yet, too feral, to be happily enclosed.* She would not endure a physical exclusivity that might become stale. She was glad Frank was married to someone else. It protected her from making promises to him she recognised she would have to keep.

There was another visceral reason she needed her absolute freedom, something else that gnawed at her, something she could usually keep well away from her conscious thoughts, but that she knew was there somewhere. It lurked, ready to be called up by the odd sensation that coursed through her body from time to time, drifting off to sleep or waking from a morning dream. She found that she could also call this feeling up just by conjuring the touch of Mosley's hand moving up her thigh that dinner five months before.

Chapter Eight

It was towards the end of January 1930 that Jennie met Mosley again. She had just made her second speech in the house, an unqualified attack on the political cowardice of her own side, the government she'd been sent to Westminster to sustain. Jennie had not exempted anyone in the Labour government. Jennie's vituperation had spared no one, not even Mosley, sitting there on the minister's front bench.

The house had not been very full that afternoon, and of the cabinet only a handful were present. Mosley was the most conspicuous of them, sprawled across three seats directly before the dispatch box and the mace. Members were beginning to stroll out for a drink in one of the palace's bars, perhaps contemplating an early supper.

"Mr Speaker," Jennie had shouted, and to her surprise, been recognised.

As she began, those strolling out stopped, turned and sat at the nearest benches. One or two who were just coming in, turned and spoke to those behind them. Soon, more flowed in from the lobbies, hoping for a bit of excitement. They were not to be disappointed.

"The government have had four months to tell us what they proposed to do about unemployment, four months during which perhaps a half a million more workers have lost jobs. The prime minster has nothing to offer these men...and women. Instead those in work are told they must work harder and be paid less for it. And why?" In a mocking tone, she continued. "So that capitalists don't take their large profits out of this country and create jobs elsewhere?" She paused for effect. "Well, they're certainly not creating any hereabouts."

The Conservatives across the floor had cheered her on, in mock support of her attack on her own side, waving their order papers. The younger ones shouted terms of endearment. The older members merely expressed encouragement.

Coming to the end, Jennie felt the need to shock once more. She looked to her left and right across the Labour benches, now fuller than when she had begun. She would address her side alone, with no pretence of addressing the whole house, or even the Speaker, as the rules required. "What's the point of Labour governing the same way the capitalists do? Better we make proposals that their lot defeat."

She gestured towards the Tories and the Liberals across the floor.

"Then we can carry them to the country, and win. The game this government is playing is not worth the candle."

Instead of sitting, Jennie trod down the steps, bowed to chair and strode from the chamber.

A handful of MPs on her side were murmuring their agreement, "Hear, hear."

A few Tories were calling after her, "Hear, hear."

Striding along the corridor, Jennie detected the echoing sound of hurrying footsteps along the flagstones behind her. Someone was trying to catch up. When she turned her head, it was Tom Mosley. He had followed her out of the chamber. Jennie slowed to allow him to catch her before she began descending the stair to the Lady Members' Room. She found herself smiling in spite of herself. Was she glad to have had an effect on someone from the front bench? Did she actually welcome his attention? Yes, she realised. Did she want others to see this glamorous figure seeking her out? She had to admit it, at least to herself.

But when he came up to her, all she said was "Yes?" in the haughtiest tone she could muster.

"I wanted to tell you that I am going to resign from the cabinet." Mosley's look was penetrating. His dark eyes searching hers for a reaction, as if to ask whether she would be glad.

Jennie wanted to be slightly provocative. "When did you just decide, just now?"

"You mean was it your speech that convinced me? No. But my reasons are rather the ones you gave in there." He inclined his head towards the chamber. "I've spent the better part of a month trying to get the cabinet to do something besides playing at Mister Macawber."

They both smiled at his Dickensian image.

She took it farther. "They'll still be hoping that something will turn up by the time the next election comes round. But why tell me?"

"Perhaps so that you might excuse me from your attack on the government."

"Well, you didn't stick it very long in the cabinet. Three months?"

"How can you condemn me for impatience after a speech like the one you just gave?"

"I suppose you're right. But I'm surprised you're quitting. It's power you want, I recall. There's none in the back benches."

"Well, I don't expect to be on them long." He looked at her gravely. "And when I return to government, I hope I'll have your support."

"You will if you earn it." She turned to walk on.

But Mosley reached out and held her arm. Jennie looked down at his hand, willing it off. It was not the way she expected to be treated, by anyone.

"Miss Lee, I can't tell if you like me or loathe me. Which is it?"

"What makes you think I give you any thought at all?"

Jennie hoped her tone conveyed indifference. But she did not turn and walk away. Suddenly she knew why. They both did. Jennie had allowed him rather too much liberty at or rather beneath Charlie Trevelyan's dining table.

"That's coming at it rather high, Miss Lee." There was a slightly conspiratorial look in his face now. They'd now reached the door of the Lady Members' Room.

Jennie could feel a tide race pulling her towards him. She needed to make a break.

She blurted, "I tell you, Mosley, I have a lover."

"And I have a wife." He loosened his grip and spoke quietly. "Makes no matter."

He had more than a wife, Jennie knew. *Why are you standing here, talking to this bounder?* But stand she did, transfixed by Mosley's penetrating stare, his winning smile, the feeling he exuded that for a moment they were the only two people in the world; the message in his whole bearing that holding her interest was the only thing he cared about, ever would care about. Jennie couldn't fathom it. She quite disliked him, and yet, for the moment, would do anything he suggested.

"Have a drink with me, Miss Lee." He took her arm gently. "Now...please." His tone was correct and seductive at the same time.

She opened the door, hoping none of the other women MPs were there, took her coat off the tree in the corner and emerged. Mosley led her out of the members' exit and across Parliament Square to a pub more frequented by Tory members than Labour MPs. Just as well, Jennie thought, no one she knew would be there.

Mosley ordered two glasses of single malt Scotch whiskey. He waited in silence until the barman had poured them, withdrew a billfold from his coat and paid. Only then did he speak.

"I dare say, Miss Lee, your speech was devastatingly accurate...it was as though you'd been sitting in the cabinet, every day since MacDonald formed the government."

Jennie wanted to be implacable. She remained silent. Mosley filled the silence between them.

"MacDonald and the rest knew what policies I advocated when they gave me a place in the cabinet. But it must have all been for show. No one's been interested in the slightest."

Jennie couldn't help herself responding to a frustration she shared as deeply.

"Whatever are they interested in?"

"Not much. They're a set of old men afraid of change, most ignorant of economics and frightened by the bankers, others are trades-union bosses bought off by big business, a few so-called socialists anxious about how to stop the unemployed shirking..."

Jennie was listening for political intelligence. "Is it true MacDonald is going to try to cut the unemployment benefit?"

Mosley nodded. "It's the only way he can balance the budget. Says we pay men more not to work than other countries pay them to work."

Jennie raised her voice. "But there is no work." Several others in the pub turned to towards them, seeking the source of the outburst.

Mosley spoke quietly. "And won't be, so long as they worry about balancing the budget. I suppose you've been listening to Lloyd George's pet economist?"

"Keynes, the one at Charley Trevelyan's dinner party last summer?" Mosley nodded. "The Liberals have what, sixty seats? Not much chance of them ever returning to power."

"But we could steal their programme. It's hardly different from what I've been arguing for anyway."

"Who is 'we,' anyway, Tom?" She found she'd used his Christian name, something she had not wanted to do.

"'We' is the Labour Party. We can make a start in the Commons. See how many backbench MPs will follow."

Jennie raised her glass. "I'll drink to that. I'd love some company rattling the old bastard's cage." She smiled bitterly, recalling the fact that Ramsay MacDonald was well known to have been illegitimate. Mosley smiled too. Then her words struck him. She wouldn't have used the word as she did if she knew she was illegitimate too. *This woman doesn't know that she is Ramsay MacDonald's bastard.* Jennie didn't notice Mosley's look of surprise. She contemplated her empty glass.

"Trouble is, rattling cages won't work. Most of the backbenchers are too timid to revolt."

Mosley smiled. "You're right of course. That's why we'll have to go over their heads. You'd be good at that, Jennie."

It was the first time he used her Christian name. Did the familiarity suit? She couldn't quite tell. Weakly she replied, "Go over their heads, what do you mean?"

"Take my policy to the party conference, override the parliamentary party!"

"Labour Party conference is eight months away. Things will get worse and nothing will be done."

"Precisely. And that's why we'll succeed."

For the third time he put his hand on her arm, now in comradeship. This time she didn't remove it.

He called to the barman. "Same again, please."

Is he already counting me into his following? I suppose he's right, damn the man. She was finding Mosley more convincing than she wanted him to be.

Mosley looked at his watch. "I say, shall we get some supper? There won't be a division in the house till late."

Jennie looked him steadily in the eye. "Don't you have a flat nearby, Tom?"

It was important they both understood this was to be no seduction. There would not even be dissimulation. He had to see that she knew all about him.

She continued. "Somewhere on Ebury Street?"

* * *

Their coupling was clinical in its equality of attention and satisfaction, both giving as good as they got, both recognising, nay, seeking a carnality uninhibited by modesty, or even ritual courtesy, still less pretended romance. It was clean and bracing, and Jennie enjoyed it thoroughly.

Afterwards, they dressed, and without discussion returned to the House.

* * *

Mosley didn't, after all, resign immediately. MacDonald actually seemed ready to listen to him. For three months a subcommittee of the most senior ministers considered his policy of public works, nationalisation of industry and high tariffs. Meanwhile he remained in the cabinet.

While the cabinet deliberated, Jennie received a steady stream of notes from Tom Mosley, written on cabinet paper during cabinet meetings, and delivered to her pigeonhole in the House. They provided a running commentary on the ineptness, cowardice and impotence of MacDonald's cabinet. A few were accompanied by invitations to his Ebury Street digs. Twice that winter, Jennie found herself accepting. She had come to understand Mosley's hold on women. They'd rendezvous at his flat. Their lovemaking was considerate, knowing, effective, but remained cool and almost surgical in its precision. There was little small talk between them and no endearments. Jennie liked it perfectly well that way. She wondered if he gave pleasure for the power it confirmed. She couldn't believe it was out of any emotion he wanted to express.

* * *

At the beginning of May 1930, Mosley finally saw further delay was pointless. He decided to resign from the cabinet.

The Prime Minister was sitting alone, in the middle of the long, coffin-shaped cabinet table at number 10. As Mosley entered, he could see that MacDonald had nothing before him—no red box, no civil service files, nothing on the blotter but his hands folded together. His chin was on his chest. *Is he asleep? Why ever not? He's in his 60s but looking like elderly man, late 70s, I should say. Should I tiptoe out and alert his secretary?* Mosley hesitated. But the noise of the double doors sliding closed behind him woke, or at any rate alerted, the Prime Minister, who raised his head and turned towards the sound. His brows were too bushy for Mosley to be able to see whether the eyes had been closed, but MacDonald was blinking in the way one woken from a nap might well do. He cleared his throat and adopted the mien of someone who had expected Mosley but was also pressed for time.

"Ah, Tom."

They'd known one another since Mosley had crossed the floor of the House to come into the Labour Party in 1926. In fact they'd been close, spending weekends at the same country houses, holidaying together, so in private it was 'Tom' and 'Ramsay.' But MacDonald must have been confused, for his next words— "Good of you to come" — suggested he'd invited Mosley, instead of the latter's seeking an interview. Mosley moved to a chair across the vast table, but MacDonald patted the one next to his.

Mosley didn't want to add embarrassment to confusion, so he ignored the suggestion that MacDonald had invited him.

"Thank you for agreeing to see me at short notice, Prime Minister." No Christian names when it was serious business to be discussed.

He pulled out the chair next to the PM, turned to face MacDonald and began. "Prime Minister, it's ground we've been over several times. I cannot continue to serve in a cabinet that rejects my proposals for dealing with unemployment. I have to resign from the government."

This was something Mosley had said before in the months during which other ministers had examined his proposals and rejected them. MacDonald must have thought Mosley was bluffing, he'd been dealing with this sort of thing in the Labour Party for almost thirty years. He didn't want to lose Mosley. The man was star of his cabinet. But he knew Mosley's proposals were anathema to enough of the front bench and seasoned trade unionists to capsize his government.

"I deprecate such a course, Mosley." The use of the surname put the distance between them this interview required. "You've only just arrived in government. You have a brilliant career ahead of you. But you need to be patient. The ocean liner can only be moved off its compass-heading a few degrees at a time."

"With respect, premier, that's all I am proposing, really!"

"No. You're proposing wholesale changes to the economy. It'll be so unsettling to expectations that business will contract even further. No. Your proposals must wait for recovery."

Mosley was desperate at the old man's obtuseness. He had to do something. He stood, resisting the impulse to take the old man by the lapels of his frock coat. But he was almost shouting. "Ramsay, there will be no recovery without my proposals."

The cabinet doors slid open and a civil servant's head was seen in the gap.

"It's quite alright, Timson." MacDonald waved the man back out with his right hand.

Cooling now, Mosley resumed his seat.

"I'm sorry, Prime Minister, I can't remain in your government." He removed an envelope from his coat, looked at it and placed it on the table. "My resignation."

MacDonald looked at him with a frown. "Fair warning, Tom. I'll have to accept it." The other nodded. "You must realise you're giving up the chance to be the next Labour prime minister. Don't you want that?"

Mosley waved his hand. "I'll get it anyway."

"That's what Parnell thought." Parnell was a name infamous in British parliamentary politics. The greatest orator and tactician of his time, forty years earlier, destroyed by the public exposure of his personal 'indiscretions.' Every politician was still familiar with the history. Revealed to be cuckolding his second-in-command, Parnell had been driven from public life.

Dudgeon rose in Mosley's face. "Is that a threat?"

"No, no, of course not." MacDonald retreated. "It's only I worry about you, Tom. Such promise, but you're giving hostages to fortune in your conduct." He paused. Mosley remained silent. "The further you go in politics, the more threatening you become to the"—MacDonald searched for the right word—"the old order, the greater the temptation of your enemies to bring you down." Both knew that Parnell had been ruined by his enemies just at the point of his greatest triumph, the only chance for home rule Ireland ever really had.

MacDonald's words had come as near to menace as the old man could make them sound. If this was a threat, Mosley needed to counter it. But it wasn't just a matter of calculation or strategy. Mosley's mind was flooded as much by the need to retaliate against the old man then and there. He put his hand inside his coat, feeling for the other envelope in his pocket, the one Lady Astor had given him. He tried to keep his tone casual. "Well, perhaps I'll avoid Parnell's fate, Ramsay. You managed it."

"What? What are you saying, Mosley?"

So, they were back to surnames. "Well, you've survived twenty-five years now without anyone learning about your 'indiscretion.'"

MacDonald face reddened. "What rot are you talking..."

"Jennie Lee."

At Mosley's words the older man's face collapsed from indignation into humiliation.

After a silence, MacDonald spoke again. "So, we're both in a position to ruin each other?" He searched Mosley's face. "Did she tell you?"

"No." Mosley could read MacDonald's wretchedness. It sapped his desire to be cruel to the old man. "I don't think she even knows."

MacDonald sought to get a grip. "Who does know? How the

blazes did you find out?"

Mosley couldn't bring himself to recount the sordid little story of Chips Channon and Lady Astor. "Just some catty gossip and a guess I decided to try on you. Don't think anyone really knows...for now."

There was no threat meant in the last two words, but too late he realised they would not sound that way. Mosley pushed the long white envelope still on to the blotter before MacDonald.

"My resignation."

Then he turned and walked from the room.

Chapter Nine

Jennie and Frank were standing at the long bar of a pub in Victoria Street just behind Westminster Abbey. They were still shaking off the rain. It had been a short walk from the palace of Westminster, down the narrow footpath between the Abbey and St. Margaret's church. But the shower caught them just as they had set out. The pub was Labour territory. The odd Tory who might find his way in was tolerated, teased and made to feel like a foreigner. Sconces above the alcove booths brightened the darkened wood of the interior. There were a dozen or more escapees from the Commons evening sitting, drinking together at the bar and among the scattered tables.

Frank ordered a lager, Jennie a gin and tonic. She was ruminating.

"What will it take to move the cabinet off its arse? There's what, two million people now without work."

Frank sighed. They were going over old ground. "Nothing. It's the 20 million union men in work *what controls* the government." The working class syntax made his point.

Jennie shook her head. "No. It's not the Union men. It's their bosses, comfortable men paid large salaries not to think beyond a company's next wage contract. We've got to find a way to reach over them."

"We can't do that." He stopped for a moment. "A couple of back benchers? Even the whole ILP faction in the House wouldn't be enough."

There were about 30 ILPs--Independent Labour Party--MPs in the House. He smiled at Jennie.

"And besides, your 'friend' Nye is right. It would split the party and bring in the Tories."

Did Jennie hear the resentment in the word 'friend'? Was her partner jealous of a meaningless liaison? She ignored it.

"But Mosley could do something."

"How can he, now he's resigned from the cabinet?"

Jennie knew the answer to this question and she blurted it. "He'll take his programme to the party conference and demand a vote."

For thirty years, once a year, in the fall, each of the political parties had repaired to different seaside resorts for a week of socialising and strategizing.

"How do you know?" Frank demanded.

"Mosley told me."

Frank was silent for a moment. He was no longer thinking about what she knew, but how she'd come to know. He feared the answer that immediately came to him. He loved Jennie Lee. He was sure she loved him. But he didn't own her, couldn't make demands on her, not when he was still married himself. In that instant, he decided he didn't want to know, couldn't bear to know. He would not speak from the inevitably rising jealousy. He would ask nothing. When he finally spoke, it was about politics.

"Jennie. I worry about relying on Mosley. He's walked across the floor of parliament too often to be committed to anything but himself."

"Just doing Churchill one better, no?" Jennie wanted to laugh the caution off. But she couldn't. She knew. "There's something personal in all this, isn't there, Frank?"

"I fear there may be, Jennie." It was the closest he would come to an admission, or was it an accusation?

Again she felt the need to reassure her lover, her friend. "Oh, Frank, it doesn't mean a thing. I love you."

But desolation had taken hold of Frank. "Jennie, I can't really go on like this."

Now a new emotion took hold of Jennie. "Does this mean you're going to break it off with me, Frank?"

He smiled.

"No." Covering her hand, he continued. "No. I'm going to ask Dorothy for a divorce. Then I want to marry you."

Tension left her shoulders, but Jennie audibly sighed.

"Frank, we've been over this ground. It won't wash. You have a calling, so do I. We're political animals. We need to be there." She nodded towards Westminster Palace, out in the rain, beyond the Abbey. She continued in a steely voice. "Divorce would destroy both our political careers. It would be senseless. Just think what the Tory papers would say...you leaving four children? Me? What gossip would they get up to publishing?"

Frank raised a hand, attempting to staunch the quiet, relentless flow of her argument. But Jennie continued just above a whisper.

"A third of my North Lanark constituency are Irish Catholics, all Labour voters. Think what their parish priest will tell them before the next election." Then she looked at him with as much love as she could muster. "Besides, Frank. I don't want to marry."

He turned away, but Jennie pulled him back. "No, listen. It's not that I don't want to marry you. I don't want to marry anyone!"

The cutting reply was out of his mouth before he could think it through. "So, you love me but you want the freedom to sleep round Westminster?"

Venom formed the words on Jennie's tongue, *How dare you?* But then she stopped herself. She did love this man. She wasn't going to wreck everything by giving him back the abuse that his pain was hurling at her. Instead, she reached up, pulled him by the lapel towards her and kissed him with an open mouth.

Then she spoke. "Listen, and try not to interrupt. First of all, I'm not forty-four, like you. I'm not even thirty-four. I'm twenty-four. And I'm afraid I attract men, especially in the men's world of politics. I can't help it. And you men, well, you all reach the point of wanting to sleep with a woman rather quickly. No matter how seriously I want to be taken, and get taken, I can't always resist either. I don't even want to resist every time. And it's not just me. It's other women my age, perhaps not many, but some."

Frank nodded and began to speak. He got no further than "But" before Jennie held up her palm and continued.

"And then there's us...together, we're wonderful. I couldn't be happier. When I'm with you I never look at another man." She had kept her fingers slowly running up and down his lapel. "But how often can we be together? There's your constituency and mine, hundreds of miles apart. There's all the traveling you do to Russia. There's your wife in Bucks with the kids. And it wouldn't be much different if we were married, not for a long time anyway...even when we lost both our seats in the scandal of a divorce."

"Jennie, I love you, I love you enough to... to..."—he searched for the word he needed, not a judgment like 'condone' or a euphemism like 'understand,' and then he chose the word—"to accept what you tell me about how you want to live."

But she still wasn't finished. "Then there's the politics. At the moment we seem to agree pretty much on the way things are gong, in the country and the party. But what if that comes apart? I've got to have my independence to say what I think and choose a course you may not agree with. I can't be your wife and do that." She stopped for a minute. A happy thought formed. "Frank, you'll be in the Labour cabinet soon. Maybe not the very next election, but the next time our lot win. It's certain. With your experience, they'll need you, perhaps even as Chancellor of the Exchequer." She shook her head, pre-empting another interruption. "I can't preside at your table, entertaining people I can't stomach, keeping my mouth shut, following your lead, being the political wife...It's not me, Frank. Not yet anyway." She put her hand up. "There, I've had my say."

She smiled and leaned over to plant still another reassuring kiss on his mouth.

Frank was silent, trying to find an argument, a consideration, an objection, a motive to which he could harness his claim on Jennie. The search for an answer was written in the knit of his forehead, chin on his hands, elbows on the bar. Jennie replied to it before his words came. "Frank. I'm yours in everything that matters, everything that matters to me. It's got to be enough." She squeezed his hand.

He nodded, cleared his throat as if to indicate the subject was closed.

He brightened. "Look, when the House rises for the summer, I'm to take a half dozen or so MPs to Moscow. After that, I've got to go south to the Caucasus for the Soviet Trade Office." Frank was a consultant for *Centrosoyus*—The Central Union of Cooperatives, which sold agricultural produce and mineral ores to British firms. "Come to Moscow. You'll see Stalin's Five-Year Plan in action. We can have a month together."

"That sounds grand, Frank. But we must be back for the fireworks at the party conference in September."

* * *

It was a chance to jump at, Jennie saw, and not just for time with Frank. The Soviet Union, everyone on the left knew, was the best hope for the future, a laboratory in which the recipe for human happiness would be perfected. Not without some false starts and some birth pains and a little unavoidable suffering. But think of socialism's future! And whom could one really trust to report on the experiment? Not the journalists owned, operated and edited by the English press barons, nor yet the members of the British Communist party subservient to the Comintern in Moscow, certainly not the gullible British political ingénues like the playwright Shaw, ready to believe whatever they might be shown by the Bolshevik commissars.

In the end, the group that went included Nye Bevan, Ellen

Wilkinson and a half dozen other Labour MPs. All eager to see what planning could do to avoid the excesses of the unfettered market, with its poverty, inequality, its wasteful surpluses of unneeded luxuries and outrageous shortages of meaningful work.

* * *

It was a warm sunny morning in July 1930 that they arrived at Moscow *Belorussian* terminal. They were met at the end of the quay by a small but energetic young man whom Frank introduced all round.

"Friends, this is Valery Kutuzov. Valery and I have been working together for a couple of years now."

Frank's friend held out a hand that was shaken by all. He had short dark hair, oval glasses and a serious face, that smiled briefly into each face as he took their hands.

"Valery is liaison between the foreign ministry and the *Centroysoyus.*"

This was the Central Union of Cooperative Enterprises Frank represented back in Britain.

Introductions completed, Kutuzov spoke, in good English. "The baggage will be sent to the hotel. I have a car waiting for us all."

He led the way through the vaulted entryway out onto the pavement where a large open vehicle stood, a red star painted on its one door, riding high on large wheels, with four benches behind a driver. His shirtsleeves rolled up, Lenin-like worker's cap pulled down over his brow, the man was smoking and looking straight ahead. He made no effort to welcome his riders, but waited silently for instructions. With visible embarrassment, Kutuzov was trying hard to make up for the wooden indifference of the driver to these foreign guests. They mounted up the car and clambered into their seats in good humour, seeing no reason why the proletarian driver should abnegate himself before dignitaries. In fact, they rather enjoyed his want of class-consciousness.

From the open government car to their hotel, they watched the streets go by, empty of vehicles save for the streetcars. These came at a steady pace, crammed with riders, some leaning from the entry steps, others having clambered on to the roof, dangerously close to the overhead tram wires.

"Valery, why so many stores boarded up?" Nye asked the Soviet official, the question the rest were thinking.

Kutuzov answered, evenly. "It's the Five-Year Plan. Things were different up till about a year ago. Then Stalin put an end to Lenin's 'state capitalism.' No more profiteering. Everything according to the plan. The little shops started disappearing in just a few months."

"That's a good thing in a poor country, isn't it?" Jennie asked. "All that shop-keeping was undermining socialism."

Kutuzov was about to answer, but Frank quickly spoke up. "Maybe it'll be a good thing in the long run."

It was not like him to interrupt rudely. The others in the car noticed. Nye Bevan was about to speak, but Frank shook his head firmly.

* * *

An hour later Jennie, Frank, and Nye were strolling down a broad but empty street towards the Moscow River. They had left the hotel in search of a tobacconist. The hotel's shop had run out of cigarettes, even domestic brands.

Moscow wasn't anything like London, not this part of it at any rate. On each side of the boulevard, more boarded-up shop windows interspersed with forlorn storefronts and almost bare shelves. It was disquieting.

No one spoke till Jennie put a question to Frank. "So, what

was that head-shaking about, Frank, back in the touring car before we got to the hotel?"

"I didn't want to get Valery into any trouble, that's all."

"Trouble?" Nye's tone was arch. "How could he have gotten into trouble, Frank?"

"Well, the driver'll be expected to report anything we say and everything Valery says to us."

Jennie and Nye spoke simultaneously. "Why?" "To who?"

"To the OGPU, because Valery is a state official and therefore not to be trusted."

Frank smiled to convey his little joke. They all knew the OGPU—the organs of state security.

"It's the way they can be sure everyone is singing from the same hymnal. Valery will have to report everything we say, and the driver's report will have to jibe with what he reports." He paused. "So, the less said, the smaller the chance of a 'misunderstanding,' right?"

The others nodded.

"That's why Valery didn't come out with us just now. It'd be too risky for him to walk round Moscow with a set of foreigners and no one to corroborate what we spoke about."

"Not even left wing Labour party types?" Jennie was earnest. She didn't want to be taken an enemy of the Soviet state.

"We might all be wolves in sheep's clothing, Jennie." Nye laughed. "I suppose that Valery knows what he's doing."

Frank nodded. "Valery has to be extra careful. Kutuzov is a famous name, and not in a good way. Valery's related to the Marshal Kutuzov, the one who beat Napoleon in 1812. Keeps having to prove he's not a class enemy."

Jennie changed the subject. "Frank, all these shops bare or boarded up. You said things were different last year. What happened? Did Stalin order them to close?"

"No. But once *Gosplan*—the state planning bureau—took control of the economy, the middlemen disappeared and the shopkeepers had nothing to buy and put on their shelves, nothing people wanted to buy."

Nye spoke. "Not even smokes? Look, we're out right now with money ready to pay. Why isn't there anybody to sell us a packet of cigarettes?"

Frank pointed down the street. "There's another tobacconist. Let's try again."

A moment later he came out shaking his head, a rueful smile on his face. He looked at his two friends and reported.

"Man said no fags anywhere in the city this week. Factory runs out of glue for the cigarette papers end of every month. You have to stock up."

Jennie was quizzical. "Run out of glue? Why don't they just order more?"

Frank frowned. "It's the plan, Jennie. Factories don't order. Planners order the factory and plans are written in stone, once a year."

"But that can't be the problem, Frank." Jennie spoke earnestly. "Planning is organising the whole economy to get everyone what they need, instead of capitalist profiteering."

"You'd think so. But a plan can't meet millions of people's wants for thousands of different things each made from dozens of parts." He stopped for a moment. "Without prices, what you called 'profiteering,' Jennie, there's no way to tell how much... cigarette paper glue is really needed. And Stalin has abolished prices."

Now Nye spoke with irritation. "Frank, we don't need a lecture on why socialism is impossible."

Jennie pulled her two companions along, an arm through each of theirs.

She had to defend her partner against her friend's complaint. "But Frank is a socialist, Nye."

"That I am." He had not been angered by Nye's provocation. "My kind of socialism is workers owning the factories they work in, Nye. The sort of cooperatives I deal with all over Russia."

Nye scoffed. "Co-ops don't make socialism! Heavy industry needs planning, not endless shop-floor discussion."

"Yes, that's what you'd think. Just ask every manager what they need and what their factory can produce, make the allocations, and let them get on with it." Frank looked up and down the street meaningfully.

"Well, what went wrong?" Jennie persisted.

"Once managers start having to tell *Gosplan* what their factories need and how much of anything they can make, every boss starts to be economical with the truth."

"Lying, to get more than his factory needs and produce less than it can?" Nye had caught on. "Just like a pit crew at the coal face." He laughed.

"Sounds like a job for the secret police!" Jennie smiled.

But Wise took the thought seriously. "They're trying it. But the coppers won't know what to look for, and they'll be bribed by the factory bosses anyway."

Jennie's tone became slightly belligerent. "What will work, Frank, capitalism?"

"Prices. What they had before this damn Five-Year Plan."

Jennie frowned. "Bring back prices, you'll end with capitalism, Frank."

Frank fell silent.

Then he replied. "Yes, I'm afraid you're right. That's the conundrum."

They were now at a bridge crossing the Moscow River.

Nye brightened. "I know where we can get some fags." He pointed. "See the Union Jack across the river? That's the British embassy. They'll have a canteen."

"Right you are, Nye." Frank smiled.

Chapter Ten

A week later, Jennie and Frank were trying to find a comfortable way to sit, lie or lean on the wooden-slatted benches of a "hard class" railway coach. They were a thousand miles south of Moscow. The rest of the Labour party delegation had gone back to Britain. After two days of watching the endless forest tracts, Frank and Jennie's train was now rumbling along vast fields, golden with wheat ready for harvest. In the early evening light, the thick line of tassels almost sparkled.

"Isn't it harvest time, Frank?"

"Actually well past it, I would have thought. I used to see farm families camped everywhere hereabouts, working past dusk to get every bushel in."

Jennie brightened. "Maybe now they've collectivised, they have combine harvesters and can start later."

"I don't think there are enough tractors to go round. But the trouble is once farms are collectivised, farmers don't own the crops they grow. So why should they work day and night to harvest them?"

* * *

The open seat coach was not crowded, but the rest of the occupants were divided between those suspicious of the two foreigners and those grateful to them for sharing what food they still had—hard sausage, black bread, and large sweet red onions.

By the time they were three days out from Moscow, Jennie and Frank had become accustomed to suspicion. It had accompanied them everywhere in Moscow, along with Valery Kutuzov, the liaison between *Centrosoyus* and the Foreign Affairs Commissariat who'd greeted them on their arrival. He'd guided them through what the party wanted them to see in Moscow.

Kutuzov had been friendly, informative, even occasionally, though quietly, candid. But just as Frank had said, he was never completely alone with these guests of the Soviet state.

Then, the night Frank and Jennie left Moscow for the Caucasus two thousand kilometres to the south, Kutuzov met them for the last time, by himself, on the quay. He seemed to Jennie a little furtive, looking behind him once or twice. Evidently, he still didn't want to be seen alone with them. He kept a brimmed hat on as they approached. Jennie sought to put him at ease, or at least express her gratitude for his hospitality.

"Thank you for all your help, Valery." She smiled as she offered him her hand. He made to remove his hat, then thought better of it, nodded and took her hand.

Then Kutuzov turned to Frank, holding out a large manila envelope.

"Here are the travel documents, for both of you." He passed them to Wise, who slipped them into a briefcase. "You will find things more...'difficult' this summer, Frank." The hesitation communicated the euphemism. "It is most important you guard the passes from the Party and the Commissariat of Foreign Affairs." Frank nodded. "We had some trouble with the OGPU."

"I understand." Frank nodded. He understood infighting between the organs of the Soviet state. "Thanks for your help, Valery."

The Russian had looked round briefly, shook Frank's hand once, and then turned on his heels and trotted off.

"He seemed worried."

Jennie looked at the man over Frank's shoulder as he lengthened his distance from them. Frank reached into his bag and handed Jennie her documents. Somehow, he knew she would want to hang on to her own.

"Everybody's got different worries. Foreign ministry's worried that we'll report what we see. If you can't get a packet of fags in Moscow, it must be much worse in the countryside.

They'll get in trouble with the party if we splash it in the English papers. Party probably fought the secret police—the OGPU—to get us the passes south. Government needs the foreign exchange my co-ops earn. That's why they let me come at all."

Jennie shook her head slowly. "This isn't the education in socialism I was expecting."

Frank spoke sharply. "Don't confuse this with socialism."

* * *

Kutuzov had been right about the 'difficulties.' It was expressed to begin with in the demand for their papers at every stop on the mainline route to Georgia in the Caucasus Mountains between the Black Sea and the Caspian. Were these spies escaping to the British in Iran or agents of the Turkish dictator, Ataturk? Who had provided them with enough food to last the week to Tbilisi? And why were they using it to win over the other occupants of the coach, people who hadn't seen a kielbasa or a kupati for a year or more? Still, their papers came from the Central Union of Cooperatives, and were stamped very clearly with a pass to all areas by the Party Central Committee in Moscow.

After the third inspection of her bag, its thin leather strap now worn to breaking, Jennie's patience had given out.

"I thought this mania would weaken the further we got from Moscow."

Frank shook his head. "Wasn't this bad two years ago. Something's worrying these functionaries."

She replied, "What's worrying everyone else seems to be getting something to eat." She glanced out the window. "Frank, we've spent two full days riding through vast fields of ripe wheat. Why the hunger?"

"Maybe it's because the new collective farms can't sell what they grow."

"Can't sell? What do you mean, Frank? Why are they growing

the stuff if they can't sell it?"

"The state just takes it. All this wheat"—he pointed out the window—"is how Russia is building a modern industrial state. It's the only thing Russia has plenty of. Stalin is going to sell Europe every bushel he can get his hands on and invest it in steel mills. That's the Five-Year Plan."

Frank glanced towards the pair of uniformed OGPU security guards, who glared back at him. "That's why this lot has to let me travel where I want, poke my nose into any hay rick I like, smell the tobacco curing in the warehouses, rub my hands on the shoe leather cow hide...I'm here because Russia really needs to sell."

Jennie thought back to Frank's exchanges with Nye in Moscow.

"Because no one back in Moscow can trust the managers to just tell the truth about what they've got and how much."

"Precisely." He smiled. "So we get a busman's holiday in Central Asia!"

Fending off begging peasants at station stops, averting their eyes from the accusing looks of hungry travellers holding emaciated children, their busman's holiday had become a grim journey into a bad dream.

* * *

Midday, the train slowed and the landscape of excavation berms and pump-derricks began to look familiar to Jennie. They were entering a coal country town, a little different from ones dotting the heaths of Scotland or the Welsh vales. She made out the Cyrillic and mouthed the word *Shakhty*, then reached for her *Baedeker*. Nothing in the travel guide.

"Know anything about this place, Frank?" She watched as a grim industrial town spread on either side of the track they were riding. It was the busiest place they'd passed through since

Voronezh halfway back to Moscow.

Frank looked up from his papers. "Nothing…probably slept through it the last time I came this way."

The brakes screeched and the train came to a halt.

"Let's see if we can buy anything to eat. We've not got much left."

Wise asked a conductor how long they'd stop. One hour.

Along the platform, an elderly woman was selling tea from a dented samovar. Two cups were attached to her trolley by a meter-long chain. Jennie approached and the woman spoke. She turned to Frank.

"Any idea what she said?"

"I think she was reassuring you that the tea is so hot it kills any germs left on the cup by the last drinker."

He turned and walked across the track into the station building.

The structure did not look promising, stained with coal dust, broken and boarded windows, doorways without doors opened to darkened spaces. Frank returned in a moment.

"Nothing to buy. Just a few beggars. But there's a cafeteria across the street. If it's for party workers, we might get a bite."

Jennie brightened. "I'll eat anything."

It was a large hall noisy with men in various uniforms, huddled over soup bowls at long trestle tables. The militia man at the door scrutinised their passes, looked towards the OGPU police sitting near by. These were the ones who'd been in their train carriage. One of them nodded slightly and the guard gestured the pair in with ill-disguised annoyance. Frank and Jennie queued without being immediately able to see anything of the steam tables behind which healthy-looking women were handing over plates. When their turn came, it was a soup-bowl of thick borscht—beetroot soup—with a dollop of sour cream. Nothing Jennie ever cared for, but it didn't matter. She would eat. They found an empty table as far from the OGPU police as possible.

Before they could even begin, Jennie and Frank were joined by three young men, all dressed in different versions of a drab brown, quasi-military tunic: buttons up each side under a cardboard Sam Browne belt too thin to carry the weight of a weapon. They smiled and politely asked permission to sit.

Hearing Frank's accent in his invitation to do so, one of the young men turned to the others, "Anglichane."

Frank and Jennie both knew this word and nodded. To their surprise, one of them began to speak English.

"Ah. You must be important Englishmen."

"Why?" Jennie asked.

"First, they let you leave Moscow. Then they let you into a Party canteen. They even let you have your own table...until now." He laughed.

Frank smiled. "You have the better of us. We are indeed important English people. But you must be important too, as you have joined us."

"No. We are merely cheeky *Komsomols*." This was the well-known acronym for the young adult's branch of the Communist Party.

"Ah, in that case, may I offer you cigarettes, since you are not allowed to smoke them?" Frank drew out his packet of Senior Service. Each took one gratefully. *Komsomols* took an oath to abstain from tobacco and alcohol.

"You are well informed about our rules, sir."

Jennie volunteered, "We know that each of you has all taken a vow to become a New Soviet Man."

The English speaker translated and one of the others replied to him.

"My friend says 'Yes, but not yet.'" They all laughed.

Jennie frowned slightly. "But without the New Soviet Man, this great experiment will fail."

"Comrade Stalin will not allow that," the English speaker replied, and then translated their exchange.

Jennie replied. "He can't be everywhere." Then she waited as the translation provoked a brief discussion among the three young men.

The English speaker turned from his friends, looked at the OGPU police and spoke quietly. "But he can frighten enough shirkers to make socialism work. Last year there was a trial here, of 'wreckers.' You know what it is, a wrecker?"

They'd heard the word once or twice in Moscow but Jennie and Frank wanted to hear more. "Tell us."

"You didn't hear about the Shakhty trial in England?" Both shook their heads. "No? It was the only news everywhere in the Soviet Union in the spring of '28, the first few months of the Five-Year Plan. There was a slowdown in coal production. The plan wasn't being fulfilled. Fifty managers and engineers in the mines and the railway were tried for sabotaging the works. Five were executed, the rest went to Siberia. Now, New Soviet Man has to be on guard against wreckers everywhere." He smiled at his mild subversion.

"So, Communism arrives courtesy of the police state? Surely not!" Jennie was adamant. "You must believe in the future of socialism. You joined the Komsomol!"

The English speaker smiled sheepishly. "It's a nice uniform, and you get to eat in party canteens." One of the three finished his soup. He rose, sauntered over to the steam tables and re-joined the line.

Frank had been quiet. Now he spoke. "Look here, friend. This trial...what was the motive for wrecking?"

"Oh. They were class enemies, in the pay of the former owners, now living abroad."

"Oh. How were they discovered?"

"Confession." The man's face remained immobile, but his eyes narrowed as they focused hard on Frank's.

"I see." It was all Frank said. He rose. "Time to get back to the train, I think, Jennie."

* * *

Ten days later, Frank and Jennie were still recovering from their travels. Frank had made stops at a dozen of the Caucasian cooperatives still selling directly to the export market—hides, tobacco, flax, even cotton in the south. None was near a town or even a village, only a railhead. None seemed to have much food, warm water, beds with mattresses, windows that closed against the evening drafts, paved roads, or even simple outhouses. Their busmen's holiday had turned into an ordeal.

Now Jennie and Frank were recovering: rested, fed, warm and clean. Both were lying almost prone in wicker lounge chairs on the terrace of a white stucco residence hall. The large building overlooked an ornate fountain, making a pleasing sound in the midst of the orderly grounds of a vast sanatorium. This was Pyatigorsk, meaning roughly "five mountains" in Russian. In Tsarist times, it had been a resort for wealthy Russians with liver complaints and enough money to subject themselves to its mud-bath treatments. Now, each of the town's sanatoria was restricted to the use of government officials of distinct ranks. Frank's connections had brought them to the most exclusive of these facilities.

Without craning their heads from where they lay, Jennie and Frank could see three of the five mountains surrounding the town that gave it its name. Visible behind them was the highest mountain in Russia, the ever-snowy triangle of Mount Elbrus.

Jennie had been subdued for some days. Frank was worried. Had something come between them? Were the hardships they'd experienced more than Jennie had bargained for? Was she tired of following him round, a mute bystander to his work? He was about to broach the subject when she spoke.

"I'm afraid this hasn't been the education I was hoping for, Frank." He waited for her to continue. "Socialism doesn't seem to be working here, does it?"

Was this why she was downcast?

"Give it time, Jennie. It's less than ten years since the end of the civil war. Only thirteen since the Bolsheviks took power. There will be wrong turns and right ones."

"No, Frank. The problem is deeper."

She sat up. She gestured towards the spread of imposing white buildings, each spa catering to a different echelon of the government hierarchy.

"What happened to the classless society? Seems like they've just substituted political power for money as the ticket into this place." Frank was silent. So Jennie went on. "What if the only way to get to socialism is at the point of a gun?"

"What makes you think so?"

"Because so far it looks like that's the only thing working here—threats, fear, punishment, making an example of 'wreckers.'"

He shook his head. "I fear you're right, Jennie. If Stalin doesn't change course, this country will turn into a vast prison."

Jennie was plaintive. "Where does that leave our socialism, Frank?"

"It's ironical, isn't it? Stalin has shown we have to surrender scientific socialism for the utopian sort we used to sneer at." His laugh was sardonic.

Chapter Eleven

Walking the terraces of her North Lanark constituency, Jennie found that the drabness did not have quite the gloom of a coal town in the Caucasus. Life in Glasgow lacked the privations she'd experienced, even in Moscow. You could buy a bolt of cloth or a packet of fags at prices anyone in work could afford. Shabby had never looked so tolerable to Jennie before.

It's not a fair comparison, she insisted to herself, every time the thought emerged. *This country's been industrialised for a hundred years. It's got to do better than one just emerging from feudalism.* But Russia had seriously disoriented Jennie. She still knew what she wanted for everyone. She just didn't know how to get there any longer. It was hard for someone who took politics as seriously as she did.

That summer, the unemployment had increased further, especially in the north and Scotland. Men milling along, no errand or chore, with vacant looks and no way to provide enough for their families. It was not something she had seen at all in Moscow. There everyone had work—had to work! *Yes, but...who's better off, the short-hours millworker here or the one with a job in the worker's state?* Then the recalcitrant voice in her head, the one that sounded like her lover, would reply, *But that's not the choice, is it Jennie?* Frank was right.

* * *

Jennie returned to her parents' in Cowdenbeath in no settled frame of mind. There, a letter had been waiting, with a Forfar postmark and no return address. Forfar was the nearest town to Glamis Castle. Jennie knew immediately that the letter could only be from Elizabeth, Duchess of York. But the envelope was plain and brown, not the gold embossing and royal franking of previous posts.

Dear Jennie,
They say you went to Russia with a Labour Party delegation. How
daring! We're at Glamis Castle for the summer. I need to talk to you.
I can drop down and meet you somewhere discreet in Edinburgh.
I'll be able to hear all about the real Bolshies.
Mum's the word, please.
Elizabeth

This time it was Jennie who was kept waiting in a pricey "tea
shoppe" she'd found on Frederick Street, just below the Royal
Scots Greys war memorial. Elizabeth Bowes-Lyons entered the
shop discreetly, no different in dress or manner from any of
the handful of young married women there already, except she
was detectably pregnant. Jennie rose, looked at her friend and
quietly congratulated her.

"I had no idea!"

Her friend spoke quietly. "Well then, you haven't been
reading the court circular!"

Jennie never did. But she wouldn't say so to her friend's face.

"I've been away longer than I realised. I was nearly a month
in Russia. When's it due?"

Her friend put her hand to her swollen midriff. "Any day
now."

She sat down gratefully and looked up at Jennie, who took
the opposite chair.

"Russia." She sighed. "Was it as grim as they say?"

"Parts of it. But I think people in the towns are better off than
they'd been before the revolution."

"Look here, Jennie, I want to hear all about your trip, but it's
not really why I asked to meet." She turned anxiously to see
whether anyone was close enough to hear.

"Where to begin? My dear, it's actually my husband" — she

mouthed the words 'Duke of York' — "who wanted me to speak to you."

"Your husband? Why can't he…" Jennie didn't need to finish the question. What might he have to say to her? "Go on." She would not interrupt, if she could help it.

"Jennie, you must understand this royal family is two different worlds. The older half — the King and Queen Mary — are formal, stiff, terribly cautious and correct. Terrifically old-fashioned in every way. But the younger set — David and Prince George — are completely out of control, behaving stupidly, irresponsibly, dangerously."

These were the oldest son, the Prince of Wales, a year older than Elizabeth's husband, Albert, and the third son, now twenty-eight, and eight years younger than Albert. Jennie said nothing. The voyeur in her wanted to learn details. Another part, the self-protective part, didn't want to hear about this at all.

Elizabeth went on. "The Prince has a suite of mistresses, latest one is Thelma Furness, but he still pines for Freda Dudley Ward. Won't think of marrying. Mauls any girl he fancies. The younger brother is worse." She mouthed another word "invert," a term recently in fashion to label the love that could not speak its name. Jennie remained stolid, resisting the temptation to ask how her friend knew. "Drugs, boys. It's too sordid."

Now Jennie could resist no longer. "Elizabeth, why tell me all this? I don't want to know…"

"I'm coming to that, Jennie. Bear with me. It's difficult, in fact it's a bit terrifying." Elizabeth gathered her thoughts again. "The King is despondent. He's afraid that David's mad He's always thought there's some hereditary weakness in the family…He's got a certain amount of evidence, I fear. For one, there were his father's appetites." Edward VII was a notorious womaniser all his life. "Add to that the Kaiser's paranoia, haemophilia in the Tsar's family. They're all Victoria and Albert's progeny. The King thinks his older brother was weak-minded."

Jennie interrupted. "Older brother? George V wasn't the heir to the throne?"

Her friend nodded. "Brother was just a year older. Turned out to be a wastrel, dunce and pervert. Albert Victor. Died in '92. We wouldn't have known about him. Too long ago." She caught her breath. "Then there's the King's fourth child, Prince John. Dead of seizures at twelve in 1919. Hushed up of course." She caught her breath. "My dear, the King feels he's fighting against madness himself!"

She stopped and Jennie felt she had to say something. All she could muster was "And?"

"The King thinks that crown must pass to Albert. He's even begun to groom him for it."

"But what about the Prince of Wales?"

"He doesn't seem to want to be king any more than his father wants him to be king."

Jennie reached out her hand. "But that means you might become queen."

"Yes."

Elizabeth now gave in and began quietly to blub. Jennie pulled a handkerchief from a pocket and handed it to her friend. She had no idea what to say. They'd been over this ground before.

"I should never have agreed to marry him. Jennie, I'm so unhappy..."

I told you so. The thought gripped Jennie. Elizabeth continued. "And now the thought of becoming queen...it's intolerable, Jennie...I can't."

"Let's hope it doesn't come to that." It was all Jennie could think of saying.

Her friend collected herself.

"Look, my dear, here's the point, the King has pretty well written off the Prince of Wales, and the Prince doesn't mind a bit of it. So, he's begun grooming Albert. Training him in government, letting him look at the boxes..." She gulped. "Jennie, this must never come out. Government would be furious."

Jennie knew that only the King was to have a key to these boxes in which the cabinet papers were sent to his majesty every day, for information and for royal warrant where needed. "Anyway, Albert has become worried, very worried, about the drift of things in the country."

"We're all worried..." Jennie wanted to say her friend's name, but she couldn't, and she couldn't call her 'Your grace,' not when she was divulging secrets of state and family.

"That's why I've come to you, Jennie. Albert wants some people in parliament to know he shares their anxiety, people who could do something, instead of letting things drift the way MacDonald seems to."

"But why me? I'm an invisible backbencher. What can I do?"

Again, Elizabeth paused, needing to gather up her courage.

"It's Tom Mosley that Albert wants to encourage. But there's no way he can do it himself."

Now Jennie began to understand. Did Elizabeth know about her 'lapses' with Mosley? She'd known about the Curzons—sisters and stepmother. Why not about Jennie as well? Who else knew? Jennie allowed herself to show brief annoyance.

"So, you told the Duke you knew someone who could be a go-between?"

"I only told him we knew each other and you were acquainted with Tom. I never mentioned what you said to me last summer, about Mosley's making a pass at you." She did not appear to notice Jennie's sigh of relief. "But he reads the papers, dear. He even reads *Hansard*." The parliamentary record went to the palace in the boxes every day. "He knows where you stand." She paused. "With Mosley and the other Labour MPs who support him."

Jennie added, "He's backed by a couple of Conservative ones too...Boothby, MacMillan."

"Albert thinks Mosley could be prime minister, the next prime minister. In fact he wants him to be."

"And the Duke wants to help make it happen? That's crossing a line that won't be tolerated at Westminster."

It was merely a matter of appearances so far as Jennie was concerned. But the appearances mattered to the men in the House of Commons. Elizabeth reached out her hand firmly and held Jennie's wrist.

"No, no, no...it's not like that at all. All Albert wants is for Mosley to know he has a friend in the palace, that's all."

"Is that all I'm to pass on?"

"Yes, but nothing more. Albert..." She began again, "The Duke...was clear on the point. He doesn't want to hear anything from Mosley. That would be crossing a line."

"Crossing a line?" Jennie sighed. "What about all the rest of what you've told me...about the old King sharing the boxes with the Duke...and what you've told me about the Prince of Wales" — she gulped and went on — "the younger brothers." She looked heavenward and hissed out the words, "Am I supposed to tell Tom Mosley all that too?"

Elizabeth looked bereft. "I don't know, Jennie. I'm out of my depth altogether in this matter. Would it help if you told him everything?"

Jennie suddenly felt sorry for her. *You can't, Jennie. It would cause terrific trouble for your friend.* "I don't see how telling him all this could help Mosley."

Elizabeth seemed relieved to have shifted the problem to Jennie's shoulders. "I'm certain you'll do what's right, dear."

"Well, I don't exactly know how I'll get him a message," she lied, but Jennie caught the fleeting look Elizabeth gave her. She knew after all, or had guessed. Her next sentence subtly confirmed the suspicion.

"To think, the future of the country may rest with that man. I only wish he wasn't such a cad." She rose. "Why are so many successful politicians like that, I wonder?"

Jennie thought she knew but remained silent. It was a subject they'd covered before, in any case. Elizabeth brightened. "Better get back. Wouldn't do to have the baby in a tea shop off Prince's Street."

Then she kissed Jennie on the cheek, a surprising gesture of closeness, and unsteadily wobbled her girth out on to the pavement. Through the shop window Jennie could see a large car immediately pull up.

You are in a mess now, dearie! Jennie realised with a surprising cheeriness. There was suddenly the electric feeling she was in the thick of it. But the thick of what, exactly, she didn't quite know. Had her friend just wrecked her parliamentary career? If anyone ever learned she'd delivered the Duke's message to Mosley, she would have to resign. The crown had to be above politics: no one from the palace could favour a politician openly. To do so secretly and be found out was worse. If someone got hold of it, the breach of an unwritten but well understood constitutional prohibition would be enough to end her political prospect. Could she refuse to carry the message to Mosley? *No!* She knew she wouldn't refuse. *You want Tom Mosley to know! He's the only chance this country has to escape its pathetic inertia!*

Only then did a really sinking weight begin to make itself felt in the pit of her stomach. Somehow, the Duchess knew Jennie was a reliable secret channel to Tom Mosley? How long before Frank Wise knows too?

Jennie rose from the table, gathered her things. She was about to pay the half crown bill when she saw the gold sovereign on the heavy linen tablecloth. She looked at the waitresses, wan in starched white collars over black uniforms. It was utopian socialism that made her decide not to wait for change. Jennie left the teashop with a rueful thought. The Duchess of York hadn't really been very interested in hearing about Russia at all.

Chapter Twelve

Jennie didn't like party conferences. In the early autumn of each year, each of them would find a different dull seaside resort for a week of socialising and infighting. They'd give the newspapers plenty to write about, without having much of an effect on anything at all. This was especially true of Jennie's party — Labour. But every MP had to be present or accounted for, herding, cajoling, flattering the activists from their constituencies when they could, protecting themselves from the embarrassment of even the whisper of a reselection fight.

This year, Labour's venue would be Llandudno, a cream-coloured stretch of hotels perched between the Welsh mountains and the Irish sea forty miles west of Liverpool. The water would be too cold to swim, the food too cooked to eat, the chairs too hard to sit upon, and MacDonald's rhetoric would be too self-congratulatory to abide. *But something important is going to happen!* Jennie reassured herself repeatedly on the all-day train journey down from Cowdenbeath. *Mosley will get his chance!*

She had to change at Edinburgh and again at Liverpool. Then there was the long ride along the River Mersey and the estuary of the Dee to the Irish Sea, all under leaden skies. Along the docks of the Mersey, empty goods wagons rusted on sidings in mute expression of the slump that now gripped the whole country. In the afternoon gloom, the small resort towns and caravan parks dotting the strands along the seacoast looked as neglected as Jennie felt.

Her newspapers were no distraction. All were filled by accounts of the crash of the R-101, the government's experimental airship — the largest one in the world, begun in the previous Labour administration five years before and now crashed to the ground in France on its first international flight, to India. Forty-eight had been killed, including the Labour government's air minister. The omens, more than one leader writer had remarked, were ominous for MacDonald's government. The R-101 had been built by the government in competition with a privately built airship, the R-100, just returned from its successful crossing and re-crossing of the Atlantic. What everyone had called the "capitalist airship" had bested the "socialist" one. Jennie threw the papers aside. Her thoughts returned to Mosley. It was no secret that now, almost five months since he'd left the cabinet, Tom Mosley would finally go over the government's heads, seek to take the party away from MacDonald to his vision for the country. It was the only thing about the week Jennie had to look forward to.

The worst of it for Jennie was there'd be no chance for any time with Frank. Like other MPs, he was duty bound to bring the wife, and she was equally obliged to play the part, which Dorothy Wise did with fervour. The days would be worse than not seeing him at all. They'd catch glimpses of one another, from a distance, even pass in corridors, nodding the way parliamentary colleagues would do. Then nothing. And nothing much for Jennie to do besides mill about the hall and be hearty with her constituency people. A week of shamming.

The one thing that she would turn over in her thoughts with any avidity was how and when she might get word to Mosley about the Duke of York's...what word should she use? Interest? Jennie would have to be patient. Llandudno was certainly not the place to pass along her message. Mosley'd be under intense scrutiny every moment. Every hack from the papers knew he was going to speak and was monitoring his every encounter, remark, gesture for a clue to what he'd say. And he'd be with Cimmie, his wife, who was also a sitting MP and at the conference in her own right, so to speak.

The second afternoon, Jennie decided to escape the meetings for a walk down to the ubiquitous seaside town pier. She paid her six pence and strolled out to the end, thinking through her quandary for the hundredth time. She knew instinctively that she couldn't tell Frank anything about her conversation with the Duchess of York. He'd have been furious at the constitutional breach. So angry he might even take it to Ramsay MacDonald. Besides, if he had any inkling of her relations with Mosley, even as much as suspected by Elizabeth—the Duchess—she had to remind herself, the jealousy would surely combine with the anger to move him to action.

"Jennie, Jennie Lee!" The voice was loud, emphatic and Welsh. "Over here!"

It was Aneurin Bevan. He bellowed in a way no Scotsman ever would, from across the wide road separating the strand from the holiday rooming houses overlooking the sea. He left a scrum of unsteady companions, all of whom looked flushed from drink, and marched directly towards Jennie, looking neither right nor left, thus forcing traffic to stop for his crossing.

Bevan was wearing the summer version of the slightly too showy style he affected in London—a straw boater over a striped coat and tan trousers. It was a look as far from the Welsh coalface as he could contrive, Jennie thought. He grasped her waist with each hand and smiled. Jennie returned the grin. He was the tonic she needed. Instantly the gloom above her vanished. "Comrade," he addressed her with a twinkle and a grin rewarding himself for his wit, "will you let me buy you supper at the most expensive restaurant in the best hotel in Llandudno?"

"You can't afford it, *Comrade*." She returned the irony of his address.

"You don't know how cheap things are here in Wales."

"I accept."

She proffered her arm and Bevan took it. An evening with Nye Bevan was the distraction she needed. She'd resist his blandishments all evening and even regale Frank with the story as soon as they were together again.

* * *

In the months since Jennie had become Frank Wise's mistress, Nye Bevan had reconciled himself to the arrangement. He'd ended the competition for Jennie that had begun soon after he and Frank had arrived at Westminster in September of '29. Nye knew in his bones he should have won. He had the assets to do so. To begin with, he was unmarried. Then there was the natural affinity that sameness of upbringing should have cultivated—both were children of the coalmines, coal miners and coal mining politics. Nye was near Jennie's age, when Frank was twenty years older. Jennie and Nye shared a political style—assertive, strident, flamboyant—where Frank Wise was thoughtful, considered, even sometimes a bit cautious.

It was always easy for Jennie to fall in with Nye. Often enough, she told herself that she should have fallen for him too.

Unlike the dour politicians of Labour Party Scotland, Nye Bevan had no problem enjoying life. When parliament was sitting, he was frequently to be seen coming back to the House in evening clothes from one or another exclusive affair, at which few Labour Party politicians would allow themselves to be seen. He'd begun by inviting Jennie to opening nights at West End theatres, even Lord Beaverbrook's charity galas. She had steadily declined.

"Nye, how can you allow yourself to be seen at these events?" Jennie asked. "Won't it destroy your reputation with the miners?" Sometimes she asked archly, "What about proletarian solidarity?"

He would reply, "Ten years at the coal face, my dear. Everyone knows my fidelity to the cause. My friends in Ebbw Vale want me to enjoy myself...it's their vicarious pleasure!"

Ebbw Vale was a mining and iron mill town, just south of the Brecon mountains in the south of Wales, much like Jennie's Cowdenbeath in the lowlands of Fife.

Knowing about Frank and Jennie, Nye had nevertheless persisted in his invitations. Occasionally, she'd accept one.

They turned back towards the pier and walked easily together towards the Grand Hotel.

Seated in the large dining room overlooking the sea, they were offered menus, Nye's with prices, Jennie's without. Offended, Jennie swiped Nye's from his hands and passed him hers.

He smiled, as she said, "Not cheap."

Nye looked towards the sommelier standing discreetly next to a heavy walnut sideboard. Instantly, but noiselessly, he swept up to their table.

"Pol Roger, please." It was a very dear champagne. Nye looked at Jennie. "The only kind Winston Churchill drinks."

Jennie turned over the menu to the wines.

"Really, Nye, you can't afford that!"

"Not so loud." Then, under his slightly beery breath, he added, "You can always live like a millionaire for five minutes."

They laughed and turned back to the menus.

When both were closed, Nye spoke again. "Where are you staying?"

"Guest house on St George's Crescent."

"I'm here in the hotel…"

As he moved his hand towards hers, she smiled. "I'm sure the view from your room is splendid, but no, I don't wish to see it tonight."

He smiled, shrugged his shoulders slightly and withdrew his hand to show he had accepted the ground rules.

"Very well, sister. No incest, just business tonight." He paused, then asked, "Are you going to listen to MacDonald tomorrow?"

"Must I? Can't abide the man."

"Well, you'll have missed nothing if you sleep in. It will be the usual cant—'everything that can be done about unemployment is being done.' There is going to be motion of censure, from the

ILP, for inaction on unemployment. I'll probably speak. So will Frank."

Jennie sighed. "It's got no chance, of course."

They both understood the block voting by union representatives of a million or more members. These votes were in the government's pockets.

Then she brightened. "But surely the main event will be Mosley?" Jennie wanted to sound offhand but didn't manage to. Nye didn't notice her enthusiasm. *He doesn't know, does he... about Mosley?*

"Yes. But I'm not much more hopeful about his motion."

Mosley would speak to the party in favour of the plan the cabinet had rejected.

"The motion wouldn't require MacDonald to resign." Jennie was trying to be optimistic.

"Don't fool yourself. If it wins, MacDonald will have been repudiated and Mosley will become the next Labour prime minister."

"And you don't think that can happen?"

"Let's order the next course."

Nye wanted to change the subject and even more the mood. But his conversation merely darkened Jennie's frown further.

"Seen Frank?"

She frowned. "Only from a distance. He's here with his wife." She fell silent.

He tried to cushion her feelings. "Constituency matters, social calls, it's all appearances."

Suddenly she had to confide. "I do understand...it's just a little harder this week, seeing them together. I can't wreck his home. I won't let him do it either." Before Nye could reply she asked, "Can it go on like this indefinitely?"

"Jennie, you know I'd do anything for you, anything to help."

He reached across the table again, and this time Jennie accepted the act of consolation and friendship.

"I keep turning things over. He can't divorce. I don't want to be married. But I love him and funnily enough he loves me."

"I'm listening." He invited her to continue. So for a quarter of an hour she took Nye on their tour of the Soviet Caucasus. But she didn't tell him how it had shaken her scientific socialism.

When she finished, Nye sighed. "Not for me, such exertions. I thought Moscow was tough enough...remember walking the streets just looking for fags?"

They were now between courses and the thought made him reach into his coat, pull out a packet of Players and offer Jennie one.

She took it, drew in a drag and exhaled through her nostrils. Jennie couldn't help it, her mind always seemed to turn back to politics.

"What'll we do if the party conference rejects the Mosley policy, Nye?"

"It depends. If the vote is close, we'll keep soldiering on... make another push, especially if things get worse."

"Get worse? There's already two million unemployed. In my constituency it's thirty per cent."

"What's the alternative? Join the Communists?"

They both laughed. Each had experienced attempts by the party to subvert their local Labour Party branches into fatuous sectarian extremism.

Jennie was thoughtful. "If the government continues to drift, the ILP contingent will start voting against it in the House."

Nye put down his knife and fork and looked at Jennie. When her eyes met his, he said slowly, "That would bring down the government." She nodded, but he continued, "Even worse, split the Labour movement. I'll never be party to that."

* * *

Walking back to Jennie's guesthouse room, she could feel the ardour rising in Nye. For all his protestation of friendship, she knew, he wanted more from her. And when he sought a kiss, a real one, Jennie gave in, enjoyed it, and began slightly to regret not having seen the view from his room.

Chapter Thirteen

The next morning, MacDonald's speech was as unctuous as Jennie feared. She'd been unable to stay away. It was a matter of morbid curiosity. When, finally, MacDonald proclaimed "Everything that can be done is being done with energy, precision and systematically" she could detect the unconcealed and audible sigh that deflated the entire pavilion.

After an endless ninety minutes, the old man subsided. Jennie needed air, as apparently did many others. People were streaming out onto the pier, muttering to one another. The hall had been dark enough that the midday overcast was blinding. Jennie turned back from the glare and saw Ellen Wilkinson behind her. Still undersecretary of health and so part of the government, she had been on the podium behind MacDonald, though too far away for Jennie to gauge any reaction in her face.

Ellen smiled as she came out of the hall into the brighter light. She grasped Jennie's hands and gave a conspiratorial shrug.

"Come have a drink before the next session?"

"Oh...I suppose." She took Ellen's arm. "Let's get that drink before this lot drain the pubs altogether."

She turned her head from side to side as people continued to stream past them.

It took a ten-minute walk, but at last they were settled in the snug of a pub, far enough away from the pavilion not to be crowded with boisterous shop stewards. Jennie brought two shandies to the table, placing each on a coaster to catch the foam still running over the glass lips. Ellen looked up as she sat.

"They're frightened, you know?"

"Who?"

"The cabinet, the government, MacDonald. That's why he left straight away after his speech. Doesn't want to be here if the party votes against him."

"But he's got a million votes in his pocket to swamp the ILP no confidence motion."

"No, I mean Mosley's motion. They're worried he could carry the conference. That would be the end for the government."

Jennie smiled. "I'll drink to that." She lifted her glass, as did her companion. "If it happens won't you be out of a job as junior minister?"

"Don't care if I am!"

"But how can Mosley pry a million votes from the Trades Union Council?"

"Sheer oratory, Jennie. You've heard him in the House. The man makes women swoon and grown men lose their reason. He'll hypnotise the crowd and call for an immediate vote. Suddenly everyone will realise he's the next leader, that he might even be able to win a majority in the country. MacDonald will never do that." She stopped. "But can he be trusted with that much power?"

Jennie wanted reassurance. "What exactly are you worried about?"

Ellen drew breath and continued. "Sir Oswald Mosley" — the titled name spat itself out — "is what I used to call a 'class enemy' when I was still a Communist. Landed family, hereditary baronetcy, officer corps in the War, with a Military Cross to prove it, still swaggering fifteen years later, society wedding, large country house, servants. Why is this man on our side?"

"You might say the same for Charlie Trevelyan. He's no class enemy!"

Ellen nodded. "Charlie comes from three generations of political men on the left of their party. His principles were his father's before him and have been fixed his whole life. He's paid for them, too!"

Jennie pulled a packet of cigarettes from her clutch and offered one to Ellen, who found a box of matches in her pocket and lit both.

Ellen exhaled and finally concluded, "Mosley's our best chance. I suppose we've got to trust him."

* * *

They were both back in their seats at the Pavilion that evening, for the last act of the conference drama. Everyone in the hall knew what was coming. It would be a tragedy whose protagonist— MacDonald or Mosley—had yet to be known.

Tom Mosley was gambling all on one throw. Everyone knew that by standing against MacDonald here he wasn't just burning bridges back to the cabinet. If he failed to carry the conference, there was no future for Mosley in politics. If he succeeded, MacDonald's premiership would be ended.

The parliamentarian hurriedly went through the motions of putting and seconding a motion and invited Mosley to come forward. As if by command, the throng quieted, took their seats, and turned their faces towards the stage. Political theatre was to unfold before them, a one-act play whose denouement was not a foregone conclusion. Mosley stepped to the stage, and stood quietly for a moment longer than anyone expected. Jennie had seen this before, in the House of Commons: Mosley's sense of presence, asserting his control of his listeners' emotions merely by making them catch their breaths.

Standing at guardsman's attention, he needed no uniform. His face shone beneath hair dark and brilliant. The officer's moustache reminded everyone he'd been in the trenches with his men. His suit was a light grey, tight-fitting, double-breasted, cut in at the waist, a sharp contrast with the celluloid wing-collars and swan-tailed frock coats of the cabinet ministers who had preceded him on the podium.

He began quietly in the silence of the vast space, every delegate feeling the shared anticipation. This, Jennie had experienced before, in the company of others and alone: Mosley's ability to make each person in the hall feel he was being addressed directly and individually. It was evident that the details of his plan didn't matter. He was hypnotising the gathering. Perhaps Jennie was slightly immune, for she found herself looking round, noticing that the delegates were rising from their seats and returning to them almost at his command. His sweeping arm motions, his fist hammering the podium, worked like a conductor's baton mobilising the orchestra of his listeners. Sometimes they remained on their feet, almost swaying to the beat of his voice. Twice, the perspiration glistening on his face made him pause. Mosley stopped, pulled the handkerchief from the breast pocket of his coat, and wiped his brow. In the silence, each of his listeners could feel the shared anxiety that he might stop when they needed him to go on, to continue to dominate them, time without end.

He was speaking about putting millions into public works, building roads, bridges, schools, hospitals, he was demanding tariff reform and Empire preference, attacking the gold standard and the craven submission of a Labour government to the Bank of England and the House of Morgan. But the two thousand or so in the pavilion were not listening to what he said so much as bathing in his energy, the anger in his voice, the pride they felt in being with him, the comradeship between them that his words instilled, the mission he would lead them on. They were no longer sober men contemplating complex issues to which there were no simple answers. They were human beings, for whom it mattered personally, and individually, that they were with Oswald Mosley. And they were prepared to be the unthinking, collective instruments of his vision. It might not last beyond the end of his speech, but while he continued, everyone was transfixed. Even Jennie could feel herself now being seduced, in a way not entirely different from what she had felt alone with him, opening to him as his ardour rose. Two thousand people in the hall banished prudence or consequences. Momentarily, they surrendered choice and responsibility in exchange for a shared feeling of membership in the grandeur that was washing over them.

Mosley came to his conclusion. He had succeeded, at least for the moment. There were no longer any sober-minded supporters of Ramsay MacDonald to be found in the pavilion.

"We are a party with our eyes on the stars, but let us also remember that our feet are planted firmly in the earth, on muddy soil, where men are suffering and looking at us with eyes of questioning and anguish saying, 'Lift us up from the mud! Give us remedies here and now!'" He paused. "Today, we may not have the majority, but at worst we will go down fighting for the things we believe in. This movement will refuse to die like an old woman in bed. We'll go down like men on the field—a better fate, and in politics, one with a more certain hope of resurrection."

Mosley stepped back from the microphone as a signal that he was now finished, and the cheering could begin. Once allowed, it came forth. It was not polite applause or the satisfied roar of the crowd on a football pitch after a home-side goal. It was the release of emotions no Englishman would ever admit to having, a sort of superlative combination of faith and resentment, untethered from lifetimes of understatement and refusal to take one's self very seriously. It was almost as if they were foreigners—Frenchmen, or even Germans, stoked to a frenzy by an orator's unconcern about the dangers of a mob.

Jennie looked about her. Would these stolid middle-aged men, stout in their three-piece tweed suits and flat caps, run amok? Where would they direct the emotions Mosley had fired? Would they begin to rip the chairs from the floor, charge the rostrum, carry Mosley from the hall on their shoulders? She looked at Ellen Wilkinson, carried away as much as the rest, standing next to her, taller by inches now as she stood erect and waved a hand in the air. Seeing Jennie's surprise at her display, Ellen sheepishly brought down the arm, shrugged her shoulders and smiled.

"Worth staying round to see?"

Jennie nodded. "Quite a show."

* * *

A quarter of an hour later the conference chairwoman came to the podium and announced the vote. A million or so for Mosley's motion. These were the blocks of votes held by people who were in the hall, who'd listened. Jennie quickly computed that Mosley had taken every one of the votes they had to give. A roar rose from the floor as others made the same calculation. Then it subsided as the realisation dawned that it would not be enough. The Trade Unions' block votes had not been there to be moved. These votes would remain with MacDonald. The speaker rapped her gavel.

"A million two hundred fifty-one thousand against. Motion defeated."

But only just. This political drama would not after all be a one-act play. Everyone present now recognised that MacDonald might yet turn out to be the protagonist of a Pyrrhic tragedy. The vote had been too close. The party was moving towards a perhaps inevitable rendezvous with Tom Mosley. That, at any rate, was the shared consensus among the emotionally drained men and women reluctantly drifting out of the pavilion into the night.

* * *

Early Thursday morning, Jennie was on the quay, waiting for a train to Liverpool and on to London. Glancing at the newsagent's kiosk, she saw the headline in the *Manchester Guardian*, "Luke-Warm Vote of Confidence/British Hitler/Continental View of Sir O. Mosley." *British Hitler? Whatever does that mean?* Herr

Hitler's National Socialist party, she knew, had come second in the German parliamentary voting the previous month, winning a hundred seats with almost twenty per cent of the vote. She bought a copy of the paper, sat down and scanned the article. It began with MacDonald's speech but then took up another thread:

> ...*one should note the re-emergence of Sir Oswald Mosley. It was, like all his set speeches, beautifully delivered and with that touch of demagogy which he adds to the effectiveness of his most popular orations. When he sat down he had an ovation and had obviously influenced many votes. We cannot resist transcribing the comments of an acute continental observer at the conference, that in Sir Oswald Mosley British Labour may yet find its Hitler. The parallel is not so absurd as it sounds, for in some respects at least the resemblance might be found between the crude aspirations of the "Nazis" and the new Socialist Imperialism. Subordinating Parliamentary institutions to its own imperative needs, to which Sir Oswald Mosley is drifting...*

Damned nonsense. Jennie stopped reading and dropped the paper to the pavement at her feet.

Chapter Fourteen

The week without Frank, watching him, sometimes just yards away and yet out of reach, had been more difficult than Jennie expected. Seeing him across a floor or a street, his wife clutching his arm, watching mere acquaintances freely seeking his company: casually saluting him, making small talk, smiling at him, shaking their heads or nodding in conversation she couldn't hear. Seeing all these people who meant so much less to him than she did, drove her to a frustration she could not hide. She would turn and make for the pier to be alone in a chill wind. *You had a month with Frank. Now let him alone for a few days.*

Jennie had consoled herself that at the end of the endless week she would have time alone with him. Sir Charles Trevelyan had invited her and Frank to spend the weekend following the conference at his grand country house, Wallington Hall, in the Northumberland countryside. His own dalliance with Jennie behind him, Charlie Trevelyan had taken a paternal interest in her. He admired Frank a great deal, thought him well matched with Jennie, and was happy to make it easy and agreeable for them to spend time together.

But then, at the Llandudno guesthouse that last evening, with the final mail delivery of the day, came the note in Charlie's hand. It warned her off the weekend at Wallington Hall. Frank's wife had suddenly insisted on accompanying her husband to Northumbria. Had Dorothy found out about Jennie? She'd certainly been a fixture on his arm for all the days of the conference. But that Jennie had credited that to Dorothy Wise's Labour Party activism. Discovery of her husband's affair would be different, not just vexatious but dangerous.

Jennie would have to change her ticket to the north for one to London.

117

* * *

Loneliness in London was a temptress. Twice in two days, Jennie found herself walking past Victoria Station, knowing full well her destination was Mosley's flat on Ebury Street. *Just going to pass on the Duchess's message?* She tried on the thought and laughed it away. *Doing this to punish Frank for not being here?* She wanted this to be the reason. He deserved punishment for taking Dorothy to Wallington Hall. Jennie wanted the emotional high ground. But she knew that wasn't the reason she was skulking round this part of London, either. The carnal motive driving her along was palpable. Telling Mosley about her meeting with the Duchess would be a prologue, a pretext.

Each time she came within a hundred feet of the narrow white stucco two-storey building, she noticed a brace of men milling about on the pavement, one with a newspaper photographer's camera. She turned around, walked away, back towards Victoria, and both times found a cinema to distract her. Two double features in two days was too much and she woke on Monday with what felt like a hangover. *All Quiet on the Western Front* had been a cure for the crowd's surge of militancy at end of Mosley's speech. But the new Greta Garbo, *Anna Christie*, cast Jennie down. It was film about a woman with a shameful secret redeemed by love. Garbo's haunted look stayed with her, troubling when it shouldn't have. Unlike Ibsen's character, Jennie's secrets were not freighted with either guilt or shame, only dangers.

The distraction of the films ended, her mood had become bleak again almost immediately after the house lights rose and the national anthem played. Resentment and self-pity brewed. She decided on the long walk from the cinema at Victoria Station back to her flat in Bloomsbury. It was not raining or even very cold and the walk would kill time.

Striding along, she tried to challenge the mood. *Come off it, Jennie. You've got what you want, don't you? Frank on your terms, not his. It's you stopping him from divorce, isn't it?* Momentarily she brightened. Then the question came. *So, why are you orbiting Ebury Street?* More than once she had tried pretending to herself that it was politics, just politics, driving her to carry the message from the palace. Her mind's eye saw through this. *Don't fool yourself, dearie. It's not a bit of revenge against Frank either. You want to see the desire in Mosley's eyes, to feel your power over his lust. It's nothing to do with love. That's why you can hide it from Frank. Isn't that right, Jennie?*

You've got two things to hide from Frank and that's the problem, isn't it? One thing he wouldn't understand—Mosley's brute allure. The other—the message from the Duke of York—he'd understand too well. It was the very sort of thing she needed desperately to talk through with Frank. But she could not, not without compromising him, as she had already been.

There'd never been anything since they'd met they hadn't been able to work through together. Walking along, she conjured a post-coital languor, turning their political lives and thoughts inside out, looking at them from every angle, comparing notes and trying to make sense of events. Frank and Jennie didn't need to agree on everything. In fact they often didn't. But everything had been in the open between them, even her freedom, at least in the abstract. And Frank didn't even try to pry.

But this business with the Palace Jennie felt her throat constrict a gulp. *You can't talk about it with Frank, ever.* Suddenly she was relieved he wasn't in London, wasn't with her. The long walk had carried her to a conclusion. She had to see Mosley and she'd never tell Frank. If he knew, before or after she did it—carry the Duke's message—Frank would be complicit in a constitutional breach that could ruin him along with her. If he advised her not to, and she rejected his counsel, there'd be a gulf between them perhaps too wide to bridge. And then would his sense of honour demand he take the matter to the Speaker of the House of Commons? Would he, could he, ruin the only thing Jennie really cared for besides him—her own political life?

Jennie heard herself argue, *It's so inconsequential a breach of the constitution.* Who really cared if the second in line to the throne had a favourable view of Mosley's politics and told him so? Then she heard Frank's quiet voice. *That's not the point, is it? It's the principle of the thing, rather.* Despite herself, she would have to agree. If anyone else had done it, the Bolshie in Jennie would have carried the matter right to the Speaker's chair. And now she was conniving at royal interference without a qualm.

She crossed through Russell Square, nearly home. Her walk and the debate in her head came to their ends. *You'll pass the Duke's message on because you have to. Because you believe in Mosley!* She was still enough of a Marxian to accept that the ends justify the means. *There may be a line somewhere you won't cross, but this isn't it! That's why you'll see Mosley before Frank gets back to town. So he can't stop you.* She had decided, and so calmly pulled out her latchkey, entered her flat and without taking off her coat reached for the telephone.

* * *

After just two rings, Tom Mosley answered with the number, "Abby 8156."

"Is that you, Mosley?" She had to keep it business-like, she knew. "Jennie Lee here."

"How nice to hear from you." Mosley was emollient.

She had to steel herself to continue. "I need to see you."

Immediately she realised this was the wrong thing to say.

"I'm so pleased." Jennie tried to interrupt but he didn't even take a breath before continuing. "Why not drop round here? I can arrange to be alone."

How to make herself clear? "It's not that, Mosley."

He sighed audibly. "It's Tom, dear."

"It's business, it's important and it's confidential. There are reporters skulking round the Ebury Street flat."

"Right you are." He cleared his throat and his tone became slightly formal. "Very well, where shall we meet?" Then the mischievous tone returned. "Your place?"

"No." Jennie tired to sound emphatic. "And Westminster is no good either." She thought for a moment. "Meet me at the National Portrait Gallery at 2 tomorrow afternoon. In front of the picture of William IV."

"Why him?"

"I'll explain when we meet."

* * *

Mosley was standing at the stipulated location, contemplating the portrait of Queen Victoria's immediate predecessor, when Jennie entered.

"Sorry to keep you waiting." She spoke quietly, looking in both directions to ensure no one was close. "I was watching from across the pavement, at the Edith Cavell memorial, to be sure you weren't followed."

"I think I shook off the press."

She looked him up and down. He was elegant even in anonymity. "Yes, but you're damned hard to miss."

"Well, Jennie..."

Quietly but firmly she interrupted him. "No names." She looked up at the portrait. "I was taught that William IV was the last monarch who actually meddled in politics."

"Yes, I recall. Tried to dismiss Melbourne even though he had a parliamentary majority."

"Succeeded, I think," Jennie observed.

"Well, what's that got to do with us?"

"Someone in the palace wants you to know that they support your actions in the Labour Party. They asked me to tell you."

Mosley was silent, digesting the meaning of her words.

Then he spoke. "And they asked you, an anonymous back bencher, to deliver this message?" Jennie said nothing, wondering if he would press her for more information.

"I suppose you shan't tell me who my well-wisher is?"

"I fear I must, having passed on his message. It's the Duke of York."

He nodded. "Yes, well, better to have his good wishes than the wastrel's."

There was no need to explain. Jennie knew this was a reference to the Prince of Wales.

Then Mosley spoke in a tone of bemusement. "I wonder if it matters?"

Jennie decided that having spent a penny she was in for a pound.

"I rather think it might. The King wants to be shot of the wastrel. Doesn't think the Prince of Wales even wants the job of being king. He's grooming the Duke to succeed."

Mosley nodded. "I see the connection to William the IV now. I applaud your historical grip—" He was about to add her name when her touch on his arm reminded him not to. "So, what am I to do with this slightly dangerous knowledge?"

"I am glad you recognise its threat. Could be used to destroy both our political careers... if it gets out."

"Unless we denounce it immediately as rank interference with parliamentary democracy." Mosley looked at her hard.

"Really, I don't think it rises to that level, do you?"

"Perhaps not." He thought a minute, then spoke. "I don't suppose the Duke of York is in regular communication with Jennie Lee, most junior, most left-wing, most republican"—he paused and shot her a look; Jennie nodded in assent—"member of the House of Commons." She caught a hint of menace in the sarcasm. "How did you come by this message?"

Jennie calculated. She'd have to answer; she was already in too deep not to.

"Duchess of York. Known her since we were girls in Scotland. I used to visit Glamis Castle in the war. Long story. I won't bore you."

"Anyone else know?"

She shook her head, recalling the two occasions on which others had noticed her receive post from the palace. Both times she'd managed to fob them off.

"Don't think so. Why do you ask?"

Instead of answering Mosley looked at her intently and then asked, "So, no one knows? Not even Frank Wise?"

She shook her head mutely. Then she asked herself, *if Mosley knows about us who else does? Frank's wife? Is that why Dorothy wouldn't let him go to Charlie Trevelyan's place in Northumberland alone?*

She wanted to ask how he knew about her and Frank. But Mosley made a point of turning to contemplate that rather bad portrait of William IV. He began stroking his moustache, evidently deep in thought, feet so close together that he swayed slightly. Jennie was about to break into his thoughts to ask about Frank again, when he turned back to her with a self-satisfied smile and a knowing look in his eye. He nodded at the portrait.

"He had ten bastards, that one, and no legitimate children at all." *You've probably had a few yourself, Tom Mosley.* "It's how Victoria became queen," he continued. "Couldn't happen anymore."

"Why ever not?"

"Illegitimacy's not much of a stain anymore." He went on, apparently giving voice to an errant thought. "Ramsay MacDonald was born out of wedlock and look where he wound up." Mosley turned to her. "But the taint is still strong in your part of Scotland. Those Irish Papists and the Presbyterian scolds...a bastard couldn't win in Glasgow, not even Ramsay MacDonald's bastard."

Jennie could not suppress a spurt of laughter. The image of

MacDonald in bed with a woman that came into her head was simultaneously revolting and ridiculous, rather like picturing one's parents in the act of sexual congress.

Tom Mosley momentarily joined her laughter. Then he regained a measure of decorum.

"Thank you, thank you for conveying the message, Jennie. You can rely on me to keep it secret. Not in either of our interests to have it known, is it?" Then he walked quickly off.

Jennie felt his sudden departure like a tight coil sprung. The relief spreading through her body made her aware of how much tension she'd been under. She had been steeling herself to resist an invitation to continue their rendezvous in a less public location, his place or even hers. She'd played a dozen mental tricks, to deflect and distract herself from the rising urge to consent to what he was sure to offer, even digging fingernails into the palms of her hands buried in the overcoat pocket, reminding her she had to refuse him. But it hadn't been necessary after all. He'd been all business. His manner had not after all turned to seduction. Now taking a breath, she went down the creaking stairs, out into the gloom of Charing Cross Road and walked back towards Bloomsbury.

There was a note from Frank on the top of that morning's post scattered at the foot of her door when she pushed it open. He'd be with her the next day. And there was a letter from a theatrical agency. Would Miss Jennie Lee, M.P., be interested in a lecture tour of the United States and Canada on the subject of her experiences in Russia? Had her trip the previous summer made the papers, Jennie wondered? More worrying, had the fact she'd been there with Frank made news as well?

* * *

Frank Wise went directly from Paddington to Jennie's flat on Guilford Street. It was late morning and the House would resume its sittings late that afternoon. He'd have several hours with Jennie. As the door opened it was evident to Frank that she'd been expecting him. Under a loosely-tied dressing gown, she wore nothing.

As they disentangled themselves from a long embrace, Jennie spoke first.

"It's been months."

"Actually, seven weeks and three days since we returned from Russia."

She was pleased he'd been counting. Taking his hand, Jennie led him to the bedroom as he pulled off the suit coat with one hand while unbuttoning his waistcoat with the other. She turned and put a hand up to his busy fingers poised above another button.

"Slowly..." she whispered, needing to savour the sensations that would drive Mosley's lingering spell from her thoughts.

When they had sated themselves, at least for the morning, both were eager to talk Labour Party politics. Jennie was too eager, seeking to distract herself from what she'd done the day before. She could not know that Frank, too, was finding excuses to put off what he had to tell her.

Jennie reached down from the bed amongst the newsprint on the floor and pulled the almost week-old *Manchester Guardian* from the pile.

Passing it to Frank, she complained, "Read the bit comparing Tom Mosley to that Hitler in Germany. Outrageous."

He began to read. In the silence Jennie assailed herself. *You fool. Why bring that up now?*

Before she could change the subject Frank replied.

"Outrageous? Maybe." Frank sighed. "But not entirely off the mark." He looked at her. She was relieved there was no accusation in his eyes. "Jennie. You were there, in that hall, weren't you?" She nodded. "You watched Mosley stir the party to its feet. Never seen people, not British people at any rate, so transported out of themselves into, into"—he thought for a moment—"into an emotional movement. They'd lost all reason for a moment and might have walked into the Irish Sea if he'd commanded it."

Jennie recalled the way she'd felt amongst the seething mass within the pavilion that afternoon in Llandudno. But Frank broke the spell.

"It was dangerous, Jennie. And with power over people's emotions like that, Mosley's dangerous."

"Spellbinding audiences makes him dangerous? No, it makes him a leader, Frank."

Frank held the page from *The Manchester Guardian* up to her and struck it with the back of his hand, reading the headline as a question.

"British Hitler?" He passed the broad sheet back to her and she reread the passage she could still remember. Frank continued. "Do they have the wrong end of the stick? I hope so. But fact is, last month in Germany that fascist got thirty per cent of the vote."

"Mosley's a man of the left, Frank. He's a socialist. Just because he's a nationalist too, that doesn't make him a National Socialist!"

Frank made no reply. They'd just had their first, their only, political row. Jennie hated it. She needed them both to show it didn't matter. She would rebuild the bridge and she'd start directly. But moving her hand halfway toward his, Jennie recognised there was something else preoccupying Frank. She pulled it back to wait. After a few moments, he leaned across the bed and took the hand that had been folded across her naked torso.

"Look Jennie, you know why Dorothy insisted on coming to the party conference?"

"She's chair of a local branch, isn't she? She'd want to attend. Isn't that why?"

"Not the only reason. She needed to send a signal."

"To whom?"

"To whom it may concern." His laugh was sardonic. "That I'm her property...poachers would be prosecuted. She won't play the Westminster game. Won't turn a blind eye to bed-hopping."

Jennie was silent. "She thinks the way you do. Divorce would be fatal to me—and to you—and she wants people to know she'll use the weapon."

Jennie recalled, "Months ago you said she suspected something. Does she know I was with you all through those weeks in the Caucasus?"

"I don't know..." Frank looked at their hands folded together on Jennie's lap, then turned to her face. "Probably." He waited for a reply. None came, so he persisted. "Look, I've decided to tell her everything, give her grounds for divorce, if you'll have me, Jennie."

She pulled his hands up her chest to her lips. "Frank, dear, we've been over this ground a dozen times. You just said it yourself. You'd be ruined. So would I."

"And if I forced your hand by divorcing her anyway?"

"You can't fritter away a brilliant political career, Frank. You're sure to be in the next Labour government. Even if Labour loses you'll be on the front bench of the shadow cabinet." She dropped his hands to her lap. "You're practically the only one in the party who understands international finance. I won't let you destroy your future. That's flat, Frank Wise!"

He was silent, contemplating her speech. What she had said wouldn't be enough, Jennie knew. She had to do something decisive to prevent Frank throwing both their futures away. She knew what it was, and it made her heart sink.

"Besides, there's a simpler solution to our problem, at least for the moment. One that will throw your wife off if she really suspects us."

"What's that?" The raised eyebrows gave Frank's face a

hopeful air.

"I'm off to North America next month. I'll be there on a lecture tour for six weeks at least. Perhaps more if it works out. Ellen Wilkinson put a lecture tour booking agency on to me. I'm to tell Americans all about Russia."

"But you're no expert, Jennie. You've spent, what, seven weeks all told in Russia?"

"Who's an expert on the subject in America? They haven't even recognised the Soviet government thirteen years after it took power." She smiled at him. "And when Dorothy finds out I'm going and won't be back for months, it'll have to allay her suspicions, won't it?"

Now she had told him her plan, and told herself as well, Jennie wanted to cushion the blow for both of them.

"I'm not leaving for a few weeks, Frank. You'll have to help me prepare a bit."

Chapter Fifteen

Jennie arrived in America with a rage against the British ruling class. When she left, it had been replaced by despairing recognition that matters could be worse. There was no class-consciousness in America. Socialism had no chance in a country where exploitation was undetected by the exploited. And the worst of the exploitation was effectively masked by colour. Everyone was oppressed by a racialism whose glare made class differences indiscernible even to those suffering the most from them.

Jennie knew that the suddenness of economic depression had made many in America much worse off than they had been. Yet now, in the winter of 1930-31, a year after it had begun, no one seemed to be doing anything about it, beyond hiding its effects. Shantytowns— "jungle camps"—were visible only from the railway tracks, soup kitchens were confined to the warehouse districts. The cheerful decorum of apple sellers at downtown corners was rigorously enforced by jocular police pretending to be hearty Irishmen, twirling their night sticks as they walked their sentry rounds.

More than once she found herself thinking back to the weeks in Moscow six months before. There were beggars along the railway lines here too.

In New Haven, Amherst and Princeton, audiences composed mainly of college professors and their wives were happy to hear Jennie's talks about the bracing changes in Russia, the rapid industrialisation of the Donbas in the south, how literacy was sweeping the country along with electricity. They were visibly less interested in the privations and suffering she reported. Students at Ann Arbor, Urbana and Bloomington were eager to learn about modernism in architecture and the *avant-garde* in theatre, film, and music—and even keener on the details about women's rights, "free love," contraception and abortion. All seemed eager to hear about the vast spaces of the Caucasus, between the Black Sea and the Caspian, which Jennie illustrated in a lantern show of maps and a dozen photos she'd snapped that previous summer.

Scattered among the middle-class academics in her audiences was the occasional union organiser. These union men Jennie sought out in the milling crowds after a talk or a lecture. It was more difficult to pick them out here in the States than at home. Their accents were no different from the businessmen or academics. Their dress wasn't distinctive, nor their demeanour. Only their questions were different. These men, and they were, she noticed, only men, wanted to find the good in the great Russia experiment, but seemed worried it was too good to be true.

One evening in Detroit, after Jennie's standard "The Soviet Union Today and Tomorrow" lecture, a young man approached.

"Good evening Miss Lee, my name is Reuther, Walter Reuther."

His attire announced him as a workingman—no tie and suit coat, just a zippered leather jacket over a plaid flannel shirt. A white vest—they called it an undershirt in America—was visible above the open collar. The hand outstretched was strong and calloused. It felt familiar to Jennie, from the pits and shop floors of industrial Britain. He was very young, not even Jennie's age, and strikingly good looking, a thick shock of dark hair swept away from his brow, a broad grin that invited friendship, dimples that made Jennie want to squeeze him. She made herself memorise the name.

"I'd like to ask you a lot more questions about Russia if I could." He looked at the crowd surrounding them. "Are you staying in town long?"

She shook her head. "Leaving for Chicago in the morning, I fear."

"Can I buy you breakfast before you leave?"

Suddenly Jennie decided to be 'forward.'

"How about a drink later, after this crowd loses interest? I've never seen a speak-easy."

"Gee, I know a blind pig in Hamtramck. It's a ways...Sure you want to go there?"

Reuther looked puzzled, as though Jennie had asked him to teach her welding.

She was not to be put off. "Yes, let's...but, Walter, what's a blind pig?"

He smiled, "It's a place that'll let me in dressed like this."

* * *

It was a streetcar ride from the hotel, down an avenue wide enough for two lanes in each direction, even though it was lined with cars parked diagonally on each side. Almost midnight and yet there was traffic—foot and motor—all along the twenty-minute route. It was almost the first time she'd been out after a lecture. The contrast between late night Detroit and a provincial town back in Britain was striking. There, everyone would be home, asleep. Here people were out, trying to forget the depression.

By the time their tram arrived, Jennie and Walter were on a first name basis. His hand under her arm almost lifted her up the high step. Jennie liked that.

"So, what do you do Walter?"

"I work at Ford."

This was going to be interesting. "Assembly line?"

"No. I'm in the tool and die shop. We make and repair the equipment on the assembly line."

"I see. Is there a union?"

"Are you kidding?" He smiled at her innocence. "Not at Ford. Not worth your life trying to organise there." He paused.

"Besides, the men don't want a union, either, not the kind we want to organise."

"'We'?"

"'We. I guess 'we' means a bunch of guys in the plant who agree with your Labour Party—socialists, refugees from the union movements in Europe, some old-time Wobblies."

Jennie was slightly amused. Would she have to explain that not everyone in the Labour Party was a real socialist? "Wobblies?" It was a word, like 'blind pig', she didn't know.

"I.W.W., International Workers of the World, the 'One Big Union' movement about twenty-five years ago, closest we ever got to English class consciousness."

"So, why are American workers so different when it comes to unions, class consciousness, and socialism, Walter?"

The Scots girl in her wanted to upbraid the use of 'English' for British, but it was a battle she knew was lost.

"I can't answer that question for sure, Jennie. But I have some guesses. People here are too well off, or they were before this depression got started. Maybe it'll change things." He stopped. "But that's part of why I wanted to talk to you. I figure the only way I'll ever find out how we should change things here is by seeing how things work other places." He paused again. "Especially Russia."

"You mean you're thinking of going? You're the first person I've met in America with that idea. How soon, Walter?"

"Not right away. I'm saving up for the trip. But you've been there, Jennie. Do you think I should go?"

"One way or the other, you have to! It's the only way to find out if it's the grand future or a hideous nightmare."

A frown broke out on Reuther's face. "Hideous nightmare? That doesn't seem a possibility you raised in your lecture."

"I didn't advise anyone to move to Russia either." Jennie took a breath. "Look, Walter, Soviet power is a huge experiment. No one knows how it's going to turn out. We have to hope for the best, but six weeks there last summer left me very worried."

"Are you saying it's dangerous?"

"Not if you keep your head down. You aren't a Trotskyist?" Reuther shook his head. "Then you'll be all right. Look, life is tough in Russia right now. We have to believe it'll get better."

He didn't seem to be listening.

"Is there real socialism—worker control, democracy on the factory shop floor? That's what I want to know. If there is, I'm sure it'll get better."

"If that's what you're looking for, Walter, you'll find some of it there." She paused. "The problem is whether Stalin will let it work." She told her companion about the trial of the 'wreckers' in Shakhty. "They were just trying to manage things between them the best way they knew how. All they got for their trouble was interference from Moscow and a lot of prison sentences."

Reuther was thoughtful for a minute. Then he rose.

"This is our stop, Jennie."

He took her arm again, as though it was the most natural act and led her out into the night. There were lights still on in a few of the long row of two-storey detached houses, a yard or two apart, each with wide porch across the front at both levels. They were wood but larger than the narrow brick housing terraces of mill and mining towns in the north of England, and Jennie could see no outhouses in the alleyways between the streets. She was about to ask Walter whether everyone had indoor plumbing. *No, girl. It'll break the mood.*

There was no sign advertising the bar, but Jennie was surprised there was also nothing much to hide the nature of the business either.

"Walter, isn't this place illegal?"

"Hi fellas." He waved a hand as he entered. A few men looked up and the bartender waived back.

"Hey, Walt."

Reuther turned to Jennie. "Yup. Has been illegal now for

about 15 years." Without catching his breath he continued. "What'll you have?"

"A pint," replied Jennie. She could tell he didn't understand. "A beer, please."

Reuther looked surprised and pleased at the same time.

"Good girl. Thought you'd ask for sherry or port or something else they don't have here. He called down the bar. "Two Labatt's, Bill."

"Not married, are you, Jennie?"

It was the very question she wanted to ask him. *How to answer?*

"No, or I wouldn't be here with you now, or even on a lecture tour alone, in another country, I suspect." She paused. "You."

"Too young, no money...wild oats to sow anyhow." He smiled.

"Let's sow some tonight." To make her meaning unmistakable, Jennie covered his hand with hers.

* * *

It was before seven the next morning when the telephone next to Jennie's bed rang. It was a wake up call. She was unused to having an instrument in her room, next to her bed at all. When it rang eighteen inches from her ear, she realised she had been in the midst of a nightmare, about to plunge into an icy sea from a transatlantic liner with no lifeboats. She was so glad to be in a cold hotel room in Michigan. But she was hung over. So, apparently, was Walter, sitting up next to her, knees drawn up, head in his hands. He smiled at her, sheepishly. Jennie couldn't suppress a laugh as she grabbed a robe and headed to the bathroom.

When she came out, he was already dressed, rubbing a day's growth of whiskers and waiting his turn for the bathroom.

"Can I buy you breakfast... Miss Lee." The formality communicated intimacy.

"My train leaves at 8:52 for Chicago."

"That's plenty of time. Terminal is across the street."

Twenty minutes later they found themselves on a pair of shiny chrome swivel stools that matched the facing of the long Formica counter. This was the sort of starkly efficient establishment they called a 'diner' in America. It was operated by one man in white, behind the counter, who, unasked, placed a mug of coffee before her.

Reuther volunteered, "I recommend the eggs easy over with a fried English muffin."

Jennie didn't know what 'easy over' was but she wanted very much to know what an English muffin was. She looked to the man behind the counter.

"Just as he said, please." Then she turned back to Reuther and smiled.

After a moment he spoke. "Coming back this way?" Then he covered her hand.

Jennie withdrew it, shaking her head. "Don't think so, not this trip."

"When will I see you then?"

"No idea, Walter."

"But, Jennie..." His face showed genuine perplexity. "I thought...last night. Well, when you invite a fella..." Reuther's words petered out.

Jennie decided to complete his thought. "When you invite a fellow up to your room and you're a woman, it must be serious... is that what you meant?" Reuther nodded vigorously. "Not this woman, Walter. It was grand, it was fun, but that's all it was, last night."

By now the short-order cook had finished his work and served up two identical plates. A companionable silence fell between them as Jennie and Walter ate. When she finished Jennie looked round and seeing that they were unobserved, leaned over and kissed him. Then she rose from the counter and picked up her bag.

"I'm off. Best of luck to you Walter, if you go to Russia."

Reuther reached out for her sleeve. "If I come through England, can I look you up?"

"I'd like that." It would have been pedantic to say she might be in Scotland, not England.

* * *

Three days later, Jennie took the late sleeper from Chicago back east. It didn't stop in Detroit. Undressing, stretching out in a berth, trying to get a night's sleep on a train—these were all new to Jennie. She could never afford the sleepers from Edinburgh to London. But her speaker fees and the prices in America brought this and other luxuries within reach, with money left over to send her parents back home.

She came back from the toilet in her dressing gown, what the Americans called a robe. She pulled the curtain, settled herself in the space wide enough for two and determined to let the sway of the train over the rail gaps lull her to sleep.

It didn't come. Perhaps it was the novelty of the Pullman car, or the strong cup of coffee her hosts had insisted upon at the end of a convivial dinner in Hyde Park. The supper was a rare occasion at which whites and Negroes shared a table on terms of equality. Jennie had seen enough of America to be surprised by it, but had also learned enough of the country's mores not to mention how exceptional the experience was. When one of the company learned she was booked on the sleeper east, he insisted on taking Jennie all the way up to the Union Station in downtown Chicago. He would put her in the hands of a personal friend, a member of the Brotherhood of Sleeping Car Porters. This was the union representing the largely black employees of the Pullman Company that owned all the sleeper coaches in the country.

As trains slid in and out of the station, their noise obliterated all conversation beyond a pace or two's distance. Jennie's companion managed to hail his friend from three cars away and they approached one another, smiling and waving. The handsome black man in the immaculate white coat and kepi of the Pullman porter put out his hand for the small case in Jennie's hand. Instead she grasped the hand warmly, shaking it vigorously. Caught off guard by this patent violation of public norms, the man searched Jennie's eyes, seeking the meaning of the gesture. Jennie's strong Scot's accent was enough to make him understand. She wasn't an American and either didn't know or wouldn't accept the rules.

She said, "Mr. Simmons, I've heard a good deal about you and your work on the way here."

He turned to his friend. "You've schooled this lady well, Fred. She didn't call me 'George.'"

Both laughed at a joke Jennie didn't understand. They now shook hands as Simmons took Jennie's larger case from his friend's hand.

"No time to socialise, we're running late on account of the weather." He turned to Jennie. "Follow me please, Miss."

Even as they spoke the train had lurched once and begun slowly to move. They mounted the car's steps quickly.

Now, an hour later, Jennie was still awake, claustrophobic between a thick shade window covering and the shrouded passageway. She struggled into her dressing gown, found her cigarettes and matches, and then carefully rose from her lower berth, ducking her head as she emerged into the narrow corridor between the curtains drawn on both sides of the coach. There at the end of the car, standing at the only uncurtained window, was the porter, Mr Simmons.

As she approached, Jennie put a cigarette to her mouth and proffered the packet to Simmons. Withdrawing a lighter he brought the flame to her cigarette, shook his head to decline her offer and spoke.

"Please excuse me," he said as he stepped past her to walk down the defile between the sleeping berths.

Jennie touched the sleeve of his upper arm.

"Must you go back to work? I didn't mean to disturb you…I only wanted to join you as you looked to be at your leisure."

Simmons sighed. "Ma'am."

Jennie had been addressed this way before, despite her youthful appearance, and always by older men, almost always black.

"I can't stand here talking to a white lady. Not if I want to keep my job."

"Why ever not?" She held his arm lightly but she could feel it was against his will.

"First man comes out of his berth for a…to use the toilet, he'll make a scene, he'll threaten me, then report me to the white conductor. No black man can be seen talking, smoking, socialising in the middle of the night with a white lady on a Pullman. No, ma'am."

He slowly pulled his arm from her hand and walked away down the corridor, leaving Jennie to contemplate the empty blackness edged by snowbanks between an occasional station lamp.

She drew on her cigarette. *I can't even talk to a black man in public? What sort of an upheaval do they fear, the white people in this country? Perhaps what really worries everyone, right down to the poorest white man, is the threat of a Negro insurrection.*

Chapter Sixteen

The thought came back to Jennie weeks later as she rode the Canadian National Railway sleeper from Toronto to Halifax, where she was to embark for Liverpool. In Montreal, she'd had to change for the sleeper to the Atlantic coast. There she noticed that the porters were white, and then she saw one carrying a case as the black man who owned it followed him onto the sleeper car. An event that couldn't have taken place in the USA.

Canada had already struck Jennie as thoroughly different from the United States, different, trying—with indifferent success—to be British. In the large towns and cities of Ontario, Jennie realised she had lost the anonymity she'd found in America. Few Americans she had met knew that Jennie was an MP. And among those who did, no one seemed to care. In Canada, matters were quite otherwise. Everywhere she was Jennie Lee, Member of Parliament for North Lanark, Scotland. It was almost as though she was on a royal tour dispensing Imperial recognition to needy colonials. Everywhere she lectured, provincial newspaper reporters asked questions. Conservative politicians were eager to dine with a member of the mother of parliament, even a Labour party MP. They asked her to tell them about Winston Churchill or Ramsay MacDonald as if they were film stars. People made speeches at her, and never left her alone long enough to meet anyone—male or female—who might take to her for whom she was instead of what she was.

Jennie was a celebrity in Canada, and she found she did not like it. Reaching Halifax she was glad to embark for home.

* * *

Taking stock, Jennie found, was an unavoidable pastime for a lone tourist-class traveller on a late winter transatlantic crossing of the Cunard *Lancastria*. A single stateroom, a table for two that no one ever asked to join, weather too awful even for a turn along the exterior boat deck, junior officers too busy to socialise in the second-class lounge, not even a bridge game to join. Most of the passengers had embarked at New York two days earlier. The "respectable" ones had already forged alliances for the duration of the voyage. And everyone seemed to be "respectable." Sitting alone in the saloon bar the first evening out from Halifax, Jennie found herself scanning the room for shipboard Lotharios. Not a one leering back at her. *Perhaps they don't travel second class?*

The *Lancastria* plied a leisurely progress through the pea soup of the Grand Banks. The predictable wail of its foghorn made a continuous night's sleep impossible for the first three days. This was inconvenient. Sleeping long and soundly was the best method Jennie could think of to make time pass rapidly. In the late morning, when she could remain in her bunk no longer, she would breakfast and take her notebook to the ship's library, always devoid of other passengers. She decided she would force herself to try to put as much of her seven weeks in North America down on paper as she could recall. Nothing came. Jennie spent the first two mornings and afternoons too often staring out of portholes into a uniform grey field, seeking a horizon line where there was none. Writing something both new and interesting for the readers of *The New Leader* seemed hopeless. On the second afternoon, she began casting her eye across the meagre shelves, searching vainly for a book she could convince herself she just had to read. There were none.

In her desperation, Jennie pulled on a drawer handle. It revealed a bin containing roughly three months' worth of the weekly *Economist*, each still folded and banded by a paper wrapper. This was a valid excuse for not writing. She needed to catch up on the political news. Jennie unwrapped each one, ordered them in a pile from oldest to newest. The most recent one was dated Friday, 10 March 1931. She decided she would ration them, read two each day cover to cover, beginning with the issue the week she'd left for America.

This resolution immediately fell to a combination of temptation and a sudden realisation that events of the greatest importance to her had transpired while she had been hiding from them in North America. None of the political events *The Economist* reported had made it to a single American newspaper she'd been able to see. It had been as though the rest of the world did not exist in the USA.

Almost immediately after Jennie had left for her lecture tour, Winston Churchill had resigned from the Conservative shadow cabinet, over India of all things. Alone in the room, Jennie had to laugh out loud even as she felt ashamed by her reaction to Churchill's outrageous word-picture of the Indian independence leader:

It is alarming and also nauseating to see Mr. Gandhi, an Inner Temple lawyer, now become a seditious fakir of a type well known in the East, striding half-naked up the steps of the Viceregal Palace, while he is still organising and conducting a defiant campaign of civil disobedience, to parley on equal terms with the representative of the King-Emperor.

The Economist must have taken great pleasure in reproducing this contemptible example of Winston Churchill's literary flair.

Much more important, by late January, there were six million unemployed in Germany, almost as many as in the USA, a country twice as populous. British unemployment was climbing beyond two and half million.

Then came the real bombshells for Jennie, news that made her realise she'd been away much too long, that matters were moving fast, too fast. The second number in the stack told her that Nye Bevan and more than a dozen other young Labour MPs had repudiated their own prime minister and climbed on the

Mosley bandwagon. The words *The Economist* quoted the radical MP, John Strachey:

> *We were tired of voting for measures which we did not believe could cope with the present situation, or against motions that seemed to us equally irrelevant; of listening to speeches half of which appeared to us meaningless, and the other half frankly dishonest; of sitting quietly in the "best Club in the World," watching from its comfortable armchairs the accelerating decline of the British industrial and commercial system and the rapid drift to disaster of the movement with which we are identified.*

All sixteen of these members of parliament had agreed that parliamentary government had to be replaced. What the crisis required was an executive "invested with power to carry through the emergency policy."

Jennie began to read avidly, turning pages in search of something, anything, that might put her further in the picture. Nothing more in this number. She shed the magazine from her lap and reached for the next wrapper, stripped it away from the folded newsprint, and began scanning the leaders and the columns of text, hungry for the next act in the drama. Had Mosley done anything dramatic, rash? Might he let it be known, by a whisper to hacks eager for a scoop, that he had support in the palace, among the royal family, from the Duke of York? *No, he couldn't!* She sought to convince herself. *It would be terrible for the Duke of York. It would be more than catastrophic for you! Surely word would have come across the Atlantic if there had been anything.* She literally exhaled when finally she found the next episode in the Mosley chronicle in the *Economist.*

He'd not gone to the palace at all. Instead, Tom Mosley had gone to the Labour Party's steadfast opponent—the greatest of Britain's industrial capitalists—and he'd gone for money, enough to pay for a national campaign, at least for a while. The article, from the end of January, was titled "Mosley motors in a Morris":

Sir Oswald Mosley has been given a cheque for 50,000 pounds by the owner of Britain's largest auto works, Sir William Morris, to fund his radical political movement.

Jennie continued to burrow into the stack before her. There, in an issue from the end of February, was the next twist in the story: Mosley had extracted a half dozen MPs from the sixteen Labour members to form something *The Economist* called "The New Party." Could that be Mosley's name for it? Jennie searched for 'Bevan' among the list of MPs who'd resigned, one after the other, to join Mosley's party. She made herself scan the list twice to be sure it was not there. It was just to be sure, but she was not surprised. However much Nye Bevan might agree with Mosley about politics, he would never abandon his miners and their party.

The last straw in this wind came in the final *Economist* number in the pile before her, from the middle of March. Mosley had not resigned from Labour. He had been expelled from the party for "gross disloyalty" before he'd had a chance to resign from it.

Jennie put down the last *Economist*. It was now early April. A month gone by. What had happened in the time between starting his "New Party" and Mosley's expulsion from Labour, she wondered? Then, her mind walked back through these political events. *What would you have done, Jennie?* She knew some of the answers to this question. *You would have signed on to the manifesto, for certain, just as Nye did. But you would have gone further, wouldn't you? You'd have bound yourself to Mosley's New Party group, wouldn't you! And if Frank had pleaded for caution, you would have argued with him fiercely and then joined anyway! Just to show Frank you weren't his creature? Would you have followed Mosley, if he had asked? Or even if he'd looked at you...that way.* Now, in the coolness of the hour, and the draughty chill of the swaying ship's library, Jennie wondered whether she'd been saved by her travels, at least for the moment, from her own impetuousness.

Chapter Seventeen

It must have been fifteen minutes after the *Lancastria* had docked, Jennie heard the knock on her cabin door.

"Come in," she said without looking up.

She was seated at the tiny desk crammed between the bunk and the opposite wall, sorting through papers, deciding what notes to keep and what to dispose of.

Still without turning, she said, "You can take the large case, but leave the small one on the bed."

"Very good, Miss." The response came from an unfamiliar voice, unexpected among the North Country accent every steward on the ship seemed to use. And then she realised it was Frank Wise who had come through her stateroom door. She rose and closed the few feet between them. She noticed as he turned the bolt on the door behind him.

"What are you doing here, Frank?" Before he could answer the question, she added, "I'm so glad to see you," and drew him down to the bunk, pushing the small case still upon it down to the floor.

Jennie began struggling against the buttons on Frank's waistcoat as he pulled the bow carefully knotted at the blouse beneath her traveling suit. The delight of slowly disrobing one another was a ritual that repeated recollection over three months separation had carved deeper into her memory. But now, it was dispensed with by unvoiced agreement. In their mutual ardour, it was surprising nothing was torn as the clothing separating them was parted.

All too soon, they were leaning companionably against pillows put up against the cold bulkhead, smoking. Now the steward's knock came with the words, "Baggage to go ashore, Ma'am?"

"Come back in five minutes," Jennie replied.

Frank rose and they both began to dress. He was silent. It was not like him, Jennie thought. She had to speak first and she didn't know where to start. She went back to her very first question. "You never said, Frank, what are you doing here?"

"Simply couldn't wait to see you. Had to be with you the first moment one could, I suppose."

"I'm glad."

She was palpably, deeply, powerfully content. She could feel it in the sudden release of the watch-spring tension that had been driving her since she had left for the North American tour. The languid feeling couldn't last long, but she knew it was real.

"However did you know it was this ship, this day?"

"Rung up your lecture tour agent. They had your schedule."

"Anyone else know I'm back?" She said it casually, as she folded away the last few things into her small valise. *Too casually?*

"Like whom?" He was quizzical.

She was thinking of Mosley and the Duchess of York but she replied, "Nye Bevan, Charlie Trevelyan, Ellen Wilkinson?"

"Hope not. If they know then it won't be long before Dorothy knows."

"Did my going manage to cool her suspicion?"

"Must have done. I've heard nothing about the matter for some time." He fell silent. "Jennie, you shan't want to hear this." Again, a pause. "The two months you were away...it was an agony for me. I can't see how I'll deal with it now you're back, except by—"

"We've been over this ground, Frank."

"I've got to make a clean breast of it with Dorothy. She knows a divorce will harm her too—"

Again Jennie broke in: "And me."

"It could be worse for her...Anyway, that's what I'm going to try to convince her of. I'll tell her everything. Get her to agree to let me live apart, without a divorce. She'll have a position, no scandal...in public, things will go on as before."

"Would she accept it, Frank?"

"Perhaps. She's not really a Westminster wife. Perfectly happy up in Bucks with her causes and the younger two."

The steward knocked again, and they opened the door. Once the trunk was gone they both left the stateroom, and joined the file of passengers moving up to the debarkation deck.

Waiting in the customs shed, Frank asked, "Well, where to? Your constituency, Cowdenbeath or London?"

"It's a bore, but I've missed a lot of sittings. Better get back to the House." She smiled, put her hand through his arm, reached down into his coat pocket and took his hand. "London!"

He nodded. "There's a boat train to Euston from Liverpool Riverside. First class, my treat."

* * *

Thirty minutes later, they were well settled into a compartment facing one another. Watching through the window as the train gathered speed beyond Liverpool Lime Street station, both silently hoped no one would join them for the balance of the journey to London. As the ranks of workmen's villas gave way to scrub along the rails, Jennie saw none of the "jungle camps" that dotted the tracks outside of cities in America. She understood why. Here, the unemployed had long ago given up any quest for jobs far from their homes. She turned to Frank.

"Catch me up then."

"How closely were you able to follow things in North America?"

"Not at all. But I had the benefit of ten weeks of *The Economist* on the *Lancastria* up to about a fortnight ago."

"Can't believe much of what they write, not about Labour politics, at any rate." Frank frowned.

"Lots of news about Mosley." Was it obvious to him that this would interest her most?

Perhaps it was. Frank seemed to sigh slightly before going on.

"There's to be a by-election at Ashton-under-Lyne. Labour member, Bellamy, PPS to pensions minister, died just after you left. Anyway, his New Party—you know about that?" Jennie nodded. "They put up a candidate and Mosley was expelled from Labour."

"So, that's why. *Economist* didn't give the reason he was pushed out." She had to ask, "Do they have a chance?"

"Dunno…Mosley has fallen quite ill. Pleurisy and pneumonia. So he hasn't been there to campaign. Left it to his wife, Lady Cynthia."

Jennie found herself not at all disquieted about Mosley's condition. He was too powerful a personality to succumb to such illnesses. Instead she thought about his wife. Jennie knew Cimmie Mosley from Parliament, she'd won a seat for Labour in the House herself in the '29 election.

"She'll do well." Frank nodded his agreement.

"Any more defections from Labour?"

"You mean Bevan?" Frank had understood her question. She nodded. "It's hard to tell actually."

"What do you mean? Either he resigned along with the others or he didn't."

"He didn't resign. But he did sign on to another of those Mosley manifesto pamphlets."

Frank stood and pulled down his trench coat from the luggage rack above the seats, reached into a pocket and pulled out a booklet. "I've got it here."

Jennie held out her hand.

"Let me see." He gave it to her and she read the tract quickly. "Nye signed on to this? Why didn't they expel him along with Mosley?"

"Too small a fish, I suspect. Labour can't afford to lose seats in the Commons, can it? Mosley was expelled for putting up a candidate against Labour. If Nye doesn't support his candidate…

well, the whips will turn a blind eye." He waited for a reply from Jennie. She was silent so he went on. "Maybe Nye Bevan's regretting signing on anyway, now the millionaire Morris is backing Mosley...I suppose you read about that?" Again he looked at Jennie.

She nodded. "Yes. It was in one of *The Economists* I read."

Frank grimaced. "Mosley is sounding more and more like Mussolini than he is like Lenin..."

Jennie had to rebut. "That's the Communist line on Mosley, isn't it, Frank?"

"Doesn't make it wrong, you know."

How to put her dissent from Frank without a quarrel?

"Can Labour afford not to make common cause, if this New Party of his catches on?"

"Maybe not. But the Ashton by-election won't be a real test for Mosley. It was a Tory seat before Bellamy won it in '29. And with Mosley ill and not campaigning himself..." He didn't finish the thought. "Look, Jennie, Mosley frightens me...worse than he did before you left."

Could she say what she thought? That Tom Mosley frightened her, and entranced her, not just by turns but at the very same time. She certainly could agree with Frank that he was dangerous.

"I know what you mean, Frank. Listening to him is like putting your fingers to a mains wire. The moment's shock should be enough to warn you off. But you keep doing it again..."

Jennie stopped for a moment, arrested by her image. Then she took her argument up again.

"But Frank, what's the alternative to Mosley? More of Ramsay MacDonald's pettifogging?"

She could feel a despond increasing its bleak hold with every mile they closed on London. In her mind's eye, she was already looking down from a back bench at Ramsay MacDonald — wing collar, frock coat, watch and fob, Labour prime minister exchanging niceties with Honourable members opposite, men who wouldn't give a tuppence ha'penny for, or even to, the working man.

"I'm ready to take the risk of a powerful drug if it stands a chance of curing the illness." She reached into her purse for a fag, lit one and drew in long. "The government's doing nothing. As it is, Labour will be blamed for the slump. The party doesn't stand a chance without Mosley. If we can't join him, we've got to get him back!"

Frank was studious, drawing on his own cigarette and allowing the smoke to emerge from his nostrils like two beams in the dust motes of the carriage air. He said nothing for a few moments. Then he spoke.

"When you get to the House tonight, you'll hear the government is hiving off its responsibilities to a committee of financiers. It's called the May Committee, after its head, president of the Prudential." This was the largest insurance company in Britain. "MacDonald's so frightened of making the wrong choice, he's asking bankers to tell him what to do."

"But everyone knows what they'll tell him: balance the budget, cut benefits, reduce policemen's salaries...and teachers." She stubbed out her fag. "Make things worse, and why?"

"To please the City and the New York bankers who are buying the government's debts so we can stay on Winston Churchill's bloody gold standard." He fairly spat the words and then lapsed into silence.

* * *

Frank had put down her case to push against the door to slide it open over the eight weeks' welter of letters, left-wing mags, adverts and handbills that had been dropped through the mail slot in her door. As he carried the bag through to her bedroom, Jennie stooped to sweep up the post. The small, square, buff envelope with the royal franking and the palace return address stood out to her eye obvious and threatening, like a letter from Inland Revenue. She had to hope Frank hadn't noticed it. Slipping it under the doormat, she rose with the rest clutched to her chest and dumped the mass on the side table, making something of a show out of beginning to sort through it.

Frank took her case through to the bedroom, still wearing his trench coat and making no signs of doffing it. Jennie was relieved. She was not at all looking forward to opening the Duchess's letter. But she had to, and she certainly couldn't do it while Frank was with her. He came up behind her, leaned over kissing her neck as his arms encircled her.

"So glad you're back."

She turned and offered her mouth. When they could both feel the ardour rising, she pushed him towards the door.

"I need a bath...See you in the House tonight?"

Without another word, but with a smile and a nod, Frank opened the door and was gone.

Jennie bent to the doormat and pulled out the envelope. It demanded to be opened by a letter knife, so she took it to the desk as uncluttered as the day she left but coated by what seemed to be fine coal dust.

The envelope was handwritten, as was the letter. The Duchess had presumably addressed it herself in the hope, almost certainly vain, that her constitutional indiscretion would be undetected.

Dear Jennie,

I was worried to have lost touch with you after Christmas. I sent a few discreet notes to the House. They were returned. When I rang up they told me you'd gone away to America for a few months. That was a pity, as so much has happened and the Duke was eager to have you pass on his encouragement to Tom Mosley. He's quite pleased about developments and especially the New Party. The Prince of Wales has come round to the same view, when he can be bothered to take any interest in public affairs. Anyhow, I hope you share

our opinion, and we certainly don't mind if you pass it on to Tom.
Please ring me the moment you get home.

The last sentence was double underlined, suggesting a royal command. But it was signed "Elizabeth B-L" instead of "Elizabeth—Duchess of York," with a telephone number so Jennie would have no excuse.

Jennie folded the letter back into its envelope. Somehow, she'd hoped that she'd been away long enough for the Duke and Duchess to find another connection to Tom Mosley. It was politically perilous. Given Frank's position, it was personally dangerous. And it was that powerful drug she had tied herself to the mast of a transatlantic voyage to resist. She simply wouldn't respond to this request, wouldn't call, wouldn't pass along any message of encouragement to Mosley.

Then the phone rang. She answered with her number. The voice in the earpiece was unmistakable. "Tom Mosley here..."

Jennie replied in a voice that she hoped suggested distance and formality. "Yes, Sir Oswald."

"Tom, please."

"I hear you've been ill."

"Much better now, thanks." The voice became less conversational, slightly urgent. "I need a favour. I rather need you to see"—he paused, evidently searching for the right description—"your royal friend as soon as possible."

"Look...Tom." She didn't want to call him that, but she didn't want to hear him insist on it, either. "I'm only just off the boat from America. Got into my flat 10 minutes ago."

"We...uh, I knew you'd been gone for some time. It makes the matter more urgent I fear. Can you see her in the next twenty-four hours?"

"No. I can't see her at all. I won't do as you ask, Sir Oswald. It's risky for me and improper too." She wanted to tell him she'd left the country to avoid the entanglement.

Before she could do so, Mosley interrupted. "Look, before you decide to burn this bridge from the palace to me, there's something you need to know."

"I'm listening."

"I'm at Ebury Street. Can you come round here?" Mosley instantly realised how Jennie would take the question. "No... it's not like that. I'm too ill and weak for any of that...touch of pleurisy. It's just I need to tell you something face to face, something important, that may change your mind about helping..." He didn't finish the sentence.

"Very well," Jennie capitulated with a sigh.

Chapter Eighteen

Before she'd even paid the taxi, the door to 22b Ebury Street was opened, not by Mosley, as in the past, but a man whose formal dress bespoke service. As Jennie was led into Mosley's bedroom, a nurse bustled out carrying a basin. The room was familiar to her but now neater and warm, very warm. Then Jennie noticed the electrical heaters on either side of the bed. Mosley was in the bed, covers drawn, wan, thinner, lying on his left side. He looked up, coughed and spoke.

"Sorry to receive you like this. Have to lie on the left side... reduces the pain."

He winced slightly. Was this for effect? Jennie wondered before supressing the thought as unworthy. Still she said noting. Mosley looked up to the servant behind her.

"That'll be all, Booth." The man quietly withdrew. "Take a pew, Jennie." He indicated a wooden chair near the bed. "I'm no longer contagious, the quacks tell me."

Still Jennie was silent, not really trusting herself. Even abed, but holding her gaze, Mosley was having his effect.

"Since you're not asking what all this is about, I suppose I'll have to begin." With a nod, Jennie bid him begin. "It was only some time after you left for America that I'd realised you were gone. I was hoping to convince you to join the New Party. Perhaps even get you to bring Nye Bevan or your friend Frank Wise into the fold."

Jennie searched for innuendo in Mosley's voice and face as he said Frank's name. She couldn't find it. Was he so fine an actor?

"Frank and Nye have both declined," she said. "Why should I have decided differently, Tom?" Suddenly Jennie was angry at herself. Why'd she called him that instead of Mosley? Was it was just that he seemed vulnerable, lying there weak, in evident pain.

Mosley pushed his elbows underneath his body and rose to sit back against the bedstead.

"Well, for you the decision to leave Labour might be rather more personal than theirs." Before she could speak he waved his hand. "No, not our relationship, Jennie. We know what that's about and it isn't political. In fact it's hardly personal." He laughed. "And we both like it that way." He waited for a signal of understanding. She gave it with a slight smile. "No, I think I can give you a better reason to leave Labour and join the New Party."

"Well?" Impatience showed on Jennie's face. She took a cigarette from her bag and began to rummage for a match.

"Please, no smoking. Not just yet." Mosley coughed. "They say it'll set back my progress."

She put the fag back in the packet and began tapping the floor with her foot.

"Look, there's no way to cushion this blow. I have to tell you straight out." He paused before plunging further. "It will come as a shock, Jennie," Again he paused. "Ramsay MacDonald is your father." Under his breath Mosley muttered, "Runs in his family..." then he looked up at Jennie's contorted face.

Jennie didn't hear this jape about MacDonald's own acknowledged illegitimacy. She was asking herself why Mosley would say such farfetched rubbish. Jennie had to show him she wasn't taking him at all seriously. He continued, seeking to convince her.

"I'm sorry but I have the Prime Minister's own admission, to me personally." If this were a lie it would be easy to uncover. As if he were reading her thoughts, Mosley added, "Ask him if you like."

Jennie hardened. "Why would you make up such a preposterous lie, Mosley?" No 'Tom,' no 'Sir Oswald, not even a Mr...just the contempt of the surname spat back at him.

"I promise you, it's the truth."

She could see sincerity in his eyes, but still Jennie resisted. "I suppose he just told you...for no reason at all, simply making polite conversation."

Mosley was calm. "I learned of it from someone else and confronted him."

Jennie absorbed this thought. "So, someone is peddling scandal about the PM and dragging an insignificant back bencher into it?"

"Actually, there's a letter from MacDonald, to your mother, that proves it. You may want to ask her."

Ask her mother if she were a bastard? Ramsay MacDonald's bastard? Impossible. But too easy a way of unmasking such a risible idea. That forced Jennie to contemplate the possibility. Mosley was going on, but she had ceased listening, absorbed only in the disclosure, trying to come to terms with it, fitting it into her own life, the family history she had lived, was still living. Trying it out to see if there was anything about her parents, her childhood, her upbringing, that this, this, this...*allegation* made sense of, was the missing piece to...Every way she turned it round the answer kept coming back, *Rubbish.*

"You're talking rot. Show me this letter!"

"My dear Jennie, I don't have it," he lied without difficulty. "I haven't seen it. The person who purloined it passed it on to... to one of our political opponents. Someone you know, actually."

"Don't tell me who." It was all she could think of as a riposte. She glared at Mosley.

"I'd hoped that once you knew the truth you'd have enough reason to join the revolt against MacDonald, leave the Labour Party and help me openly."

Jennie wasn't following Mosley's train of thought. She couldn't, wouldn't think about what all this meant between her and her mother, her parents. It was too filthy a thought. It had to be stamped out, obliterated by another. But a dawning recognition made matters worse. *If it comes out, no one will ever listen to another of your attacks on the government without thinking, 'MacDonald's bastard.' You'll be a laughing-stock, the butt of jokes. People will put your politics down to personal animosity.* She realised that Mosley was right: at least if it came out, she could have nothing further to do with the Labour Party. *You'd be a constant reminder, a badge of the leader's misconduct. You'll be a pariah in the House. You're certain to be deselected in your puritanical Glasgow constituency. Never mind what happens to Ramsay Mac.* The hard-political calculation was effective in driving the domestic shame, humiliation, disgrace from her thoughts. Mosley was right. If it came out she'd have no future in the Labour Party.

Then she conjured an image of the old man. A wave of contempt swept over her as she thought about the abuse she'd heaped on MacDonald for a half dozen years…her own father. There was no emotion of chagrin in her, she noticed. Just the surprise, the shock, and now dizziness. All this time she'd been standing at the side of Mosley's bed. Looking behind her, she collapsed into a bedside chair.

"Who else knows?"

"Jennie, your secret is safe with me, I promise." He smiled. "We're on the same side, surely!"

Now she was angry, angry enough to need to act, to take sides, to strike out at the fates—the ones she'd struggled against in her past, and this new threat to her political life, the one she cared about the most.

"But if I join your New Party and it comes out—about me and MacDonald. It will certainly distract the tabloids just as much as if I were to stay in the Labour Party." She didn't add, *And ruin me.*

"I'm going to see to it that it doesn't come out. Not even from the Tory press." He raised hand. "Don't ask how. I've a way with hacks and their editors and with the handful of people who're in the know." He paused. "And actually, we can't have you joining the New Party, not just yet. There's something you're needed to do that makes that impossible."

"Something you need me to do?"

"You know about the Ashton-under-Lyne by-election?" She nodded. "It's why I called. We need some reliable, untraceable go-between to the palace, to the Duke. And you are the only one we've got."

The words brought her back to the present, into the room, back to immediate reality. She drew a breath.

"Very well. What am I to do exactly?"

"Just get in touch with the Duchess, today if possible. She'll want to meet and give you something for me. A small package. Bring it here as soon as you have it."

"Why the urgency?"

"It's to do with this Ashton by-election." Jennie was silent. Mosley indicated the instrument on the night table. "You can call from here."

"I don't have the number."

"I do." He passed her a scrap of paper and indicated the instrument, atop the small table cluttered with medicines next to his bed.

Jennie lifted the receiver. It was a new, single-piece listening/ speaking handset. She dialled and waited. A woman's voice she recognised answered.

It was not a servant or a switchboard operator, but sounded like Elizabeth herself, giving her number, "Victoria 6408."

"Elizabeth." Jennie didn't use the words 'Duchess' or 'your grace.' "Jennie here. Got your note. Just back from abroad. Can we meet today?"

There was a pause. "Let me look at my book..." After a pause the voice went on. "Nothing till six. Then I have to dress for dinner."

Jennie didn't want to hear more. "When and where, Elizabeth?"

Momentary silence on the line. Then she spoke. "Remember

the tea shop on Kensington Church Street? I'll have my chauffeur drive me by in three quarters of an hour. Give you enough time to get there? Just come to the kerb-side car window. Is that all right?"

Did the Duchess not want to be seen, or was she simply pressed for time? Jennie wouldn't ask. She looked at her watch. Forty-five minutes. She could practically walk there from Ebury Street. "See you then." Jennie replaced the instrument.

Mosley pulled a bell rope at his bedstead. "My man will get you a cab."

He reached across to the desk and found three half crown coins. He proffered them.

"For the fare."

Jennie glared at him and left.

* * *

It hadn't taken much thought to work out what was going on. Jennie's immediate guess, formed on the walk to Kensington, was confirmed almost immediately. The Duchess's car was waiting. Without speaking, she had rolled down a window and handed Jennie a parcel wrapped in brown paper and tied off neatly by a string. Then Elizabeth tapped the glass between her and the driver. The car moved off into the scant traffic.

* * *

Why hadn't her friend said even a single word? Sitting in her cab on the way back to Ebury Street, Jennie answered the question for herself. She needed merely to measure its dimensions in her hand spans, bend the package and heft it to realise she was carrying a sheaf of five-pound banknotes, about three inches thick. How much would that be? She had no idea. But it would certainly fund Mosley's New Party through the Ashton-under-

Lyne by-election and probably beyond it.

How did you get this deeply into such a vortex, Jennie? It wasn't foreseeable. Was it inevitable? She hadn't chosen to be Ramsay MacDonald's child...if she really was. An hour after she'd been informed, she was having trouble believing it. She hadn't chosen to be thrown together with Elizabeth Bowes-Lyons at twelve years old, or to like her well enough to remain her friend. She hadn't chosen the politics of her parents, for that matter. Together, these treads had drawn her to this cab ride, carrying a thousand pounds to a politician too charismatic to trust, doing something probably illegal and certainly unconstitutional, something she'd have to hide from her lover, her friends, her political allies, everyone. It had all happened without malice of forethought. But it wasn't that she'd had no choice. *Why are you searching for excuses to do what you are going to do anyway, Jennie?* There was a frisson of excitement about it all. More than a frisson. It made her feel she was at the centre of something, something that could turn out horrible or wonderful. But something in which she had a real role, not just the role of an oddity, a freak—the hectoring young woman in the House to whom no one listened, except for fun. The danger was a stimulant. It made her life matter, and not just to her, but even, a little bit, to history. The hard part, she knew, was keeping all this secret from the man she loved. *For his sake? Somehow to protect him? Fooling yourself again, Jennie. That's not why you can't tell him. He'd make you stop. You want him and you don't want to stop.*

Back at Ebury Street, she told the cab to wait, got out and rang the bell. When Mosley's man answered, she handed him the package and told him to pay off her cab. Then she walked away down the street towards Victoria and the tube. She still wanted to turn up at the Commons that evening.

Swaying in the crowded underground back to Guilford Street, Jennie found herself contemplating her newly discovered real father. She was anonymous enough that there'd be no interruption. Letting the notion become real inside herself, her mind, in her thoughts about herself and the world, she searched for the feelings it would elicit. Back at Ebury Street, it had been brief shame, embarrassment, anger, guilt. But now, these emotions were gone. *I should feel something powerful, but I don't, and I can't make myself feel the emotions I suppose I should feel...How exactly do you feel about it?* The answer came into her head. *Droll! It's a nice bit of irony, that's all. It doesn't add to my contempt—no, not the right word—my scorn for that old man. Now it's settled in my mind, it doesn't make me hate him more, does it?* She reflected on the matter. However had it happened? When and where? Her mother with this wizened, bent pathetic white-haired figure in a wing collar. She found herself unable to conjure up his shape, his manner, his look 25 years before. Knowing she was his child somehow just didn't make a difference to her. *Perhaps you don't really believe it, Jennie?* But she did.

Then it struck her. How must Ramsay MacDonald have felt, listening to her in the House of Commons over the last two years? Not Ramsay MacDonald, Prime Minister, politician accustomed to abuse, invective, hyperbole, from opponents on his left as well as his right. *How did your father feel about his own child's harsh invective, the contemptuous tone, the visceral expressions of personal animosity, perhaps even hatred that had driven your Parliamentary speeches, Jennie?* He had sat there, stolid, unprovoked, calm. *But what was he feeling?* Now, the notion wasn't droll to Jennie anymore. An emotion was welling up, and she felt her eyes glisten with tears. Jennie took out a handkerchief. No one noticed. It could just as well have been a bit of soot in the eye.

She constructed the image in her mind's eye again—her, standing above him on the back benches, lashing out, and him, below, before the dispatch box, knowing it was his own child condemning him, as she sought to get others to share the anger, the animosity her politics was driving. *Is that something you should be ashamed of? The hurt Ramsay MacDonald had to keep hidden?* Suddenly, she could taste ash in her mouth. *How ever will you be able to stand up in the Commons again, as long as he's the prime minister?* That night in the Commons, she sat silently through the evening sitting.

* * *

Having taken an invisible hand in the Ashton-under-Lyne by-election, Jennie followed the last weeks of the campaign in the papers.

Ashton seemed favourable ground for Mosley. It was a midlands town east of Liverpool, with a deep and deeply unprofitable coal mine, a large number of textile mills unable to compete with Britain's Indian colonies, a real Colonel Blimp as the Conservative candidate, and a do-nothing trade union boss sitting as the Labour member. Until the last week before the poll, Mosley was too ill to speak at the New Party campaign rallies, but Cynthia Mosley did. Jennie wondered, was it her glamour and beauty that drew large crowds, or her evident sincerity? Then, with only six days to go, news broke that Mosley was well enough to speak. A hall was booked—one large enough to accommodate thousands—and a speech announced.

The morning after, Jennie was avid for the papers. She strode down Guilford Street to the newsagent at the Russell Square underground and bought all three papers, the *Herald,* the *Times* and *The Manchester Guardian.* The meeting had been a great success—6800 people, a spellbinding speech, all three papers agreed. There were photos in the *Herald* catching him pacing across the platform. Never tethered to the rostrum, Mosley had dealt effectively with the Labour hecklers, calling them Communists, securing wave after wave of loud cheering. Was he going to win? Parliamentary sketch writers were preparing their readers.

Night of the poll, Jennie sat by the wireless till the last news report without learning the result. So, again the next morning she rushed out for the papers. The *Times* gloated that the Tory, Colonel Broadbent, had beaten the Labour sitting-member by more than 1000 votes. The New Party's candidate had come third with 4500 votes. The *Herald* complained that Mosley's candidate had deprived Labour of a victory. But the bigger news, reported by the Liberal-supporting *Manchester Guardian*, was the riot outside the town hall after the result had been announced. Leaving the announcement of the returning officer, Mosley and a small group of supporters had waded directly into a sea of angry Labour Party supporters, courting harm and establishing an instant reputation for courage. Jennie knew immediately this was an action Mosley had decided to take with calculation.

Towards noon, her telephone rang.

Jennie expected to hear Frank's voice and began to think what she should say about the news. "Bloomsbury 7208," she said in a neutral tone.

It was Elizabeth, Duchess of York, certain that Jennie would recognise her voice and not even waiting for a response.

"Jennie, dear, did you see the results? Wasn't it exciting?" She paused for agreement. Hearing nothing she went on. "I just had to talk about it with someone we can trust."

"I've just been reading about the fighting afterward—"

"Yes. I was terrifically worried for Cimmie." This was Mosley's wife, Cynthia. "She was at the returning officer's announcement. Then there was that mob..."

Of course, Jennie remembered, the Duchess of York would have known the daughter of Lord Curzon well and for a long time. She recalled the casual way Elizabeth had first mentioned Tom Mosley's indiscretions with Cynthia Mosley's sister, and her step-mother—his mother-in-law. The Duchess hadn't been worried about that, not a bit of it. In fact, she'd sounded slightly jealous not to be party to such a ménage. But now, it occurred to Jennie to ask herself, *If Elizabeth knows Cimmie Mosley so well, why do they need me to be go-between?* Then she had a disobliging thought. *Is it because Lady Cynthia Mosley has more constitutional scruples than I do?* Did Cynthia Mosley herself even know about the improper campaign funding? Jennie couldn't work it out and was not going to ask. But the question remained: why *were* Mosley and the palace using Jennie as an intermediary? An extra link in the chain between them was just a risk they wouldn't take unless they had to.

Chapter Nineteen

The New Party hadn't won the by-election, but it had raised enough hopes and enough dust to begin to look like a movement that would last. The result, Jennie knew, would be more clandestine meetings with the Duchess, and more deliveries of discreet financial support from the palace to Mosley. Through the spring of '31 everything worsened, and still the government temporised. It would do nothing radical in fear of a fatal blow from Wall Street and the City. The half measures the Trades Unions allowed it to take were both ineffective and offensive. Jennie seethed. *You've got to do something, and this is all you can do for the moment.* The thought was enough to absolve of the only real guilt she felt: keeping the secret from Frank.

* * *

What Jennie really couldn't understand was the hold international capital held over a supposedly socialist government. Why should millions of men and woman be made miserable in order to satisfy J. P. Morgan in New York? What did he care about how much gold bullion there was in the vaults of the Bank of England, anyway? The papers were full of dire warnings about runs on the pound, but what did they really amount to, and why did it matter?

She could see the Labour frontbench—MacDonald, the PM, Snowden, the Chancellor, Thomas the minister of Labour— motionless, hypnotised day after day, paralysed, in thrall to the flow of dollars, franks, guilders and gold in and out of the Bank of England. Once upon a time, Jennie had learned why economists demanded every pound be backed by an ounce or two of gold, but she couldn't for the life of her remember what that reason was.

Finally, she decided to admit her ignorance to Frank. They were sitting in his large Bloomsbury flat. His two girls had gone back to Bucks for the Easter holidays, so he and Jennie could enjoy the rainy spring weekend. They'd decided to go nowhere, see no one, do nothing but enjoy one another. It was a rainy Sunday afternoon. They found themselves in the drawing room, turning the pages of the broadsheet papers, reading aloud from leaders and columns that struck their fancies. As one read, the other would survey the lush green of the growing foliage in the square, framed by the mullions of the rain-streaked windows.

"Gold standard? Why should we care, Frank?"

He put down his paper. "Fixed amount of gold about. Government can't issue more pound notes than there is gold to back 'em."

"So?"

"Fixed amount of pounds, but more things to buy with the same amount of money... Well, prices have to fall. That goes for the price of labour, Jennie. Wages go down and stay down."

Jennie smiled ruefully. "So, if you've got lots of money, the gold standard keeps making you richer and richer as it makes prices fall."

Frank now frowned. "And if you don't have much money, you're worse and worse off."

"You're telling me we have to get off the gold standard as soon as possible, aren't you, Frank." Then the thought came, *That's Mosley's policy, isn't it?* Jennie wasn't going to bring that up and risk spoiling a long rainy Sunday afternoon indoors.

* * *

Jennie hadn't been able to bring herself to speak in the House of Commons all that winter and into the spring. She didn't have the stomach for Ramsay MacDonald's sorrowful countenance. She could see he felt himself powerless before the black tides washing over the country, and now she wouldn't add the pain of a child's reproach.

First Frank, and then Nye Bevan had noted her reticence. She shrugged them off. One day in the smoking room when she was alone with Ellen Wilkinson, her friend wondered aloud if Jennie was losing heart. It seemed to Jennie a good excuse for her silence.

"What's the point, Ellen? Government won't listen, and the other ILP members are already convinced. Should I address the Tories or the Liberals?" It was a convincing reason. And it worked pretty well till one day in early June.

She'd come into the Lady Members' Room. There was no one present but Lady Astor, and her maid, helping her out of a glittering evening dress and into the sombre suit and tricorn hat Nancy Astor affected on the Conservative back benches.

She looked round from behind the screen where she was changing and hissed, "Ah, Miss Lee. Have you heard what your party's government is about to propose in the Commons?"

What are you outraged about now, Lady Astor? Jennie waited, knowing if she didn't know she'd soon learn.

"They're going to try to cut the budget deficit on the backs of women."

Nancy Astor was glaring at her as she strode forth from behind the screen in her parliamentary battle armour.

"Don't you want to know?"

Jennie nodded, supressing the reply almost on her lips: *You'll tell me soon enough.*

"I have it straight from the PPS for that Bondfield woman." This was the MP serving as parliamentary private secretary to Margaret Bondfield, the minister of Labour, the only woman in MacDonald's cabinet.

Jennie lost patience. "Well, what's she done? Spit it out."

"She's going to announce that unemployed women will no longer be eligible for national insurance payments."

"But, but...working women have been paying into the unemployment insurance scheme. How can they be cut out of it?"

"Simple, just pretend they don't need the money because their husbands work, or, if they're not married, because their families can support them." She caught her breath. Before Jennie could think of anything to say she continued. "Besides, your lot don't want women working anyway, just crowds out men's chances to find jobs."

Both of them knew she was right. The Trades Unions behind Labour were fervent in their opposition to women in work.

"Will you speak against it, Miss Lee?"

Jennie replied with a touch of venom. "Will you?"

"Perhaps. But you won't, not since you came back from America. You'll want to go easy on your fa—" Jennie heard the word form on Lady Astor's lips, which then spat out the word "party" instead.

So, she knew. Had Mosley told her? Had she told others? Who else knew? Nancy Astor was continuing to speak, perhaps covering her slip, trying to distract Jennie, but Jennie was no longer listening. Instead she was conjuring a frightening image. Standing in the House, catching the Speaker's eye, rising from the back benches to heap scorn, derision, abuse on Ramsay MacDonald, while all round her the men sat, knowing she was attacking her own father. She flushed the deepest crimson.

Lady Astor watched Jennie's face and ceased her diatribe. The two women were now standing only a few feet apart, glaring at each other.

Just above a whisper, Jennie said, "How do you know?" And without waiting for a reply added, "Who else knows?"

Nancy Astor's tone changed, softened by the intimacy of the matter.

"I don't know who else knows." She sighed. "My source was rather a nosey parker, but he's an American, a society snob who doesn't travel in your circles, so perhaps no harm's been done on your side of the aisle."

Her glare belied the comforting words even as she mouthed them.

Lady Astor reverted to her accusation, "That really is why you've been silent ever since you came back from America? Did someone there tell you?" she answered her own question. "No...I don't think anyone in America could have known."

If Nancy Astor had noticed Jennie's reticence, who else had? And seeking explanations of her silence, had people begun to speculate? Did Jennie need to worry that anyone would hit upon so far-fetched a reason why she had ceased her merciless attack on the Labour front bench? Her glare became even fiercer.

"Who have you told?" She added venom to her words.

But even as she asked, one answer came to Jennie. *It was you who told Tom Mosley, wasn't it?* The realisation was instant. That had to be how he knew, or at least it was Jennie's best guess. Was Nancy Astor clever enough to realise that it was Mosley who'd told Jennie? She didn't seem interested in knowing how Jennie had learned that MacDonald was her father. Why not? *Because she thinks she knows?*

Without answering Jennie's question, Lady Astor strode from the room, leaving her maid to fold away the party gown and carefully place the rings, tiara and necklace in their fitted traveling case. Jennie sat down on the worn chesterfield. It was then that real anxiety began to creep up on her. Lady Astor had told Tom Mosley and Tom Mosley had told Jennie. What if Nancy Astor began to be interested enough in why he had told Jennie? Once this question dawned on her, another thought came and now Jennie was properly frightened. She remembered that first afternoon, here in this very room, when a message arrived for her from the palace. Nancy Astor had noticed and asked. Jennie hadn't replied, but was that the end of the matter? Probably not for the Viscountess Astor. She'd make a point of learning what connection the little Scottish socialist might have with royalty.

Had she already done so? Might she put the palace, Jennie and Mosley together and make real trouble out of it? That Jennie was MacDonald's bastard was a matter of mere gossip. But what if Nancy Astor's insatiable curiosity revealed that Jennie was bound up with constitutional mischief, uncovered the secret transmission of money, Royal interference in politics? Jennie instantly calculated that every loyalty of Lady Astor's—gentry, party, ruling class, her husband's newspaper interests—every one of them would be sucking secrets like this from her lips the moment she learned it. It would sink Jennie, certainly in her North Lanark constituency, if not in the party altogether. It would destroy any chance of Mosley's New Party and whatever chance he had of righting the sinking ship. Jennie had committed herself on this bet at stakes far higher than she had ever meant to, or could afford. She had to distract Nancy Astor and anyone else who was wondering about her silence in the house. She'd have to speak in the debate. *But that wouldn't be enough of a distraction from what was really happening, would it?* She had to warn Mosley as well. If it had been Nancy Astor who'd put him onto Jennie's bastardy, he'd have to find a way to lead her off any other trail it might put her onto.

* * *

Jennie was in her usual place as far back from the government benches as she could be, up against the back wall in the shadow beneath the Strangers' Gallery overhang. But she was wearing a bright green dress, which shone even in the dim light passing between the carved wooden support pillars. Members would certainly notice her. Would the Speaker?

Margaret Bondfield had just put the question of her "Anomalies" bill. Jennie rose. The Speaker of the House had evidently noticed her. Perhaps he'd also remarked her seven weeks absence and then her silence in the months after she returned from America. The second time she rose to catch his eye he recognised her.

Jennie knew she had to make something of a storm in her attack on the government, though the subject was the rights of women workers alone—married at that, and not all workers. It wouldn't be hard. She looked at Bondfield, deciding how to begin. It was customary to refer to an MP in one's own party as 'my honourable friend.' But Jennie would not adopt the hypocrisy. She would be rude.

The minister of labour, the very first woman to ever hold a cabinet post in this country, has, shamefully I say, decided to sacrifice the interests of her sex to maintain the support of the Trades Union bosses in this country. Removing three hundred thousand married working women from the protection of a pittance in unemployment insurance that their own contributions have earned is shameful enough. But to do so simply to prevent reductions in the amount paid to unemployed men...well, that is not something socialists could ever have expected their own government to demand they vote for.

There was a jeer. Was it from her own benches or the Tory side?

"When did you last vote with this government anyway, Jennie?" Laughter swept the house; even Ramsay MacDonald smiled.

"Order, order," the Speaker's voice boomed. When quiet had been restored, he turned back to Jennie. But she had resumed her seat, and next to her Ellen Wilkinson rose and was recognised to continue the attack.

Jennie looked across the aisle, seeking out Nancy Astor. Was she in the house? Yes, easy to spot in her accustomed place behind the opposition benches as far as possible from Winston Churchill, now himself a backbencher.

At the division on the motion to adopt the minister's bill, Jennie joined a dozen or more other Labour MPs in opposition. She noticed as she passed the teller that Mosley hadn't been in the house at all. But Cimmie Mosley was, voting with Jennie and the other ILP members against their own government. Jennie approached her from behind as they passed the tellers.

"Lady Mosley," she said quietly. "Can you pass a message on to your husband?" Without turning her head, Cynthia Mosley nodded. "Tell him that Lady Astor knows what he told me and she may know that I am in communication with the Duchess. He will understand."

Cynthia Mosley turned to Jennie and frowned. Suddenly Jennie began to worry. Did Mosley's wife know about his arrangement with the palace? Did she approve?

Chapter Twenty

And then Jennie's world changed completely. It took only a month, August 1931, a month that announced itself as the annual parliamentary interregnum everyone expected, when the House rose for summer recess. By the end of that month, everyone else's world in Britain had also taken a radical turn.

* * *

It was late that Saturday morning that the papers arrived at Wallington Hall, the grand country house of Sir Charles Trevelyan high up in the Northumbrian countryside, a half dozen miles inland from the North Sea. Jennie and Frank Wise were Charlie's guests that first weekend of the parliamentary summer recess. Frank would shoot grouse with Charlie, an activity Jennie couldn't begin to understand. She was going to read, first Virginia Woolf's *To the Lighthouse*, and if it was too difficult, the latest instalment of *The Forsythe Saga*, secure in the knowledge that Galsworthy had been praised by the Writer's Union in Moscow.

Breakfast was over and all three were in the Library, each at a writing table, scratching away with pen and ink, dealing with constituency correspondence. The wainscoting and bookshelves of the ample room were brightened by the morning light, streaming in through three large windows from which curtains had been drawn, billowing slightly in a breeze coming off the Northumbrian plain.

A valet entered quietly, laid a salver with the morning's post at Sir Charles' elbow and placed three newspapers on the library table. Frank rose, picked up one and then the other.

They heard him mutter, "I say..." as he picked up the other two and turned. "Better look at this. The May Report is out, and it's a bit of a bombshell."

The others understood immediately. Everyone in politics had been waiting for this shoe to drop ever since March.

The May Committee had begun its sittings work just as Jennie returned from America. After more than a year in office, Ramsay MacDonald had admitted to his cabinet colleagues that he was "baffled" by the ever-increasing unemployment numbers and how to cope with them. The admission had been the last straw for Charlie Trevelyan, who had quit the cabinet. He did not hide MacDonald's admission in cabinet from his friends. The evening he'd sent in his resignation to MacDonald, he met Frank, Nye and Jennie coming into the house. Charlie was beside himself.

"Baffled, he said. As though it were a crossword puzzle!"

"Poor, pathetic creature...like a child paralysed before a cobra." Jennie had been unable to say more.

In his bafflement, Ramsay MacDonald had asked a wealthy financier, Sir George May, to convene 'experts' who might tell him what to do in this ever-worsening economic crisis. Everyone knew that the conclusion of this charade was foregone: austerity, belt-tightening, sacrifice, stiff upper lip. Now, three months after it began, everyone in Westminster knew the May Committee's shoe had to drop at any moment. Now it had.

The other two rose and each took up a paper.

Trevelyan spoke first. "They're predicting a run on the pound and a deficit of 120 million pounds for the year."

Frank sighed. "Well, publicising a prediction like that will certainly make it happen. How foolish...unless they mean to destabilise the government."

"Why's the prophecy self-fulfilling, Frank?" Jennie asked.

"A dozen reasons. For one, it'll frighten investors to sell treasury bonds, cease any investment at all, take their money out of the country, and so push up the unemployment rate. That'll require more unemployment insurance, making the deficit worse."

Jennie glanced back at the papers. Now she spoke. "No it won't. They want to cut the unemployment benefit by 60 million pounds. How much is that off the weekly dole, Frank?"

"I don't know, maybe fifteen, twenty per cent."

Jennie put down her paper. "No wonder the two Labour men in the Committee refused to sign."

Frank sat down, paper in his lap. "There is nothing new here. MacDonald didn't need the May Committee to give him these ideas. Snowden could've told him the same thing six months ago." Philip Snowden was the Chancellor of the Exchequer, once a man of the left, now a stalwart for Churchill's gold standard.

Charlie spoke. "All the blighter ever did in cabinet was natter about retrenchment, let the market work itself out…"

Frank replied. "It's all wrong, damn it. Trouble is there's no one in the cabinet to challenge the May Committee. No one with any economics, not MacDonald, not the Trades Union folk. There won't be anybody who'll stand up and refute this stuff. Wish you hadn't resigned, Charlie." There was a tinge of anger in his tone.

The older man looked surprised. "I couldn't have done it. I'm no political economist."

"Sorry…you're right of course."

Jennie looked towards Frank. "You'll just have to do it from the pages *The New Statesman* and *The Herald*."

These were the most widely read periodical and newspaper on the left.

"I suspect Keynes won't need any help from me in *The New Statesman*." Then he looked at Trevelyan. "Do you think the cabinet will wear the cuts May's demanding?"

Charlie Trevelyan began counting on his fingers.

"I can think of about five stalwarts who will certainly reject cuts to unemployment insurance, and a couple who are keen to soak the rich at least a little. But that leaves more than a dozen who'll be loyal to Ramsay MacDonald come what may."

There was no need to enumerate them. Jennie and Frank knew who they were as well as Charlie.

Jennie spoke the conclusion they had all reached by now.

"It all depends on MacDonald then."

They were silent for a moment. But the other two couldn't know how the sinking feeling weighed on her. Jennie knew in her viscera what her father would do. She felt somehow that she shared his shame, and she hated him for it.

Trevelyan spoke. "I wonder if he knew this damn May report was about to come out when he recessed parliament for three months."

Jennie grimaced. "It certainly keeps the pressure off...no muttering cabals in the corridors of the house."

"Not a bit of it, Jennie." Frank was firm. "The City will begin to react to this report on Monday. Mark my words, in ten days, there will be the most god-awful crisis in the financial markets, MacDonald will have to do something. Only question is what."

"Well then, you and Jennie had better change your plans."

They had organised another trip back to Russia. Frank had his work for the *Centrosoyus*. Jennie would travel separately and meet him, perhaps gather material for another lecture tour of America. They'd have a month together.

Frank looked towards Jennie with a grim smile. "Maybe it won't come to that. It's three weeks till we sail for Leningrad."

Charlie Trevelyan rose. "I think we might just have time to get some grouse hunting in."

Jennie produced a mock frown. "Is that before lunch or before the collapse of the pound, Charlie?"

* * *

Frank was right in his prediction, of course. By midweek the papers were reporting a roiling crisis in the City.

* * *

It was pouring rain when they left Wallington Hall the next Wednesday, towards noon. In silence, Frank and Jennie watched the metronome paths of wiper blades sweeping down across the windscreen, behind a driver too well-trained to make conversation. Fifteen dreary miles past lush but sodden pastureland on one side and deeply leaved treelines on the other, in the steady downpour to the Morpeth Station. Its creamy sandstone had been washed clean by eighteen hours of steady rain. The entry was closely framed by thick foliage that had thrived in the rain and now added its own drops to the shower in a gust as they pushed the door open.

"I'll just get the tickets, shall I?" Frank asked as he started towards the booth beneath a wall map of the London North Eastern System.

Jennie reached out to stop him. "I'm not going to London just yet. Got to go home briefly."

She hadn't wanted to tell Charlie, or even discuss with Frank why she had to go. But through the last days of the brief holiday, it had become evident to Jennie that she couldn't much longer put off confronting her parents with what she'd learned. Was it a truth they'd known for twenty-six years and kept from her? If it was, she had to know more, she had to know why, before she threw herself into the political storm that now had to come. She would do what she had to do to bring down MacDonald, if she could, and make Mosley prime minister. If it required her to tell the world who her father was, so be it. But it had to be the truth, and the only way to establish it was to go home and confront her parents. From the moment she had decided she had to do it, a dread had descended upon her. *What will you say? How can you even ask?* These questions kept forming themselves in her mind, no matter what tricks she tried to banish them. But no thoughts formed themselves into any question she could actually put to her parents at all. Instead there were emotions, coming in waves—shame that she should even ask, fear that it would really be true, all carried along by waves of anxiety she couldn't suppress.

If Frank noticed he said nothing. Now, before the station entrance, he stood there a moment, nodded, searching her face, kindness and concern in his eyes, and understanding that didn't ask for explanation. *Does he know?* She briefly wondered and then recognised it was just the look of someone who loved her. Then he walked into the station to buy the tickets.

Their trains would arrive moments apart. Standing underneath the platform roofing, shaking umbrellas and unbelting trench coats, each looked into the gloom towards a different direction: Jennie to the south for her train to Edinburgh, Frank for the train to Newcastle coming in from the north. For the moment, there was nothing more to say. Jennie tried hard to imagine what Frank was anticipating from Dorothy Wise: stony silences, abrupt requests, curt responses, ritual courtesies. *All the reasons not to marry anyone!* Then she thought, *He's no idea what I'm to face.* She thought it through again one last time. *You can't tell him just this one thing about your real father, without unravelling everything. You've no convincing answers to any next question he might ask that won't open floodgates. So more lies between you and your lover, your friend.* She wanted to cry but wouldn't.

Frank saw her face contort just enough to hold back the tears, mistook them for sadness at parting and hugged her tightly to him. Holding her at arms' length, he slid his hands down from her arms and reached hers squeezed them firmly.

"It's only a few days." She nodded.

The rumble coming from both directions, rising through their feet, broke into their reverie. When they looked up, the six great wheels of an A1 steam locomotive where sliding, apparently not rolling, down the platform track. It was Jennie's Edinburgh-bound train.

* * *

Three hours later, Jennie was sitting, not in the small kitchen of the terrace house she'd been raised in, not facing her parents across the same wooden table at which she'd grown up. Instead she was alone with her mother—just them, no father—sipping tea in a shabby café, below the elevated trestle of the railway tracks that bisected the Cowdenbeath high street. The rain had stayed with Jennie as she rode north, heavy enough to make both shores invisible as her train trundled across the Forth Bridge. Matching her mood, the storm showed no sign of weakening as the train moved inland through Fife.

Jennie had wired ahead and Euphemia Lee was waiting at the station. As Jennie's train pulled in, she could be seen under the cover of the platform shelter, not quite gaunt, but serious, unsmiling, mouth a thin line, and yet the face still unwrinkled, a cigarette in her hand, and two or three fag ends stamped out at her feet. Smoking on a railway platform was not something her mother was wont to do, Jennie thought. Euphemia Lee was alone. She'd mounted the stairs to the platform and was waiting. *She means to intercept me, alone. Could someone have told her why I was coming?*

Euphemia's greeting was surprisingly warm, at least by Scottish standards. She took hold of her daughter's arms, held her back for a good look, and then hugged her. *Perhaps she was eager to see me, that's all.*

Euphemia spoke. "You must be tired from the long journey."

"No, Mum, I've been in the north of England for some days. It was only a matter of a few hours getting here."

Her mother was obviously not listening. Preoccupied, she took Jennie's case and led her down the stairs. Under the railway bridge, at the High Street she turned in the opposite direction from their home. Before Jennie could ask why she spoke.

"Let's get a cup of tea at the caf', dear." Jennie nodded, and her mother went on, "I wanted to talk to you before we see your father."

Jennie stopped. *But he's not my father*. The thought was in her eyes as she glared at her mother. Euphemia Lee looked back into them hard, her face softened and her eyes pled for a little understanding. Jennie read them and softened.

"Yes, let's get a cup, I'd like that, Mum."

Face to face, at a small round table, in a dark alcove, neither woman seemed to know how to begin. Suddenly, sitting there, it came to Jennie, a question that tacitly assumed enough to open the subject they both had to address.

"How did you find out I knew?"

Her mother withdrew an envelope from her coat pocket. Jennie recognised the manila of a government envelope with official franking and no stamp. She placed it on the table and smoothed it out. The return address was now clear, No. 10 Downing Street.

"He wrote to warn me the secret was out. Politics being what it is, I guessed you'd find out soon enough."

"MacDonald wrote to you. Ramsay MacDonald? You're in touch with him?"

The thought almost bowled Jennie out her chair. She grasped the edge of the small table with both her hands.

Her mother answered, matter-of-factly, "Occasionally, not more than that, perhaps once a year."

This was beyond Jennie's ken. "But why? Whatever for?"

Euphemia withdrew a packet of Woodbines, offered one to her daughter, who took one from her mother, perhaps for the first time in her life. Lighting up, the older woman drew on the cigarette, flicking a loose bit of tobacco from her lip with her tongue and spoke.

Her voice remained unemotional, "He's your...real...father. He cared about you. He was proud of you. But he could never talk about it to anyone...except me."

Jennie wanted to challenge her mother. Her real father was James Lee, the man who'd raised her, loved her, pushed her into a man's world, made her the woman she'd become. But Jennie wasn't going to argue about the words 'real father.'

"How long has MacDonald known? Since I was born?"

Euphemia shook her head. "No. He didn't find out till you were three. He'd come back to Cowdenbeath for a meeting, and met you for the first time."

"But he knew…about me?"

"Not till then."

Jennie paused, working up the courage to invade the intimate life of another person, her mother's. It wasn't just unnatural, it was more than unpleasant. It would be repugnant, but she had to know. "How did…it…happen?" She couldn't bring herself to go beyond the pronoun.

"Must you know?" Her daughter could only nod. Euphemia fortified herself with another draw on the fag. "He seduced me…one night while you father was at the theatre next door."

She waited for a reaction. Seeing her daughter's eyes narrow in anger she went on.

"Of course, I could never tell your dad. He'd have killed MacDonald sure as we're sitting here."

"Why did you never tell me?" Even as she asked the question Jennie realised how silly it was.

Her mother replied nonetheless. "Tell you? Don't be daft! Tell you when? When you were a bab'? When you were a schoolgirl? When you were in the 'varsity, already deep into our politics, girl?"

"Sorry, Mum. T'was a stupid question."

But her mother was going on. "Besides for a long time I admired him, we admired him, your dad and me both, especially in the war when he gave up everything."

Both mother and daughter knew that Ramsay MacDonald had resigned as party leader and actively opposed the Great War against his entire party for four years, till its end vindicated him triumphantly.

"There wasn't a reason in the world to tell you, even if you could have kept it from your dad." She looked hard at her daughter. "And you must never say anything to him, do you hear?"

Jennie reached for her mother's hand. "I swear." She took another cigarette from the packet on the table, lit it and smiled inwardly, while keeping her face immobile. *Thanks, Mum, you've given me what I really need, a personal anger I never really had. You've dispelled any pity for the doddering old man.* Her mind sought the right word for how she felt. Then it came. *You've made me Nemesis.*

As if she were reading her daughter's thoughts, Euphemia Lee spoke. "Jennie, once his politics changed, when he became a trimmer, a compromiser, we began to despise Ramsay MacDonald. By the time he showed how comfortable he was round the wealthy, once we began to despise his politics, you were already with us. There was never any need to make you hate him for what he did to me."

The women rose. Jennie left a few bob on the table. By tacit and mutual consent, the conversation was over, the matter was closed, the subject was not to be broached again. As they walked out into the rain, struggling with umbrellas against the gusts, Jennie couldn't deny the feeling that there was something she hadn't asked, something she still needed to know, a loose thread she had not tugged at. *Whatever could it be? It will come to you, Jennie. But it will be too late to ask, won't it?*

Chapter Twenty-One

Each day through the middle weeks of August, the news was worse. Each day, the Tory press proclaimed the rising onslaught on the pound, the inexorable closures—mills, mines, shipyards, foundries, factories. All accompanied by the same front-page leader, in one variant or another, over and over: *Government Must Take Action!* Almost any action would suffice, just to show the government understood it was in crisis.

After a few days with her parents, Jennie found reasons to nurse her constituency and went off to Glasgow. North Lanark was more depressing than it had ever been. The August weather was fine. But the warm and sunny spells made the days worse for Jennie. She'd watch from the train crawling slowly out from the centre of Glasgow, as housewives came out of tenements and terraced houses to hang sodden laundry or pluck weeds in a kitchen garden. Choosing a different stop each day, she began walking, promised herself she'd spend the week finding her way from one end of the constituency to the other, meeting voters wherever she could find them. There was little enough work and the strips of urban allotments Jennie passed were teeming with men, each preening his vegetable trellis, sometimes right up to the evening's dusk after nine. Jennie wanted to talk, but the men were shame-faced and sullen. Each evening, she'd manage to catch the last train from Motherwell back to Queen Street Station in Glasgow.

MacDonald had returned to London from his own Scottish constituency on the 10th of August, the day Jennie had left Cowdenbeath for Glasgow. But then, for another few days, nothing much happened in Whitehall that the papers could report. Jennie expected nothing more than the drumbeat of front-page leaders in the Tory broadsheet dailies: the persistent demand that the burden of a failing economy be shouldered by the unemployed. Finally, on the 19th, MacDonald called his cabinet together. The next day, when the London papers arrived in Glasgow, there was no hiding that the government was at an impasse. The cabinet was evenly divided on the cuts, and MacDonald grasping at some compromise that would keep his government in office and him as prime minister.

That evening, as Jennie walked into the shabby hotel on George Square, the desk clerk turned to the pigeonholes and pulled out several pieces of paper.

"People 'been calling for you and sending you wires, Miss Lee."

He handed her two telegrams and a handful of notes. One of the telegrams was from her mother: *Labour MPs seeking you. Stop. Go to London. Stop. Mum.* Another was from Ellen Wilkinson in London: *Need you here urgently. Stop. Take next train.* The note was from her local constituency committee head: *MPs trying to reach you. I've given them your hotel's name.* The trunk call phone messages were from Nye Bevan—typically extravagant, Jennie couldn't help thinking—and from Frank. *He wouldn't have called from home. Either he went to a post office or he was already in London for some reason.* She looked up from the bits of paper in her hand.

"Do you know when the night train for London goes?"

"11:33. But booking hall's already closed."

"Never mind. I can get a ticket on the train. Only I won't want a sleeper."

Can't afford one, can I? She laughed out loud. It would be seven and a half hours to London Euston, sitting up, if the 2d class compartment was full. *Nothing for it.* Jennie shrugged.

"Please prepare my bill."

She moved to the stair and began a trudge to the third floor. There had been no explanation in any of the messages. But surely it was political, not personal. *Everything political is personal to you, Jennie,* the voice in her head was knowing.

It was 3:40 AM, when the bright lights on the quay during the

Liverpool station-stop woke her from a deep sleep. Jennie had actually found an empty compartment and a conductor who was a Labour Party stalwart. He knew the name, even pretended to recognise her from the papers and promised to keep passengers from joining her as long as he could. Now, as she awoke and realised where she was, the trace of the dream she'd just woken from remained with her. It was unmistakably the face of her father—her real father, Ramsay MacDonald—nothing more. Then it evanesced. Was the face threatening, angry, had it leered at her? She couldn't conjure it again. She leaned back, tilting her head against the side cushion, and tried to sleep again. Five minutes later, she gave up. She thought about her mother and Ramsay MacDonald. Jennie found herself, for the first time since her conversation with her mother, actually conjuring the image of Ramsay MacDonald, twenty-five years younger, seducing an equally younger Euphemia Lee. What must it have been like? She could somehow paint an image in her mind of the tall, thin, handsome man with a sort of ludicrously lascivious grin. It came along with a rising anger at him. But it was the woman she couldn't put in the picture.

Euphemia Lee was a person of great strength, rather unbending, with a mind that could not be changed. She'd been the stalwart in their small family, making the decisions, and enforcing them: firm with her daughter and firm with her husband. Single-mindedness had been her chief character trait. The notion that a man might have seduced her just didn't fit easily with her character.

Jennie tried again to make the seduction happen in her mind. Could Euphemia Lee have been attracted to the politics MacDonald represented? He was already a personality in Labour Party circles back then. Might she have been star-struck, seduced as much by his celebrity? No, Jennie had to admit, her mother was just too dour for that and too unsentimental about the politics she shared with MacDonald too.

No, it couldn't have been seduction. The notion of 'Ramsay MacDonald—seducer' was preposterous. *If it wasn't seduction, what was it?* She made herself think things through, repugnant things. Still, things that just didn't sit right. It was like a jigsaw with a puzzle piece forced in somewhere. *Could it have been worse than seduction? Could it have been assault?* The word formed in her mind. *Rape? And then afterwards hidden, suppressed, denied, allowed by both parties to become mere 'seduction'?* In her rage against MacDonald, she wanted to make this the truth. But she knew the pieces of the puzzle didn't really fit this way. He was even less capable of rape than he was of seduction.

Then the question came to her, the one she'd failed to form and so failed to ask that afternoon in the shabby café beneath the railway bridge over the high street in Cowdenbeath. *Mum, why ever did you tell MacDonald about me at all? Three years later, or ever after, for that matter? Why did you even allow yourself again to be in the same room with the man…if it had been rape or anything even remotely like it?* She had to ask herself: would her mother not feel the violation every time she saw him, heard from him, in fact every time she looked upon her daughter? She paused on this problem in her train of thought. *Would a man who'd raped or even seduced a woman stay in touch with her, visit her in her husband's home, carry on a correspondence with her for years?*

The coach began, almost imperceptibly, to move along the Liverpool station platform. Once it picked up enough speed, the rhythmical sway of the carriage began to urge her back to sleep against her will. She didn't want to give in to it. She had to think things through. She rose, reached for the packet of fags in the coat rolled on the rack above her head. Jennie remained standing. Balancing against the rhythm of the train as she lit up and let the smell of the smouldering Virginia tobacco waken her completely. Then she sat.

It wasn't rape. Couldn't have been. So it had to have been seduction. Could it have been the other way round? Might your mother have been seductress, and MacDonald the seduced? This at least made a kind of sense to Jennie. She had no trouble seeing herself seducing a man. She'd done it in fact, would have seduced Mosley just for the fun of it if he'd put up the slightest resistance instead of a more than willing participation. *But your mother seducing someone, anyone? And under her own roof? Just out of desire? Out of the question. The dour Presbyterian in your mum wouldn't have allowed it to herself.* Euphemia Lee had never done anything merely for fun. *Could it be your mother wanted Ramsay MacDonald's child?* Jennie had been an only child, and had complained of it more than once growing up. Her friends and schoolmates all had brothers and sisters, some had too many for their family's own good. She knew how long her parents had been married before Jennie arrived. And she knew equally well that her mother had never taken any precaution against pregnancy. 'Family planning' had been as much a watchword among socialist ladies in Scotland as women's suffrage. Euphemia Lee had introduced her daughter to contraception before she went up to university in Edinburgh. But there was, to Jennie's secret adolescent inspection, no sign of a diaphragm or other such device in her mother's most intimate cabinets or drawers. Either she didn't need one, or her marriage was chaste, or...*Wanting a child by MacDonald, then telling him and conducting a correspondence with him for years. Surely your dad would have learned of it...unless he knew all along?* The alternatives and the possibilities were jumbling in her mind. *If Dad knew, why had Mum sworn me to secrecy from him?* It was becoming hard to follow one possibility without others cutting across and leading her in quite different directions. Then, quite against her will, Jennie fell asleep.

She was still sleeping deeply when the train came to its final halt at King's Cross London. As the conductor shook her gently awake, Jennie instantly experienced a rush of relentless anger. She couldn't explain to herself why, but the political rage against Ramsay MacDonald she'd harboured was now strengthened and made much more personal. And it had broadened to her mother, and her father. It didn't matter that she couldn't frame an exact reason why she was now so angry with the world that had created her.

* * *

Back in her flat, Jennie went to her phone. *Who to ring up first? Ellen, Nye, no, Frank of course.* He answered at the first ring and before he could say anything, she spoke.

"I'm in town, Frank."

"You know about the cabinet crisis meetings?"

"Yes, it's why I'm back. Took the night train."

"You must be knackered." He paused but before Jennie could respond he spoke. "The ILP is trying to rally every Labour member we can—Trades Union Council, Fabian Society, anyone we can to get the ministers to resist the cuts."

"What can I do?"

"Looks like there's eight or nine members of the cabinet on our side. Not enough yet. I'm going to try to teach Parmoor some economics." This was the government's leader in the House of Lords. "Ellen thinks you could give Lees-Smith a bit of backbone. She's going to talk to Margaret Bondfield." This was the only woman in the cabinet. Frank smiled. "Doesn't think you can help much there."

They both chortled, recalling Jennie's slashing attack in the commons less than two months before.

Jennie replied, "Lees-Smith? Didn't he replace Charlie Trevelyan at the Board of Education last winter?"

"That's the man. Likes to buck authority too. You're not old enough to remember, he read that poet Sassoon's anti-war letter on the floor of the house in the middle of the Great War. Stood his ground against the jingo mob."

"Any more? Just those three?"

"The rest are already pretty solid one way or the other. But we'll talk to all of them. The real question is whether the Trades Union Council will resist the cuts. If they do, MacDonald will be able to hold out against the City and Wall Street."

Jennie replied, "If he wants to…"

Frank was momentarily silent. *That's ominous,* she thought.

"Look, come round to Bedford Square tonight after you've seen Lees-Smith, will you, dear."

Bedford Square was Frank's flat. She'd hope to hear those words.

"Yes, of course," she replied, brightening a little for the first time that day.

* * *

It was about three in the afternoon when Jennie found herself at the door of the president of the board of education. She'd been before, when Charlie Trevelyan had held the post. He'd resigned in the winter, to protest MacDonald's bewilderment and the government's inaction. She gave her name to the male secretary-gatekeeper, who told her he'd see if the minister was available. A few minutes later Hastings Lee-Smith poked a head out the door, smiled broadly and ushered Jennie through. She followed the back of his frock coat. Over the coat, a celluloid collar stiffly rose, horizontally bisected by the black ribbon of a City Banker's bow tie. The office was small, rather dimly lit, with a few leather-bound volumes in a glass bookcase behind a desk, at which Lees-Smith seated himself. He slid his palms over the flat, uncluttered surface as if smoothing it out and looked up at Jennie.

"I'm expecting to be called to a second cabinet meeting this afternoon, Miss Lee, so I may have to be brief."

"I'm here to lobby you, sir."

"I expected as much. And I am aware of which side you're

on." He smiled—was it in agreement? "Naturally I can't divulge cabinet matters. But I can tell you no decisions have been made."

Jennie nodded. "Is it safe to say the sides are fairly evenly divided, sir?"

"Quite." Lees-Smith sat impassive. He would volunteer no more.

"You're an economist, sir. You must have considerable influence in the discussions."

"Well, Miss Lee, whether I do or not, it's precisely because I'm an economist that I am so worried. I see the chancellor's arguments. He says that in the deflation the purchasing power of the unemployment payments has increased forty per cent. How is anyone to answer that?"

Jennie's answer was ready. "Rather simple, sir. Ask the Chancellor of the Exchequer to live on fifteen bob a week." She paused. "Or twelve, if he has his way with the cuts." Then she asked, "Have you given any thought to Keynes' plans"—she paused— "or Mosley's?"

"Pointless. MacDonald can't get the Liberals to support him and Mosley's bolted the party entirely. Spending won't wash with the government anyway. Snowden hates Keynes and Lloyd George. I can't ever repeat the names he calls them when ladies are absent."

The telephone rang. Lees-Smith picked up, listened for a moment.

Then he said, "On my way."

Rising, he held his hand towards the door. The interview was over.

"Cabinet secretary's office. We're beginning again."

They rose and walked out together. Until they were alone on the pavement, out of anyone's earshot, they were silent. Then Lees-Smith spoke.

"Tell you what I'm afraid of, Miss Lee. It's not like 1924 when MacDonald made his government resign over a trifle."

It has been five years and Jennie couldn't recall the history. Lees-Smith set off on a trot. Jennie reached out a hand to slow him down.

"Very sorry, I didn't follow. What did you mean?"

He turned for a moment, "This time MacDonald will do anything to stay in office."

Then he marched off down Whitehall with a bearing that brooked no more conversation.

* * *

Frank was not alone when Jennie arrived at his Bedford Square flat, towards seven in the still bright daylight. A dozen MPs, all ILP members, were sitting round Frank's drawing room, filling the chesterfield, a couple of wing chairs and some side chairs that had been dragged from the dining room. She searched for Nye Bevan, but he wasn't there. Maybe the reason was political. He wasn't ILP and he had sided with Mosley on everything till the latter had been expelled from the party. Still, she wanted badly to know what Nye was thinking. *Maybe he's not here because he knew I'd be here and I'd stay the night with Frank.*

Each briefly reported on their respective missions to wavering cabinet ministers. Few had even the limited success Jennie could report. She ended her report with the minister of education's last words.

"He may have been giving something away." She wanted to use the very words. "Said that it wasn't like 1924, when the Labour government resigned over a trifle." She paused. "Then he said MacDonald would do anything to stay in office."

One of the older MPs recalled, "In '24 the first Labour government resigned on a technicality. They didn't have to go, but MacDonald refused to give an inch for a compromise."

Now Frank spoke. "Well, if MacDonald is trying to find a way to stay in power, that makes our jobs a bit easier."

Chapter Twenty-One

"How so?" It was a Yorkshire voice, someone who hadn't spoken up yet.

Frank looked towards the man. "Just keep the pressure on. He'll need every vote in the cabinet… and every Labour vote in the House." He looked round the room. "Let's meet again here tomorrow morning. See where we are. We may need to do a lot more lobbying."

* * *

Jennie woke about eight the next morning. She was quietly dressing when Frank spoke.

"Where are you going, dear?"

"Sorry, didn't mean to wake you. I want to go home and change. before the others return. Wearing exactly what I had on here last night would be rather rubbing things in their face, no?"

"Suppose so. Hadn't occurred to me."

"Men." She smiled and left the room.

Chapter Twenty-Two

It was a short walk from Bedford Square back past the British Museum, across Russell Square to Guilford Street. Jennie had not gotten much past the Russell Square Underground station stairs, when she saw the large grey and black saloon car parked at what looked like the street door of the block of flats where she lived.

Immediately, she knew to whom the vast Daimler saloon belonged. Seeing it there at seven thirty in the morning was remarkable enough. But there, across the pavement, was Elizabeth Bowes-Lyons, standing at Jennie's front door. Approaching, Jennie could see her arm repeatedly rise to the bell for Jennie's flat. She turned as Jennie approached.

"There you are! I tried to ring you a hundred times."

As Jennie came closer Elizabeth rushed forward, almost falling into Jennie's arms.

There was no one on the street except the chauffeur standing at the Daimler, but Elizabeth held her close and whispered, "The Duke sent me. I don't have much time."

She pulled Jennie towards the car and almost forced her into the back seat. The chauffeur had opened the door to the dark leather depths of the coachwork. Closing it firmly on them, he receded down the straight, as if making a show of giving them complete privacy.

Jennie was sitting back on the seat. The Duchess had folded down a jump seat so that they could face one another.

"We've just heard. The King is coming back from Scotland tonight."

So what, Jennie thought. But all she said was, "And?"

"Don't suppose you'd know. He only ever went to Scotland two days ago, told the Prime Minister he'd be gone for a fortnight. Now he's coming back, forty-eight hours later. Means something is going to happen. Soon."

"Why are you telling me this, Elizabeth?"

"Because we're worried, the Duke and I, that something terrible is about to happen. Or maybe there is a chance that something wonderful can happen. But only if the right people know what's going on. And you are the only person we thought we could tell who'd get the information to" — she hesitated — "the right people." They both knew whom she meant.

"Very well, what is it?"

Elizabeth took a breath. "The King is in league with the Tories to bring down the government. That's why he's coming back."

"How do you know?"

"I'm in the palace, dear. I can see who's coming and going — Baldwin, Chamberlain, the Conservative front bench, bankers, City people. The Duke travelled up to Scotland with the King. Listened to him all the way up in the train. Called me when they got there. The King thinks we're heading for economic collapse. Said he'll stop at nothing to get Labour out."

"But that would be unconstitutional."

"They're trying to cook up a scheme to dish Labour but keep MacDonald as figurehead prime minister."

"Why would they want to do that?" Jennie wondered aloud.

"Don't you see dear, putting the Tories in but keeping MacDonald as figurehead, they could say it was a Labour PM making all those terrible cuts. The thing they're frightened of is demonstrations, a general strike, a revolution like in Petrograd in '17, chaos."

Jennie was shaking her head. "How can the King do that, keep the Prime Minister and jettison the government?"

Then she recalled Lees-Smith's words 'This time MacDonald will do anything to stay in office.' Could he be induced to betray the cabinet he created, the government he led, the party he'd founded 40 years ago, to do so? *Has he already done so?*

"Has the King been in touch with MacDonald, Elizabeth?"

Elizabeth thought for a moment. "I don't think so, not yet. But the Duke thinks this is Tom Mosley's chance. If they can tempt MacDonald to betray the Labour party and people found out in time, Tom could claim the leadership in one go!"

Suddenly Jennie saw. Her eyes widened. She sucked in a breath.

"He could, couldn't he…if MacDonald were to abandon the party."

"That's why I've come to see you. Someone has got to get him to come back from the South of France. The Duke and I have discussed it. We can't…"

Jennie snapped. "Why not?"

"To begin with, every call in the Palace goes through the switchboard. If one of us made a trunk call, the King's private secretary, Wigram, would know almost instantly." Jennie nodded. "If anyone found out it would be the end of any back channel out of the palace, altogether."

"You're right."

Elizabeth searched her face. "You'll do it?"

Jennie nodded. Then the enormity of what she had just agreed to rose up before her. *You'll have to tell Frank everything. No, you can't.* A tissue of lies stretching back months, it would destroy everything between them. She began to backtrack.

"Look, Elizabeth, how can you be sure? Couldn't it just be talk? Your father-in-law's an old man. He may just be fuming at his impotence."

The Duchess looked at her watch. "Look, I must go. I told them I was going to a dentist." She touched her cheek in mock pain, "Sudden abscess."

Jennie couldn't help laughing. "At this hour?"

"Dentists will do anything for a duchess."

She leaned forward and opened the door, calling to the driver standing twenty feet from the car, "Schaeffer." She got in and looked back at Jennie standing by the car.

"If I learn more, I'll ring you for another talk."

* * *

Now, Jennie had to tell Frank things she'd been withholding for months, things that would make him furious, things that could cost them both their political lives, things that she never wanted to reveal to her lover. Things none of the others who were to return to Frank's flat that morning could know, ever. Where to begin and what exactly to say?

There was no time to change her clothes after all. She found a cab.

"Bedford Square, please."

It should have been a journey of five minutes, but morning traffic was already heavy. It was almost nine when the taxi pulled up at Frank Wise's door.

Frank was already dressed when he answered the doorbell. He looked at her.

"You've not changed."

As he said it his face turned to concern. Something was wrong. He pulled her in and led her to the kitchen, where a small percolator was still bubbling on the stovetop. He drew a chair from the table for her and, without asking, he poured another cup of coffee. As ever he was imperturbable.

"What is it, girl?"

Jennie hadn't been in a hurry to speak, still at a loss for how to begin. There was nothing for it but tell him everything.

"Frank, we've got to talk, now, before the others come." She caught her breath and began. "I've been told that the King and the Tories, and"—she nodded her head towards the square— "the bankers...are going to try to get MacDonald to betray the party."

"What do you mean?" Before she could answer he added in a tone of disbelief, "How do you know?"

"Duchess of York told me not an hour ago."

"Duchess of York?" Eye brows raised, he drew in a breath. "Jennie, you better start at the beginning."

"You'll be furious, Frank. I wanted to tell you everything, but I couldn't...couldn't compromise you."

"Time you started then." The words came out with a distaste in his voice she hadn't expected.

"Very well. You know about my relation with Elizabeth Bowes-Lyons?"

"A little. You knew her in the war, when you were a child?" She nodded. "Go on."

"Well, for the better part of this year I've been her go-between with Tom Mosley, or rather she and I have been links in a chain between her husband, the Duke of York and Mosley."

"Go-between? What exactly have you been doing, Jennie?"

"Carrying packages, mainly. Probably cash, stacks of five-quid notes."

"But that's corruption, Jennie." Then the penny dropped. "It's worse. Its royal interference in politics, choosing sides between parties, favouring politicians. And you made yourself a party to it?"

"Frank, I'm not prepared to defend myself." There wasn't time to argue.

"So, you did nothing but pass on money?"

"No. I listened." She thought for a moment. "She said some shocking things. Swore me to secrecy. Things about the royal family. The King doesn't trust the Prince of Wales or the Duke of Clarence. Said the Prince isn't interested in anything but women...Duke of Clarence is a drug addict and probably a homosexual!"

Frank looked exasperated. "Palace scandal...what's it matter?" There was more impatience in his voice.

"It matters because the King's grooming the Duke of York to succeed him, not the Prince of Wales. Lets the Duke see the boxes."

Frank understood immediately and better than Jennie. "My God! All the state papers, all the cabinet minutes? No one at the palace is authorised to look at that stuff but the King!" Jennie remained silent. "So, the Duke of York knows everything the King knows?"

She nodded. "Probably. But here's the thing. The Duke is no Tory. He and the Duchess seem to be on our side. At any rate they support Tom Mosley's New Party."

"Now, Jennie, tell me again what the Duchess told you this morning, word for word if you can."

"The King told MacDonald he was going to Scotland a few days ago. The King got there and turned round a day later. He's coming back to London. Elizabeth said"—she saw Frank look blank for a moment—"the Duchess of York said the King thinks the country is about to go under and he'll do anything to put a Tory government in."

"Without an election? How?"

"By getting MacDonald to trash his cabinet and switch parties!"

Franks eyes widened. "And MacDonald has agreed?"

"Duchess thinks he doesn't know what's being stitched up between the Palace and the Tories." Frank nodded. "And she said something else, Frank. They both—she and the Duke—- think that the crisis is a chance for Mosley."

Frank thought for a moment. "I see. If MacDonald bolts from the party, Mosley could rally it. It's playing with fire. Still, Mosley might just make a difference."

"But he's in Antibes, the Riviera." She hesitated. "The Duchess asked me to call him. I'm to tell him what's happening and get him to come back."

Frank's look was searching. Jennie could see he wanted to know everything, even if it hurt. "How did you find yourself in this tangle, Jennie?"

She wouldn't, couldn't, tell him what he really wanted to know. *No, Jennie, you must.*

"Tom Mosley knew something, something about me, something I didn't even know. That's what got me into this" — she used Frank's word—"this tangle."

Anger grew in Frank's face. "Are you politely telling me he blackmailed you?"

"No! He convinced me, made me see what I had to do...but I knew I couldn't compromise you, couldn't tell you anything."

But you're not asking what he told me, Frank. She needed Frank to ask. He wouldn't. *He's afraid to know.* Instead, he looked at his watch.

"The others will be getting here any minute."

What hold does he think Mosley has over me? One too intimate, too hurtful for Frank, my lover, to bear? You can't let him suffer. Tell him a truth, a devastating truth, one that spares him, and yourself, from the other truth about you and Mosley. She gulped.

"Somehow he found out that Ramsay MacDonald is my real father...and told me" She stopped to let it sink in. It would be obvious to Frank that Jennie would be ruined if it came out, make her a laughingstock in the House, Typhoid Mary in Scottish politics, end her career. She waited for Frank to speak. He was silent, looking at her in disbelief. She took Frank's hand. Holding it in her lap, she repeated herself, so he'd make no mistake.

"Ramsay MacDonald is my father. My mum confirmed it. That's why I went home. I had to find out."

Frank remained silent. Then the doorbell rang. He rose from the table went to answer it, knowing full well he could say nothing to anyone about what he'd just learned. Jennie moved to the lounge and found an inconspicuous seat. Perhaps the arriving MPs wouldn't notice she was already there, still there, had never left? They'd have the tact not to draw attention to a fact that might embarrass Frank. Nine men trouped into the room and took roughly the places they'd left the night before.

Chapter Twenty-Two

When they were settled, Frank began.

"Look everyone," Frank said to them, "Things seem to have changed since last night." The words secured everyone's attention. "The King is coming back from Scotland this morning. So obviously there's a crisis coming."

More than once voice spoke, "How'd you know, Frank?"

The lie was immediate. "Hack called me this morning from the *Evening Standard*."

This was one of Beaverbrook's papers. It was a plausible lie.

The voices spoke again, competing against one another with questions, guesses, suggestions.

"Perhaps the PM's going to ask for a dissolution."

"An election, now? That's a terrible risk."

"Not if we're really going to do something, the government needs a fresh mandate."

"Has Ramsay Mac suddenly found some guts?"

Frank kept a poker face, though he knew all these responses were terribly wrong. He raised his hands.

"Friends, we've no idea what's going to happen." The others made no reply. "Let's wait another day. Let's meet again tomorrow morning, shall we? Then we can see where we are."

Jennie and Frank could feel the deflation, as their friends' excitement about action, any action, waned. Frank went to the door and the others took the signal, filing out into the square, some going left, others right.

Frank waited till they were well away from the door. He turned back toward Jennie standing at the threshold of the lounge.

He spoke quietly, "I think you should get in touch with Mosley. Tell him to come back."

"Yes. I was going to do that, actually."

She wouldn't tell Frank how, but she'd already decided to go round to Ebury Street and ask to use the instrument there. Mosley's man would know how to reach him, and besides, a trunk call from his flat would not arise suspicion.

* * *

It wasn't difficult to get Mosley to the telephone. The connection across the Channel and down to the Mediterranean was surprisingly clear. The servant passed the instrument to Jennie.

Before she could speak the voice came, "Mosley here."

"Look, Tom, the Duchess asked me to say that you're to come back to England straightaway. Things are afoot politically and there may be an opportunity for you."

"For the New Party?" Mosley sounded hopeful.

"I don't know, maybe for your party, maybe for you to re-join Labour and—"

"Won't do that, Jennie."

"Listen, Tom, to re-join Labour as leader, replace MacDonald, perhaps even succeed him as prime minister."

"What are you saying? Is there really going to be a crack-up straightaway?"

"Looks very much like it. We'll know more in the next twenty-four hours."

"Very well. I'll fly tonight. Be there in the morning."

"Fly? Didn't know you could. Be careful."

Chapter Twenty-Three

It was the very same morning that the King's sleeper pulled into Kings Cross. He'd slept poorly, anxious about the intervention he was now committed to. In all his years as King, since the death of his father Edward VII, in 1911, George had tried to be cautious, correct and disinterested. Even at the worst of the Great War, when the politicians were at each other's throats and ambition regularly overbore the nation's interests, he'd kept aloof. But now he couldn't, wouldn't. Someone had to think of the country first, instead of his own interests. Only he could do that, George knew, just because his interests and the nation's interests were one and the same! All night long on the journey south, he thought back to his cousin, the Tsar, how the socialist revolution had destroyed his country and taken his life in the same paroxysm. He could still remember how innocently it started, the dispatches from the legation at Petrograd, day after day, a drip that became a stream and then a torrent, culminating in the news from Yekaterinburg that Nicky and all his family had been murdered by the Reds—the socialists. He'd been right, he knew, to refuse Cousin Nicky asylum when the Reds offered to send him. They might have been brothers, but George would not allow Nicky's contagion to endanger his crown. Now it was happening again, and to him. *Make no mistake. It's the thin edge of the same wedge.* He said it over and over to himself until he was satisfied that he was convinced. *It jolly well isn't going to happen here.* He was going to take matters into his own hands. *Constitutional niceties be damned!*

Coming down the steps from the sleeper coach he saw his private secretary, Colonel Wigram, waiting a few feet down the quay. George appreciated his sensitivity. *The man just knows instinctually how much space to give his sovereign.*

"Well, Wigram, any news?"

"Prime Minister's duty, sir, and he's coming to see you this morning. Thinks it's the usual weekly audience. I've set an appointment for 10, sir." He paused and took the silence as an invitation to continue. "I've had several calls from people taking soundings — Stanley Baldwin, and Dawson of *The Times* has rung several times. Told me to speak to deputy governor of the Bank of England for an opinion."

"Deputy? Why not Montagu Norman himself?" This was the Governor of the Bank.

"Ah, he's retired ill to Canada for a long rest. Said he couldn't take the strain and left last week."

"Well, what did…"

Wigram supplied the name, "Harvey, the deputy governor."

"Go on man, what did he say?"

Wigram looked up and down the quay. No one was in earshot.

"Actually, he telephoned me before I could ring him. J.P. Morgan wired him from New York, asking whether the cabinet was going to accede to the May Report recommendations. That's why he rang me."

"Well, we may know this morning, eh?" The King almost snorted his irritation. He led the way to the Palace Daimler, ignoring the London policemen saluting as he passed.

* * *

An hour later the King was in a naval uniform waiting in a sitting room from which the dustsheets had been pulled moments before he entered. Wigram knocked and entered, followed by MacDonald, looking almost sheepish, a boy brought before the headmaster for a beating he knew was richly deserved. He bowed and brought the King's right hand to the vicinity of his lips. This sufficed for George V.

Knowing what his Prime Minister was about to tell him, all the King said was, "Well?"

"Your majesty, I regret to report that the cabinet have not yet be able to come to a conclusion about the budget cuts the May Committee has recommended."

"Not yet? What the blazes are you waiting for, man?" Then he calmed down. "Please take a seat, Prime Minister."

MacDonald did so, but not before the King seated himself.

"See here, MacDonald. You're the indispensable man. It's your duty to make your cabinet take the hard decision." He looked for some glint of appreciation in the man's eye, some spark in his doleful countenance. "Only you can bring the country out of this impasse peacefully."

There was only resignation in MacDonald's voice. "But, sir, I can't impose the cuts required without half my cabinet resigning. I'll certainly loose any vote of confidence in the Commons."

The King now responded with almost a flourish, as though he were a magician making a rabbit materialise from nothing.

"Not if the Conservative opposition support you."

MacDonald's eyes widened involuntarily. "Why should Mr Baldwin allow that? If my government falls, there'll be an election and he stands to win."

"We can't afford an election, MacDonald, and we can't risk losing your leadership. I think I can get Mr Baldwin and the rest of the Conservative leadership to agree to that. Perhaps even the sounder Liberals."

"Can you?"

MacDonald was already acquiescing, the King could see. He hadn't immediately said what the King had expected him to say — "You can't do that." But then the King's constitutional breach dawned on MacDonald. "But sir, the sovereign can't discuss government matters with the opposition."

"I can with your knowledge and consent, Prime Minister." The King saw he was winning MacDonald over. "Look, Prime Minister. Go back and try again with your cabinet. Meanwhile, I'll talk to the opposition...with your agreement, of course. Come back and see me tonight."

He rose, signalling the end of the interview.

* * *

When his secretary returned from showing MacDonald out of the private apartments, the King addressed him.

"Wigram, get the Conservative and the reliable Liberal leadership here as soon as you can, but discreetly."

The reliable Liberal leadership of course excluded Lloyd George, the former prime minister, desperate to return to power but beyond the pale of any government with Conservatives in it.

A few hours later, matters had been agreed nicely. Baldwin, the Tory leader, and Herbert Samuel, recognised leader of the "reliable" Liberals, had concurred. If MacDonald couldn't make his socialists see reason, the King would invite him to lead a "National Government" — there was a nice ring to it. The Prime Minister would have "support" from all the Conservative MPs, those Liberals who could be pried away from Lloyd George and such Labour MPs as might follow him. Now, all they had to do was wait for the Labour government to destroy itself. Freed from the socialists, MacDonald would certainly do the right thing!

A good morning's work done, the King invited his son, the Duke of York, to luncheon. He would tell the Duke what had been accomplished. It would be a lesson to him in how the sovereign could make a difference in the country's interests.

* * *

Jennie had been sitting by the telephone all that afternoon and early evening. Frank and Charlie Trevelyan had both been ringing up with developments leaked from the cabinet meetings. Each had a different source, but they were in agreement on the deadlocked discussions. There had been two cabinets already that 23rd of August, and another one expected in the evening. Now, towards 4:30, the instrument jangled again. She lifted it to her mouth.

"Museum 6428."

Instead of Frank or Charlie, it was a woman's voice.

"Meet me at the Kensington Church teashop, soon as you can." The Duchess rang off almost before Jennie had recognised her voice.

Jennie dialled Frank's number and spoke briefly. "I may have some news in a bit. I'm going out now to meet...her."

She didn't want to say the name, as though she feared someone at some switchboard somewhere might be listening.

Jennie heard Frank say, "Very well," and hung up.

Immediately the instrument rang again.

She lifted the received and began to give the number, "Museum..." Before she finished, she heard Tom Mosley's voice.

"I'm back. At Ebury Street."

"Very well...I may have news tonight. I'll ring."

* * *

The Duchess' Daimler was nowhere to be seen as Jennie walked down Kensington Church Street. She'd taken the tube to Notting Hill Gate again—faster than a cab. Entering the shop, she saw Elizabeth at a small corner table, still looking no different from the other young matrons taking tea. This time, she did not rise but beckoned with a gloved hand. Jennie drew out the chair, sat and poured a cup from the china pot at the table, added milk and looked at her friend.

"Tom Mosley is back. He just rang me."

"Good. Look, Jennie, things are moving fast against your people. But Albert thinks there's still a chance for Mosley." Jennie made no reply. "The King's confident he's convinced MacDonald to stay on without Labour. He's arranged matters with Baldwin."

Jennie drew her breath. *This is your father, about to betray everything he had ever stood for. Everything I stand for.*

All she could mutter was, "What?"

"MacDonald's coming back to the palace tonight. The King's to tell him to tender his government's resignation and immediately invite him to form a new cabinet full of Tories and tame Liberals."

Evidently, the Palace's plan was being carried off without a hitch. The working classes would blame the swinging cuts on a Labour prime minister, or at any rate an ex-Labour prime minister. The Tories would have their cuts and not pay a political price. Anger and despondency choked Jennie's voice.

"What can we do about it?"

The question wasn't addressed to Elizabeth Bowes-Lyons, but to Jennie's whole world.

"The Duke says you're to tell Tom Mosley."

Jennie looked at her friend, suddenly realising she was dealing with a complete innocent.

"Is that all? Isn't there a plan? Does anyone have an idea of how to stop this?"

Elizabeth sighed. "Perhaps Tom Mosley'll know what to do."

Jennie looked at her. "Your grace, Mosley commands the loyalty of six MPs, including his wife, Cimmie. What can he possibly do about this?"

Suddenly, she was the Duchess, unwilling to be cross-examined.

"I've no idea, dear. I'm just delivering a message from my husband."

She squeezed Jennie's hand, rose from the table and left.

Jennie remained, finishing her tea and thinking hard. When she tried to pay, the waitress told her it had already been taken care of. Out in the street, she found a cab immediately.

"22 Ebury Street please."

As she sat watching the streets go past, something like a counterattack began to formulate itself in her head.

* * *

Mosley was in the front room when she arrived. He rose from a wingback chair as she entered. Hair oiled, body scented, his double-breasted suit, as ever, tight to his body, a regimental tie at his collar, three points of a kerchief emerging from the coat's pocket. He looked exactly as she'd expected. A cologne had even made him smell attractive. Apparently, he couldn't resist the urge to be seductive, even in a political crisis.

The room was dark but for the lamp above the chair. There was a cigarette burning in an ashtray full of them and a cloud of tobacco hovered below the ceiling. He'd evidently been sitting there for some time, waiting. Stewing? Inaction did not sit well with him.

"At last," were first words he uttered as she entered.

Mosley reached out for her. But Jennie did not approach. She took a seat on the chesterfield opposite. He read her mood and gracefully returned to his chair.

Quickly, Jennie went over the events of the last few days—the telephone calls, the meetings, the conversations with the Duchess. Then she paused to allow him to respond. But he remained silent. Was he thinking things through, Jennie wondered? No. He was at a loss.

"Well, it looks like I've come on a fool's errand. The King has scuppered us, Jennie. Don't see what we can do about all this."

Jennie rose, walked over to the side table and took a cigarette from the box, lit it herself before he could even rise from his chair. She was slightly triumphant, thinking *I know what to do!* The cab ride had been just long enough to think the matter through. It was the only way. But she couldn't do it herself, not the smallest part of it. Mosley couldn't do much of it alone. It would take quick work, several others, and a great deal of persuasion. She had to first persuade Mosley and then Lloyd George. And that would be the easy part.

"Tom, how well do you know Lloyd George? Can you get a meeting with him tonight?"

"I can try." He thought for a moment. "He's almost certainly down in Surrey, at his place in Churt." Lloyd George had lived there since his time as prime minister in the Great War. "I can ring him there."

"How far is Churt?"

"About an hour and a half or so by motor. Tell me what you have in mind, will you? Otherwise I won't know what to say."

"Very well. There's only way to stop this palace coup, and make no mistake, that's what it is. We've got to find a majority in the House to put a stop to MacDonald's betrayal. That means the parliamentary Labour Party and your lot—the New Party MPs— and as many Liberal MPs as Lloyd George can command."

"I see. Yes. Of course."

"But that won't be the hard part. We'll have to get the Speaker to recall parliament. And he's a dyed-in-the-wool Tory."

Mosley understood. "One step at a time." He picked up the receiver. "Operator, trunk call please, to Churt, Mr Lloyd George."

There was a wait and then he was talking again, first to a servant, then evidently to Lloyd George himself. Jennie only heard Mosley's half, but it was obvious the call was not unwelcome. He nodded.

"About an hour and a half. Cheerio."

Jennie wondered, *Do these people really talk like that?* Mosley rose.

"Come along. I've got a fast roadster in the mews."

She followed him into the hall where he reached for two flat caps and handed her one.

"Try it on." Jennie did so. "Looks fetching."

Chapter Twenty-Three

He smiled and led the way towards the back of the flat. Jennie made no reply.

Opening the small car door for Jennie, Mosley swiftly moved round the small, bright-blue car and athletically, even theatrically, hopped into the driver's side. Pushing the choke in and pressing the starter button, he said the wrong thing.

"MG model M — gift of Morris, don't you know."

It only reminded Jennie of the 50,000 pounds the owner of Morris Motors had given Mosley to start his new party in the winter. Money that was evidently gone by the time the palace began using Jennie to fund its by-election campaign. She shivered and Oswald, noticing, put his arm over her shoulders and drew her to his warmth.

Jennie shook her head and moved away. "I'm alright."

Mosley seemed to understand. He reached behind her. "There's a blanket in the boot."

Chapter Twenty-Four

Once they were out of London, the roadster moved at speed and the noise in the open car was too great for conversation. Jennie was glad. She didn't want to make conversation with Mosley and she needed time to think through what she was to say to Lloyd George.

A large and friendly Saint Bernard greeted them at the door when the butler opened it.

"I'm to take you in directly, sir."

He took their flat caps with the ceremony due to opera hats, hanging them at a coat tree. It was near ten in the evening but the old man was still dressed in a light tweed Norfolk jacket, wearing walking boots, muddy enough to signal that, despite his sixty-five years, Lloyd George was still strong and active. It was widely known that he'd been in hospital for some surgery only the week before. His visitors were to understand he was still vigorous.

The accent had remained unashamedly Welsh. "Well, Mosley, you didn't say you'd be bringing anyone with you." He turned to Jennie. "I recognise you, you're MP for…" He thought a moment. "Glasgow East? No. I err…it's North Lanark. Miss Lee, isn't it?"

Jennie couldn't help beaming. "Yes, indeed sir."

"Come sit by me, Miss Lee."

He patted the chesterfield with a grin Jennie recognised as unreservedly lascivious. Lloyd George evidently had no qualms about competing with Mosley for her attentions, as many of them as he could secure. Not for nothing was he called the Old Goat and he was hiding nothing of his reputation. He looked back at Mosley.

"Well, Tom, no beating round the bush. What brings you here?"

Would Mosley cede to Jennie or would he pretend the mission

was his, Jennie wondered. He surprised her.

"Actually David, I'm rather the chauffeur for Miss Lee, who has startling information and, I believe, a proposal."

Now, will the former prime minister listen to a slip of a girl? She cleared her throat and began. "The King has interfered with the constitutional process and convinced MacDonald to do a bunk."

She stopped to gauge the effect. Lloyd George blinked twice, suggesting it was his eyes he didn't believe and not his ears. She rose from the chesterfield, looked down into Lloyd George's quizzical face and went on with heat.

"Tomorrow, he's going to obtain his cabinet's resignations, resign himself and then be asked by the King to form a new government with the Tories and any other rats he can induce to desert Labour. King's organised it with Stanley Baldwin. He's conspired with Liberals too, like Samuel."

Herbert Samuel was officially deputy leader of the Liberal Party. He had been an ally of Lloyd George's before the Great War, but was now on the party's right wing. As she spoke, her anger rose, making Jennie's voice quaver.

"I can see why you'd be angry, Miss Lee. But calm down. Please tell me how you know all this. I don't doubt your word, but your sources will affect how we proceed."

Jennie relaxed slightly and sat down again. *He's going to take me seriously.* She looked towards Mosley, who took her cue.

"Actually David, she had it all from Elizabeth, Duchess of York."

"Anything in writing?"

Was he suspicious, Jennie wondered? Before she could answer, Mosley spoke again.

"Miss Lee has been a regular conduit between me and the palace. She—"

"I don't have any of that in writing," Jennie interrupted.

As much for her own sake, Jennie had to prevent Mosley from saying more about what she'd been doing.

"It all happened today. But I have a file of my own private correspondence with the Duchess that goes back almost fifteen years."

"So, I'm to believe you then." He sighed.

"'Fraid so." She smiled.

"I suppose you've come to me with this information because you want me to do something?"

"Don't you…want to do something?"

Was she really going to have to convince him?

Mosley spoke. "It's the most blatant violation of the constitution in a hundred years. Someone's got to put a stop to it."

"What do you want of me?" There was annoyance on his face. "Am I to tear the mask of disinterested-monarch-above-politics from the King? Not worth it!"

He shook his head emphatically.

Jennie knew what would move him. Power. *Why doesn't Mosley know?*

"No," she said. "That's not it, sir. We want you to take back your place on the government front bench. Regain the premiership."

Lloyd George's eyebrows rose. "How so?"

"The maths is simple, sir." Jennie looked back at Mosley. Couldn't he say anything? "Labour have 280 seats in the house. Tom here has half a dozen in his New Party and still commands a lot of support amongst Labour MPs. You've got fifty-nine Liberals. Add them up and it's a workable majority in the House." She paused for the effect and then drove the argument home. "It's more than enough to enact the policy you and Tom have both been advocating in the Commons for almost two years now."

Lloyd George looked across to Mosley. "Is this girl talking rot, Tom?"

"Don't think so myself, or I wouldn't be here. Look, if you'll throw in with the plan, my people will certainly back it. We've nothing to lose."

Lloyd George was now pulling at his moustache, running his mind over the initial possibilities. "But will Labour stand still for an alliance with me?"

The words brought a surge of relief to Jennie. She'd landed him. Lloyd George was already thinking about things in the first person. She'd baited her hook with power and brought home the big fish.

"They've no alternative." On this matter Jennie felt confident. "Half the cabinet refuse to make any concession to the May Committee and Wall Street. MacDonald will carry no one along with his betrayal, except perhaps Snowden."

Lloyd George interrupted. "It was probably Snowden's gambit to begin with."

Jennie smiled. *Right you are!* "The ILP are against cuts. The Trades Unions have refused to accept them. Bevin hates MacDonald anyway."

Lloyd George snorted. "Nye Bevan, that popinjay upstart? He doesn't carry many people with him."

Jennie expected the mistake. Many made it.

"No, not Nye Bevan, Ernest Bevin—IN, not AN, general secretary of the Transport and General Workers Union. Went along to cabinet yesterday himself to warn them off cutting the unemployment benefit."

Mosley brightened. "How do you know, Jennie?"

"Cabinet leak." Jennie was bluffing, but her political instincts told her it ought to be true.

Lloyd George slapped his two hands on his thighs.

"Very well. We might have a workable majority in the house. But how do we put a stop to MacDonald's plot?"

Jennie added, "And the King's." If her plan was to work, she had to keep focus on the Palace. "Seems to me there's only one chance. And it's very much up to you, sir." She looked at Lloyd

George with all the gravity she could muster. "You've got to go to the Speaker, sir. And demand he recall parliament."

The name came to Lloyd George straightaway. "Captain Fitzroy? That old stick."

Edward Fitzroy had been deputy speaker and then speaker of the House of Commons for a half dozen years. Before that, he'd spent twenty years keeping out of debates on any subject bar agriculture and violence in the Ireland.

"Haven't talked to him for years."

Did she dare tell the former prime minister what to do?

"You must see him and demand parliament be recalled. Tell him that between you, Tom here and Labour, you'll have a majority in the Commons and the right to try to form a government!"

Lloyd George was thinking. "What if MacDonald asks for a dissolution and the King grants it?"

"That's why you have to go to the Speaker tomorrow. Tell him about the King's interference."

Mosley added, "Appeal to his sense of fair play. We've got to be given a chance."

"It's not sport, old man," Lloyd George observed. "But it is an affront to the House. If I know the Speaker, he won't wear it, even if he is an old Tory!" Egoism now took hold of Lloyd George. "Not if I put it to him that way."

"You have another threat, sir." Jennie spoke calmly. "If the King's interference comes out, the monarchy will be undermined badly."

Mosley now added, "The Duke of York will be ruined...the way his wife's been leaking to Jennie here. And with that pathetic Prince of Wales, the King is relying on the Duke. He needs him." Jennie couldn't help smiling. *You're shameless, Mosley. It's you who've put the Duke in this position, by taking his money for your schemes.*

Lloyd George suddenly looked doubtful. "What are you

talking about, Mosley?"

"Tell him the rest, Jennie."

"Very well." She sighed. Then for three minutes she detailed what the Duchess had told her about the King's oldest and youngest sons.

Lloyd George evidently knew nothing of this palace gossip. "You can't expect me to retail all this tittle-tattle to the speaker?"

Mosley spoke. "Not unless you need to. It should be enough for him to know the King is letting someone else look at the boxes. That's breach of trust enough. Just asking Wigram if it's true will get right back to the King."

Jennie was perplexed. "Wigram?"

Lloyd George responded. "King's private secretary. Old school. Would be mortified if it came out about the boxes, dereliction of his duty." He thought for a moment. "Wigram's an old friend of the Speaker...in the Guards together before the Great War. Would make it easier to get the King to climb down if the Speaker can get Wigram on side."

Jennie whispered to herself, *Old boys' club.*

Aloud she said, "Will you approach the Speaker, sir?"

"I bloody well will." Lloyd George rose. "Mine will be the first voice he hears tomorrow morning, bright and early. Hold yourselves in readiness."

It was their signal to leave.

* * *

Captain the Right Honourable Edward Algernon FitzRoy was as old a man as Lloyd George. Thirty years now he'd been a member of the House of Commons, never a minister, almost invisible on the Conservative back benches, absent for years at the front during the Great War. For the last half dozen years, he'd been neutered, first as deputy speaker and now as speaker of the House. FitzRoy preferred to think of himself as permanently aloof from party politics. Others thought that 'aloof' did not describe the man as well as dour, unbending, humourless. All agreed, he was perfect for the Speakership!

Lloyd George was not looking forward to his interview with FitzRoy. There would be no small talk, nothing to warm the chill bounds of formality that had fated FitzRoy to the role of a sterile fixture in Westminster. One could only trade on his loyalty to the House of Commons and the unwritten constitution of the realm.

It had taken Lloyd George but little effort to track the Speaker down that morning. He was in London. Why, Lloyd George wondered, was he there three weeks after the House had risen for the summer? Had he been recalled from his estate in Northamptonshire? A meeting in the Speaker's office in the House was out of the question. Despite the need for discretion, to which the former prime minister had alluded, FitzRoy evidently wouldn't receive him at home. Not a good omen. Instead he suggested Whites in St. James's. When he suggested they meet there, did FitzRoy recall voting against Lloyd George's membership in the club twenty-five years before? The black ball still rankled the former PM.

Lloyd George agreed and motored up to town straight away. It was just before noon when he arrived, but London streets were still somnolent in the summer Monday morning. As the car came round Pall Mall into St James Street, he leaned forward.

"Benson, don't hang about. Come back in an hour."

"Very good, sir."

The car came to a halt, and before the club's footman could come to the kerb, Lloyd George was out and striding into the hall. He looked at the Commissionaire.

"FitzRoy here?"

"Yes sir. He asked I take you in directly. It's just in the back, sir. Very private."

He led his charge through a brace of narrow corridors. This room was very much off the clubman's beaten path. *Just so, won't do for anyone to take notice of this meeting. Or does he not want to be seen with me?* Lloyd George smiled to himself.

The servant knocked twice and withdrew.

At the command, "Come," Lloyd George entered. At the far side of the small room, overlooking a back garden visible through the mullioned window, sat FitzRoy, dressed formally, folding a copy of *The Times*. Looking at the attire, Lloyd George thought, *I'm one down already.* He was dressed in summer weight country tweeds.

They'd known each other slightly for thirty years. For most of those years, Lloyd George had gleamed with a stellar magnitude, while Fitzroy had been burned into a lump of cold charcoal. In the war, FitzRoy had briefly joined a right-wing splinter party in revolt against Lloyd George's coalition. All sides had later pretended it hadn't happened, but probably both of them remembered well enough.

Now, the former prime minister had no very clear idea of exactly how to approach the man. No notion of whether FitzRoy would treat him as a statesman or a blackguard. Lloyd George settled into the chair opposite. Only then, in a moment of reflection, did he decide how to proceed.

"Mister Speaker, I come to you as one privy councillor to another." He tried to gauge the effect. But the other man's face remained immobile. "On a matter of constitutional urgency."

He paused again, hoping for an expression at least of interest. Nothing.

"Today the Prime Minister will ask for his cabinet's resignations, carry them to the King, and be asked by his majesty to form a new government, mainly of members of the current opposition party."

This was FitzRoy's party, of course, and one with a profound distrust of Lloyd George, dating to well before his premiership in the Great War.

"MacDonald will carry no one from his own party with him,

except his chancellor of the exchequer."

"Very well. So, MacDonald is going to change sides. What's it to do with me?"

"The entire business is the result of gross interference in government by the King, conniving together with the opposition. It's unconstitutional. And you are the only one who can put a stop to it." Lloyd George's voice rose at the crescendo of his little speech.

FitzRoy was not moved. He raised his hand. Then in a voice laced with scepticism he asked, "May one know how this intelligence came to you?"

Lloyd George wouldn't lie unless he had to, but he had no compunction about misleading. "From a member of the royal family." The suggestion of direct knowledge was unambiguous.

"Which one, if I may ask? The egregious Prince of Wales retailing titbits to his mistresses?"

"No." He plunged. "From the Duke of York."

Lloyd George could see the other man was now beginning to believe him.

"Supposing I believed you for a moment, sir, what would you have me do?"

"Recall parliament."

"Before the Prime Minister asks me to? Why should I do that?"

"To give the House of Commons an opportunity to repudiate MacDonald's action and show that Liberals and Labour can form a government."

"Why should I lift a finger to let the socialists continue to misgovern?"

FitzRoy had finally shown his political colours. It was what he was waiting for.

"Because it won't be a socialist government. It will be a Lloyd George Oswald Mosley government."

FitzRoy's torso rose in his chair. He drew his hands from

his knees, placed his elbows on the chair arm and brought his fingers together beneath his chin.

After a moment of silence, he asked, "How will that be arranged?"

"Quite simple really. I have fifty-nine MPs. I won't fall in with Labour unless they choose Mosley as leader. And if you recall the Labour Party conference last year, Mosley carried all before him till the block voting. He has the confidence of the parliamentary party. Between us, we'll have a solid majority—340 or so—in the House, even if MacDonald takes a half dozen MPs with him."

There was sarcasm in FitzRoy's voice as he replied, "So, I am to be a stalwart of democracy, recalling parliament to frustrate the machinations of the King?" He shook his head. "You can't expect me to embarrass the monarch."

"Wrong end of the stick, Mr Speaker." Lloyd George smiled slightly. "If you act, it needn't come out that King George interfered." Was the threat of the public disclosure enough to seal FitzRoy's agreement? "The King will be grateful to you for protecting the crown."

Lloyd George rose from his chair with the hope that FitzRoy would see where his interests lay.

Chapter Twenty-Five

The Right Honourable Edward Algernon FitzRoy, speaker of the House of Commons, secured his immortality in British political history the next day. The early editions of the London papers had reported the Prime Minister's interview at Buckingham Palace on the previous evening, the 24th of August. The King had accepted MacDonald's resignation and that of all his ministers. He had then graciously invited MacDonald to remain as prime minister, forming a National Government of all parties to deal with the economic crisis.

Reading the papers, FitzRoy saw that Lloyd George had been right.

Arriving at the House of Commons, FitzRoy summoned his clerks and ordered the immediate recall of parliament. Then, without further explanation, he left the palace of Westminster and was not to be heard from again for the following seventy-two hours. The next time he was to be seen in public, it was alighting from a train at King's Cross and hailing a cab to take him to the House for the parliamentary sitting he had ordered.

The recall of parliament had thrown the entire political world into confusion. MacDonald had been trying to form a "National" ministry with the Tory leader, Baldwin; Samuel, the tame Liberal; and Snowden, his Chancellor of the Exchequer. The King had been about to return to Scotland. The Labour Party leaders, out of office only for a day, still in London and reeling from MacDonald's betrayal, met at party headquarters. They seethed at their former leader but had no idea of how to proceed. Only Lloyd George knew what he was about. By the late afternoon of the day before parliament was to be recalled, he'd convened a closed-door meeting of the Liberal parliamentary party. Only one or two, hoping for seats in MacDonald's National Government, had refused to attend.

"Gentlemen, tomorrow in the House, I will propose a want of confidence in MacDonald's new cabinet." Voices were raised. "Yes, yes, I know we have no idea now who will be in it. But we know its policy well enough—retrenchment in government, cuts to the unemployment benefit, and preservation of the gold standard." His caucus quieted down and Lloyd George continued. "When I make this motion, Labour will join us and we'll defeat the MacDonald government even before it is fully formed."

Here a voice emerged from the men seated before Lloyd George.

"If he's defeated, he'll just get a dissolution from the King. There'll be an election..."

Lloyd George raised both his hands and successfully quieted the group.

"No. There won't be a dissolution or an election."

He couldn't tell them he had the Speaker in his pocket, but he knew FitzRoy would not ask the King to dissolve parliament, no matter MacDonald's demands. He'd already burned his bridges recalling the House.

"Gentlemen, parliament won't be dissolved for two reasons. First, the crisis is too grave. The nation can't afford six weeks of electioneering and indecision. Second, we will have a workable majority in the present House of Commons."

The chatter in the room had by now subsided. By what magic had Lloyd George contrived a governing majority out of fifty-nine seats?

"We shall form a government with Labour, supported by upwards of 340 members. And it will carry out our policy, not a socialist one! But I need your complete assent. We hold the balance but only if we are united."

* * *

Two hours later, the House of Commons convened. MacDonald was still sitting on the front bench, deserted by his former Labour ministers, flanked by Baldwin, Neville Chamberlain, and one Liberal, Herbert Samuel; rather what Lloyd George expected. Oddly enough, the Labour MPs were still ranged behind MacDonald in the seats they'd occupied for the better part of two years. The level of chatter rose as members filled the chamber, speaking to one another of their complete perplexity.

At the appointed hour, the Speaker gavelled order and MacDonald rose, expecting to be recognised. Instead the Speaker nodded towards Lloyd George already standing.

"Mr Speaker, I beg to move that this house has no confidence in any government led by the right honourable member for Seaham."

This, all knew, was MacDonald's constituency near Manchester. The hush in the chamber ended in an explosion of shouting by Labour members from behind MacDonald, as order papers were thrown into the air and began to drift downwards over his front bench.

Jennie was sitting on the rear most bank of benches, with Frank to her right and Ellen Wilkinson to her left. They had come along with only slightly more knowledge than most others of what might transpire. Now, they were to witness the rarest of events in the House of Commons—debate on a motion of no confidence. It was one they thought might last days, depending on the members' urge to speak. In the event it was over in a day. By midnight the House had divided and Ramsay MacDonald's betrayal had failed.

Three speeches Jennie remembered afterwards, each significant in a different way. To begin with, there was MacDonald's catastrophic attempt to save his new ministry. He stood and was recognised by the Speaker first. Realising the votes he needed were behind him on the Labour benches, he turned from the dispatch box, and pled his case, clothing an appeal for loyalty and trust in his personal history of fidelity to Labour. There was enough nostalgia in the parliamentary party at least to listen for a while in silence. And for once the Tories opposite were not interjecting with cruel japes at the stooped, weary and pathetic figure whose back was turned to them. But then, he began to explain that the bankers on Wall Street had given him no choice, that J.P. Morgan himself had been on a transatlantic radiotelephone to explain that without the cuts demanded by the May Commission the pound would collapse.

Jennie turned to Ellen. "He's lost all touch if he thinks Labour MPs will want to please the House of Morgan."

As she said it, the first cry of "Shame!" rose from Labour, in a strong Welsh. Was it Nye Bevan? And then interruptions of "No surrender to the bankers!" interspersed with FitzRoy's voice shouting "Order!" as he gavelled the arm of his chair that rose high up between the two sides of the chamber. But MacDonald had lost the House. There were shouts of "Miners first, Morgan later." Even some Conservative backbenchers began to join in the jeering.

Late in the afternoon, Frank rose to speak. No one who had spoken before him had his grasp on finance and economics. No one who spoke after him could refute his arguments or match his mastery of detail. In that single speech, Frank Wise made himself the Chancellor of the Exchequer in the government Lloyd George and Tom Mosley were to form. He began quietly and calmly, in a tone that suggested understanding and sympathy for the government's predicament: the budget deficit, the level of unemployment, the deflation that was wrecking business and work. Then he came to the gold standard. Once or twice Frank looked towards the gallery above the House. Jennie followed his gaze till it reached Maynard Keynes, the Liberal economist, wearing a Cheshire cat's grin. Having brought the whole house with him in his exposition of how the gold standard was supposed to work, Frank now reflected on the history of its failure since Churchill had brought it in, and then demonstrated the irrelevance of the 19th century economist's theory of the gold standard to the economic reality of the 20th century. It was as if the whole House of Commons were a set of university students, held wrapped by a brilliant lecturer. Finally, Frank took the House through a tour of the policies offered over the last years by Lloyd George for the Liberals and by Mosley when he had been a Labour minister, showing how they responded to the realities the country actually faced. He sat down to cheering and shouts of "Hear him! Hear him!" from the Liberals and some Tories as well.

The Labour members were largely silent, until one among them shouted the demand: "Answer, Snowden. Answer!" Twice Chancellor in Labour governments, still sitting beside MacDonald on the front bench, the man had no choice but to rise. He knew that the fate he shared with MacDonald was at stake. Everyone else in the House knew it too.

Unused to contradiction of his expertise on so many different fronts, Snowden looked down at a scrap of paper on which he had made a few notes. Evidently, he couldn't decide which of them to put first, or to put at all for that matter. All he could say in the end was that everything he had done was in accord with sound principles of public finance and orthodox economics, what was required to ensure confidence. The interruptions began: "Whose confidence, the House of Morgan's?" and they did not cease until Snowden sat down, recognising his defeat.

Late in the evening, with few members still rising to seek the notice of the chair, Mosley rose dramatically from his seat. He stood still and made no gesture, waiting as others became still, took their seats, and looked towards him. Only when he knew he had the attention of the whole house did he raise his hand to seek the notice of the Speaker. The speech he then gave hardly addressed the motion of no confidence. By that time of night, its passage was a foregone conclusion. Every Liberal who had spoken supported Lloyd George's motion, no Labour member had spoken for MacDonald, and the handful of Tories who intervened mocked their leaders for seeking shelter behind a broken leader of the party they had long opposed. Even if the whips could impose their discipline, every nose-counter came up with the same figures. The motion would carry by at least twenty votes, perhaps double that. It was no surprise then, that Mosley would use the last moments before the division to claim the leadership of a revolution that was sweeping away the old order.

He began by announcing that the New Party would vote for the motion of no confidence and would then dissolve. He would seek readmission to Labour and urge all his followers to do likewise. He went on to reiterate the programme of public works spending, job creation, and economic planning that he had advocated, first in MacDonald's cabinet, again in his resignation speech, and for a third time at the party conference of 1930. Mosley went on to generously credit the same policy to Lloyd George and to offer his personal support for any government in which the wartime prime minister might now be persuaded to join. It was, Jennie thought, a clever way to signal to those who feared socialism. Lloyd George was no socialist, alas. But then Mosley launched into a peroration that people would quote for a year:

Better the great adventure, better the great attempt for Britain's sake, better a great experiment in strong leadership than strutting and posturing on the stage of little England, amid the scenery of decadence, until history, in turning over a heroic page of the human story, writes the contemptuous postscript: 'These were the men to whom was entrusted the Empire of Great Britain, and whose selfishness, ignorance and cowardice left it a Spain.' We shall win or we shall return upon our shields.

Lloyd George rose, and with evident confidence demanded the vote: "I beg leave to move the previous question."

The Speaker called upon the House to divide, yeas to his left, nays to his right, assigned the tellers and left the chair. It was soon obvious that the motion would carry.

Sitting there, high up in the chamber, back against the wall, as distant from the front bench as one could be, Jennie Lee looked to her right and her left. No one had turned in her direction. No one in the maelstrom of a parliamentary division was paying Jennie the slightest attention. But she had been the Scottish Valkyrie, had chosen her victim and killed him off. *That he was your father, well, that didn't matter...or rather, it did. It turned vindication into revenge.* Jennie rose from her seat, and moved down the steps to the lobbies where she would add her vote to end MacDonald's political life. *You can revel in it all, but you can't reveal any of it.* It didn't matter. It was enough.

* * *

Jennie, Nye Bevan, Ellen, and a dozen other ILP members, including Frank, were seated on chesterfields and wingchairs pulled together round a low table in the Smoking Room of the House. They were speculating on the shape of the next government, waiting for the Speaker to recall the members and announce the vote. Then, a commissionaire approached and whispered in Frank's ear. He rose and excused himself.

"I'm called to a meeting with Lloyd George, Mosley, Henderson and the Speaker."

Arthur Henderson had been foreign secretary in MacDonald's government and had led opposition to the cuts in the cabinet. He was as old as Lloyd George and had been interim Labour Party leader twice before, in a period that went back to before the Great War. All assumed he would again become interim leader.

Forty minutes later, Frank returned, looking a bit dazed. He sat and all fell silent, waiting for his news.

"The Speaker's told MacDonald he'll advise the King to deny any request for a dissolution."

"Didn't realise he'd be on our side." It was Nye Bevan who spoke words others were thinking. No one noticed Jennie's smile.

Frank continued. "Says he'll tell the King there's a working majority and it should be given a chance to form a government. Pretty confident he'll get the King to agree."

"With Henderson as prime minister?" The natural assumption was voiced by Ellen Wilkinson. Everyone knew Labour had almost five times the number of seats Liberals held.

"Don't think so. Lloyd George said unless he gets the premiership, he won't let his people support the government."

They spoke at once. "The old devil! Rank opportunism." "He expects to govern?" "How many seats in the cabinet does he want?"

Frank answered the last question to everyone's surprise. "He wants only one seat in the cabinet for his party."

"One seat, at the head of the table, eh? Clever."

Frank added, "And Mosley agreed to it, at least until he's elected leader of the Labour Party."

"We can probably sit still for Lloyd George that long." It was Jennie who gave voice to the reasonable view. "Why did they ask you to meet with them, Frank?"

He drew a breath, smiled sheepishly and spoke in a quiet voice. "They want me to be Chancellor." The others rose to clap him on the shoulder, but not before each emitted an audible expression of joy.

Chapter Twenty-Six

Once he was appointed, it was almost a month before Jennie and Frank could spend a night together. Their first weekend alone in Jennie's flat was a languorous passage of mornings and afternoons in bed, punctuated only by forays out for the morning and evening papers. Repeatedly, at moments of passion, some thought would remind one or the other of an event or an exchange, a conversation, a development in Whitehall or Westminster. And then they would both be deliciously distracted from their passions, recalling reactions, opinions, speculations, assessments pent up over a month of enforced separation.

* * *

It had been weeks of frenetic activity in government, in politics and the economy. There was a lot in the papers, but Jennie learned most of it from brief encounters with Frank. She knew the King had, with great reluctance, given in to admonitions, bordering on blackmail, that he accede to the Speaker's advice. He didn't much like Lloyd George, but the prospect of a brief premiership and the chance to appoint Mosley as his successor was, as he said to Wigram, his secretary, "not unattractive."

Lloyd George had been received, kissed hands, and formed a cabinet composed mostly of members of MacDonald's Labour cabinet, save for Snowden and Thompson, who had both abjured the party along with MacDonald. Lloyd George's Liberal colleagues were pleased not to have to risk their political lives in the experiment that was now to be conducted. The Labour cabinet ministers were glad enough of places in government both to fall in with Lloyd George's policies and to demand the loyalty of their Labour Party colleagues.

The parliamentary Labour Party had met on the morning

after the vote of no confidence, and, by acclamation, elected Sir Oswald Mosley its leader. Lloyd George had immediately made him leader of the House and Lord President of the Council, a seat in the cabinet with no department reporting to him. But Lloyd George had also invented a new position—deputy prime minister—to which he appointed Mosley, giving him space in the Cabinet Office round the corner from Downing Street. The symbolism was clear to all. Mosley was to be as close to prime minster as one could get.

Much of the press's attention had fallen on the previously little known MP, Frank Wise, who had shown such mastery of the economy in the want-of-confidence debate that destroyed MacDonald's hopes. Now, as Chancellor of the Exchequer, Frank's first act had been to take the country off the gold standard. And the sky had not fallen. In fact, after falling enough to make British coal suddenly competitive again, the pound had stabilised at a level that required no intervention by the Bank of England. Economists couldn't understand it, but they couldn't deny it. Badgered by the press about the May Report, he had wisely said nothing, leaving parliamentary sketch writers to speculate about the new government's policies.

Ministries continued to tick over, but almost everything that went on at Number 10 involved planning a vast programme of public works, especially road maintenance and widening, targeted to cities, towns and regions with the highest levels of unemployment. The Tory press complained that these were regions in which better roads were not needed as nothing was moving on the current roads. But the Prime Minister told planners to ignore such complaints. "We'll bring traffic back to those places by paying the road builders." Lloyd George's pet economist, Keynes, was now spending so much time at Number 10 that Frank offered him a guest room next door, in the Chancellor's flat at Number 11. Frank had no wish to live there at all, for reasons that were clear to Jennie and no one else.

He could never be with her at all if he had to live at Number 11. Keynes' main function was to advise the Treasury on how to fund its radical departure from economic orthodoxy. Taxation and inflation were the order of the day. It would be months before anyone could tell whether the plan was working, but with no better place to keep their money, the rich had not yet deserted. Meanwhile cuts in the dole, unemployment insurance and pay for teachers, sailors and the police were off the table.

For all his visibility in government, Mosley was not to be found in cabinet meetings, on the floor of the Commons, or even in the smoking rooms of the House. He had presented Frank with copies of the previous Spring's *Mosley Manifesto* and said he'd support anything consistent with it. Then he left London. All that first month in office, Mosley swept up and down the country, giving fiery addresses to large meetings, promising swift action, taking hold of the Labour Party and putting his stamp upon it, making fun of Tory resistance and Liberal qualms.

The large public meetings were marred only by clashes between Mosley's supporters and Communists, of whom the slump had created large numbers. Now, their numbers falling and in fear of a government that might rob them of the discontent fuelling their movement, the party needed to provoke a quarrel.

* * *

It wasn't until Sunday afternoon of that first weekend they'd managed to share that Frank and Jennie found themselves in disagreement, exchanging cross looks and sharp words. The subject was Mosley's national speaking tour, or perhaps it was a pretext.

Sitting side by side in bed, neither dressed at all, they were surrounded by the Sunday papers. Jennie had been reading *The Times'* report on Mosley's meeting in Leeds. She put the paper before Frank.

Chapter Twenty-Six

"Still worried about Mosley?"

Her tone suggested there was no reason for disquiet, that Frank's former anxieties about him had been wrong.

"His crowds are huge. He's going to win the next election for us."

Frank looked up from his paper. "Yes, he's quite the demagogue."

"Demagogue? I'd call him a real leader. Someone we desperately need after ten years of Stanley Baldwin and Ramsay MacDonald."

"I grant you his magnetism."

Jennie searched for innuendo in his voice. Was it there? *Is he making an observation of Mosley's effect on the electorate, or on me?* They'd never actually allowed themselves to admit shared knowledge of her 'infidelity' with Mosley. What had never been explicitly admitted, they could both pretend never happened at all. Frank knew he had no right to demand an account from Jennie. He couldn't even call what she had done 'infidelity.' She was unable to think of these few couplings as betrayals of her love for Frank. But she knew that, as a man, Frank couldn't really ever shake himself free from sexual jealousy. It was a difference, a barrier between men and women Jennie thought unbridgeable. The frank truth about what Mosley meant to her should have allayed all Frank's fears, but in fact would simply inflame them. She knew exactly how she felt about Mosley, and she could still call up the feeling. Remarkable how she could dredge the body's sensations from unknown depths of memory, even now, months since she'd had anything to do with him that way. It had been a pure, thoughtless, fleeting, hedonic oblivion, nothing to do with what was really important to her—the fulfilment she felt being with Frank. And yet telling Frank any of that was impossible. He wouldn't be able to understand that these pleasures came unaccompanied by any enduring feelings, commitments, loyalties, anything he should be jealous of. She would treat Frank's remark as political, not personal.

"Doesn't the country need his magnetism? Don't we need to feel that something is being done?"

He frowned. "I suppose so. I'm frightened of what will happen when he tires of the adulation and begins to involve himself in governing."

"What do you mean?"

"I've said it before. Mosley thinks parliamentary democracy is inefficient. Produces nothing but half measures. He'll lose all patience once he begins seeing the way government really works. Then he'll try to use his support to cut through the compromise, the horse trading."

"Nothing wrong with that, is there? We've seen enough pointless parliamentary wrangling for ourselves, haven't we?"

"Still don't get it, do you? You've ditched MacDonald and you're going to end up with Mussolini, or worse, that German demagogue, Hitler!"

Jennie rose from the bed in dudgeon. She stood before him, nude, hands on her hips, her voice quavering.

"Look, I ditched MacDonald and he was my own father. If Oswald Mosley looks to turn into Benito Mussolini, I'll do no less."

Frank was silent for a moment. He had worked hard to supress the knowledge, to unknow what Jennie had told him about her and MacDonald that morning six weeks earlier, just before the upheaval. He'd nearly succeeded in forgetting. But now, she was making him face it again.

Suddenly feeling naked, Jennie reached for a dressing gown.

"I wish I didn't know. If only Mosley hadn't told me. Either I should have been told before I chose a political life or never have been told at all. Now I've got to live with this fact."

Frank couldn't remember ever having seen Jennie cry. He was about to. Rising from the bed, he slipped into his dressing gown and sought to bring Jennie to him. She resisted, then moved away. He watched her now, seeking a look, a mannerism, a movement, something that would make Jennie the daughter of Ramsay MacDonald. There was none. She came back to the bed, and they both sat down on its edge.

"He was a hero in my family once. But for years now he's just seemed like an unctuous old sell-out." Frank let her go on. "Then to discover the pathetic old man envenoming me was my own flesh and blood...well, it's made me feel even more poisonous, I'm afraid." She shivered and he wrapped an arm round her. "Frank, the worst of it is that every time I try to put the pieces together it looks horribly like a conspiracy of MacDonald and my parents. As though I was some political creation, not their child at all."

She could see Frank wanted an explanation, but he wasn't going to demand one. She led him through the reasoning that had preoccupied her now for months. At each link he nodded.

When she finished, Frank spoke quietly. "And so you paid him off, well and truly. You destroyed him, Jennie, and a good job too."

Only a handful of people knew Jennie's catalytic role in 'the coup,' as they called the events that brought MacDonald down and Lloyd George and Mosley to power.

"Doesn't make me happy, Frank. Not now it's done. I can't help thinking the cold dish of revenge isn't to my taste." She looked at him. "I want to feel that I did it for the right reasons, not because he..." She couldn't find the words to finish her sentence.

Suddenly Frank was troubled. "Jennie, you never needed to know about all this, about MacDonald and your parents. Why ever did Mosley tell you?"

Jennie was past protecting herself or anyone else. She needed to answer, to tell Frank everything now. She wanted his absolution.

"Mosley knew about my friendship with the Duchess of York.

He wanted me to be his conduit to the palace. I suspect he told me because he rather thought it would induce me to go along. I was reluctant."

Frank let out a low whistle. "Are you saying he blackmailed you...if it had come out, the truth might not have ruined MacDonald. Certain would have wrecked your political life."

"Not exactly, Frank. It wasn't a *quid pro quo*."

"But he would have used it against you, if you hadn't agreed to help him. You mustn't trust him, Jennie, in private affairs or public matters. He's no honour. There are no limits to the means he'll help himself to."

Jennie frowned. "Double standard, Frank?" She went on: "It's alright for you to serve in cabinet with him. But I'm not to trust him?"

"Perhaps neither of us had much choice. But we're riding the tiger, that's for certain."

Jennie had the last word. "And so far it's headed in the right direction."

Chapter Twenty-Seven

Unlike Frank Wise, Jennie's political twin, Aneurin Bevan had no qualms and only enthusiasm for Tom Mosley. Like Jennie, he was both too young and too unreliable to be even contemplated as cabinet material. So he found himself spending long afternoons and evenings on the backbenches, where he would always contrive to be sitting as close to Jennie as possible. When she rose for refreshment, a smoke or a breath of air along the terrace of the House, he was usually to be found doing the same, trying hard not to look too much like a loyal canine. He knew about Jennie and Frank, had reconciled himself to their abiding relationship, but never stopped making clear to her that he remained available. More than once, he reminded her of his reply when she had remarked they might as well be brother and sister: "Yes, with a tendency to incest." Jennie showed him she was flattered by his attentions, even tempted. Besides, she liked Nye Bevan as a great friend, a political fellow traveller, and the only real *bon vivant* in her life. But Nye knew nothing of Jennie's role in the coup, nor how exactly it had happened. Those few who did know worried that Nye might be tempted to leak the details to his pal Beaverbrook. From him it would get to *The Daily Express*, for certain.

Jennie and Nye were standing together on the terrace on a November evening, almost three months after 'the coup.' Neither was wearing a coat, letting the wind off the river clear the cobwebs of a long sitting. There was no river traffic, not even a coal barge. Behind the bare trees on the embankment opposite, the long ribbon of the St Thomas hospital buildings was dark.

"I've been invited to speak at one of Tom Mosley's rallies, in East Hull, next week. Want to come?" Nye smiled conspiratorially.

Jennie chortled. "Actually, they invited you because I turned them down."

It would be another rare weekend escape for Frank from the Treasury and from his wife.

Jennie wondered aloud. "Hull's a fairly safe seat. Why's Mosley speaking there?"

"Now he's party leader, he's cleaning out the stables, Jennie. Sitting MP, Kenworthy, he's not reliable. Was anti-Lloyd George when he was a Liberal."

"That doesn't make him unreliable now, does it?"

"Mosley's trying to bring some discipline to the party, purge the wayward nonconformists. Seems like a good idea."

"I don't much like it, Nye. If our party had demanded ideological conformity, you and I would never have been allowed to stand for parliament."

"It's different times, Jennie. If we're going to succeed, we'll have to sing from one hymnal."

"Conducted by one choir master?" She recalled Frank's worries about Mosley. "You're frightening me rather, Nye."

Bevan didn't respond. He must have been thinking of something quite different. Flicking his fag into the Thames, he turned to Jennie and smiled.

"There isn't going to be a vote on anything important tonight. Let's play truant. I'll buy you dinner at the Café Royale."

"You can't afford it!"

"I'm a Bollinger Bolshevik, my dear...we'll just forget we didn't pay the bill."

Jennie shrugged. "Very well, I'll let you steal me dinner."

* * *

They were settled into a red-plush semi-circular booth at the Café Royale. Nye was nodding in a friendly way at too many of the other diners for Jennie's comfort. She made a show of putting the menu up to hide her face.

"Don't worry, Jennie. People here are discreet."

"How can you be sure?"

"I come with a different woman every night and so far there's been nothing in the scandal sheets." He began to scrutinise the wine list.

"Every night and they still let you walk out on the bill?"

"I usually send it to Lord Beaverbrook...and he always pays!" Nye smiled and Jennie couldn't decide it he was serious or not.

He put down the wine list and reached for Jennie's hand. He did not hold it but only squeezed it in a decidedly fraternal manner.

"How are things...with Frank?"

Suddenly she felt a rush of gratitude towards Nye.

"Thanks for asking."

The need to tell someone had been weighing for days, weeks now. He waited.

"You know the saying, 'Be careful what you wish for.' Everything's going swimmingly."

"Swimmingly? Is that political or personal?"

For Nye, the past three months in the House had been pure fun, watching Tom Mosley, and Frank Wise for that matter, standing at the dispatch box making fools of old men like Churchill, Neville Chamberlain and Stanley Baldwin. No one even bothered to jape at MacDonald, shunted off to a corner of the opposition bench with his son, almost the only Labour MP besides Snowden who had followed him out of the party. One look at Jennie and he knew it hadn't been quite the same for her.

"I'm miserably lonely." She looked forlorn. "I never see Frank anymore, that's the problem."

"Has his wife twigged?"

"Long ago now. But that's not the problem anymore. Once he became Chancellor of the Exchequer, she turned a blind eye altogether."

"Any idea why?" Nye was surprised.

"I don't know. Perhaps she wants this government to succeed.

A scandal would harm it."

"So, she's happy to be the wife of the Chancellor of the Exchequer, to be taken up by the cabinet wives club as a very senior member."

"That's not Dorothy Wise, Nye. It's not like that at all. She's more of a bluestocking. I think she believes in what her husband is doing and she's decided she doesn't mind about me. You know, women aren't driven by jealousy about sex like you men."

"Well, I'm jealous of you and Frank."

"No, Nye, you're envious. But you shouldn't be. We haven't seen each other, Frank and me, for a month now. He's too bloody busy with government. That's why I'm miserable. I'm pretty sure he's miserable too. That's my consolation."

Nye pushed a menu towards her. "Let's order. And if you're still miserable after dinner we can try to do something about that."

Instead of a kick under the table he won a sly smile from her. "And I'll explain the difference between jealousy and envy."

* * *

Jennie spent much of that winter with Nye, and also with Ellen Wilkinson, along with other members of the parliamentary Labour Party who were not in the cabinet. There was much opportunity for talk, for writing and reading articles for the left-wing rags, but also for meals and pints during long sittings of the House. And between Jennie and Nye there was even a little time for the distractions of the flesh. It wasn't as electric for her as being with Tom Mosley, and it lacked the emotional intensity, security and refreshment of making love with Frank, falling asleep with him, waking up with him. Still, she needed the attention and the release an afternoon or evening with Nye provided.

Too often, when she and Frank were able to meet it was

in some public place—the smoking rooms of the House or a Labour Party function. Always, there were others with them, or arriving to interrupt them. Once, he complained that he had not had a home cooked meal in a fortnight, and that had been 'tea' prepared by the wife of a senior civil servant while they worked.

It was only just after the New Year, in January of 1932, that Frank and Jennie were able to share a weekend together. Frank had asked to hide out from reporters, civil servants and cabinet colleagues at Jennie's flat on Guilford Street. He was holding two red boxes, with a third under his right arm, when he came in. Jennie took one at the door and led him into the sitting room.

She closed and locked the door, leaned back against it and let her eyes drink in his presence. For his part, Frank lowered the two cases to the floor, turned slowly and smiled shyly, like a truant. Then, without a word they came together in the middle of the room, disrobing one another. The flat was cold, but they didn't notice. Both had been heavily dressed: Frank against the elements, Jennie to save on coal in the flat. By mutual agreement, the process of undressing each other had begun at speed, but slowed down as the final layers were removed.

An hour later, Jennie was back in the lounge rustling up two whiskey and sodas, when her eyes fell upon the boxes again. She returned to the bedroom with the drinks and stood before the bed. "Those damn boxes. You brought work, didn't you?"

"Got to." Frank frowned. "Have to start writing the budget speech...Worse news." He paused. Jennie put down the glasses and reached for the bedstead, bracing herself. "I suspect this is the last weekend we'll have together for months."

"Months? How can that be?" The distress twisted her face.

"Mosley wants an election...to break up the government, make himself prime minister. He's going to use the budget to break up the coalition."

Jennie repeated his words with invective. "He's going to use the budget? You're Chancellor, not Tom Mosley! It's your budget."

"Don't fool yourself. He's leader of the party. I couldn't stop him even if I want to."

"Do you? Want to stop him?"

"No, not yet anyway. We've agreed a budget, Mosley and I have." He sighed slightly. "Pillow talk, Jennie?"

She knew what the interrogative tone meant. He would divulge cabinet discussion if she promised secrecy. So far, she had been as good as her word.

He spoke two words. "Tariff reform."

Jennie threw the words back in mockery. "Tariff reform? Who the blazes cares about tariff reform when there are two millions unemployed?"

"Lloyd George does. His party does." Frank looked at Jennie, hard. "Don't you see? It will force Lloyd George's resignation, as PM. He'll pull his sixty members out of the coalition. There'll be an election, one we can win outright."

"Over tariffs? They'll withdraw over import duties?"

"Free trade's been a fixed point for Liberals almost for a hundred years, Jennie. They'll never give it up." He stopped, evidently deciding whether to divulge more. "And it's not just tariffs Mosley wants. It's 'Imperial Preference,' free trade with the White dominions—Canada, Australia, New Zealand, South Africa. Tariff wall against everyone else—Europe, the USA."

"I still don't understand, Frank. What's so radical about… what did you call it, Imperial Preference?"

"It's Mosley's idea, actually. Steal a plank from Tory policy. Up the empire and all that. Wrap Labour in the Union Jack. Get Beaverbrook's papers to our side…"

Jennie understood well enough. "Why should the Tories hoover up all the patriotic vote, eh?"

"His very words." Was there a hint of suspicion in his words? Always Jennie listened for the hint of suspicion.

Jennie smiled. "Just a coincidence." She leaned against him

suggestively.

Frank put his arm round her. "So, yes. This election means we probably won't have another day together for months."

* * *

Frank was right, but things moved so fast they were almost too busy to notice how little time they had together.

* * *

A week later, Frank made his budget speech, weathering the attacks by Churchill and Snowden as previous chancellors. But then he had to listen while Lloyd George withdrew his sixty MPs from the coalition, with a tirade about the sanctity of free trade. Mosley followed as leader of Labour, with a speech that began soberly but ended in a fusillade, delivered with such venomous effectiveness it had Labour members cheering for a combination of socialism and nationalism never before heard in the House of Commons. The party had found its firebrand.

Amidst the cheering, Frank turned from front bench and scowled up at Jennie sitting as far behind the front benches as she could. His look spoke clearly. "You see the risk..."

Sitting well back in the chamber, Jennie noticed. But like others she'd surrendered to the emotions Mosley was creating on his side. She revelled in the shocked, indeed cowed faces opposite on the Conservative benches. *We're going to win this election*, suddenly she was sure.

* * *

The next day, parliament was dissolved, and the election campaign of 1932 commenced. As in 1929, Jennie was in demand as a speaker across the Labour seats of Scotland and the border constituencies. Meanwhile, Frank was the party's sober statesman in the Home Counties round the capital.

But, eclipsing them and all other speakers across the political firmament, Mosley swept like a shooting star, tracing a fiery path from one constituency to another. He spoke everywhere with an incandescent combination of anger against the old order, Conservative, Liberal and Labour; an order that had been completely ineffective against the decade-long labour slump. He combined the attack with a word picture of Britain's Imperial future, binding its white dominions closer together, all protected from the rest of the world by a high tariff wall that guaranteed a job to every Briton who wanted to work. But the perorations of Mosley's addresses were a series of threats against those who were not with him and his people in this crusade. These, the enemies of Britain, would themselves suffer for the suffering they had long imposed. At first, Mosley focused on finance capitalism, Wall Street, the City; those who had slaved Britain to the gold standard. But then, seeing how accusations of conspiracy stirred his listeners, he sought other enemies.

Jennie followed the reports of his meetings, digesting the transcripts of the speeches, even as she crisscrossed the narrow waist between lowland Scotland down to the Ridings of Yorkshire, speaking at colliery pits and union halls. She searched for reports of other Labour speakers, especially Frank and Nye. But all were invisible in Mosley's penumbra. Jennie was eager to draw her themes from her leader. She understood that inflammatory rhetoric would catch fire, and that it might even burn some.

Others were reading Mosley's speeches too, especially those who in the last year of MacDonald's reign had joined the Communist Party out of anger and desperation. Now, a few were at Jennie's events, always holding signs and placards, that began at the rear of the crowds but moved forward as her speeches reached climax, challenging her control of the meetings. Their signs and their interruptions condemned the Labour Party's new leader as a Fascist. Jennie didn't like the choice she faced of ignoring them or treating their charge as even worth refuting. She'd enough experience with Communist labels—Scab, Back leg, Trotskyite—however, to answer them back with some effect.

One evening in Dundee, hecklers finally pushed Jennie too far.

"That's right, anyone who disagrees with you must be a Fascist, especially if what they are doing threatens to work! Threatens to make workers better off, to make'm see your lot for the sorry Stalin-stooges you are."

Some behind Jennie on the stand gasped at her red-baiting. Comrade Stalin was not an object of general obloquy on the left. In fact, the venom of her riposte had rather surprised herself. Her visit to the Soviet Union had had its effect after all. Her hecklers stunned into mute fury, Jennie carried on her address, condemning MacDonald's failed attempt to thwart democracy, the failure of the Tory's conventional nostrums, the promise of the new spending to put men in work again.

But that evening, when she had a chance to glance at the London papers, Jennie saw that Mosley had begun to lend credence to the charges of the Communist hecklers, ones it would be hard to fob off the next time a heckler made the claim. There was an article on the front page of *The Times*, one of Harmsworth's papers that had been kind to Mosley throughout out his career:

Labour Leader Sees Vast Foreign Conspiracy in Opposition

Facing an apparently well-organised body of Communist hecklers, Sir Oswald Mosley stunned a large meeting at London Olympia into silence tonight when he identified his opponents on the right and the left as part of a single conspiracy, organised by international Jewry. As he neared the end of his remarks, Sir Oswald said, "We know well the saying, the enemy of my enemy is my friend. Well, the combined opposition we face from international finance and world communism is more than that. It's not just that they both need us to fail in our quest to save Britain. It's not merely that each will do well out of the failure of the Labour Party for its own reasons. No, we are dealing with the same invisible hand manipulating both the House of Morgan and the Comintern, whispering in the ear of both J.P. Morgan and Comrade Stalin. It is conspiracy of a powerful cabal of Jews that we must overcome if we are to build the New Jerusalem. Do not mistake my words or confuse what I say with the hysterical rot of Herr Hitler in Germany. It's not all Jews, or most or even any British Jews who seek to defeat our movement, who would stand to gain from our failure. Jews in Britain have nothing to fear from a government I lead, from a Labour government. No, it's the Baron Rothschild's and the Comrade Radeks who have between them financed our enemies, crafted their strategies, demanded their loyalty, out of a deep plan to control everything.

The article went on to identify Baron Rothschild as a well-known French banker and Karl Radek as one of the leading members of the Soviet Politburo.

Jennie knew that linking capitalists to communists via the Jews had long been a common thread among nationalist politicians throughout Europe. But it was not a theme any politician had ever tried to exploit in Britain. Surely Mosley couldn't sincerely credit the absurdity. But then why was he saying these things? Was it merely to excite credulous voters, to somehow add xenophobic 'patriots' to the Labour Party's natural constituency?

Jennie turned to the Labour Party paper, *The Herald*. There on the front page was another worrying story.

Leader Calls For Party Security Teams

The Labour Party leader, Sir Oswald Mosley, has called for volunteers to provide protection against Communist disturbances at Labour Party events. Citing repeated attempts to break up meetings round the country, and especially his own speeches, Mr Mosley has offered to provide training, uniforms and paid employment to suitable persons prepared to participate in units to be deployed at meetings round the country during the last three weeks of the parliamentary elections. The establishment of such a force he notes has been a common response in European countries to Communist provocations.

She put the paper down. Then she reread both articles slowly. Had she missed something? She hadn't expected disapproval in *The Times*. But there was no hint of dissent from Mosley's remarks in *The Herald*; not in the reports, not in the leaders, nowhere. Who's writing for the party's favourite newspaper now, she wondered? The inescapable thought formed. *There's too much smoke here for there not to be a fire, or at least one smouldering. Only one thing to do. You've got to confront Tom Mosley.* Jennie didn't want to, but she had to come face to face with him, and demand answers to a half dozen questions. He might not answer, or answer truthfully, but she had to gauge his eyes, his voice, his demeanour. Then she'd know, or know enough to decide what to do herself.

* * *

The next morning, Jennie put a trunk call through to Labour Party Central Office in London. Mosley, she learned, was in the Midlands. He'd be in Newcastle that night, not so far from North Lanark. Jennie might miss a meeting, but she had to see Mosley. By noon, she was on an express from Glasgow, thinking through the way she would have to confront him.

Chapter Twenty-Eight

There was only a single man, lounging in a chair, before the hotel room occupied by the leader of the Labour party. He rose and politely introduced himself as a detective inspector and asked Jennie's business, then stood aside as she knocked.

Mosley opened the door to his hotel room and she was greeted with the vision of a theatrical set for a play starring John Barrymore. He stood before her in a florid dressing gown over what looked like silk pyjamas. Over his shoulder, she could see a sitting area before a warm coal fire. Without a word, he allowed her to follow him in. He paused before a drinks tray and spoke.

"I know it's early, but would you like something?"

She shook her head and looked round. The four-poster bed was turned down under subdued light, the curtains drawn against the sombre late afternoon light, the room smelled of Virginia tobacco as smoke curled from a lit cigarette in an ashtray between two padded armchairs ranged before the fireplace. Mosley poured a small whisky for himself, perhaps to encourage her to change her mind. Then he spoke.

"I was about to take a nap. It will be a long evening—meeting, speech, dinner..."

"Sorry to disturb you, Sir Oswald."

He frowned slightly. "I should think we're still Tom and Jennie?"

It was not the tone of a blackmailer. Jennie made herself recall their last meeting.

"As you wish," she replied and immediately began to worry about the slippery slope she always found herself on with Mosley. "I came on a matter of politics, Tom. I need some clarification."

He pointed to one of the chairs, and sat himself. "Very well. Tell me."

"I've read two accounts of your speeches in the papers.

They're…troubling. Look, I've never accepted other people's criticisms of you." Jennie felt a twinge, thinking of Frank. "But when you begin to sound like that beast in Germany, I worry they're on to something."

"Beast in Germany? That Hitler fella? Clever blighter. I'm told he doesn't take seriously half of what he says, but it works." He paused. "Look Jennie, no one believes everything they put out in a political speech. You don't yourself, do you?" He didn't stop for an answer. "The papers probably quoted me accurately. But I'm trying to win an election…for us. If I have to engage in a little demagoguery to bring in voters who might not always support Labour or even vote at all, I've got to whip them up a bit, right?"

He paused, waiting for her acquiescence. It did not come, so he continued.

"Think about who we're fighting. A Tory party that was perfectly willing to do much worse! These are the people who forged that letter supposed to be from the Soviets to defeat us in '24."

He was right about that, Jennie had to admit. Two days before the 1924 election, *The Daily Mail* had published a letter it claimed to be from the Soviet government to the British Communist party ordering them to support Labour. By the time the forgery had become known, the Conservatives had swept Labour from its first government.

"But, Tom, you're giving opponents a stick to beat you with. They call you a Fascist and you are giving them the ammunition they need."

Mosley picked up his glass and downed the whiskey. "Fascism is a coming thing. Look at Mussolini's success in Italy. There are half dozen fascist groups in England already. It does no harm to make them think the Labour Party is a home for their mixture of nationalism and socialism."

"I can't agree, Tom."

"You have that luxury, Jennie. You're not party leader. I've had to do a number of things I haven't liked or wanted to do. All those MPs who were deselected in favour of ex-soldiers, farmers, small holders. Do you think I liked it?"

"I can tell you I didn't like it. You packed a lot of local party constituency meetings and swamped people who'd been loyal to the party their whole lives."

"Yes, and it cost a pretty penny too. But without them we'd never have a chance of winning. Now we do. Don't you see, Jennie? You can have clean hands and lose. Or you can do what it takes and really alleviate suffering."

There was an earnestness, a sincerity in his eyes that disarmed her, if it didn't quite convince her.

Jennie sighed. "So, my qualms are misplaced and I'm not to take what you have to say to win as what you really believe? Well, I suppose I can do that. But I can't bring myself to say the same."

"I'm not asking you to, Jennie. You couldn't dissimulate if you tried. And you don't need to, to win those seats in the Scottish coal fields."

He leaned towards her, smiled, and put a hand on her knee. Jennie immediately knew he was wordlessly changing the subject, recalling to their memories his gesture the first time they met.

She did not immediately move her knee but instead kept his gaze. It was all the encouragement he needed to lean forward and bring his mouth to hers, not aggressively but ardently enough to make her know his desire was strong. It was just what Jennie feared was going to happen. *Or was it just what you hoped was going to happen?* She could feel unmistakably what her body was telling her, and telling Mosley as her tongue responded to his kiss. *Why not? Why should you hold back when he isn't? It will be as good for you as for him, you know that.* It was a secret, but an undeniable equality she shared only with this man, taking her pleasure as he did, without any question of further meaning.

Chapter Twenty-Eight

Then she stopped. *It's not why you came, but if you carry on, it will be!*

"No, Tom, not today, not this time." She stood. "You've a speech to think about giving. I've got to go back to Scotland."

He rose in acquiescence, smiled gamely, led her to the door. There he brushed her cheek with his lips and squeezed her hand. He had understood that this part of their relationship was ever to be wordless.

* * *

Jennie was able to convince herself she'd been unnecessarily anxious, that Oswald Mosley had probably been right. In that late winter election of 1932, Labour had finally won a majority of seats in the House of Commons. It was a slim majority, 321 out of 615, but a real one. What's more, Mosley as Prime Minister brought along almost all the cabinet ministers who had refused to accept MacDonald's betrayal back the previous summer. True, the Liberals were no longer any part of the coalition. But Frank Wise, reappointed as Chancellor of the Exchequer, was still able to consult Keynes freely. And he did so in drafting a budget for the new government. Keynes had again broken ranks with the academic economists, acquiescing in a tariff, thus losing the ear of Lloyd George, but gaining influence with Mosley.

Though consulted on the Speech from the Throne, that would open the new parliament, Frank was spending a well-earned post-election holiday. After a week in Bucks, where the press had found him preparing the garden with Dorothy and cycling with his daughters, he'd quietly come back to London. Slipping out of the rear of his Bloomsbury residence, he'd walked the back streets to Russell Square and Jennie's flat. A few days with her and then he'd make a show of visiting Charlie Trevelyan for the early spring partridge shoot. Afterward, Jennie would arrive separately and, if possible, without notice.

That first evening together after the election, Jennie and Frank had so much to say to each other they couldn't stop even after turning out the lights. In the dark, they talked through the campaign for hours, staring up at the ceiling, sharing cigarettes, voices disembodied, freed from smiles and frowns, raised eyebrows and wrinkled brows. Unchecked, somehow their thoughts escaped into words before second thoughts could stifle them. Lying together for the first time in months, talking quietly side-by-side, they found desire over and over that night. The intimacy made Jennie and Frank both want to share everything. But they knew they couldn't do that. Frank had secrets to keep, was sworn to them by his seat in the cabinet. Jennie too had to keep her secrets, just to be her own person, independent, autonomous, unchecked by the constraint of other people's permission, approval or consent.

Watching the occasional headlight catch their cigarette smoke, forming iridescent columns that moved in arcs across the ceiling, Jennie came as close as she dared to the subject she had to avoid.

"Frank, you're still worried about Mosley, aren't you?"

She wanted to tell him about her meeting with Mosley. She knew what his answer would be but this was a way to bring it up.

He made rather a show of pausing to consider. "I'm afraid so. You heard the campaign speeches."

"But that was only rhetoric, Frank."

"How can you be sure?"

In the stillness and the quiet, the very words she'd used once before escaped, "Because he told me."

Frank was silent, but now, in the dark, somehow she could feel the twinge of jealousy crossing his face. He would not say anything. It was understood between them that she had the right to do as she pleased. She responded to the look on his face she could feel without seeing.

"Yes, I went to see him, when he was in Newcastle." She had to forestall Frank's reaction. "But I didn't stay the night. I hardly took off my coat. We spoke for less than an hour. I put it to him he was sounding like a Fascist, especially attacking Jews and organising a strong-arm squad."

Then she thought, *You didn't actually mention either one, did you, Jennie?* She reproached herself. *But he knew what I was taking about!*

Frank did not respond immediately. Then he spoke in a neutral tone. "What did he say?"

Jennie repeated her conversation with Mosley. Frank's deep breath announced his relief and Jennie took it for political vindication, until he spoke.

"Can't deny I'm glad you didn't spend the night." He went on. "But, Jennie, I fear he was just fobbing you off...keeping you on side."

"Why? He didn't seem to repeat that stuff again, not that I read anyway."

"Well, you weren't the only one in the party upset by the Jew-baiting."

"And you're still worried? Why did you join the government?"

"That's obvious. Power." His honesty was numbing. "But there were conditions, Jennie. Some of us—Atlee, Lansbury, Morrison"—these were three of the most senior members of the Labour parliamentary party—"we told him we wouldn't serve if he insisted on a junta."

"A junta?" Jennie wanted the label justified, or at least explained.

"A handful of men governing without parliament. No debate, no compromise, just decisions. That's the scheme that's worried me from the start. You can't run a country like that, certainly not an economy like ours. Remember what we saw in Moscow?"

In the dark, Jennie frowned. She wouldn't dispute the matter yet again, but she couldn't accept Frank's qualms. Two years on the back benches had done nothing to shake her conviction, that parliament was an obstacle to change when it wasn't simply a charade. She drew on her fag and sent another column of smoke rising into the dark.

"So, what will happen?"

"For the moment, we'll go on pretty much as before, when Lloyd George was PM, and Mosley was in charge of spending money on public works—roads, schools, railway repair, anything that soaks up unemployed men." Jennie wanted to intervene to remind him women needed work, but she didn't. "Except we'll add Mosley's tariff. It probably won't help create any industrial jobs, but it'll be popular."

In the dark she laughed. "Frank, it's me you're talking to. This isn't a press briefing."

She leaned on an elbow, looming over him in the gloom, then pulled on the lapel of her dressing gown, opening it with a smile he could just discern. Frank reached up, cupping her proffered breast, and brought his mouth towards hers.

Chapter Twenty-Nine

After an evening of frustration, seeking the Speaker's eye without success, Jennie realised she'd been in the chamber too long and was losing the thread of the debate. She wanted badly to ridicule the Conservative speakers. Each had reflexively attacked the policies outlined in the Speech from the Throne that had opened parliament. Serious debate had given way to hours of mock indignation, hyperbole and adolescent japes. It was fun listening. This mockery was Jennie's metier too. She wanted badly to intervene, but wasn't given the chance.

She left the floor of the House and wandered into the members' lounge. Looking round and seeing no one, she went to the bar, asked for a gin and tonic and carried it to a chesterfield. She lit a cigarette and let the smoke exhale through her nostrils. It would ward off the fatigue of the session, she knew.

She'd not been seated for a minute, when she saw Nye Bevan come into the bar, look round and make directly for her. She hadn't seen him in the Commons, but he must have been there, perhaps annoyed that she had not spotted him. *Typical man. Thinks he's the main sight in the House.* Bevan arrived at the chesterfield and, without asking, deposited his large bulk on the leather cushions, sighed and took Jennie's hand, in a brotherly embrace between his two large miner's paws.

"Jennie. At last. I've been looking for a moment to speak to you. Wanted to know why you hadn't gotten so much as parliamentary private secretary's post?"

"Why should they offer me anything?" Jennie was perplexed.

"Because..." Was Nye going to say 'Because of Frank'? No. He started again, "Because you're a thorn in the side of the Tories."

Jennie frowned. "There are three or four Labour women who have a much better claim on a job than me—Ellen Wilkinson for one."

The real reasons she'd been ignored were obvious to Jennie: the Speaker of the House probably had full knowledge of her role in the conspiracy that destroyed her father. But she could hardly mention any of this to Nye. She changed the subject.

"What about you? You supported Mosley from the start. I expect that sort of loyalty would be repaid. But here you are, still a back bencher."

"He offered. I declined."

"Oh Nye! Whatever for?"

"The job was of no interest. Something to do with the post office." He paused, looking at Jennie. "Besides, something doesn't smell right. Can't explain. Instinct."

Jennie thought a moment. "Nye, is it too late to change your mind, or at least to tell them you'd accept another offer?"

"I suppose not. Why?"

"Well, you are not the only one with suspicions, and inside the government you'd learn a little more than outside."

"Max Beaverbrook used the same argument on me."

"Naturally, he'd love someone on the inside feeding titbits to *The Daily Express*. You must do it."

"Very well, if they ask again. I'll do it, for you, sister." He winked. "But if you ask me, you should be in a better position than I am to keep a finger to the pulse."

Jennie reddened slightly. *Does he know about Mosley and me?*

Nye went on. "After all, was you who engineered this whole thing, wasn't it? Getting Lloyd George and Mosley to scupper MacDonald's scheme." *How does he know? From Mosley? From Frank? From the Speaker or Beaverbrook? Could it be known in Fleet Street?* "Don't deny it and don't ask how I know."

Jennie was now worried. *Is this what he meant when he said something doesn't smell right?* "How many people know?"

"Know you had a hand in destroying MacDonald? Can't be many. It's too good a story not to make the papers. It hasn't, so your secret is probably safe."

Not just my secret, Jennie thought. *There's the Duchess, the Duke, the King for that matter.* She dared not ask how much more Nye knew.

He was going on. "Anyway, it gives you a hold over the PM that should land you some job in government you're qualified for."

Quite the contrary, Jennie thought. *Far too dangerous. If I got a plum job, people would begin to ask why. And that could be a disaster.*

Instead she replied, "I'm too young, I've got no particular qualification. I've only just arrived at Westminster." She looked at her friend. "But you're a man. A big, boisterous, loud, opinionated man. You must have something for your loyalty to Mosley!"

"You're all of that too, Jennie, including most of the man-bits! But I see your point about not drawing attention after what you did."

What I did? Jennie was listening carefully to Nye's words, gauging how much was knowledge, surmise or bluff.

Nye went on. "But you needn't go all silent, as you did in the last session. We need those fiery speeches you gave when you first got here."

"Can't get the Speaker's attention." Jennie knew why she couldn't. FitzRoy blamed her for the Labour victory, she was certain. Now, she realised that everything she'd done to thwart MacDonald, to support Mosley, had made her almost completely invisible.

Jennie looked up. There, looming above both of them, was Sir Charles Trevelyan—Charlie, now back in government as Mosley's Lord President of the Council. It was the third time Charlie Trevelyan had held this post, which made him responsible for the government's education policy. He was holding a pint of dark ale in one hand and a file of order papers in another.

"May I?"

Nye smiled. "If you care to be seen with the small fry." He

patted the chesterfield.

Charlie sat heavily and smiled at Jennie. It was the conspiratorial smile of a former lover, now friend. Nye Bevan decided he didn't want to compete for Jennie's attentions, whether chaste or not. He waved his hand in the direction of a knot of men at the bar, and rose, turned first to Jennie and then to Charlie Trevelyan. "Must be off."

Charlie sighed after he'd gone. "How much does he know?"

Jennie frowned briefly. "How much do you know?"

"Frank has pretty well put me in the picture. I made him, once Mosley asked me to come into the cabinet again. Had to know what I was in for." He gestured towards the departing Nye Bevan. "So, how much does he know?"

"Well, I think he knows I went to see Lloyd George with Mosley. Not much more."

"But he hasn't asked why you went with Mosley? Rather dim of him."

"Clever of you to have twigged to it, Charlie." She patted his hand. "Perhaps Nye has too. That would explain why he didn't ask me about Tom Mosley. Nye Bevan fancies me. He can't have me." *No one can.* Silently, she said the words to herself. "But he doesn't want to know about my"—she searched for the right word—"my attraction to other people. Not for you"—again she reached out a hand to his—"and certainly not to Mosley. Nye would never ask a question that presumed…intimacy."

"But what about you and Frank? Surely he knows."

"Nye Bevan is prepared to lose me to Frank Wise. Frank is that much older than either of us, he thinks the relationship is almost paternal."

"Well, I'll answer your question. How much do I know? I'm in the picture pretty completely, Jennie…all the way up to Buckingham Palace."

"Then you know why I've been thoroughly frozen out here at Westminster." Trevelyan was silent. Jennie concluded, "Perhaps

I'll just resign. It's a safe Labour seat. My successor may be able to do more good than I can."

"Don't be foolish, Jennie Lee." Trevelyan put an avuncular hand on her knee. "You're the future of this party. You may not have a role now, but you've got to prepare for one in the future."

"How?"

"It's all well and good to give rousing speeches in the Commons. But government means drafting laws, arguing about them on the floor of the House, and defending them in the courts." Jennie opened her mouth to protest. But Trevelyan raised a hand. "Jennie, you're being a self-indulgent revolutionary. It's time to grow up. We need trained solicitors, Jennie. You read law at Edinburgh along with the teacher training. But you've never qualified. You need to find a firm, here in London that'll take you on as an articled clerk, and learn the practical bits of the law."

"Not for me, shuffling papers or rearranging subordinate clauses in contracts."

"Well then, become a barrister. Pleading before a judge or jury suits your skills at advocacy."

"And sit those tedious dinners at the Inns of Court?" Jennie frowned. "Never. Besides, I can't afford it, not an MPs salary."

He looked at her hard. "Jennie. If you make a start, I'll pay the fees, and I'll find someone to serve as your pupil-master too."

It would, Jennie recognised, be at least a stopgap, a next step, a way that might lead her out of the impasse she'd found herself in. Studying had come as natural to her as speaking. It would certainly take up her days, but leave her evenings free for the Commons. And Charlie Trevelyan was right. It might equip her for something more than rousing rabbles in the coalfields. Then, of course, there were hardly any women barristers. The prejudice against them was fierce. But as a sitting MP she'd be in a stronger position to get briefs, to resist discrimination in court or make it public. Like politics, it might be another field in which

Jennie could do as much as any man could.

"Very well, Charlie. I'll think about it."

* * *

The image of herself as a barrister appealed to Jennie. *You can be as aggressive as you want.* It was a thought that ran through her head. There had only ever been one woman barrister so far, Jennie knew. She'd had to struggle merely to secure the title. Indeed that an act of parliament had been required to make it possible for her to serve as a barrister at all. Knowing all this made the whole prospect even more attractive to Jennie. That, as a woman, she might never attract a brief with real money behind it didn't discourage her over-much. After all, Charlie Trevelyan would be paying for her training. Jennie giggled a bit when she thought of herself in a black academic gown with a white, curled wig on her head, showing mock deference in a law court. But still, the idea appealed to her. She might do in a courtroom what she probably could never do in the House of Commons—take something important from start to finish and undeniably get the credit for it.

And then so many things changed that the opportunity seemed to turn into an inevitability. Suddenly there was nothing much else to do but swot up the law.

* * *

The budget had been passed, not even narrowly. None of the handful of Liberals left had supported it, but a dozen Tories defied their Whips and voted with Labour.

Then, once he'd gotten the government's marching orders through the Commons, Mosley struck.

In a speech that combined invective and cold reason, he rose and carried the House through a withering criticism of its day-to-day politics, its decade of ineffectiveness, its waste of words, paper, and most of all, of time. His voice dripping with contempt, the Prime Minister hurled abuse on the pettifogging of the opposition; the endless meetings of the House as committee of the whole, hearings that offered MPs opportunities to grandstand for the press, select committees writing endless white papers and blue books, the obstruction of permanent secretaries in every ministry and the legalism of the solicitor general's office. It was Mosley at his rhetorical best, a performance that hypnotised even those who would disagree with every word.

"The crisis we face does not allow us the luxury of parliamentary debate suitable in its courtesies and prerogatives to the wit of a Disraeli and the temporising of a Gladstone."

He looked across the House, to the elderly men still ranged in frock coats and detached collars on the opposition bench.

"As was said long ago to another rump of parliament, 'You have sat here for too long for any good you have done. In the name of God, go.'"

They were the words of Oliver Cromwell every English schoolboy learned. He turned to his own backbenchers.

"All of us must go. And let the government get on with the task of saving our country."

As he spoke, the almost morbid fascination of his listeners grew, their attention was rapt, their emotions drained away, their very wills surrendered. Mosley disarmed even the most fervent defenders of the mother of parliaments. When Mosley had finished, Winston Churchill had risen. Called on by the Speaker, FitzRoy, he had been shouted down, and not just by Labour Party MPs supporting their PM. As Churchill rose again, seeking once more to secure the attention of the House, Mosley stood, turned his back, bowed briefly to the Speaker and strode from the chamber. It was an expression of contempt, so well timed that most of his backbenchers rose and made to leave with their leader.

Swept along with the others by Mosley's emotional torrent, Jennie too left the chamber to the opposition, flailing in its frustration. At the door of the House, Jennie halted, turned back and began looking for Frank. Mosley's voice had held her so firmly she had not even watched Frank to gauge his reaction to the speech. Now she could see him, still standing at the dispatch box along the government bench, in fierce argument with another man, presumably another cabinet minister, though she couldn't tell whom. She decided to wait. But ten minutes later he walked right past her without noticing, still arguing.

That night, Frank called, well after midnight to say the cabinet were meeting.

"In the middle of the night?" It was all Jennie could think to say.

"'Fraid so, got to go." He rang off without saying anything more.

Too disturbed to sleep, Jennie cast round for someone else to ring up, someone to talk to. She needed to try her thoughts out against someone else's. Had others been swept away as she had been? Were they still swept away in the cool quiet of the middle of the night? She tried Nye, Ellen, even Charlie Trevelyan. None were answering telephone calls, no matter how long she allowed the instrument to ring. Finally, she took three fingers of Scotch and threw herself on the bed.

* * *

Looking at the alarm clock, she realised with a start it was nearly ten thirty in the morning. Quickly, she dressed and made for the newsagents, next to the Russell Square tube stop. From ten feet away she could make out the huge font in the tabloids, "Commons Recessed." Buying the three broadsheets, Jennie retreated to her flat, glancing at the articles as she walked. The Leader of the House had announced at eight thirty that morning the recess of parliament "until further notice." She couldn't wait but began reading the details, even as she fumbled with her latchkey. The three papers expressed themselves almost identically: "The Prime Minister, Mr Mosley, has announced that having passed a budget, both Houses of Parliament will be recessed, and the government will begin implementing policies by Orders in Council."

Yes, Jennie thought. *That's it, that's the way to get things done.* Framed as an Order in Council, a cabinet decision would need only *pro forma* Royal Assent to come into legally binding force. The excitement of decision, action, movement welling up in her, the same emotions that had animated her listening to Mosley the night before. *Hurrah,* she found herself thinking. *He won't let himself be hobbled by endless, pointless debate. He won't waste time, suspend principles or dilute legislation to secure compromise. Things will really change now.*

Jennie dropped the key on the hallway table and, without taking off her coat, found a chair and sat, scanning the front pages for reaction. She found it in Harmsworth's *Times.* Thoroughly conservative, even right-wing, the paper had occasionally approved of Mosley's politics before he became Labour leader, but not since then. It crowed in a front-page leader that he had wisely followed a trend sweeping Europe. Everywhere, notably in Italy and Germany, strong governments had shut down talking shops in order to get on with the business of recovery. Now, Britain too had seen that the crisis was too serious for politics as usual.

Where is Frank? She reached for the telephone again, dialled the number and waited. No answer. Nothing, at 11 in the morning? Jennie put down the papers and rose. Taking her latchkey from the side table and putting it her pocket, she strode out the door, turning left towards Russell Square. She would stand at Frank's door on Bedford Square all day waiting for him, if she had to. And she didn't care who might see. Entering the building she mounted the stairs to his flat, knocked and waited. Nothing. Descending, she walked to the kerb, looking up to see whether there were lights on in the flat. In the daylight, there was no way to tell. *Where are you, Frank?*

After a few moments, discretion drove Jennie to the other side of the street. It would never do to be seen if the Chancellor of the Exchequer arrived at his digs trailing newspaper reporters. Facing his door, with her back against the railings of the garden in the open square, Jennie began to wait. *This is no good.* She sought a gate in the wrought iron fence, and, entering the green space, she found a bench with a good view of Frank's door. There was enough foliage to hide her from the pavement and the street. She wondered if she could smoke without arousing the attentions of a policeman. *It's the middle of the day. Bobbies aren't expecting floosies to ply their trade here and now.* She lit up a fag and then sat, for almost an hour, in the sharp cold of the early spring day, until a cab finally drew up and a very tired-looking Frank alighted. He was carrying nothing but a trench coat, no red boxes, no dispatch case, not even a hat. He was still fumbling for his latchkey as she mounted the three steps to where he stood at his door. Jennie beamed with relief at finally seeing him, eager to share the excitement, enthusiasm that the morning's news had kindled in her. But, as he turned to face her, his wan smile offered no match for her mood. Frank sighed, slumped into her arms, holding on to her in a manner that signalled fatigue, regret and anxiety. *What's gone wrong?* Jennie asked herself the questions as her own warm emotions quickly subsided. She followed him inside saying nothing.

Frank made to hang his trench coat on one of the hooks at the door. When it fell to the ground, he merely looked down with indifference, making no gesture towards retrieving it. Instead, he shuffled into the lounge and sat heavily in an armchair. Jennie picked up the coat, hung it securely. She looked back at the door, noticing several days post below the letterbox. It was evident

Frank had not been in the flat for some time.

Before she could say anything, he looked up at Jennie, and made an offhand gesture.

"Well, I'm out…and not a moment too soon." There was no real sound of relief in his tone.

Jennie was certain she'd misheard. "What do you mean, you're out? Out of what? What's happened, Frank?"

"Out of government. I've resigned as Chancellor."

There was a silence between them as Jennie absorbed the meaning of his words. She fell to her knees before him.

"But why…why now, just when everything is finally moving in the right direction?" She looked up at his face, willing him to share her optimism.

"No, Jennie. They're not. Not so far as I can see. Things are moving in dangerous directions. Directions I can't support."

"I don't follow, Frank. You were in the House yesterday. The party is completely behind Mosley. Recessing the House is a brilliant coup." She stopped. "Isn't it?" Had she missed something? He was silent and Jennie was becoming impatient. "Wasn't it?"

Frank exhaled, as though he'd been waiting for a chance to speak. "It was a coup, I'll give him that. Everyone knows how the opposition would try to slow things down."

Jennie nodded. "I saw some Tories cheering the PM…Boothby, MacMillan. And the way the house turned on Churchill. It was grand."

Momentarily enjoying the feeling her recollection had stoked, Jennie sought Frank's face. Did he share it? Evidently not. She mulled his grudging agreement.

"If you approved, why ever did you resign, Frank?"

"It wasn't the recess. The cabinet could have governed at least for a while without having to meet parliament every day. The recess would have given us all time to get on with our jobs. But that's not why Mosley did it." He paused. "And it's not why

I resigned."

Jennie could scarcely keep a moderate tone. "So, why then?"

"Mosley wants to rule alone, or near enough. Told the cabinet he's got the King's approval to establish a small inner group, four or five ministers, like Lloyd George's war cabinet in 1916. It's to be prime minister, chancellor of the exchequer, minister of works, minister of war, first lord of the admiralty, minister of labour."

"But that's fine, Frank." She brightened. "You'll be in the thick of it."

There was exasperation in his voice. "Didn't you listen, Jennie? I resigned!"

"Surely it's not to late. You can tell him you changed your mind."

"Don't you understand? I won't be party to it."

"To what?" She did not hide the belligerence.

"The unravelling of democracy. Centralised power answerable to no one." His voice rose. "Look, Jennie, it's not even the innocent delusion that a government can control an economy. It's dictatorship he wants, like in Italy or Russia."

"That's rubbish." Jennie had finally had enough of Frank's doubts, cautions...his middle-aged moderation. She rose and stood before him. She thought for a moment about Mosley's speeches during the campaign, the one's he'd fobbed off as mere posturing. She had to banish her anxiety. Otherwise nothing would ever really change.

"Frank, it's not going to be Stalin or Musso. It's to be a war cabinet, as you said, just like Lloyd George's in the Great War."

"It'll be Mosley, three toadies and Bevin."

Jennie misheard. "Aneurin? That's wonderful but—"

Frank interrupted with exasperation. "No, not Aneurin Bevan. No. Ernest Bev*in*," he emphasised the 'in'. "Goddamn head of the Transport Union. Right-wing bastard—against the general strike, anti-Semitic to the bone, hates parliament..." His voice dropped off.

"It doesn't matter, Frank. We've got to" — she paused — "got to see it through. We've done too much to turn away now."

What Jennie was saying to herself silently was *I've done too much...risked too much to give up now, to turn back.*

"It's not a good enough reason to quit, Frank. It's not practical politics."

She wanted him to argue. She needed him to treat her like an equal as he always had, to take their politics seriously, and really understand one another. But it was obvious he wasn't going to. Not this time. He wasn't even answering her. Why not?

"Is there something else, something you're not telling me, something...personal?"

She wanted to add *something personal again?* But somehow knew she shouldn't.

Frank was about to speak. Then decided not to. He merely shook his head slowly. It seemed to Jennie he had nothing to say, he wouldn't argue, he couldn't, wouldn't defend what he had done. It was a Frank she'd never known. Defeated, perhaps even frightened?

Now Jennie realised that since they'd walked through the door into the flat, neither of them had reached out for the other. It was as though suddenly they'd found themselves on opposite banks of a river flowing too fast to ford. She gulped, knowing what it meant. For all the disagreements of their life together over almost three years, it had never come to this. She began sternly to address herself. *Jennie, you can't let politics do this. You love this man.* Then another voice in her head answered back. *Yes, but he's giving up. And he won't tell me why. I can't make him tell me. I won't make him tell me.* Neither of them had ever forced the other to do or say anything. Both had kept secrets. Neither had pried. It had never been like that. Jennie was not going to start now — wheedling, imploring, threatening. She waited, certain, convinced that the love between them would force his real reasons into the open between them. She thought of all her own silences, secrets, reservations, ones she'd kept to protect Frank. No, not only to protect him, but to keep her own freedom.

It came to her with a rush. *He wants to break with you Jennie, or perhaps you to break with him. Why? He hasn't changed his mind, his feelings, certainly not about you, you can feel them still. So, why?*

She spoke the word, "Why?"

There was no answer from Frank across the space that separated them. Perhaps a slight shrug, almost imperceptible, perhaps involuntary—a silent sob suppressed? But he only stood, stoical, resigned, not from a job, but to a fate, like a stranded mountaineer, all hope of rescue surrendered.

"I see." It was all she said. The only response was a wan smile.

Mournful, subdued, Jennie turned, looked round for her bag and coat. Then, realising she hadn't removed her coat, plucked up her bag, turned and walked quietly to the door. She took one more last look round and walked out.

Chapter Thirty

The break with Frank was as much what pushed Jennie through the gates of the Inns of Court as the suspension of parliamentary sittings. Even as she walked slowly away from Frank's flat, she began contemplating the vast potentially empty space of hours, minutes and days that she faced. A desert landscape of inactivity was not something Jennie could cope with. She needed to be doing, accomplishing, participating in events. If it wasn't government, or even the sham of participation in the ineffectual debates the House afforded, it had to be something. She had hoped to spend the summer in Russia with Frank, and then lecture in the States during the normal parliamentary recess in the fall. But that was not to be. She couldn't go with Frank, and the lecture-booking firms wouldn't offer her a tour with no new material to deliver.

So, Jennie told Charlie Trevelyan that she would take up his offer to read for the bar. She had studied Scottish law at university. At 29 she was not too old to start again. Indeed, she thought herself a better student now, a little more patient, a little more thorough. She needed to make a good fist of it. *Begin as you mean to go on*, Jennie told herself that first day she entered the precincts of the Middle Temple. It had been a long, damp and cold walk from Russell Square. Jennie had used the time to steel herself to this task.

Passing a dozen newsagents, she would not let herself buy a newspaper, despite the headlines on the hoardings, "PM's New Charges" bold across the newsprint. She wouldn't look! She had to focus on immediate matters, lest she find herself thinking of Frank, or Tom Mosley, what Nye might be doing back in Wales or whether she should be in Glasgow protecting her parliamentary seat. Reading the papers, in the days immediately after breaking with Frank, she found some political vindication. Most of what

Mosley was doing seemed right to her. But then, some of what he began saying was strange, worrying, even slightly un-British. He'd refused to cut unemployment benefits, began a vast scheme for road building, ordered the Treasury to freeze assets that might flee, forced unions and companies to bring their disputes to government for settlement. But then, in military uniform, all his Great War medals gleaming, Mosley had spoken before the British Legion. No prime minister had ever kitted himself out this way before, not even in wartime. After reviving the worst of his campaign rhetoric, he had announced that, hereafter, Great War veterans and their families would have the first claim on benefits. Those who had not served, those who had profited without serving, and finally "people foreign to our culture" — unnamed but unambiguous in his reference—and those in the thrall of such people would not be allowed to profit from the recovery his government was affecting. *Just words*, Jennie thought when she read them. And indeed there were no policies behind them, at least so far.

As she passed more and more newsstands on her way down the Holborn, the hoardings vied for her attention. Finally, she picked up a *Daily Herald*, the Labour paper and began to read.

Prime Minister's Charges
In a speech before the Trades Union Council, Sir Oswald Mosley accused an unholy alliance of Bolsheviks and Financiers of seeking to destroy the economic recovery that his government has begun to achieve. Sir Oswald asserted that Jewish banking houses, seeking revenge for Britain's abolition of the gold standard, were working together with the Jewish leadership of the Soviet Union attempting to foment labour unrest in the United Kingdom. When he held aloft copies of the Protocols of the Elders of Zion and The Communist Manifesto, the Prime Minister was joined at the lectern by Mr Ernest Bevin, who now combines the posts of Minister of Labour and Chancellor of the Exchequer.

As Jennie scanned the rest of the *Herald's* front page, there was no hint of dissent reported. Still standing at the kiosk, she spread the paper open and turned to the Leaders. There, at the top, was an editorial approving Mosley's remarks, and even noting their similarity to statements by the German Chancellor, Herr Hitler.

You can't read this, Jennie. It's not going to help you and there's nothing you can do about it. She had to keep away from the papers if she was not to go mad. Throwing the newsprint into a bin, she walked down the Strand towards Middle Temple with the best resolve.

* * *

In retrospect, it was never clear to Jennie whether her education as a barrister could really have succeeded. Was it overtaken by events, or were the traditions of the Inns of Court just too fustian for her to bear? She didn't last as a student more than a few months, let alone the three years required. It wasn't so much the arcana, or the gowns and wigs, still less the exams, which, in fact, would satisfy Jennie's competitive instincts. As she had joked to Charlie Trevelyan, it was the required dinners that slowly broke Jennie's spirit. After just a term of boring evening meals, sitting at the women's table at the Middle Temple, Jennie had just about enough.

A dozen dinners in all, she would have to face, over several terms, gowned and formally dressed, presence required before grace, and remaining even after the post-meal grace had been intoned. That first term, gliding across the perfectly kept lawn golden in evening twilight, entering the timbered hall, she had studied the ruddy faces of the rather beefy leaders of the bar. Jennie would involuntarily shudder, thinking about the misery on the London streets surrounding the closed off quadrangle of the Middle Temple. Frowned upon by hundreds of portraits of dead judges, serried in ranks against the wainscoted wall, Jennie would come upon the same three women pupils, fated to share her "mess." They were segregated at a lady's table and subjected to a sort of Coventry by the rest of the students and the pupil masters, who watched over punctilious observance of ritual—remember, no shaking of hands, bowing only—that had nothing to do with advocacy before the bar.

It was all going to be too much to bear, and when, on the night of her third required Middle Temple dinner, the message from the Duchess of York came, Jennie did not hesitate to change her plan.

She hadn't heard from Elizabeth once since the election of '32, a year and a half before. And she was rather glad of it. The liaison was too dangerous to both of them. But then, the envelope had come, to her pigeonhole in the Middle Temple students' post boxes. Someone at the palace had been keeping tabs on her. But, evidently, precautions had been taken. The heavy linen envelope with the royal crest embossed at the top had been stuffed into a large buff envelope suitable to a legal brief. It carried neither postage stamps nor franking. *So, it had to have been hand delivered*, Jennie realised as she withdrew it. Standing among the milling bar pupils, she pulled the linen envelope out and immediately recognised the handwriting of the word scrawled and underlined across the cream-coloured paper: <u>Confidential</u>. Jennie looked up. It was the unmistakable hand of Elizabeth, Duchess of York. There were a dozen men, only men, within a few feet. She couldn't read the note then and there. Pushing it back into the larger envelope, Jennie thought for a moment and then turned in the direction of the women's public toilets. There were none at the Middle Temple for female students. It was a journey of several minutes.

Closing and locking the stall door behind her, Jennie dropped her case and opened the envelope again.

Dear Jennie,

This is my second note. Perhaps my first did not reach you. It's urgent we meet. I have something important to give you. I will have my car driven by your flat on Guilford Street at 7:00 next Wednesday, 22 June. Turn your lights and pull your window blinds down if you are home and can receive me privately.

Elizabeth

Jennie had to think. The Duchess hadn't really thought things through. Would her lamp lights be bright enough to be noticed on an early spring evening? The sun would still be high in the sky at that time. Were there even blinds on Jennie's front windows? She'd literally never noticed. It was Tuesday, so she'd have an evening to experiment. But the next day, the day Elizabeth had demanded they meet, that Wednesday, was an obligatory dinner at the Middle Temple. *I'll just have to miss it*, she thought with a smile.

Every light and lamp was on in Jennie's first floor flat on Guilford Street and the shades—yes, there were some on the front windows—were down. In fact, a discerning observer might have made out the shadow of Jennie's profile against one of them as she waited for the Duchess to arrive. A few minutes after seven, it was quiet enough for Jennie to hear the Daimler pull up. One heavy limousine door closed, another closed, and the car pulled away into the evening traffic.

Jennie rushed out of her flat, descended the stairs and threw open the front door to find Elizabeth Bowes-Lyons searching among the doorbell labels for the name 'Lee.'

She was dressed in a dark suit and had a cloche hat pulled down on her head. Besides her handbag, the Duchess was carrying what looked like a finely worked portfolio case.

"Thank Goodness, Jennie." She breathed a sigh as she swept through the doorway. "I didn't want to stand out there a moment longer than I had to. Can't be spotted, don't you know."

"Are you in danger?" Jennie's question was issued in a tone of gentle mockery.

The Duchess didn't notice the jibe. "Might be." She moved hastily into the hall. "Cloak and dagger stuff, really."

Jennie led the way up the stairs and closed the door behind them, threw the bolt in a gesture of complicity, and then leaned against it. Her friend began to look round. *Is she sizing up my digs or looking for someone to take her hat and gloves?* Jennie suppressed the catty thought and waited. Her guest turned round and dropped her bag on a side table. Then, Elizabeth marched back to the door, put out both her hands and grasped Jennie's arms.

"My, but I'm glad to see you. Haven't had a word since the election, I dare say."

"It was well before then, your grace…"

Elizabeth raised a hand as if to ward off the title. "None of that, Jennie. We're alone, gloriously alone." Then she turned, sought a chair, dropped the folio she'd been carrying on the floor beside it and looked back at Jennie. "May I?"

Jennie nodded and Elizabeth sat. "Of course." She went to the saggy chesterfield opposite.

Nodding towards a sideboard, she offered, "Sherry?"

"Yes, thanks." Elizabeth pulled her folio off the floor and unzipped it, as Jennie poured the sherry into two cut glass glasses. *Can she manage not drinking from crystal?* Jennie couldn't help forming the thought. *Stop it!* She commanded herself, came back to the seats, put one glass on the small table next to Elizabeth and downed hers standing.

"Very well, Elizabeth. You have the floor. End my suspense."

The Duchess pulled a grey file from the portfolio and pulled at the bow tied in the middle by purple ribbons. There were several pieces of paper in the folder.

"My husband"—she stopped, evidently searching for a word— "purloined this file." The ribbon-tied oak tag was marked "Most Secret." She handed the file to Jennie, who opened it. "Have a good look."

There were about a dozen papers, mostly onionskin flimsies, endorsed by marks in fountain pen with initials. The top two sheets, however, were evidently Photostats. They both were in Italian, one with a letterhead *Ambasciata d'Italia nel Regno Unito* above a London address, the second's letterhead read *Ministro degli Affari Esteri, Roma.* Jennie looked up from these two sheets.

"I don't read Italian."

Elizabeth smiled. "Neither does the Duke. There's a translation of each. There's also a letter in German, with a translation."

Jennie found the German letter. It was also onionskin, of a weight used for airmail letters, and had a heading in embossed black letters, *Fritz Thyssen, Duisburg-Hamborn, Deutschland.* She put it aside with the Italian Photostats, and turned to the documents in English. Three had an MI6 — counter-intelligence — heading and the others were apparently documents from SIS, N-section. SIS Jennie knew was the Secret Intelligence Service, running British spies overseas. She had no idea what N-section was. MI6 was an organisation she knew and one she distrusted. It spied on Britons in Britain and had a reputation for infiltrating and undermining left-wing movements, on the pretext they were under Soviet control. Both memos were marked in dark bold capital letters that had been underlined, **NOT TO BE TRANSMITTED TO CABINET OFFICE. FOR HM's EYES ONLY.**

She began with the SIS N-section memorandum.

N-section has removed copied and replaced the attached letter to the Italian ambassador from the Italian diplomatic pouch.

This letter, copy attached, marked 'ambassador's eyes only' is from Signor Benito Mussolini, the Italian Duce, acting as minister of foreign affairs.

It states that Signor Mussolini has authorised the Italian ministry of foreign affairs to advance moneys to Sir Oswald Mosley, in amounts of 25,000 pounds sterling per month from December 1930.

The letter directs the Italian ambassador at London to provide these funds personally and directly to Sir Oswald Mosley or his designated representative and to request no receipt. The chancery administrator will be reimbursed for these funds with a fortnight's delay.

Owing to the post Sir Oswald Mosley now occupies, it will be inconvenient to the work of this office should he become aware of its knowledge of his affairs. Accordingly this memo is to be retained in files and not circulated.

The understatement in the SIS memo was breath-taking. Tom Mosley, the Prime Minister, was in the pay of a foreign government, a fascist one at that, and no one was to know. Jennie turned to the next SIS memo. It too was marked '**NOT TO BE TRANSMITTED TO CABINET OFFICE. FOR HM's EYES ONLY.**'

SIS Section VII

It has come to the attention of our agents in Germany that certain industrialists hitherto associated with the German National Party, but now supporting the National German Socialist Workers Party candidate in the presidential election, Herr Hitler, are also seeking to make contributions to British political parties and movements.

The attached letter from Fritz Thyseen, director of the Vereinigte Stahlwerke AG, [United Steel Corporation] to the Italian ambassador in Berlin expresses knowledge of payments by the Italian government to Sir Oswald Mosley and offers to add additional support, on the condition that Mosley confirms that Italian authorities do not take advantage of Thyssen's support to reduce their own.

We are unable to monitor the Prime Minister's personal correspondence or the Italian diplomatic correspondence to establish whether or not such undertakings to Thyseen have been made by the Italian government, or whether payments have been made.

Jennie let both memoranda drop to her feet on the floor. *So, you were right, Frank, righter than you knew.* She looked up at Elizabeth. Her tone was incredulity.

"The Prime Minister is in the pay of foreign powers." She caught her breath. "And not just any foreign powers, but the Italian Fascist government and the capitalists bankrolling that Hitler fellow in Germany?"

Elizabeth nodded.

"And how did you come by these documents?"

"I told you, the Duke slipped them away from the King's desk."

"Will he miss them?"

"I doubt it. Albert says the King looked them over and then just kept working through his boxes. It was as though he didn't care...or already knew, or wasn't surprised. Anyway, that's how it seemed to the Duke."

"And why did the Duke swipe them, exactly?"

"Well, the King had put them into one of the red boxes. The box would have gone back to the PM's office."

Jennie saw immediately. "Absentminded old fool. Mosley would have seen them after all, the very man SIS and MI6 wanted them to be kept from." Jennie drew in a breath pondering the enormity of the next question. "But the King knows...?"

Elizabeth could only nod.

"And you brought these documents to me? Whatever for? What do you want of me?"

"I don't really know, Jennie...I'm...we're at a loss what to do. We can't take this to the government—that's Mosley. We can't take it to the Prince of Wales or the military, the civil service, the newspapers. We can't take it any—"

"Not without Mosley finding out," Jennie interrupted. "Not without risking the King's wrath, if you're right about him." One more thought intruded. "Not without destroying the monarchy if it becomes known the King is condoning treason."

No bad thing that, the Republican in Jennie said to herself.

"The Duke thought about going back to the people who wrote these briefs. But we don't know who they are. And if the heads of SIS and MI6 are loyal to the government, or support Mosley... well, the game would be up. We're at a complete loss."

"Elizabeth, where do you and the Duke stand in all of this? You had no qualms about supporting Mosley, even when the King was trying to maintain MacDonald as a figurehead."

"Isn't it obvious, Jennie? We were wrong! We helped create a monster. We should never have interfered. But now we have no idea how to stop it."

"And whatever makes you suppose I agree with you about Mosley?"

Elizabeth's eyes opened in fright. Had she made a terrible mistake? Was her friend about to betray her to Mosley, to the King?

Jennie couldn't let her twist in the wind. She smiled. "No, it's alright, dear. I'm with you. We've both made a frightful mistake about Mosley." Then her look clouded. "But what can we do?"

"We're at a stand, the Duke and I. And you're the only person I could safely talk to about this...this...disaster."

"Well, you can talk safely enough, Elizabeth. But I can't see what I can do."

Elizabeth rose. "Got to get back. Always worried I'll be missed and people will ask where I've been." She glanced down at the papers and the folio on the floor between them. "Jennie, will you keep these papers for us?"

"Must I? They're dangerous."

"That's why they're safer with you than me."

Jennie looked to the grate. "We could just burn them?"

"No!" Elizabeth's face showed resolve. She bent down and began to gather them up. "If you won't keep them I'll have to..."

"Very well." Jennie gripped her friend's hand and then took the papers.

They both heard the low growl of an idling motor in the street. Both knew it was the Duchess's car signalling its return.

When her friend had gone, Jennie began to think, *where to cache the folio? In the grate! Just as she had suggested to Elizabeth.* Carefully, she moved the grate and swept away the lining of ash and dust beneath it, laid the folio down, swept the ash over it and replaced the grate. Then she sat down before it, contemplating the problem of what to do. The answer came back, with a dread fatalism: nothing to be done.

Chapter Thirty-One

Every morning that week, Jennie was woken in the dark, long before dawn, from an apparently dreamless sleep, with the same gnawing hollow of anxiety in her stomach. She knew why, instantly. But for all the focus on the problem—what to do with the papers and the knowledge she was hiding—no answer came to her, at least nothing that she was willing to act on.

She tried to fob the documents off as forgeries, plants, like the Zinoviev letter that destroyed the Labour Party's chances in 1924. But whose interests would such a forgery serve? More likely these letters were real and dangerous, like the Zimmerman telegram—German's attempt to ally itself with Mexico against the USA during the Great War.

They have to be real, alas. But then she had to do something with them. *Make them public? Destroy the monarchy? Destroy the Labour Party along with Mosley?*

None of that would happen. You'd not be believed for a moment, Jennie. There'd be a campaign to discredit or silence or even make you invisible, orchestrated by the press barons now fawning over Mosley.

She'd start over, thinking through another strategy.

Go to Mosley with them? Threaten him? Absurd. That would just get you back to the first dead end, disbelieved or worse.

Jennie would roll over in bed and try to clear her mind of the problem, to steal a few more hours' sleep, to think it through afresh in the morning. It didn't work, night after night. *You need to work this through with someone else. With Frank.* Making contact, Jennie knew, would almost certainly be detected by his wife. With parliament in recess and having resigned his cabinet seat, Frank had gone back to Bucks and his family. *But you can explain, girl. It's a matter of state, of national importance!*

And what if the documents aren't genuine? You may have wrecked his marriage for nothing.

No, Jennie. You've already decided they must be real. You can't take that step back.

Then go to him in Bucks. Jennie had never been there, never wanted to confront Dorothy Wise, never wanted to make Frank choose. *But now, he's got nothing political to lose if she finds out. No, that's not right. Frank has a future in politics, when all this is over. But it's one that could still be destroyed by scandal.* Each night, when her thoughts came to this point, Jennie acknowledged to herself that she still loved Frank, wanted to wind back the clock and recreate what they'd had, that she never should have broken with him. Worst of all, she acknowledged that he'd been right about what was happening to their country. The reckoning made her feel even worse, angry, frightened, alone.

On the fifth morning after Elizabeth's visit, Jennie picked up the telephone and called Charlie Trevelyan's London home. A servant answered with the number. Jennie asked for Sir Charles.

"Sir Charles is at Wallington Hall."

Jennie replied, "Shooting?" She knew this was a frequent pastime of Charlie's.

"I believe so, miss."

She was about to ask whether there were guests, but immediately realised the servant would not reply even if he knew.

After a pause the voice carried on. "Is there a message, miss?"

"Thank you, no message." Jennie sat down and wrote a short note to Charlie Trevelyan.

Charlie,
If Frank Wise is with you shooting, please ask him to call me here in London. If he's not with you but you can reach him, please tell him <u>discreetly</u> to ring me in London. He'll have my number.
Jennie Lee

Should she say any more? Should she label the envelope

'personal'? No, it was enough simply to underline the word 'discreetly.' *Now, perhaps you'll get a night's sleep.* With that thought, she rose, collected her case and left for the Middle Temple law library.

It was near midnight, two days later, that her phone rang. Jennie was still awake, dreading the prospect of waking again as she had each night for a week or more.

She lifted the receiver, giving her number, "Museum 6428."

The operator spoke. "Trunk call. Putting you through. Go ahead."

Then she heard Frank's voice. The tone was quiet, almost as though he were whispering.

"Jennie. Got your note. I'm here at Charlie's place." Wallington Hall was hundreds of miles north in Northumberland. "Can't talk now. Here with Dorothy and the boys. Look, I'm coming back to London Monday week."

"That's five days. Can you make it sooner? It's urgent...It's, it's...business." She hoped he'd understand it wasn't pleasure or desire that was demanding his return.

"Can you tell me anything, Jennie?"

"Only that you were right...right about—"

Before she could add the name Frank interrupted. "I see." He must have understood completely. "I'll call if I there's a way I can come sooner."

He rung off before she could say anything more. He'd asked nothing, nothing at all. Suddenly Jennie began to wonder, *What does he know? Does he already know what I've got to tell him?*

* * *

Jennie had to fill those five days, waiting and worrying, finally, wondering whatever Frank and she could do, anyway, once he came. She spent more time in the law library than she needed to. She caught up with her damnable dinners. By Friday she'd even taken to wandering round her flat sorting things out, folding clothes away in drawers, clearing her dishes from the sink... she'd taken a tea towel to her drinks glasses as though she were a barman polishing them to a gleam.

Finally, she sat at her desk facing a typewriter that *The New Statesman*'s editor had given her, in fact, had delivered, just to encourage her to write for the mag. It had been weeks since she'd even tried to say something about national affairs or European ones. In the winter after the British election, she had written about the appointment of Hitler as German chancellor even though his party had lost seats in the national elections. Then another piece about the fire that destroyed the Reichstag and gave Hitler the excuse to govern without a parliament at all. Now, as an MP supporting a government doing much the same thing in Britain, what was there to write about? It was no good. She had nothing to say. *Maybe you should take back your attack on Herr Hitler, Jennie?*

If only Nye, or Ellen, or...anyone were around. *I'd settle for an argument with Lady Astor!* The wry laugh was no comfort.

It rained Saturday morning. Looking at the bland reports in the papers consumed only a little time. Jennie turned to the film adverts. Losing herself in an Odeon had passed time before, even forestalled temptations. There, on the page next to the largest advertisement, for a picture with the intriguing name, *The Bitter Tea of General Yen*, was a notice and an article, "Board of Censors Requires Cuts." The film, about a love affair across the white/yellow colour line, was in places too much for English sensibilities. *Well*, she thought, *that's for me*. Felling better for something to do, to occupy her afternoon, to distract her from the weight of that damn folio beneath her grate, Jennie was able to count the hours till she could leave her flat for the cinema. By noon, the rain had stopped, and Jennie decided that the two miles to the Regal at Marble Arch would do her good, distract her longer. She set off in a blithe spirit, with an almost carefree step.

Jennie knew London well enough to find the shortest way to Marble Arch, through the zigzag of differently named streets that made a hypotenuse of the triangle, bounded by Tottenham Court Road and Oxford Street. By the time she had turned from Windmill Street to Percy Passage, she was pretty confident that she was being followed. The same nice-looking young man, in conservative clothes, a bowler and tightly rolled umbrella, had been walking down exactly the same streets for nearly a mile now. No moustache, no special military bearing, plain-faced and just a pair of oval horn-rimmed glasses. Stopping at a shop window mirror, stooping to tie a shoe, even doubling back once, made her shadow evident. The man kept well back, however, and showed no sign that he'd been detected. Jennie decided to lose him in Selfridge's.

She did so, but as a result had cut it too fine. As she arrived, the vast organ—only one of its kind in a London theatre, as every moviegoer in that city was well aware—had just come to the end of its pre-programme concert. Slowly, it dropped from the stage as the lights went down. Sweeping her torch from side to side in a show of annoyance, the matronly usher showing Jennie to her seat made it obvious that she was offended by the discourteous tardiness.

As a distraction from her mood, her problem, her affairs—personal and political—*The Bitter Tea of General Yen* was a frightful, comical, absurd mistake. A woman separated from her husband by unrest in Shanghai is saved and held hostage by a handsome, powerful, unscrupulous warlord, who falls in love with her, but whom she betrays. All portrayed by visibly western, Caucasian actors in rather transparent makeup and stereotyped accents. It was too easy, indeed hauntingly inevitable for Jennie, to see in the film, the entire cast of characters, in her real-life drama. She remained to the end, desperate to learn what the protagonist's fate, and allegorically, Jennie's own would turn out to be. The warlord, betrayed and deposed, learns that his captive loves him and then dies by his own hand. The kidnapped heroine returns to Shanghai. *Hollywood, Jennie! You should have known better.*

She rose, stood for the national anthem and then made for the tube station. By the time she'd arrived at the steps down to the tube, Jennie had decided to march back the way she'd come. This time, she could detect no following friend. But she had kept to the crowded streets of a Saturday evening Oxford Street. There was no reason to hurry home to an empty flat, where she'd just have to continue waiting till Monday.

* * *

The loud and persistent rapping at the door finally penetrated her deep, dreamless sleep. Jennie lifted her head to look at the alarm clock: seven twenty-five. So early on a Sunday morning? She pulled the dressing gown from the covers and slipped her arms through it as she rose. By the time she'd reached the door, she knew the voice. It was Charlie Trevelyan.

She threw the door open. Trevelyan literally staggered in.

"Charlie, what are you doing here? You look a fright." She couldn't suppress the thought.

"Traveling all night. Wanted to get here as soon as I could… before you saw the papers." She took his coat and hat, turned back to him to see sheer agony on his face. He reached out to her arms and held them for a moment.

There was no preface. Charlie just began to speak. "Jennie, Frank is dead." In the silence he went on. "Shooting accident, yesterday afternoon."

All she could say was "How?"

"Not sure. He was alone, at a stile. Gun must have discharged as he climbed over."

Now, he pulled her to him, to absorb the grief about to overtake her. It came, in waves of sobs and moans. For long moments, he held her as her hands closed about the folds of his coat and pulled violently at them, her head pounding on his shoulder until he had to have been able to feel the pain beneath the layers he wore, in his collarbone.

She couldn't compose herself. She wouldn't compose herself. She did not want to do so. She needed to lament, to weep, to howl. It felt to her that, somehow, she had killed her lover, her partner, the person she cared for most in the world. She didn't know exactly why she was responsible, precisely how she'd done it or at what moment. She just knew it was all her fault. She had walked away, made the breach, and over what? A trivial disagreement about politics? No, a deep disagreement and one about which she'd been completely wrong. That's what made her responsible.

Her mind wandered back and forth through these thoughts and images...all accompanied by pain, all over her body, down to her hands and fingertips, throbbing as she clutched at Charlie's coat. The enormity of the loss came again, in a new way. Never again to look at Frank, to smile at him and be smiled at by him, to feel him with her, inside her, calming her or making her want to do things, teasing and being teased, sharing thoughts, memories, stories, emotions, all barriers down, long into nights. She'd never have any of this again.

Feeling Trevelyan's rough, unshaven cheek for a moment, she thought, *This isn't fair to Charlie. This is making it harder for him.* She didn't care.

It must have been a quarter of an hour that they stood there. Her friend, her mentor, her long ago occasional lover, held her, without a word, without a gesture of impatience or emotional fatigue, without taking a step to staunch her lamentation or express his sympathy or comfort her, beyond holding her as long as she wanted to, needed to, cling to him. Charlie Trevelyan knew exactly what Jennie needed at this time, and more than anything he wanted to provide it.

The lassitude of sadness finally submerged the violence of her grief. Jennie slowly released him, dropped her hands and, without turning, allowed herself to collapse into an armchair, still covering her face with her hands. Charlie dropped before her to his knees and forced a white kerchief into an unwilling hand. Then he rose and took a seat on the chesterfield opposite. There he waited until she was ready to look at him.

"Jennie. There's something we have to do." She was puzzled but said nothing. "I've got the latch key to Frank's flat. Is there anything of yours there?"

Jennie nodded. "Some clothes, toiletries."

"Any letters from you to Frank?"

"Don't know. Perhaps."

"We've got to get them out. Before Dorothy finds them. I want to spare her feelings. I'm sure you do too. And it wouldn't do to make matters public, anyway, would it." Jennie shook her head.

She rose and went into the bedroom to dress.

* * *

By Monday, the papers had the details of Frank's accidental death. The trunk calls were coming in, from Nye in Wales, from Ellen in the North, from the few others who knew. After declining the first few, Jennie simply ceased to answer the telephone. There was nothing to say. She didn't want to be consoled.

But then, a week later, the letter came. The sender wanted Jennie to have no doubt about who it was from. "Dorothy Wise" was written in a firm hand and a wide pen point on the return of an envelope bordered in black. Jennie noticed her hands shake as she pulled it open.

My dear ~~Miss Lee~~ Jennie,
I do understand how hard it must be for you, who have no official
'right' to be considered, and who must carry on as if it were only a

great friend and not more you have lost.

I feel rather a humbug getting all the official condolences—but for his sake and the children's I've got to go on playing the game of not letting the world know—and especially the few who half-knew and look to see how I take it.

I think it makes it very much easier for me that you know I did care. If I hadn't cared at all I might have made it easier for you both. If I had cared more, loved him more, I suppose I could have carried on, could have shared him with you, or at least loved the part of him he gave me. How does one blame oneself now for not living up to the bigger selfless outlook that I got a glimpse of?

At Wallington Hall, Frank and I agreed to not blink at these issues, to face them in a spirit of friendly compromise and live our lives more separately. I know how much he meant to you.

Now, I face a separation that will be easier for me to bear than the other might have been. I know it will be much harder for you.

Please meet me a Frank's London flat any time next week. I will be there to pack his things away and will want to give you a token or two to remember him.

Dorothy Wise

Jennie read the note twice, trying to piece its full meaning together. Dorothy Wise seemed to have learned everything, and to have learned it after Jennie had broken with Frank. Why had he told her, why had they agreed to live separately? What might it have meant for them, for Jennie and Frank? Could Dorothy Wise answer any of these questions? Jennie didn't think so.

Chapter Thirty-Two

The door to the building was propped open, and the door to Frank's flat was open as well, when Jennie arrived. Men had been moving packing crates and furniture into a van at the kerb. As she entered, Jennie could see from the looks of the flat that they had just about completed their work.

There, in the midst of the lounge, stood Dorothy Wise, surveying what remained to be shifted. There were some traveling cases with papers on the window seats that overlooked Bedford Square. She was a large, middle-aged lady, hair parted in the middle and held in a bun, wearing grey mourning dress with a black crepe arm band. Frank's widow looked very much "in charge," dealing with matters and movers firmly. Jennie had only ever seen her at a distance, in the gallery of the House and even then had not looked at her long enough to hold her glance or even to notice whether Dorothy Wise was watching her. Now she was. Jennie entered and was met with neither a frown nor a smile, but a look she would have called 'business-like.' *Could have been worse*, Jennie thought.

"Ah, Miss Lee..." Dorothy Wise cleared her throat.

Jennie wondered if she was about to launch into something.

"Jennie... please."

She hoped the meaning in her voice was clear. *We've got to be friends to one another now*.

"I shall. I'm to be Dorothy then."

Jennie nodded. She was about to go on when a removal man came in again. She fell silent as he moved his luggage trolley under the last of the crates. He paused, looked round and spoke to no one in particular.

"Well, that's it then."

"Yes, thank you."

Dorothy's tone was dismissive...or perhaps she was just eager to be left alone with Jennie. She waited a full few seconds after hearing the trolley start to clatter down the steps. Then Dorothy led her into the bedroom, now bare and unfamiliar-looking, Jennie noticed with relief. There was, she suddenly realised, nothing left of Frank Wise in the flat that she could have taken to remember him by. Had Dorothy simply forgot why she'd invited Jennie? Had Jennie left it too late coming, when everything had already been packed or disposed of. *It doesn't matter,* she thought to herself.

"Miss...uh, Jennie, I need to talk to someone about a very difficult matter. And it might as well be you. You may have a stake in the matter."

"What is it, Mrs...Dorothy?"

"Come, let's sit."

She drew Jennie to the window seat, on which there was a large manila envelope. The woman planted herself and patted the wood as an invitation. Jennie did as she was bidden, trying to decide which of her questions to ask first. Dorothy was holding herself, as if in an iron grip.

"I have to tell you, Jennie, I fear that Frank was murdered." Before Jennie could reply a firm hand was placed on her thigh, as if to say, let me go on. "In fact I'm sure he was."

Eyes widening, Jennie could only gasp. "Oh..."

Everything else she'd wanted to know about Frank's last days had now lost any interest to her.

"It had to have been murder," Dorothy repeated, and then held up three fingers to count off her reasons. "First of all, Frank would never have crossed a stile with cartridges in barrels of a shotgun. I know. I hunted with him sometimes. He taught me always to unload before doing that." Jennie nodded. "Second, the spent cartridges in the gun were the wrong size shot."

"Wrong size?" Jennie did not understand the words.

"Exactly. The gun belonged to Frank and when they gave it back, the spent cartridges couldn't have been his. He only ever hunted ground birds at Wallington Hall. When I got the shotgun back the cartridges were marked LG." Jennie looked confused. Dorothy explained. "L.G.—large grape, as in 'grape shot.' The kind you use for larger animals, deer." Jennie nodded, wincing as she imagined their effect at close range. "And finally, the barrels were clean, both of them." Before Jennie could ask what that meant she explained. "They'd not been fired at all that afternoon!"

"Not fired? But then how was he killed?"

"Don't you see? Someone killed Frank, with a shotgun firing LG shot then took the spent LG cartridge and put it in Frank's weapon, to make it look like he'd shot himself. But whoever it was, the man knew nothing about shooting, or at least how our people do it."

Jennie understood, *Our people, the upper class, the landed gentry, people you'd expect to run into at a weekend house party where there was a shoot.*

"What did the police say?"

"I was already back home when the gun came back to me. I put two and two together and called the Chief Inspector in Newcastle. He listened politely and promised to call back. Haven't heard a thing in ten days."

All this was making sense to Jennie, and making no sense. "But, Dorothy, who could have wanted to kill Frank?"

"Yes, that was my question. Then I found something among his effects at home."

She reached over to the envelope lying next to Jennie. Jennie reached out, but Dorothy held it close and continued.

"Some months ago, just before he resigned from the cabinet, Frank had a visitor, someone from Russia. You know, Frank worked for the Soviet Cooperative Societies."

Jennie could hardly tell her she knew this from the experience of traveling in Russia with Frank. She merely nodded.

"Well, Frank knew this man well. I'd never met him before,

but Frank greeted him warmly and made him stay to dinner. I've tried to remember his name. Kuznezov? Something like that."

The name jogged a memory for Jennie. *The little man who guided us round Moscow two years ago.*

"Kutuzov, perhaps?" she offered.

"Yes, that's it." Dorothy went on. "Anyway, I found these papers hidden in Frank's office a few days ago."

"Hidden? Where?"

"They were beneath the middle drawer of a desk that came out while I was reaching for its deepest contents. Drawer fell to the floor and as I bent down to pick it up, I saw the envelope."

Now, finally, she handed it over. There was Cyrillic writing in the upper left hand corner. Jennie opened the envelope and pulled out a sheaf of papers. Even before she began to rifle through them, she knew. These were the same papers the Duchess of York had brought to Jennie, papers Elizabeth wouldn't even take back, made Jennie hide, papers that could destroy the Prime Minister.

"Dorothy, I've seen all these papers before. In fact I have copies of them. Don't ask me where I got them."

Jennie stopped to think. *Yes, this is why Frank was murdered. There's a Soviet spy in MI6—or maybe in SIS—filching the same documents that came to the King. Someone at the Russian embassy wanted Frank to know. Frank must have confronted Mosley with the information.* "Have you shown these papers to anyone else? Charlie Trevelyan, anyone?"

The other woman shook her head and bit her lip, no longer looking so formidable. She whispered, "There's a motive here, isn't there...for killing Frank?"

Jennie sat very still, trying hard to recall every word she'd exchanged with Frank the night he'd resigned from government and she had broken with him. He'd never told her why he'd quit in so many words. He'd simply denied it was over politics. She'd said he'd not given a good enough reason to quit. She'd asked if it were not something else, something personal. It hadn't been personal. It had been secret, dangerous, explosive. It had been treason in the pursuit of power, perhaps much worse, and certainly what Frank had feared. That's why he had said nothing, had let her go without a word of explanation.

Jennie looked at the woman next to her. She knew what had to happen.

"Dorothy, you've got to destroy these papers. Forget you've ever seen them. You have children. You and they may be in danger if anyone knows you've even seen them."

"And what am I to do about my murdered husband?" She was belligerent.

"Nothing. There's nothing we can do, either of us. Not without risking our lives too, I fear."

"What are you talking about?"

"Please, please, just leave it alone."

Your husband, my lover, died because he knew about Mosley, and confronted him. And then the thought overwhelmed Jennie, *You've done this all, it's your fault, you pushed the first stone down the mountainside when you destroyed MacDonald. This avalanche is all your fault.* She gulped. The tears came and all she could do was reach across and hold on to the older woman as she began to shudder. Dorothy Wise mistook the tears for sorrow, sadness, a shared mourning. *If she knew what I was guilty of?* Jennie shuddered again. *Can you live with the guilt?* The answer came back immediately. *No, I can't. Well then can you expiate it?*

Jennie rose, looked down at Frank's widow.

"Let me try to...to..."

She didn't know how to finish the thought—to make it right? Make Dorothy Wise and her children whole again? Impossible! Revenge Frank? How would that help? Undo what she had done? Somehow turn the clock back to before all this disaster? Rewrite history? What could she do? And then she knew what she could do.

Jennie finished her sentence. "Let me try to do something."

"What?"

The voice was steady. Dorothy's question was not laced with anything ironical, rhetorical, challenging. She simply wanted to know what Jennie had in mind.

"I don't know." She had to make it work, she had to stop Dorothy from taking matters further herself. "I don't know *yet*. But I promise. I will do something. You'll know when I do."

Perhaps Dorothy grasped what she would have to do to fulfil this promise. She handed Jennie the envelope.

"Be careful."

Then she rose from the window seat, walked into the hall, took her coat from the hook behind the door, and left the flat. There was nothing for Jennie to do but follow her out into the street. Dorothy Wise mounted a cab at the kerb without looking back. Jennie couldn't blame her.

As the taxi drove off, Jennie couldn't help notice there, across the road, was that owlish face in the horn-rimmed glasses who'd followed her to the films the day before Frank's death — *no, his murder*, she now reminded herself. He was standing with his back to the shrubbery of Bedford Square. Quickly turning his face away, he drew out a newspaper from under his arm. His studious efforts to look like he was waiting for a bus were betrayed by the absence of a bus stop anywhere nearby. When Jennie strode off towards Montague Place, almost immediately he turned and followed her. *A rank amateur*, Jennie thought. *Let's confront him.* Walking briskly, she turned away from the direction of her flat and instead circumnavigated the British Museum until she reached its main entrance on Great Russell Street. Then, she entered the gate and moved up the stair into the building. *Let's see, Room 40, great books. There are bound to be commissionaires about there, protecting the Guttenberg Bible.*

The cavernous interior was cold and gloomy in the late November afternoon. Jennie mounted the broad stair from the grand lobby and turned into the great hall of manuscripts, codices, folios and incunabula set out under poor light in glass cases. She knew her shadow had come with her, at least as far as the steps up the temple-shaped portico of the museum. She'd turn round once she arrived in the exhibit room and steal a glance to see if he were still there.

"Jennie? Jennie Lee?"

The query carried in a loud and quite foreign voice. The accent was decidedly American and it came from a man striding towards her from well inside the room, the direction opposite to her stalker's expected entrance. The youngish man was handsome, brown hair thrown back from his forehead in need of cutting, a wide face but with narrowed eyes, dressed in a neat but definitely non-English style—cotton trousers, a lumberman's checked shirt beneath a short, zippered leather coat. He had a flat cap in his hand. *At least the cap's British,* Jennie thought. He repeated her name, again much too loud for an Englishman in a public place and well before he had reached her. Jennie knew the look on her face made it clear she hadn't the slightest idea who this person was. He read the look, slowed his progress towards her, momentarily worried, perhaps, that he had mistaken her for someone. But as he got closer he became certain. Then it came to her, this was the young man she'd met in America, more than two years ago, the factory worker who'd wanted her advice about Russia. The one she'd decided to take to bed, one cold evening in Detroit, Michigan, the one who'd taken her to breakfast the next morning. *What was his name, damn it?* Arriving before her, he thrust forward his right hand.

"Reuther..." and before he could repeat it, the first name came to Jennie.

"Walter!"

His face brightened into an infectious grin. "Yes. How great to see you. The only person I know in London."

Jennie smiled. "This is a surprise"

She was glad to see him. His energy, directness, innocence, was a mood-changing distraction from her problems. It would also protect her from whomever was following. She looked round the room. With characteristic good manners, no one in the room showed any sign of having noticed the small commotion the American had risen. And the owl, as she had come to think of her trail, was nowhere to be seen.

"What are you doing in London, Walter?" They began walking along companionably.

"I'm on my way to Russia. Here for a week waiting for my visa. Can't get one in the States. We don't recognise the Soviets."

She remembered his plan and his questions.

"I see." On impulse she put her arm through his. "Walter, there's a tea shop across Great Russell Street. Let me buy you a cup."

He smiled broadly, as if to signal it was exactly what he'd hoped for.

"Well, if I can get coffee, I'll be glad to accept." He took her arm in a manner Jennie felt a little too proprietary. But it was not the moment to disabuse Walter Reuther.

* * *

The coffee had been served. Reuther withdrew a packet of American cigarettes from the shirt pocket beneath the leather jacket and offered Jennie one. The sight of a cardboard matchbook and the taste of a Camel suddenly took her back to America, to the gleaming silver diner in Detroit...

"So, you're going to Russia after all."

"Yes, I am."

"Hope you're ready for it. Things are a bit worse than they were when I went two years ago."

Reuther replied, frowning slightly. "The collectivisation?"

So he knows. Good. Jennie had been following Stalin's drive to force the peasant farmers onto vast state farms. The result had been catastrophic, according to Frank. Production hadn't increased. Convinced the farmers were withholding grain, the state was beginning to extract every bushel they could find, leaving the rural population to starve.

Reuther looked at her hard. "Do you think it's as bad as the papers say?"

Jennie nodded. "I'm afraid so. Some independent sources. Wish it weren't true."

"Lots of arguments about it in the Party back home."

"The Party? I thought I remember you saying you were not a Communist Party member."

He smiled. "Almost right. Actually you asked me if I was a Trotskyist. And I said no, I wasn't, and I'm still not."

"Remind me what you'll do in Russia, Walter."

"Stay as far away from collective farms as I can." He smiled knowingly. "My brother and I are going to work in a plant Ford is building a couple hundred miles east of Moscow. See for myself how Communism works."

"That's wise, Walter. Will you tell me what you learn?"

"I sure will." The smile was both infectious and sincere. "We're going to Germany for a few weeks on our way to the Soviets. My dad was born, grew up there."

Jennie's expression changed to concern. "It could be dangerous there, especially for a party member. You mustn't look for trouble, Walter. The Brown shirts were killing Communists before this Hitler became Chancellor. Now they've a hunting licence from him."

Reuther lowered his voice. "I know. We've been worried about it. Going to see some…friends…in Berlin. They've asked us to bring in"—he fell silent—"something to defend themselves." He withdrew a folded paper. "Do you know where this is?" He unfolded the note and read the address as he passed it. "42 Glamis Road, near Cable Street."

Jennie smiled, thinking to herself, *Glamis. It all started with Glamis, didn't it?*

"Yes, I know where that is, actually. Glamis Road's named after a castle in Scotland I used to visit. And Cable Street's a thoroughfare in the Jewish"— 'slums' was the right ward, but she didn't want to use it— "district." Then, not even reflecting, "I can take you there if you want."

"That'd be great! But I wouldn't want to put you out."

"Not a bit of it. When do you need to go?"

"Tomorrow early. Around eight in the morning, when there's a lot of foot traffic in the area, they told me."

"Right. Where are you staying?"

Walter brightened. "Just around the corner from here at the Gresham Hotel. 36 Bloomsbury Street."

Jennie rose. "See you at seven fifteen tomorrow morning."

She put out her hand, feeling rather American. Reuther shook it with a slightly disappointed look. *What were you expecting, Mister?* Her inner voice even sounded American.

Chapter Thirty-Three

"It's a thirty-minute tube journey from here." Jennie was optimistic the next morning as she led her new friend back from Bloomsbury Street to Russell Square. "We'll change at King's Cross." He didn't appear to notice as she searched the pavement before and behind. She had left her flat by the rear garden. She couldn't chance being followed again.

Reuther sounded eager. "Haven't been in the subway here yet."

She tried to make her correction gentle. "Underground, Walter. A subway is what you Yanks call an underpass." She laughed. "Made that mistake in Chicago. I said something about a subway we were going through and they told me they didn't have one."

They plunged into the surging morning crowds at King's Cross. Jennie was pleased, certain that the crush was covering their tracks. Reuther covered her gloved hand with his as they stood in the Hammersmith Line train. Jennie liked it. At Whitechapel they alighted.

"We've a bit of a walk now," Jennie observed.

Reuther looked at his watch. "Will we get there on time? The guy was pretty specific about how long he'd wait."

It was ten past eight by the time they'd covered the mile or so down the Commercial Road and Lukin Street to Cable Road.

Jennie pointed to the small side street, "Glamis Road." Reuther nodded with relief.

"Why don't you wait here, Jennie? You don't need to be party to this...transaction."

"Very well. I'll nip into St Mary's." She nodded towards the grey stone church streaked in coal dust. "When you've finished, I'll be the one inside praying for your safety in Germany." They both laughed grimly.

A rather longer time elapsed than Jennie expected. Enough time for Jennie to think through one more time the opportunity that might have presented itself, the opportunity to solve her problem, to put the world back to right, or at least set it on another course, a course she might be able better to live with. She'd been running through this line of thought since leaving the teashop the day before. The train of reasoning and imagining had each time carried her to exactly the same outcome. *Not a very reliable guide, your reasoning, is it, Jennie,* she couldn't help thinking. *Where has it gotten you so far?* Perhaps this time things might go as she hoped. *If not, well, it's your life to do with as you like, isn't it?* The thought comforted.

When Walter finally sat down next to her, he was carrying what looked like a considerable package, wrapped in brown paper, tied professionally with string, innocent in the way a package of books from Foyle's might have looked.

"Walter, how are you going to smuggle that package into Germany?"

"Well, first I'm going to unpack it, take the guns apart. Then my bother and I will spread the parts out in both our bags. But mainly we don't expect to be searched at the German border at all, Jennie."

"How can you know?"

"Because we're going through the Saar." Everyone knew about *Saarland*. This was the coal-rich German statelet the French had detached and occupied after the Great War. It was now the last refuge of Hitler's visible opponents.

"German customs won't inspect bags coming from Saar because that would admit it's foreign territory."

"Clever."

"Walter, do you know how to use a pistol?"

"Yup, I do." He indicated the package. "These are actually a couple of revolvers, not pistols. Webley's...standard British Army."

"Can you teach me how to use one?"

Reuther raised his eyebrows. "We'd need a firing range."

"I don't think so. All I need to know is how to load, take the safety catch off, and fire...I don't need to practice aiming." She smiled. "After all, I am not going to fire at anyone, am I?"

"Well I can do that anywhere...anywhere the police won't see, that is."

"How about my place?"

"That'll be fine." They both rose and began walking back to Whitechapel Tube stop.

Walking side by side, not facing each other, not looking into one another's eyes, Jennie felt able to ask the really important question.

"Walter, can you lend me one of those...Webleys, for a day? Loaded."

He was silent. "Jennie, we hardly know each other. Why are you asking me to do this?"

She drew closer to him, putting her arm through his. It felt good, natural, warm, companionable. "It's because we hardly know each other—in fact, so far as the world is concerned, there's no trace of our acquaintance at all. It's the best reason to ask you."

"I'm probably a fool. But somehow I trust you, Jennie Lee."

She smiled. "You should."

* * *

Back at Jennie's flat on Guilford Road, Reuther unwrapped the package on the desk. Inside were two wooden boxes. He opened one box and removed the weapon.

"Standard British Army revolver, I'm told." He hefted it, checked to see it was empty and handed it to Jennie. She held away from herself with both hands, the first firearm she'd ever touched—it was as heavy as it looked, rugged, with a hexagonal barrel about four inches long—and handed it back with an inquiring look.

It took Reuther a few minutes to explain a double action/single action revolver to Jennie. But when she understood that all she ever needed to do was pull the trigger firmly—no chambering a round, no safety catch, no cocking the gun—she was pleased. Handing her the revolver, he let Jennie fire it dry a few times, but then stopped her.

"It's bad for the firing pin, Jennie." He thought a moment. "Remember, the recoil is serious on these Webleys. And unless you take some practice rounds, you'll feel it. And without practice your second shot will probably be way off."

Then he broke the revolver and showed her how to load and unload.

Removing the cartridges, he asked, "How many do you need, Jennie?"

"One."

He handed it to her. "Alright, let's see you load and set the barrel so that one bullet will be in the right place in the chamber." Jennie took the weapon, broke it open expertly enough, but then had trouble rotating the barrel. She looked up at her instructor.

"Sticky wicket? Is that what you people say?"

They laughed together, reducing the tension. Then he took the revolver back and showed her how to move the barrel again. The second time was a charm.

"Wish you could really fire it a few times."

"Won't be necessary, Walter. I merely intend to frighten someone."

"Then you won't be needing any bullets, right?" He'd called her bluff. Jennie smiled and held out her hand. He placed two in her palm. "Insurance."

Then Jennie turned serious. "Walter, I like you very much. But I think the less time we spend together the better for both of us. It wouldn't do for us to be seen by anyone."

Chapter Thirty-Three

"Jennie, I was already planning to take the back way out, if there is one."

"I'll show you."

He looked down at the Webley on the table. "How long are you going to need the piece?"

"I'm not sure. A few days, perhaps a week. Is that too long?"

"No, no. My brother and I are going up north to visit some factories in Manchester and Liverpool. We'll be gone at least a week."

"Walter," she took the lapel of his leather jacket. "We won't see each other again. I'll leave the box, wrapped up at your hotel, sometime before you get back."

He nodded and then Jennie pulled his head towards hers and kissed him. It was not a fraternal kiss.

* * *

In the event, it took Jennie a bit longer than she expected. When she called Number 10, and identified herself, the secretary told her the PM was to be at Cliveden Hall, Lady Astor's home, for the weekend and would be back on Monday.

Should you call him there? No reason not to. Jennie tried to think calmly. *They already have logged your call in Whitehall. Yes, well... there's no reason to make the matter look urgent.*

But after the call, she found herself breathless and trembling when she put down the receiver. It was Mosley who had Frank killed. That was sure. Could he have guessed that she knew? She had to convince herself he had no idea. Regardless of her resolve, she couldn't control the fright that now began to assail her. *But there's no way he knows that you know.* She had to convince herself.

Thursday to Monday? There was nothing to do but wait. She couldn't leave her flat. She might miss a call from the PM's office. She might be followed again. She cast her eye round seeking a way to kill time. Legal tomes that held little fascination for Jennie at the best of times were completely useless distractions now. She sat down at her desk among them, some open, others on the floor, even beneath the table. She was condemned to waiting, staring at the wooden box holding the Webley revolver. She had no desire to take it from the box, heft it, load it, do anything with it. As she gazed at it, the box it became a coffin, and then a tombstone that marked the end of her life.

Write your last will and testament, Jennie. She pulled a piece of paper from the desk drawer and rolled it into the typewriter. The fingers moved and the letters appeared across the page: I Jennie Lee, being of sound body and...she stopped. *This is silly. You have nothing to leave and no one to leave things to.* She could write a political testimony, an explanation of what she was about to do and why. *No, you can't. There are too many people to protect for you to tell the truth.* In fact, now she realised she'd have to destroy the documents, both the ones Elizabeth had given her and the duplicates she'd received from Dorothy Wise. *No, not both. You'll need one set, you'll take it with you when you see Tom Mosley.* The childishness of the notion came to her. *Why? To confront him with his treason, his villainy, before you kill him? You're envisioning a melodrama, Jennie.*

She rose from the desk, poured herself a large neat whiskey and removed the folio Elizabeth had given her from beneath the grate. Then, she crumpled some newsprint and threw it into the fireplace, withdrew from the desk the manila envelope she'd taken from Dorothy. Once she'd arranged the two sheaves of paper on the grate, Jennie sat before the fireplace, lit a cigarette, sipped her whiskey and thought matters through once more. *You won't need them. You are not going to ask him to explain, justify, excuse. You're certainly not going to vindicate yourself to him and then kill him.* She'd seen too many films in which such grandiloquence allows the victim time to escape. She struck a match, bent down and kindled the newsprint. Soon the papers were burning nicely and after a few moments they were ash. She rose and finished the drink. Then Jennie returned to the sideboard and poured herself another, larger one.

* * *

The importuning, unceasing ring of the telephone woke Jennie at quarter past eight on Saturday morning. Looking round she saw she was not in bed, but sprawled on the chesterfield, still dressed, with a blanket pulled over her against the chill. She rose, and knocked over an empty whiskey bottle. Now, everything snapped back into place. On her feet, unsteadily advancing on the jangling instrument, she began to feel the hangover throb in her temples. Jennie couldn't help reaching for her forehead with one hand as she grasped the receiver with the other. She paused to remember her number...then it came.

"Museum 6428."

She heard an operator speaking. "Putting you through now, Cliveden."

"That you Jennie? It's Tom Mosley here." Suddenly she was completely awake. "Private office told me you rang." He did not wait for a response before going on. "Haven't heard from you in ages. How are you?"

Does he suspect? Is that why he's called?

"Fine, Tom, fine."

She had to call him Tom, she knew. It would be a signal. She covered the mouthpiece and cleared her throat. Looking down at wrinkled clothes and then across the room at her face in a mirror, Jennie was glad he could only hear her voice.

"I wondered if we might see each other."

Was this too much out of the blue? Was it too subtle? Would he understand the choice of words, see each other instead of her asking to see him?

He understood what she was proposing instantly. "Yes. I'd

like that." And before Jennie could ask when, it all fell neatly into her lap. "Look, I'm at Lady Astor's. Convenient to call you from here."

She understood that there'd be no logging of the call, or even a trace of anything but the trunk call charge.

"Damn boring weekend. Wanted to get away from business. But it's all they'll talk about here." She let him go on. "Nancy's dry and the drinks are bloody awful. Look, there's nothing on here till dinner. What if I motor into town?"

"Today?" Jennie gulped. "That might work, Tom." She made herself sound casual and even a bit hesitant. Pretending to leaf through a diary, she replied. "Let's see...No, nothing. That's fine. Your place, Ebury Street, still have it?"

"Indeed." Enough silence to look at a wristwatch. "Might be a bit tricky on this end. I'll have to slip out of here after luncheon, without anyone noticing. Let's say three."

"Very good. See you then."

She put down the receiver with a smile. It was the waiting that had made things so difficult, reduced Jennie to drunkenness. Now Mosley's own impetuousness, ardour...no, his lust had annulled the time. *But you look a slattern, Jennie. Will it matter? Yes. You've got to get in the door, into the bedroom perhaps.* The first thing Jennie needed was a bath, if only to warm up. She let the water run high and soaked for a long time, thinking through her plan. Then she chose the gown she'd worn that night at the Trevelyans', when Mosley had first laid a hand on her thigh. Would he remember?

At one fifteen she strode down the steps of the block of flats, carrying a sack with the Webley in its box. She had tried to place the revolver in her coat pocket. It was simply too large, and too heavy to secure in a belt, she'd tried that too. Carrying it in the bag just seemed risky. What if it fell out, or the bag dropped or was ripped? What if she tripped and the bag opened? No, she'd have to carry the gun in its case.

Cab or tube? *A cabbie might remember you. Will it matter? Of course, if you want to get away with it, if you want to protect Walter. The Underground then.*

Chapter Thirty-Four

Jennie recognised the little MG roadster at the kerb in front of Mosley's Ebury Street house. But there was no one about and the street was quiet. She mounted the two steps and rang the bell. She could see through the glass at the side of the door that it was Mosley himself coming to the door, not a servant.

"It's open!"

She heard the words, pushed on the door and found it giving way.

Tom Mosley was before her, in the same dressing gown he'd worn the afternoon she'd gone to see him in the midlands during the election. She remembered how she'd resisted temptation, how he'd fobbed off her concerns, how she'd allowed herself to be captured by her hopes. *It wasn't so long ago, was it?* The recollection raised a strengthening anger in her. He reached for her sack and Jennie almost recoiled. But it was an innocent gesture. Without noticing its heft, he put it on the side table and took her coat. Then, saw the dress and smiled almost shyly. They moved together into the lounge, a room still sparsely furnished, with wide windows giving out onto the narrow street. It was obviously a room Mosley spent little time in, even less now he was PM. "Drink?"

"Sherry, please."

"Rather demure, Jennie. Can't I offer you something more... fortifying?"

"Very well, a whiskey and soda." She tried to smile.

They stood facing each other, sipping their whiskeys in silence. *He's probably impatient to move to the bedroom,* Jennie thought. *Well I can't just go to the entry and take out the gun.* She needed him to give her a few moments alone. *But he's waiting for me to make the advance, why?* Deciding on action, she moved towards him, reached for his hands, she placed one on each of her breasts and opened her mouth as she moved her face up towards his. This was, she knew immediately, exactly what Mosley was waiting for—her desire, her carnal appetite to match his own. He didn't want to have to seduce, he didn't have the time, the patience for it. He'd never needed it with Jennie. She could feel his body responding as he moved his hands over her body. Then he took her by the hand to lead her to the bedroom.

On one side of the double bed lay a silk negligee in blue and a matching silk robe. She moved to that side. Once they were standing on opposite sides of the bed, his look willed her to undress. She did so, as she'd done before, slowly but without unnecessary suggestiveness. She let the gown drop from her shoulders. She wore nothing beneath it, nothing at all. Nude, she raised the negligee over her head and let it slide down her body. She did not bother with the robe, letting his eyes continue to rove across her body. But Jennie was doing everything by calculation, not as before, by naked desire. *Can he tell? No, he's too absorbed by his own feelings to notice mine just now.*

Mosley began to loosen his dressing gown.

"Just give me a minute, will you Jennie?"

He turned for the bathroom. *This is your moment.* She made for the hallway, pulled the box from the sack, opened it, checked the position of the cartridge in the barrel. Then she placed the revolver in the sack, carefully, so she could reach in and grasp the gun's handle as she withdrew it. Then she walked back into the room holding the sack at her side.

Her pulse racing, her head throbbing, Jennie could not hear the front door of the flat open behind her as she moved back into the bedroom. Entering, she saw Mosley come out of the bathroom still wearing his florid dressing gown, now tied loosely, with his bare chest visible between the broad lapels. It was the way he stared past Jennie, mouth agape, that made her realise there was someone behind her. She turned her head. There, standing in the doorway, was the man who'd been following her for weeks, the man with the owlish glasses, in a heavy coat, with his hat—a homburg—in his hand. *No, it's not in his hand. It's covering his hand,* she immediately realised. Mosley saw it too and understood immediately, for he raised his hands in a gesture of surrender. There was a weapon beneath the homburg. The man's arm was held out at a right angle from his body, and it was casting the hat back and forth on an arc between the two others.

Mosley dropped his arms to his sides. He looked at each of them for a moment and spoke. "Jennie, apparently you don't know Malcolm MacDonald, formerly MP for...a Nottingham constituency." Sounding casual and utterly composed, he continued, "Which one was it, Malcolm?"

The man now spoke. "Bassetlaw, Sir Oswald, north of the town."

Mosley turned towards Jennie. "Jennie Lee, MP for North Lanark. You two really should know each other. Malcolm is the son of our former leader and PM, Ramsay MacDonald." Jennie turned to look at the man. He was her half-brother.

Mosley knows. Does this MacDonald know?

Her unvoiced question was answered immediately. "I know who Miss Lee is." The voice was calm, factual, steely. "She's my sister." He corrected himself, "My half-sister. And she ruined my father...her father."

Jennie watched his arm move towards her. *Gesture or threat? Revenge is a dish best served cold...hadn't you told yourself the same thing?*

As MacDonald's arm moved toward Jennie, Mosley smiled slyly, in a show of *sangfroid*. "Look here, old man. I helped."

"Shut up." MacDonald's tone was malevolent. *Or was it dismissive?* Jennie couldn't tell. Watching them both, he began speaking to her. "Once you knew he was your father, you set out to destroy him."

Words of reply were forming in her mouth even before Jennie realised what he'd revealed. *Mum told him, told Ramsay*

MacDonald, told him I knew, told him after I visited Cowdenbeath.
It came back sharply, her mother's admission in that grim little
café beneath the railway bridge. *And then she wrote to tell him?*
Why? Jennie had to reply. "No, that's not why I did it at all. I
wish I had never known."

Mosley was missing something. "When did you find out,
Malcolm?" Jennie was taken aback by the familiarity. *Is he using*
the man's Christian name to make common cause?

MacDonald did not turn towards him but remained fixed on
Jennie. He addressed his reply to her.

"After the defeat...my father showed me a letter from your
mother. Then he told me about your"—he paused, looking at
each, while distaste spread on his face—"relationship."

Jennie and Mosley glanced at each other. *Does he know about*
the Duke and Duchess of York, the back channel from the palace?
But then Jennie realised there was something now much more
important he might know about—Mosley's treason. *Could he*
know that too? No, he doesn't, he can't. And she no longer had the
papers to prove it to him. *Damn! Would he even care? It's me he's*
going to kill.

As if he'd read her mind, MacDonald now shifted his stance
directly towards Jennie.

"The shame, the suffering, the pain you caused my father,
after fifty years of trying to serve the working people of this
county. To be turned out of office as a traitor to his people, his
party, his honour, when all he wanted was to save the country."
He stopped, pointed the hand in homburg at her. Still, the hat
did not fall from the weapon beneath it. "And destroyed by the
hand of his very own daughter."

If she was going to discharge her mission, Jennie couldn't
wait a moment longer. Her right hand reached across to the sack
she held, grasped the Webley and withdrew it as she stepped
up to Mosley. She pushed the barrel at his neck and pulled the
trigger. His eyes seemed to bulge in their sockets just before

Mosley crashed to the floor.

The recoil was so great it knocked her back and she never heard the report. When she reopened her eyes there was a body on the floor and she was covered, literally covered with the man's viscera. Her stomach immediately began to churn as she wiped what could only be grey matter from her eyes. She looked at MacDonald. He was motionless and still held the concealed weapon towards her. She waited for him to pull the trigger. Seconds passed, half a minute. They stood facing each other. When nothing happened, Jennie walked to the bathroom. She had to cleanse herself, no matter how little time she had left. As she closed the door, she realised she was still holding Walter Reuther's revolver. Now she'd never be able to return it. Found carrying it, he would become an accessory after Mosley's murder.

Two minutes later, she re-entered the room, naked, having left the gruesome negligee on the floor at the foot of the bathtub. MacDonald was still there, his feet still fixed to the floor, his face quizzical. Unashamed, again she waited for him to shoot. When he didn't, she walked round the corpse oozing on the floor. She reached her clothes and began to dress. *What is he waiting for? Perhaps he no longer has the stomach for it, having witnessed one shooting already.* She was having trouble not vomiting herself. *How can he just stand there?* But there he was, motionless contemplating what had just happened.

Jennie picked up the sack, went back into the bath for the Webley and strode past MacDonald into the hall. Then she spoke. "Very well. I'm leaving now." Silence.

The street was as deserted as when she'd arrived. Apparently, no one had responded to the sound of a gun firing. Jennie walked off towards Victoria Station and the tube. In its anonymity no one had seen her come or go.

* * *

Sitting at the desk in her darkened flat, Jennie was startled by the telephone next to her. It was about nine o'clock, or at least she'd just heard some bells tolling out the time, bells she'd never noticed before. She took the receiver from the cradle but said nothing, waiting.

"Jennie, is that you? It's Nye. You won't have seen the papers? I'm at Beaverbrook's office at the *Evening Standard*. The late editions have just gone out. Not on the street yet."

"What is it?" Her voice was a monotone.

"Mosley's dead. Suicide."

Suddenly she was awake and alive again. "What? Suicide?"

Nye must have had a paper in his hands. He began reading from the copy:

The Prime Minister, Sir Oswald Mosley, was found dead in his London flat this evening. The body was discovered by his manservant returning to his duties from a day off. Sir Oswald had evidently shot himself with a Webley service revolver that was found in his hand. There was no suicide note or other indication of why he had killed himself. The Prime Minister had been spending the weekend at Cliveden, the home of Lord and Lady Astor. Neither his absence from that estate nor his presence in London was known to anyone. Sir Oswald had evidently arrived alone, as his two-seat roadster was found parked at the kerb before his Ebury Street flat.

Nye stopped reading. "Well, what'd you make of that, Jennie?

"Nye, be a good fellow, come and see me...right away."

She put the receiver back down. *Nothing for it but to keep on living.* She rose from the desk and began turning on lights.

Now the questions came. Why had MacDonald done it, covered up everything, even leaving a revolver of the same kind as her own at his side? Did he have the stomach to kneel over the corpse and put Mosley's finger round the gun butt? Had he removed her negligee and robe? Were the police covering matters up, as apparently they had in the case of Frank's death? A hundred answers came to her. Perhaps MacDonald had no stomach for another killing, he couldn't kill a woman, not his half-sister, he knew more than he was letting on, or surmised it after following me for days.

Or perhaps when I killed Mosley he began to think there was much more to all this than he knew.

Then she saw the sack, still standing on the side table by the door. *The Webley. They won't be looking for it after all, will they?* It was a ten-minute walk to the Gresham Hotel on Bloomsbury Street. There was no one at the registration desk to receive the package for Mr Reuther. So, she left it in the sack with a note bearing his name. Jennie was back well before Nye arrived.

"You're a brave man, to want to marry me, Nye Bevan."

* * *

The *cons* seemed very much to have the better of the *pros*, Jennie thought. Inside, she still loved Frank, and grieved for him so deeply she felt there was little emotion left for anything or anyone else. But she knew Nye loved her, and she liked him awfully. It would have to be enough. She didn't want to be lonely anymore, or even as much alone as she had been when Frank was still... still there.

More than once she'd asked Nye why they had to marry. "Can't we just live together quietly, discreetly?"

Nye was firm. "It won't wash, Jennie."

"You mean the prudes in our constituencies might get wind?"

"No. I mean my parents won't allow me to live 'in sin.' It's that simple."

"Big bro Nye Bevan, frightened of his mum?"

"You've met her, girl. Will you cross her?"

"Very well, I'll marry you. But I won't wear a wedding ring and I'll not take your name."

* * *

He'd begun courting Jennie the moment she'd asked him to come to her flat that day Mosley had died. Nye had diverted her, entertained her, brought her out of herself, first cautiously and slowly and soon more actively. And somehow, he did it without ever intruding on her grief about Frank. About her hand in Mosley's death, it was obvious he knew nothing. Nor, apparently, did the rest of the world.

She could only ever think of Mosley as dying...not being killed, still less killed by her. And she would no more tell Nye what had actually transpired than she would have gone to Scotland Yard. It would have made him an accessory. Besides, she felt no guilt, none whatever. It was enough that Malcolm MacDonald had held her fate in his hands for a moment. Had silently judged her, pardoned her, and then disappeared entirely from her life, not even nodding to her as they passed in the Palace of Westminster once parliament was recalled.

Somehow, Nye knew how to pursue Jennie now, what she needed after Frank's death. She wanted Nye as a friend, a companion, and fellow stalwart. He was not ardent, at least not immediately, never pressed, showed Jennie that he would never even try to domesticate her. He had watched her too long and too closely to make a conventional marriage, or even a confining one.

* * *

There were a few reporters hanging about, mainly from the Beaverbrook press, the morning Jennie and Nye emerged from the Holborn Registry Office on a day late in October 1934. The newspapers' interest was unsurprising. By now, the pair were well known fixtures in the parliamentary sketch writers' columns. No longer in the Speaker's Coventry, Jennie had resumed her full-throated voice on the Labour back benches, aiming her barbs in counterattack almost exclusively at Tory complaints about waste in public expenditure. Nye had become a parliamentary private secretary to the minister of Labour, the unbending and very reluctant Labour minister Ernest Bevin. This had given the hacks daily opportunities to record how each man was confused for the other in their Whitehall offices.

As the flashbulbs popped, the reporters shouted questions at both of them.

"No hat, no gloves, no veil, how can we tell who the bride is, Jennie?"

Jennie's smile broadened into a grin as she held up her left hand.

"No ring either, boys."

"Did you forget to buy one, Nye?" It was the reporter from the *Daily Express*.

Jennie answered for him. "I just don't like rings, boys."

"Mrs Bevan, will you be giving up your parliamentary seat?"

Nye stepped forward and raised both hands in the air. "I wish to announce that if anyone addresses a political question to this lady" —he turned to beam at Jennie— "as Mrs Bevan, the question will not be answered."

At this point Jennie stepped in front of Nye. "The question wasn't addressed to you, Nye." Then she looked at the hack, pointing her thumb behind her at Nye. "What he said is right. And to save your breath, the answer is no. In fact, I'll be leaving tomorrow to go to Geneva with the Prime Minister."

None of the reporters noticed Nye's double take. It had obviously been news to him, try as hard as he might to pretend otherwise to the reporters.

* * *

A quarter of an hour later, they were sitting at a table in The Ivy on West Street near Covent Garden, toasting the wedding with the two witnesses they'd found in the registry office.

"Jennie, were you going to tell me about this trip to Switzerland?" Nye's face betrayed a combination of pride and pain in her news.

"Just heard this morning." They'd both learned from the papers the previous day that the Prime Minister, Arthur Henderson, was going to Geneva to rally the League against Mussolini's threats to Abyssinia. Departing from previous government policy, he had announced a demand that the League impose an oil embargo on Italy and offered the British Mediterranean fleet to back it up. Henderson was finally Labour prime minister, after serving as temporary leader of the party three times in the previous fifteen years. He had always been a stalwart for the League of Nations, even winning the Nobel Peace Prize for his support of the League's disarmament work.

"I'm glad he's making a stand against Musso." Nye paused. "But why take you?"

"I have no idea, Nye."

* * *

Sitting in the Prime Minister's first class compartment, both Arthur Henderson and Jennie Lee felt slightly out of place. First class was a rare luxury for a Labour member of parliament. Worse, to be found out traveling first was a major embarrassment in the culture of the Labour Party. Henderson had not yet become entirely comfortable with the practice, despite a year or so in office. Jennie had only ever ridden first on Frank Wise's largess.

They were on the boat train rolling through Kent to the coast and a channel steamer at Folkestone. Just past Maidstone, Henderson had excused his parliamentary private secretary from the compartment and the permanent secretary as well. But then he remained silent for further minutes, watching the tidy pastureland glide by. For a change, Jennie did not think it her place to break the silence.

This was to be their first conversation since Henderson had been appointed prime minister. His audible throat clearing announced that it was about to begin.

"Miss Lee, you have no idea why I asked you to join me on this mission to the League Headquarters. You can't have, as I have told almost no one." Jennie could only nod. "Well, a little background. You know of course that Labour governments can have little confidence in our security services as presently constituted."

"Yes sir, everyone knows about the connivance of SIS in the Zinoviev letter."

This was the forgery of a letter of support for Labour from the Soviets in 1924. Jennie knew as well about how SIS had suppressed the evidence of Mosley's treason, but she couldn't reveal it. Probably Henderson didn't know himself.

"Alas, there are other examples. I won't trouble you with them now. What it means, however, is that foreign governments and others friendly to the Labour government sometimes approach the prime minister's office directly, avoiding all civil service contact. Sometimes, we learn things that way the permanent secretaries don't want us to know." He paused, awaiting a question.

But Jennie understood. "I shan't ask for any details, sir."

"I'm afraid I must put you in the picture, however." He drew a breath. "There are people in the Soviet Commissariat for Foreign Affairs who have offered to provide us with information, secret information, about Italian and German policy. Do you know the name Kutuzov?"

Jennie swallowed. She certainly did know that name and it frightened her immediately. This was the name of the Russian she'd met with Frank in Moscow, the man who had brought him the documents about Mosley that Dorothy Wise had found, the documents that led to his murder, the same documents Jennie had already had from the Duchess of York. What did Henderson know of the matter? Hoping the Prime Minister would not notice the sweat forming above her lip or the trembling his question had set in motion, Jennie had to lie.

"Kutuzov... Kutuzov...No. I don't think so."

"Well, Kutuzov is a member of the Soviet delegation coming to the League meeting next week." The Russian government had joined the League of Nations only a fortnight before. "Rather a low level bureaucrat actually, but says he has documents about the Italian plans in Abyssinia and he says, about German violation of the Treaty of Versailles—rearming, with Russian connivance."

"And you credit him? You don't think it's a provocation, or a trap or even a plant, like the Zinoviev material?"

Henderson shook his head. "No, Miss Lee. He's already provided some startling information to prove his *bona fides*." Jennie waited in apprehension. Now her fears were to be realised. He went on. "Evidence that Mosley was in the pay of the government of Italy and of German industrialists. Slipped it to our League representative when he was here last month arranging the Soviets' membership terms."

Does the PM know? About Frank, about me? The questions absorbed her so completely she'd stopped listening. Now Henderson leaned forward, breaking the reverie.

"That brings us to you, Miss Lee."

She looked up at his rather kind grey face, readying herself for his revelation.

"What's it to do with me, sir?"

"That's the odd part of the story. This Kutuzov fellow sent word that he will give the documents only to you. Said to tell you he's sure you'll know what to do with them."

"So, that's why I've been put in the delegation going to Geneva." Jennie felt relief. "What exactly am I to do, sir?"

"Make yourself conspicuous." He chortled. "That should be no trouble, Miss Lee. Kutuzov'll find you. If you can get the papers and they tell us what I think they will, I may be able to use them to get the League to take action, not just against Mussolini, but against this Hitler fellow too. Nip his adventurism in the bud." Smiling broadly, he patted her knee in a fatherly way. "Who knows, Miss Lee, you might just change the course of history."

Jennie beamed and then she said something Henderson never understood at all.

"Third time lucky."

The End

Dramatis Personae

Almost all persons mentioned in this work really lived. Most actually did a good deal of what is credited to them in the narrative, at least before the British political crisis of August 1931. In that month the Prime Minister, Ramsay MacDonald switched sides, joined with Tories to impose a harsh austerity on his country and embarked on a half dozen years of appeasement.

All these persons are now long dead. A brief description of each of them is provided below in roughly the order of their appearance in the narrative. The major events in the narrative described in the book depart from actual history as from August 23, 1931. The descriptions below do not reflect those departures.

Ramsay MacDonald, leader of the Labour Party, Prime Minister of Great Britain, 1924, 1929-35

Euphemia Lee, mother of Jennie Lee, member of the Independent Labour Party

James Lee, father of Jennie Lee, mine safety officer, member of the Independent Labour Party

Jennie Lee, born 1904-1988, MP 1929-1931, 1945-1970, married to Aneurin Bevan 1935, Minister for the Arts, 1964-70

Sir Charles Philip Trevelyan, 3d baronet, Liberal and then Labour MP, President of the Board of Education (Minister of Education) Labour government of 1924, 1929-1931

Lady Mary Katherine Trevelyan, Charles Trevelyan's wife, half sister of Gertrude Bell, influential British Arabist

Lady Nancy Astor, Viscountess, American, married Waldorf Astor, 2d Viscount, first woman to sit in the British House of Commons

Henry "Chips" Channon, American expatriate, social climber and diarist, Conservative MP, 1935-1950, identified by W. Somerset Maugham as the model for Elliot Templeton in *The*

Razor's Edge. His diaries were expurgated when published.

Ellen Wilkinson, Labour MP for Middlesbrough, 1924-1931, Jarrow, 1935-1947, Minister of Education in the Atlee Labour government, 1945-1947, chairman of the Labour Party, 1944-1945, labour union organiser and founder member of British Communist Party in 1920, left party 1924.

Winston Churchill, Chancellor of the Exchequer, 1924-1929, out of office thereafter until 1939

Elizabeth Bowes-Lyons, daughter of the Earl of Strathmore, raised at Glamis Castle in Scotland, subsequently the Duchess of York, married to Albert, second son of King George V, became Queen on the accession of Albert as George VI, after the abdication of her brother-in-law, David, later styled Edward VIII, mother of Elizabeth II and queen mother until her death at 102 in 2002

Oswald Mosley, 6th baronet of Ancoats, officer, British Army, Royal Flying Corps, Conservative MP 1918-22, independent MP, 1922-24, Labour MP, 1926-31, member of Ramsay MacDonald's cabinet as Chancellor of Duchy of Lancaster, 1929-1930. Founder of New Party, 1931 and leader, British Union of Fascists, 1932-1940, received subsidies for party from Italian Fascist government from 1931 onward, married his lover Diana Mitford 1936 (witnesses to marriage included Adolf Hitler), interned by British government during WW2, unsuccessful parliamentary candidate for fascist and racist parties until his death in 1980.

John Maynard Keynes, world famous economist, associated with Liberal party, author of two influential works in the period: the bestselling *The Economic Consequences of the Peace*, and the subsequent tract, *The Economic Consequences of Mr Churchill*, echoing the title of its predecessor

Lydia Lepokova, Russian ballerina, married to Keynes

Harold Macmillan, unorthodox Conservative MP for Stockton, 1924-29, 31-45, and for Bromley, 1945-1964, early supporter of Sir Oswald Mosley, subsequently Foreign Secretary, Chancellor of the Exchequer and Prime Minister of Great Britain, 1957-1963.

Dorothy Macmillan, wife of Harold, involved for over thirty years in an affair with Macmillan's friend and ally, Robert Boothby, MP

Frank Wise, barrister, civil servant, economic adviser to Prime Minister Lloyd George, then Labour MP, 1929-1931, from 1923 representative of the Soviet Union Cooperative Foreign Trade bureau in Great Britain

Aneurin Bevan, after Clement Atlee, most important Labour politician of his time. MP for Ebbw Vale (South Wales) from 1929 to his death in 1960. On the left of the Labour Party, was the sole sustained opposition to the Churchill wartime government. As Minister of Health and concurrently Minister of Housing, established the NHS and organised the greatest home building programme in British history after the Second World War. Married Jennie Lee in 1934.

Walter Reuther, American union organiser, and liberal leader, president of United Automobile Workers, after 1940 a leader of the Congress of Industrial Organizations, from whom he expelled members of the Communist party in the late '40s, probably joined Communist party briefly in the early 1930s, travelled to Europe in 1933 and worked in Soviet auto plant, Gorky, 1933-1935

George V, King and Emperor from his father's death in 1910 until his own in 1936, famously predicted of his son David, Prince of Wales, and afterward King Edward VIII, "After I am dead, the boy will ruin himself within twelve months," he is also known to have said, "I pray to God my eldest son [David, afterward Edward VIII] will never marry and have children, and that nothing will come between Bertie [his second son Albert, afterward George VI] and Lilibet [his eldest grandchild Elizabeth, afterward Queen Elizabeth II] and the throne."

David Lloyd George, MP, 1890-1945, Cabinet Minister and then Prime Minister of Great Britain 1916-1922, leader of the Liberal Party. 1926-1931. Widely suspected of selling titles to secure financial support for his party during and after the war, so widely reputed to be a womaniser that he was called "the goat."

Cynthia (Cimmie) Mosley, wife of Sir Oswald Mosley, Labour Party MP, 1929-1931, daughter of Lord Curzon, Viceroy of India and Foreign Secretary, 1919-1924, in despair about her husband's infidelity during their marriage, not sympathetic to her husband's politics after 1931, died after surgery for appendicitis 1933.

Edward Fitzroy, Conservative MP for Northamptonshire North, 1900-1918 and for Daventry, 1918-1943, Speaker of the House of Commons, 1928-1943, captain in British Army during WW1.

Malcolm MacDonald, MP for Bassetlaw, 1929-1935, son of Ramsay MacDonald, Minister of Health, 1940-41 and other offices mainly in foreign affairs, including last colonial governor and only governor general of Kenya, 1963-1964

Arthur Henderson, MP, three separate times leader of the Labour Party, 1908-10, 1914-17, 1931-32, Foreign Minister in MacDonald's 1929-31 government, recognised Soviet Union, chaired League of Nations Disarmament Conference 1932-34, winner of the Nobel Peace Prize, 1934

About the Author

In addition to *The Intrigues of Jennie Lee,* Alex Rosenberg is the author of two other historical novels, *The Girl from Krakow* and *Autumn in Oxford,* as well as many books of non-fiction, mainly philosophy. He is the R. Taylor Cole Professor of Philosophy at Duke University in Durham, North Carolina. He lives there in the winter. In the summer he's in France, near Geneva, Switzerland. Some of Alex's writing, for *The New York Times, Time Magazine, Salon.com, 3AM,* and other media can be found at his website, www.alexrose46.com.

Top Hat Books

Historical fiction that lives

We publish fiction that captures the contrasts, the achievements, the optimism and the radicalism of ordinary and extraordinary times across the world.

We're open to all time periods and we strive to go beyond the narrow, foggy slums of Victorian London. Where are the tales of the people of fifteenth century Australasia? The stories of eighth century India? The voices from Africa, Arabia, cities and forests, deserts and towns? Our books thrill, excite, delight and inspire. The genres will be broad but clear. Whether we're publishing romance, thrillers, crime, or something else entirely, the unifying themes are timescale and enthusiasm. These books will be a celebration of the chaotic power of the human spirit in difficult times. The reader, when they finish, will snap the book closed with a satisfied smile.
If you have enjoyed this book, why not tell other readers by posting a review on your preferred book site.
Recent bestsellers from Tops Hat Books are:

Grendel's Mother
The Saga of the Wyrd-Wife
Susan Signe Morrison
Grendel's mother, a queen from Beowulf, threatens the fragile political stability on this windswept land.
Paperback: 978-1-78535-009-2 ebook: 978-1-78535-010-8

Queen of Sparta

A Novel of Ancient Greece

T.S. Chaudhry

History has relegated her to the role of bystander, what if Gorgo, Queen of Sparta, had played a central role in the Greek resistance to the Persian invasion?

Paperback: 978-1-78279-750-0 ebook: 978-1-78279-749-4

Mercenary

R.J. Connor

Richard Longsword is a mercenary, but this time it's not for money, this time it's for revenge...

Paperback: 978-1-78279-236-9 ebook: 978-1-78279-198-0

Black Tom

Terror on the Hudson

Ron Semple

A tale of sabotage, subterfuge and political shenanigans in Jersey City in 1916; America is on the cusp of war and the fate of the nation hinges on the decision of one young policeman.

Paperback: 978-1-78535-110-5 ebook: 978-1-78535-111-2

Destiny Between Two Worlds

A Novel about Okinawa

Jacques L. Fuqua, Jr.

A fateful October 1944 morning offered no inkling that the lives of thousands of Okinawans would be profoundly changed—forever.

Paperback: 978-1-78279-892-7 ebook: 978-1-78279-893-4

Cowards

Trent Portigal

A family's life falls into turmoil when the parents' timid political dissidence is discovered by their far more enterprising children.

Paperback: 978-1-78535-070-2 ebook: 978-1-78535-071-9

Godwine Kingmaker

Part One of The Last Great Saxon Earls

Mercedes Rochelle

The life of Earl Godwine is one of the enduring enigmas of English history. Who was this Godwine, first Earl of Wessex; unscrupulous schemer or protector of the English? The answer depends on whom you ask...

Paperback: 978-1-78279-801-9 ebook: 978-1-78279-800-2

Messiah Love

Music and Malice at a Time of Handel

Sheena Vernon

The tale of Harry Walsh's faltering steps on his journey to success and happiness, performing in the playhouses of Georgian London.

Paperback: 978-1-78279-768-5 ebook: 978-1-78279-761-6

A Terrible Unrest

Philip Duke

A young immigrant family must confront the horrors of the Colorado Coalfield War to live the American Dream.

Paperback: 978-1-78279-437-0 ebook: 978-1-78279-436-3

Readers of ebooks can buy or view any of these bestsellers by clicking on the live link in the title. Most titles are published in paperback and as an ebook. Paperbacks are available in traditional bookshops. Both print and ebook formats are available online.

Find more titles and sign up to our readers' newsletter at http://www.johnhuntpublishing.com/fiction

Follow us on Facebook at https://www.facebook.com/JHPfiction and Twitter at https://twitter.com/JHPFiction